A Dirty Job

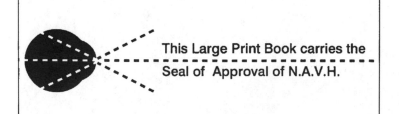

This Large Print Book carries the
Seal of Approval of N.A.V.H.

A Dirty Job

Christopher Moore

WHEELER
PUBLISHING

Published in 2006 by arrangement with William Morrow, an imprint of HarperCollins Publishers.

Wheeler Large Print Hardcover.

The text of this Large Print edition is unabridged.
Other aspects of the book may vary from the original edition.

Set in 16 pt. Plantin by Carleen Stearns.

Printed in the United States on permanent paper.

Library of Congress Cataloging-in-Publication Data

Moore, Christopher, 1957–
    A dirty job / by Christopher Moore.
        p. cm.
    ISBN 1-59722-316-6 (lg. print : hc : alk. paper)
    1. Large type books.   I. Title.
PS3563.O594D57 2006b
813'.54—dc22   2006014627

This book is dedicated to Patricia Moss, who was as generous in sharing her death as she was in sharing her life.

AND

To hospice workers and volunteers all over the world.

Contents

PART ONE

The Sorry Business

What you seek, you shall never find.
For when the Gods made man,
They kept immortality for themselves.
Fill your belly.
Day and night make merry,
Let Days be full of joy.
Love the child that holds your hand.
Let your wife delight in your embrace.
For these alone are the concerns of man.
— *The Epic of Gilgamesh*

1

Because I Could Not Stop for Death — He Kindly Stopped for Me —

Charlie Asher walked the earth like an ant walks on the surface of water, as if the slightest misstep might send him plummeting through the surface to be sucked to the depths below. Blessed with the Beta Male imagination, he spent much of his life squinting into the future so he might spot ways in which the world was conspiring to kill him — him; his wife, Rachel; and now, newborn Sophie. But despite his attention, his paranoia, his ceaseless fretting from the moment Rachel peed a blue stripe on the pregnancy stick to the time they wheeled her into recovery at St. Francis Memorial, Death slipped in.

"She's not breathing," Charlie said.

"She's breathing fine," Rachel said, patting the baby's back. "Do you want to hold her?"

11

Charlie had held baby Sophie for a few seconds earlier in the day, and had handed her quickly to a nurse insisting that someone more qualified than he do some finger and toe counting. He'd done it twice and kept coming up with twenty-one.

"They act like that's all there is to it. Like if the kid has the minimum ten fingers and ten toes it's all going to be fine. What if there are extras? Huh? Extra-credit fingers? What if the kid has a tail?" (Charlie was sure he'd spotted a tail in the six-month sonogram. Umbilical indeed! He'd kept a hard copy.)

"She doesn't have a tail, Mr. Asher," the nurse explained. "And it's ten and ten, we've all checked. Perhaps you should go home and get some rest."

"I'll still love her, even with her extra finger."

"She's perfectly normal."

"Or toe."

"We really do know what we're doing, Mr. Asher. She's a beautiful, healthy baby girl."

"Or a tail."

The nurse sighed. She was short, wide, and had a tattoo of a snake up her right calf that showed through her white nurse stockings. She spent four hours of every workday massaging preemie babies, her hands threaded through ports in a Lucite incubator, like she was handling a radioactive spark in there. She talked to them, coaxed them, told them how special they were, and felt their hearts fluttering in chests no bigger than a balled-up pair of sweat socks. She cried over every one, and believed that her tears and touch poured a bit of her own life into the tiny bodies, which was just fine with her. She could spare it. She had been a neonatal nurse for twenty years and had never so much as raised her voice to a new father.

"There's no goddamn tail, you doofus! Look!" She pulled down the blanket and aimed baby Sophie's bottom at him like she might unleash a fusillade of weapons-grade poopage such as the guileless Beta Male had never seen.

Charlie jumped back — a lean and nimble thirty, he was — then, once he realized that the baby wasn't loaded, he straightened the lapels on his tweed jacket in a gesture of righteous indignation. "You could have removed her tail in the delivery room and we'd never know." He didn't know. He'd been asked to leave the delivery room, first by the ob-gyn and finally by Rachel. ("Him or me," Rachel said.

13

"One of us has to go.")

In Rachel's room, Charlie said: "If they removed her tail, I want it. She'll want it when she gets older."

"Sophie, your Papa isn't really insane. He just hasn't slept for a couple of days."

"She's looking at me," Charlie said. "She's looking at me like I blew her college money at the track and now she's going to have to turn tricks to get her MBA."

Rachel took his hand. "Honey, I don't think her eyes can even focus this early, and besides, she's a little young to start worrying about her turning tricks to get her MFA."

"MBA," Charlie corrected. "They start very young these days. By the time I figure out how to get to the track, she could be old enough. God, your parents are going to hate me."

"And that would be different how?"

"New reasons, that's how. Now I've made their granddaughter a shiksa."

"She's not a shiksa, Charlie. We've been through this. She's my daughter, so she's as Jewish as I am."

Charlie went down on one knee next to the bed and took one of Sophie's tiny hands between his fingers. "Daddy's sorry he made you a shiksa." He put his head down, buried his face in the crook where the baby met Rachel's side. Rachel traced his hairline with her fingernail, describing a tight U-turn around his narrow forehead.

"You need to go home and get some sleep."

Charlie mumbled something into the covers. When he looked up there were tears in his eyes. "She feels warm."

"She is warm. She's supposed to be. It's a mammal thing. Goes with the breast-feeding. Why are you crying?"

"You guys are so beautiful." He began arranging Rachel's dark hair across the pillow, brought a long lock down over Sophie's head, and started styling it into a baby hairpiece.

"It will be okay if she can't grow hair. There was that angry Irish singer who didn't have any hair and she was attractive. If we had her tail we could transplant plugs from that."

"Charlie! Go home!"

"Your parents will blame me. Their bald shiksa granddaughter turning tricks and getting a business degree — it will be all my fault."

Rachel grabbed the buzzer from the blanket and held it up like it was wired to a bomb. "Charlie, if you don't go home and get some sleep right now, I swear I'll buzz the nurse and have her throw you out."

She sounded stern, but she was smiling. Charlie liked looking at her smile, always had; it felt like approval and permission at the same time. Permission to be Charlie Asher.

"Okay, I'll go." He reached to feel her forehead. "Do you have a fever? You look tired."

"I just gave birth, you squirrel!"

"I'm just concerned about you." He was not a squirrel. She was blaming him for Sophie's tail, that's why she'd said squirrel, and not doofus like everyone else.

"Sweetie, go. Now. So I can get some rest."

Charlie fluffed her pillows, checked her water pitcher, tucked in the blankets, kissed her forehead, kissed the baby's head, fluffed the baby, then started to rearrange the flowers that his mother had sent, moving the big stargazer lily in the front, accenting it with a spray of baby's breath —

"Charlie!"

"I'm going. Jeez." He checked the room, one last time, then backed toward the door.

"Can I bring you anything from home?"

"I'll be fine. The ready kit you packed

covered everything, I think. In fact, I may not even need the fire extinguisher."

"Better to have it and not need it, than to need it —"

"Go! I'll get some rest, the doctor will check Sophie out, and we'll take her home in the morning."

"That seems soon."

"It's standard."

"Should I bring more propane for the camp stove?"

"We'll try to make it last."

"But —"

Rachel held up the buzzer, as if her demands were not met, the consequences could be dire. "Love you," she said.

"Love you, too," Charlie said. "Both of you."

"Bye, Daddy." Rachel puppeted Sophie's little hand in a wave.

Charlie felt a lump rising in his throat. No one had ever called him Daddy before, not even a puppet. (He *had* once asked Rachel, "Who's your daddy?" during sex, to which she had replied, "Saul Goldstein," thus rendering him impotent for a week and raising all kinds of issues that he didn't really like to think about.)

He backed out of the room, palming the door shut as he went, then headed down the hall and past the desk where the neo-natal nurse with the snake tattoo gave him a sideways smile as he went by.

Charlie drove a six-year-old minivan that he'd inherited from his father, along with the thrift store and the building that housed it. The minivan always smelled faintly of dust, mothballs, and body odor, despite a forest of smell-good Christmas trees that Charlie had hung from every hook, knob, and protrusion. He opened the car door and the odor of the unwanted — the wares of the thrift-store owner — washed over him.

Before he even had the key in the ignition, he noticed the Sarah McLachlan CD lying on the passenger seat. Well, Rachel was going to miss that. It was her favorite CD and there she was, recovering without it, and he could not have that. Charlie grabbed the CD, locked the van, and headed back up to Rachel's room.

To his relief, the nurse had stepped away from the desk so he didn't have to endure her frosty stare of accusation, or what he guessed would be her frosty stare of accu-sation. He'd mentally prepared a short speech about how being a good husband and father included anticipating the wants and needs of his wife and that included bringing her music — well, he could use the speech on the way out if she gave him the frosty stare.

He opened the door to Rachel's room slowly so as not to startle her — anticipating her warm smile of disapproval, but instead she appeared to be asleep and there was a very tall black man dressed in mint green standing next to her bed.

"What are you doing here?"

The man in mint green turned, startled. "You can see me?" He gestured to his chocolate-brown tie, and Charlie was reminded, just for a second, of those thin mints they put on the pillow in nicer hotels.

"Of course I can see you. What are you doing here?"

Charlie moved to Rachel's bedside, putting himself between the stranger and his family. Baby Sophie seemed fascinated by the tall black man.

"This is not good," said Mint Green.

"You're in the wrong room," Charlie said. "You get out of here." Charlie reached behind and patted Rachel's hand.

"This is really, really not good."

"Sir, my wife is trying to sleep and you're in the wrong room. Now please go before —"

"She's not sleeping," said Mint Green. His voice was soft, and a little Southern. "I'm sorry."

Charlie turned to look down at Rachel, expecting to see her smile, hear her tell him to calm down, but her eyes were closed and her head had lolled off the pillow.

"Honey?" Charlie dropped the CD he was carrying and shook her gently. "Honey?"

Baby Sophie began to cry. Charlie felt Rachel's forehead, took her by the shoulders, and shook her. "Honey, wake up. Rachel." He put his ear to her heart and heard nothing. "Nurse!"

Charlie scrambled across the bed to grab the buzzer that had slipped from Rachel's hand and lay on the blanket. "Nurse!" He pounded the button and turned to look at the man in mint green. "What happened . . ."

He was gone.

Charlie ran into the hall, but no one was out there. "Nurse!"

Twenty seconds later the nurse with the snake tattoo arrived, followed in another thirty seconds by a resuscitation team with a crash cart.

There was nothing they could do.

2

A Fine Edge

There's a fine edge to new grief, it severs nerves, disconnects reality — there's mercy in a sharp blade. Only with time, as the edge wears, does the real ache begin.

So Charlie was barely even aware of his own shrieks in Rachel's hospital room, of being sedated, of the filmy electric hysteria that netted everything he did for that first day. After that, it was a memory out of a sleepwalk, scenes filmed from a zombie's eye socket, as he ambled undead through explanations, accusations, preparations, and ceremony.

"It's called a cerebral thromboembolism," the doctor had said. "A blood clot forms in the legs or pelvis during labor, then moves to the brain, cutting off the blood supply. It's very rare, but it happens. There was nothing we could do. Even if the crash team had been able to revive her, she'd have had massive brain damage. There was no pain. She probably just felt sleepy and passed."

Charlie whispered to keep from screaming, "The man in mint green! He did something to her. He injected her with something. He was there and he knew that she was dying. I saw him when I brought her CD back."

They showed him the security tapes — the nurse, the doctor, the hospital's administrators and lawyers — they all watched the black-and-white images of him leaving Rachel's room, of the empty hallway, of his returning to her room. No tall black man dressed in mint green. They didn't even find the CD.

Sleep deprivation, they said. Hallucination brought on by exhaustion. Trauma. They gave him drugs to sleep, drugs for anxiety, drugs for depression, and they sent him home with his baby daughter.

Charlie's older sister, Jane, held baby Sophie as they spoke over Rachel and buried her on the second day. He didn't remember picking out a casket or making arrangements. It was more of the somnambulant dream: his in-laws moving to and fro in black, like tottering specters, spouting the inadequate clichés of condolence:

We're so sorry. She was so young. What a tragedy. If there's anything we can do . . .

Rachel's father and mother held him, their heads pressed together in the apex of a tripod. The slate floor in the funeral-home foyer spotted with their tears. Every time Charlie felt the shoulders of the older man heave with a sob, he felt his own heart break again. Saul took Charlie's face in his hands and said, "You can't imagine, because I can't imagine." But Charlie could imagine, because he was a Beta Male, and imagination was his curse; and he could imagine because he had lost Rachel and now he had a daughter, that tiny stranger sleeping in his sister's arms. He could imagine the man in mint green taking her.

Charlie looked at the tear-spotted floor and said, "That's why most funeral homes are carpeted. Someone could slip."

"Poor boy," said Rachel's mother. "We'll sit shivah with you, of course."

Charlie made his way across the room to his sister, Jane, who wore a man's double-breasted suit in charcoal pinstripe gabardine, that along with her severe eighties pop-star hairstyle and the infant in the pink blanket that she held, made her appear not so much androgynous as confused. Charlie thought the suit actually looked better on her than it did on him, but she should have asked him for permission to wear it nonetheless.

"I can't do this," he said. He let himself fall forward until the receded peninsula of dark hair touched her gelled Flock of Seagulls platinum flip. It seemed like the best posture for sharing grief, this forehead lean, and it reminded him of standing drunkenly at a urinal and falling forward until his head hit the wall. Despair.

"You're doing fine," Jane said. "Nobody's good at this."

"What the fuck's a shivah?"

"I think it's that Hindu god with all the arms."

"That can't be right. The Goldsteins are going to sit on it with me."

"Didn't Rachel teach you anything about being Jewish?"

"I wasn't paying attention. I thought we had time."

Jane adjusted baby Sophie into a half-back, one-armed carry and put her free hand on the back of Charlie's neck. "You'll be okay, kid."

"Seven," said Mrs. Goldstein. "*Shivah* means 'seven.' We used to sit for seven days, grieving for the dead, praying. That's

Orthodox, now most people just sit for three."

They sat shivah in Charlie and Rachel's apartment that overlooked the cable-car line at the corner of Mason and Vallejo Streets. The building was a four-story brick Edwardian (architecturally, not quite the grand courtesan couture of the Victorians, but enough tarty trim and trash to toss off a sailor down a side street) built after the earthquake and fire of 1906 had leveled the whole area of what was now North Beach, Russian Hill, and Chinatown. Charlie and Jane had inherited the building, along with the thrift shop that occupied the ground floor, when their father died four years before. Charlie got the business, the large, double apartment they'd grown up in, and the upkeep on the old building, while Jane got half the rental income and one of the apartments on the top floor with a Bay Bridge view.

At the instruction of Mrs. Goldstein, all the mirrors in the house were draped with black fabric and a large candle was placed on the coffee table in the center of the living room. They were supposed to sit on low benches or cushions, neither of which Charlie had in the house, so, for the first time since Rachel's death, he went downstairs into the thrift shop looking for something they could use. The back stairs descended from a pantry behind the kitchen into the stockroom, where Charlie kept his office among boxes of merchandise waiting to be sorted, priced, and placed in the store.

The shop was dark except for the light that filtered in the front window from the streetlights out on Mason Street. Charlie stood there at the foot of the stairs, his hand on the light switch, just staring. Amid the shelves of knickknacks and books, the piles of old radios, the racks of clothes, all of them dark, just lumpy shapes in the dark, he could see objects glowing a dull red, nearly pulsing, like beating hearts. A sweater in the racks, a porcelain figure of a frog in a curio case, out by the front window an old Coca-Cola tray, a pair of shoes — all glowing red.

Charlie flipped the switch, fluorescent tubes fired to life across the ceiling, flickering at first, and the shop lit up. The red glow disappeared. "Okaaaaaaay," he said to himself, calmly, like everything was just fine now. He flipped off the lights. Glowing red stuff. On the counter, close to where he stood, there was a brass business-card holder cast in the shape of a whooping crane, glowing dull red. He took a second to study it, just to make sure there wasn't some red light source from outside refracting around the room and making him uneasy for no reason. He stepped into the dark shop, took a closer look, got an angle on the brass cranes. Nope, the brass was definitely pulsing red. He turned and ran back up the steps as fast as he could.

He nearly ran over Jane, who stood in the kitchen, rocking Sophie gently in her arms, talking baby talk under her breath.

"What?" Jane said. "I know you have some big cushions down in the shop somewhere."

"I can't," Charlie said. "I'm on drugs." He backed against the refrigerator, like he was holding it hostage.

"I'll go get them. Here, hold the baby."

"I can't, I'm on drugs. I'm hallucinating."

Jane cradled the baby in the crook of her right arm and put a free arm around her younger brother. "Charlie, you are on antidepressants and antianxiety drugs, not acid. Look around this apartment, there's not a person here that's not on something." Charlie looked through the kitchen passthrough: women in black, most of them middle-aged or older, shaking their heads,

27

men looking stoic, standing around the perimeter of the living room, each holding a stout tumbler of liquor and staring into space.

"See, they're all fucked up."

"What about Mom?" Charlie nodded to their mother, who stood out among the other gray-haired women in black because she was draped in silver Navaho jewelry and was so darkly tanned that she appeared to be melting into her old-fashioned when she took a sip.

"Especially Mom," Jane said. "I'll go look for something to sit shivah on. I don't know why you can't just use the couches. Now take your daughter."

"I can't. I can't be trusted with her."

"Take her, bitch!" Jane barked in Charlie's ear — sort of a whisper bark. It had long ago been determined who was the Alpha Male between them and it was not Charlie. She handed off the baby and cut to the stairs.

"Jane," Charlie called after her. "Look around before you turn on the lights. See if you see anything weird, okay?"

"Right. Weird."

She left him standing there in the kitchen, studying his daughter, thinking that her head might be a little oblong, but despite that, she looked a little like Rachel. "Your mommy loved Aunt Jane," he said. "They used to gang up on me in Risk — and Monopoly — and arguments — and cooking." He slid down the fridge door, sat splayed-legged on the floor, and buried his face in Sophie's blanket.

In the dark, Jane barked her shin on a wooden box full of old telephones. "Well, this is just stupid," she said to herself, and flipped on the lights. Nothing weird. Then, because Charlie was many things, but one of them was not crazy, she turned off the lights again, just to be sure that she hadn't missed something. "Right. Weird."

There was nothing weird about the store except that she was standing there in the dark rubbing her shin. But then, right before she turned on the light again, she saw someone peering in the front window, making a cup around his eyes to see through the reflection of the streetlights. A homeless guy or drunken tourist, she thought. She moved through the dark shop, between columns of comic books stacked on the floor, to a spot behind a rack of jackets where she could get a clear view of the window, which was filled with cheap cameras, vases, belt buckles, and all manner of objects that Charlie had judged worthy of interest, but obviously not worthy of a smash-and-grab.

The guy looked tall, and not homeless, nicely dressed, but all in a single light color, she thought it might be yellow, but it was hard to tell under the streetlights. Could be light green.

"We're closed," Jane said, loud enough to be heard through the glass.

The man outside peered around the shop, but couldn't spot her. He stepped back from the window and she could see that he was, indeed, tall. Very tall. The streetlight caught the line of his cheek as he turned. He was also very thin and very black.

"I was looking for the owner," the tall man said. "I have something I need to show him."

"There's been a death in the family," Jane said. "We'll be closed for the week. Can you come back in a week?"

The tall man nodded, looking up and down the street as he did. He rocked on one foot like he was about to bolt, but kept stopping himself, like a sprinter straining against the starting blocks. Jane didn't move. There were always people out on the street, and it wasn't even late yet, but this guy was too anxious for the situation.

"Look, if you need to get something appraised —"

"No," he cut her off. "No. Just tell him she's, no — tell him to look for a package in the mail. I'm not sure when."

Jane smiled to herself. This guy had something — a brooch, a coin, a book — something that he thought was worth some money, maybe something he'd found in his grandmother's closet. She'd seen it a dozen times. They acted like they've found the lost city of Eldorado — they'd come in with it tucked in their coats, or wrapped in a thousand layers of tissue paper and tape. (The more tape, generally, the more worthless the item would turn out to be — there was an equation there somewhere.) Nine times out of ten it was crap. She'd watched her father try to finesse their ego and gently lower the owners into disappointment, convince them that the sentimental value made it priceless, and that he, a lowly secondhand-store owner, couldn't presume to put a value on it. Charlie, on the other hand, would just tell them that he didn't know about brooches, or coins, or whatever they had and let someone else bear the bad news.

"Okay, I'll tell him," Jane said from her cover behind the coats.

With that, the tall man was away, taking great praying-mantis strides up the street and out of view. Jane shrugged, went back and turned on the lights, then proceeded to search for cushions among the piles.

It was a big store, taking up nearly the whole bottom floor of the building, and not particularly well organized, as each system that Charlie adopted seemed to collapse after a few weeks under its own weight, and the result was not so much a patchwork of organizational systems, but a garden of mismatched piles. Lily, the maroon-haired Goth girl who worked for Charlie three afternoons a week, said that the fact that they ever found anything at all was proof of the chaos theory at work, then she would walk away muttering and go out in the alley to smoke clove cigarettes and stare into the Abyss. (Although Charlie noted that the Abyss looked an awful lot like a Dumpster.)

It took Jane ten minutes to navigate the aisles and find three cushions that looked wide enough and thick enough that they might work for sitting shivah, and when she returned to Charlie's apartment she found her brother curled into the fetal position around baby Sophie, asleep on the kitchen floor. The other mourners had completely forgotten about him.

"Hey, doofus." She nudged his shoulder with her toe and he rolled onto his back, the baby still in his arms. "These okay?"

"Did you see anything glowing?"

Jane dropped the stack of cushions on the floor. "What?"

"Glowing red. Did you see things in the shop glowing, like pulsating red?"

"No. Did you?"

"Kind of."

"Give 'em up."

"What?"

"The drugs. Hand them over. They're obviously much better than you led me to believe."

"But you said they were just antianxiety."

"Give up the drugs. I'll watch the kid while you shivah."

"You can't watch my daughter if you're on drugs."

"Fine. Surrender the crumb snatcher and go sit."

Charlie handed the baby up to Jane. "You have to keep Mom out of the way, too."

"Oh no, not without drugs."

"They're in the medicine cabinet in the master bath. Bottom shelf."

He was sitting on the floor now, rubbing his forehead as if to stretch the skin out over his pain. She kneed him in the shoulder.

"Hey, kid, I'm sorry, you know that, right? Goes without saying, right?"

"Yeah." A weak smile.

She held the baby up by her face, then looked down in adoration, Mother of Jesus style. "What do you think? I should get one of these, huh?"

"You can borrow mine whenever you need to."

"Nah, I should get my own. I already feel bad about borrowing your wife."

"Jane!"

"Kidding! Jeez. You're such a wuss sometimes. Go sit shivah. Go. Go. Go."

Charlie gathered the cushions and went to the living room to grieve with his in-laws, nervous because the only prayer he knew was "Now I Lay Me Down to Sleep," and he wasn't sure that was going to cut it for three full days.

Jane forgot to mention the tall guy from the shop.

3

Beneath the Number Forty-one Bus

It was two weeks before Charlie left the apartment and walked down to the auto-teller on Columbus Avenue where he first killed a guy. His weapon of choice was the number forty-one bus, on its way from the Trans Bay station, by the Bay Bridge, to the Presidio, by the Golden Gate Bridge. If you're going to get hit by a bus in San Francisco, you want to go with the forty-one, because you can pretty much figure on there being a nice bridge view.

Charlie hadn't really counted on killing a guy that morning. He had hoped to get some twenties for the register at the thrift store, check his balance, and maybe pick up some yellow mustard at the deli. (Charlie was not a brown mustard kind of guy. Brown mustard was the condiment equivalent of skydiving — it was okay for race-car drivers and serial killers, but for Charlie, a fine line of French's yellow was all the spice that life required.) After the funeral, friends and relatives had left a mountain of cold cuts in Charlie's fridge, which was all he'd eaten for the past two weeks, but now he was down to ham, dark rye, and pre-mixed Enfamil formula, none of which was tolerable without yellow mustard. He'd secured the yellow squeeze bottle and felt safer now with it in his jacket pocket, but when the bus hit the guy, mustard completely slipped Charlie's mind.

It was a warm day in October, the light had gone autumn soft over the city, the summer fog had ceased its relentless crawl out of the Bay each morning, and there was just enough breeze that the few sailboats that dotted the Bay looked like they might have been posing for an Impressionist painter. In the split second that Charlie's victim realized that he was being run over, he might not have been happy about the event, but he couldn't have picked a nicer day for it.

The guy's name was William Creek. He was thirty-two and worked as a market analyst in the financial district, where he had been headed that morning when he decided to stop at the auto-teller. He was wearing a light wool suit and running shoes, his work shoes were tucked into a leather satchel under his arm. The handle of a compact umbrella protruded from the side pocket of the satchel, and it was this that caught Charlie's attention, for while the handle of the umbrella appeared to be made of faux walnut burl, it was glowing a dull red as if it had been heated in a forge.

Charlie stood in the ATM line trying not to notice, trying to appear uninterested, but he couldn't help but stare. It was glowing, for fuck's sake, didn't anyone see it?

William Creek glanced over his shoulder as he slid his card into the machine, saw Charlie looking at him, then tried to will his suit coat to expand into great manta-ray wings to block Charlie's view as he keyed in his PIN number. Creek snatched his card and the expectorated cash from the machine, turned, and headed away quickly toward the corner.

Charlie couldn't stand it any longer. The umbrella handle had begun to pulsate red, like a beating heart. As Creek reached the curb, Charlie said, "Excuse me. Excuse me, sir!"

When Creek turned, Charlie said, "Your umbrella —"

At that point, the number forty-one bus was coming through the intersection at Columbus and Vallejo at about thirty-five miles per hour, angling toward the curb for its next stop. Creek looked down at the satchel under his arm where Charlie was pointing, and the heel of his running shoe caught the slight rise of the curb. He started to lose his balance, the sort of thing we all might do on any given day while walking through the city, trip on a crack in the sidewalk and take a couple of quick steps to regain equilibrium, but William Creek took only one step. Back. Off the curb.

You can't really sugarcoat it at this point, can you? The number forty-one bus creamed him. He flew a good fifty feet through the air before he hit the back window of a SAAB like a great gabardine sack of meat, then bounced back to the pavement and commenced to ooze fluids. His belongings — the satchel, the umbrella, a gold tie bar, a Tag Heuer watch — skittered on down the street, ricocheting off tires, shoes, manhole covers, some coming to rest nearly a block away.

Charlie stood at the curb trying to breathe. He could hear a tooting sound, like someone was blowing a toy train whistle — it was all he could hear, then someone ran into him and he realized it was the sound of his own rhythmic whimpering. The guy — the guy with the umbrella — had just been wiped out of the world. People rushed, crowded around, a dozen were barking into cell phones, the bus driver nearly flattened Charlie as he rushed down the sidewalk toward the carnage. Charlie staggered after him.

"I was just going to ask him —"

No one looked at Charlie. It had taken all of his will, as well as a pep talk from his sister, to leave the apartment, and now this?

"I was just going to tell him that his umbrella was on fire," Charlie said, as if he was explaining to his accusers. But no one accused him, really. They ran by him, some headed toward the body, some away from it — they batted him around and looked back, baffled, like they'd collided with a rough air current or a ghost instead of a man.

"The umbrella," Charlie said, looking for the evidence. Then he spotted it, almost down at the next corner, lying in the gutter, still glowing red, pulsating like failing neon. "There! See!" But people were gathered around the dead man in a wide semicircle, their hands to their mouths, and no one was paying any attention to the frightened thin man spouting nonsense behind them.

He threaded his way through the crowd toward the umbrella, determined now to confirm his conviction, too far in shock to be afraid. When he was only ten feet away from it he looked up the street to make sure another bus wasn't coming before he ventured off the curb. He looked back just as a delicate, tar-black hand snaked out of the storm drain and snatched the compact umbrella off the street.

Charlie backed away, looking around to see if anyone had seen what he had seen, but no one had. No one even made eye contact. A policeman trotted by and Charlie grabbed his sleeve as he passed, but when the cop spun around and his eyes went wide with confusion, then what appeared to be real terror, Charlie let him go. "Sorry," he said. "Sorry. I can see you've got work to do — sorry."

The cop shuddered and pushed through the crowd of onlookers toward the battered body of William Creek.

Charlie started running, across Columbus and up Vallejo, until his breath and heartbeat in his ears drowned all the sounds of the street. When he was a block away from his shop a great shadow moved over him, like a low-flying aircraft or a huge bird, and with it Charlie felt a chill vibrate up his back. He lowered his head, pumped his arms, and rounded the corner of Mason just as the cable car was passing, full of smiling tourists who looked right through him. He glanced up, just for a second, and he thought he saw something above, disappearing over the roof of the six-story Victorian across the street, then he bolted through the front door of his shop.

"Hey, boss," Lily said. She was sixteen, pale, and a little bottom heavy — her grown-woman form still in flux between baby fat and baby bearing. Today her hair happened to be lavender: fifties-housewife helmet hair in Easter-basket cellophane pastel.

Charlie was bent over, leaning against a case full of curios by the door, sucking in deep raspy gulps of secondhand store mustiness. "I — think — I — just — killed — a — guy," he gasped.

"Excellent," Lily said, ignoring equally his message and his demeanor. "We're going to need change for the register."

"With a bus," Charlie said.

"Ray called in," she said. Ray Macy was Charlie's other employee, a thirty-nine-year-old bachelor with an unhealthy lack of boundaries between the Internet and reality. "He's flying to Manila to meet the love of his life. A Ms. *LoveYouLongTime*. Ray's convinced that they are soul mates."

"There was something in the sewer," Charlie said.

Lily examined a chip in her black nail polish. "So I cut school to cover. I've been doing that since you've been, uh, gone. I'm going to need a note."

Charlie stood up and made his way to the counter. "Lily, did you hear what I said?"

He grabbed her by the shoulders, but she spun out of his grasp. "Ouch! Fuck. Back off, Asher, you sado freak, that's a new tattoo." She punched him in the arm, hard, and backed away, rubbing her own shoulder. "I heard, you. Cease your trippin', *s'il vous plaît*." Lately, since discovering Baudelaire's *Fleurs du Mal* in a stack of used books in the back room, Lily had been peppering her speech with French phrases. "French better expresses the profound *noirness* of my existence," she had said.

Charlie put both hands on the counter

to keep them from shaking, then spoke slowly and deliberately, like he was speaking to someone for whom English was a second language: "Lily, I'm having kind of a bad month, and I appreciate that you are throwing away your education so you can come here and alienate customers for me, but if you don't sit down and show me a little fucking human decency, then I'm going to have to let you go."

Lily sat down on the chrome-and-vinyl diner stool behind the register and pulled her long lavender bangs out of her eyes. "So you want me to pay close attention to your confession to murder? Take notes, maybe get an old cassette recorder off the shelf and get everything down on tape? You're saying that by trying to ignore your obvious distress, which I would have to later recall to the police, so I can be personally responsible for sending you to the gas chamber, that I'm being inconsiderate?"

Charlie shuddered. "Jeez, Lily." He was continually surprised at the speed and accuracy of her creepiness. She was like some creepiness child prodigy. But on the bright side, her extreme darkness made him realize that he probably wasn't going to go to the gas chamber.

"It wasn't that kind of killing. There was something following me, and —"

"Silence!" Lily put her hand up, "I'd rather not show my employee spirit by committing every detail of your heinous crime to my photographic memory to be recalled in court later. I'll just say that I saw you but you seemed normal for someone without a clue."

"You don't have a photographic memory."

"I do, too, and it's a curse. I can never forget the futility of —"

"You forgot to take out the trash at least eight times last month."

"I didn't forget."

Charlie took a deep breath, the familiarity of arguing with Lily was actually calming him down. "Okay then, without looking, what color shirt are you wearing?" He raised an eyebrow like he had her there.

Lily smiled and for a second he could see that she was just a kid, kind of cute and goofy under the fierce makeup and attitude. "Black."

"Lucky guess."

"You know I only own black." She grinned. "Glad you didn't ask hair color, I just changed this morning."

44

"That's not good for you, you know. That dye has toxins."

Lily lifted the lavender wig to reveal her close-cut maroon locks underneath, then dropped it again. "I'm all natural." She stood and patted the bar stool. "Sit, Asher. Confess. Bore me."

Lily leaned back against the counter, and tilted her head to look attentive, but with her dark eye makeup and lavender hair it came off more like a marionette with a broken string. Charlie came around the counter and sat on the stool. "I was just in line behind this William Creek guy, and I saw his umbrella glowing . . ."

And Charlie went through the whole story to her, the umbrella, the bus, the hand from the storm sewer, the bolt for home with the giant dark shadow above the rooftops, and when he was finished, Lily asked, "So how do you know his name?"

"Huh?" Charlie said. Of all of the horrible, fantastic things she might have asked about, why that?

"How do you know the guy's name?" Lily repeated. "You barely spoke to the guy before he bit it. You see it on his receipt or something?"

"No, I . . ." He didn't have any idea how

he knew the man's name, but suddenly there was a picture in his head of it written out in big, block letters. He leapt off the stool. "I gotta go, Lily."

He ran through the door into the stockroom and up the steps.

"I still need a note for school," Lily shouted from below, but Charlie was dashing through the kitchen, past a large Russian woman who was bouncing his baby daughter in her arms, and into the bedroom, where he snatched up the notepad he kept on his nightstand by the phone.

There, in his own blocky handwriting, was written the name William Creek and, under it, the number 12. He sat down hard on the bed, holding the notepad like it was a vial of explosives.

Behind him came the heavy steps of Mrs. Korjev as she followed him into the bedroom. "Mr. Asher, what is wrong? You run by like burning bear."

And Charlie, because he was a Beta Male, and there had evolved over millions of years a standard Beta response to things inexplicable, said, "Someone is fucking with me."

Lily was touching up her nail polish with

a black Magic Marker when Stephan, the mailman, came through the shop door.

" 'Sup, Darque?" Stephan said, sorting a stack of mail out of his bag. He was forty, short, muscular, and black. He wore wraparound sunglasses, which were almost always pushed back on his head over hair braided in tight cornrows. Lily had mixed feelings about him. She liked him because he called her Darque, short for Darque-willow Elventhing, the name under which she received mail at the shop, but because he was cheerful and seemed to like people, she deeply mistrusted him.

"Need you to sign," Stephan said, offering her an electronic pad, on which she scribbled *Charles Baudelaire* with great flourish and without even looking.

Stephan plopped the mail on the counter. "Working alone again? So where is everyone?"

"Ray's in the Philippines, Charlie's traumatized." She sighed. "Weight of the world falls on me —"

"Poor Charlie," Stephan said. "They say that's the worst thing you can go through, losing a spouse."

"Yeah, there's that, too. Today he's traumatized because he saw a guy get hit by a bus up on Columbus."

47

"Heard about that. He gonna be okay?"

"Well, fuck no, Stephan, he got hit by a bus." Lily looked up from her nails for the first time.

"I meant Charlie." Stephan winked, despite her harsh tone.

"Oh, he's Charlie."

"How's the baby?"

"Evidently she leaks noxious substances." Lily waved the Magic Marker under her nose as if it might mask the smell of ripened baby.

"All good, then," Stephan smiled. "That's it for today. You got anything for me?"

"I took in some red vinyl platforms yesterday. Men's size ten."

Stephan collected vintage seventies pimp wear. Lily was to be on the lookout for anything that came through the shop.

"How tall?"

"Four inches."

"Low altitude," Stephan said, as if that explained everything. "Take care, Darque."

Lily waved her Magic Marker at him as he left, and started sorting through the mail. There were mostly bills, a couple of flyers, but one thick black envelope that felt like a book or catalog. It was addressed to Charlie Asher "in care of" Asher's Secondhand and had a postmark from Night's Plutonian Shore, which evidently was in whatever state started with a *U*. (Lily found geography not only mind-numbingly boring, but also, in the age of the Internet, irrelevant.)

Was it not addressed to the care of Asher's Secondhand? Lily reasoned. *And was she, Lily Darquewillow Elventhing, not manning the counter, the sole employee — nay — the de facto manager, of said secondhand store? And wasn't it her right — nay — her responsibility to open this envelope and spare Charlie the irritation of the task? Onward, Elventhing! Your destiny is set, and if it be not destiny, then surely there is plausible deniability, which in the parlance of politics is the same thing.*

She drew a jewel-encrusted dagger from under the counter (the stones valued at over seventy-three cents) and slit the envelope, pulled out the book, and fell in love.

The cover was shiny, like a children's picture book, with a colorful illustration of a grinning skeleton with tiny people impaled on his fingertips, and all of them appeared to be having the time of their lives, as if they were enjoying a carnival ride that just happened to involve having a gaping

49

hole being punched through the chest. It was festive — lots of flowers and candy in primary colors, done in the style of Mexican folk art. *The Great Big Book of Death*, was the title, spelled out across the top of the cover in cheerful, human femur font letters.

Lily opened the book to the first page, where a note was paper-clipped.

This should explain everything. I'm sorry.
— MF

Lily removed the note and opened the book to the first chapter: "So Now You're Death: Here's What You'll Need."

And it was all she needed. This was, very possibly, the coolest book she had ever seen. And certainly not anything Charlie would be able to appreciate, especially in his current state of heightened neurosis. She slipped the book into her backpack, then tore the note and the envelope into tiny pieces and buried them at the bottom of the wastebasket.

4

The Beta Male in His Natural Environment

"Jane," said Charlie, "I am convinced by the events of the last few weeks that nefarious forces or people — unidentified but no less real — are threatening life as we know it, and in fact, may be bent on unraveling the very fabric of our existence."

"And that's why I have to eat yellow mustard?" Jane was sitting at Charlie's breakfast counter eating Little Smokies cocktail sausages out of the package, dipping them in a ramekin of French's yellow. Baby Sophie was sitting on the counter in her car-seat/bassinet/imperial-storm-trooper-helmet thingy.

Charlie paced the kitchen, marking off his evidentiary points in the air with a sausage as he went. "First, there was the guy in Rachel's room that mysteriously disap-

51

peared from the security tapes."

"Because he was never there. Look, Sophie likes yellow mustard like you."

"Second," Charlie continued, despite his sister's persistent indifference, "all the stuff in the shop was glowing like it was radioactive. Don't put that in her mouth."

"Oh my God, Charlie, Sophie's straight. Look at her go after that Lil' Smokie."

"And third, that Creek guy, got hit by a bus up on Columbus yesterday, I knew his name and he had an umbrella that was glowing red."

"I'm so disappointed," said Jane. "I was looking forward to raising her on the allgirls team — giving her the advantages I never had, but look at her work that sausage. This kid is a natural."

"Get that out of her mouth!"

"Relax, she can't eat it. She doesn't even have teeth. And it's not like there's a moaning Teletubby on the other end of it. Oh, jeez, it's going to take major tequila to get that picture out of my head."

"She can't have pork, Jane. She's Jewish! Are you trying to turn my daughter into a shiksa?"

Jane snatched the cocktail sausage out of Sophie's mouth, and examined it, even as the fiber-optic strand of drool stayed connected to the tiny kid. "I don't think I can eat these things ever again," Jane said. "They'll always conjure visions of my niece blowing a terry-cloth puppet person."

"Jane!" Charlie grabbed the sausage from her and flung it into the sink.

"What?!"

"Are you listening at all?"

"Yes, yes, you saw some guy get hit by a bus so your fabric is unraveling. So?"

"So, someone is fucking with me?"

"And why is that news, Charlie? You've thought someone was fucking with you since you were eight."

"They have been. Probably. But this time it's real. It could be real."

"Hey, these are all-beef Lil' Smokies. Sophie's not a shikster after all."

"Shiksa!"

"Whatever."

"Jane, you're not helping with my problem."

"What problem? You have a problem?"

Charlie's problem was that the trailing edge of his Beta Male imagination was digging at him like bamboo splinters under the fingernails. While Alpha Males are often gifted with superior physical attributes — size, strength, speed, good looks

53

— selected by evolution over the eons by the strongest surviving and, essentially, getting all the girls, the Beta Male gene has survived not by meeting and overcoming adversity, but by anticipating and avoiding it. That is, when the Alpha Males were out charging after mastodons, the Beta Males could imagine in advance that attacking what was essentially an angry, woolly bulldozer with a pointy stick might be a losing proposition, so they hung back at camp to console the grieving widows. When Alpha Males set out to conquer neighboring tribes, to count coups and take heads, Beta Males could see in advance that in the event of a victory, the influx of female slaves was going to leave a surplus of mateless women cast out for younger trophy models, with nothing to do but salt down the heads and file the uncounted coups, and some would find solace in the arms of any Beta Male smart enough to survive. In the case of defeat, well, there was that widows thing again. The Beta Male is seldom the strongest or the fastest, but because he can anticipate danger, he far outnumbers his Alpha Male competition. The world is led by Alpha Males, but the machinery of the world turns on the bearings of the Beta Male.

The problem (Charlie's problem) is that the Beta Male imagination has become superfluous in the face of modern society. Like the saber-toothed tiger's fangs, or the Alpha Male's testosterone, there's just more Beta Male imagination than can really be put to good use. Consequently, a lot of Beta Males become hypochondriacs, neurotics, paranoids, or develop an addiction to porn or video games.

Because, while the Beta Male imagination evolved to help him avoid danger, as a side effect it also allows him fantasy-only access to power, money, and leggy, model-type females who, in reality, wouldn't kick him in the kidneys to get a bug off their shoe. The rich fantasy life of the Beta Male may often spill over into reality, manifesting in near-genius levels of self-delusion. In fact, many Beta Males, contrary to any empirical evidence, actually believe that they are Alpha Males, and have been endowed by their creator with advanced stealth charisma, which, although awesome in concept, is totally undetectable by women not constructed from carbon fiber. Every time a supermodel divorces her rock-star husband, the Beta Male secretly rejoices (or more accurately, feels great waves of unjustified hope), and every time a beautiful movie star marries, the Beta Male experiences a sense of lost opportunity. The entire city of Las Vegas — plastic opulence, treasure for the taking, vulgar towers, and cocktail waitresses with improbable breasts — is built on the self-delusion of the Beta Male.

And Beta Male self-delusion played no small part in Charlie first approaching Rachel, that rainy day in February, five years before, when he had ducked into A Clean, Well-Lighted Place for Books to get out of the storm, and Rachel granted him a shy smile over a stack of Carson McCullers she was shelving. He quickly convinced himself that it was because he was dripping with boyish charm, when it was, in fact, simply because he was dripping.

"You're dripping," she said. She had blue eyes, fair skin, and dark loose curls that fell around her face. She gave him a sideways glance — just enough consideration to spur his Beta Male ego.

"Yeah, thanks," Charlie said, taking a step closer.

"Can I get you a towel or something?"

"Nah, I'm used to it."

"You're dripping on Cormac McCarthy."

"Sorry." Charlie wiped *All the Pretty*

Horses with his sleeve while he tried to see if she had a nice figure under the floppy sweater and cargo pants. "Do you come here often?"

Rachel took a second before responding. She was wearing a name tag, working inventory from a metal cart, and she was pretty sure she'd seen this guy in the store before. So he wasn't being stupid, he was being clever. Sort of. She couldn't help it, she laughed.

Charlie shrugged damply and smiled. "I'm Charlie Asher."

"Rachel," Rachel said. They shook hands.

"Rachel, would you like to get a cup of coffee or something sometime?"

"That sort of depends, Charlie. I'd need you to answer a few questions first."

"Of course," Charlie said. "If you don't mind, I have some questions, too." He was thinking, *What do you look like naked? and How long before I can check?*

"Fine, then." Rachel put down *The Ballad of the Sad Café* and counted on her fingers.

"Do you have a job, a car, and a place to live? And are the last two things the same thing?" She was twenty-five and had been single for a while. She'd learned to screen her applicants.

"Uh, yes, yes, yes, and no."

"Excellent. Are you gay?" She'd been single for a while in San Francisco.

"I asked you out."

"That means nothing. I've had guys not realize they were gay until we'd gone out a few times. Turns out that's my specialty."

"Wow, you're kidding." He looked her up and down and decided that she probably had a great figure under the baggy clothes. "I could see it going the other way, but . . ."

"Right answer. Okay, I'll have coffee with you."

"Not so fast, what about *my* questions?"

Rachel threw out a hip and rolled her eyes, sighed. "Okay, shoot."

"I don't really have any, I just didn't want you to think I was easy."

"You asked me out thirty seconds after we met."

"Can you blame me? There you were, eyes and teeth — hair, dry, holding good books —"

"Ask me!"

"Do you think that there's any chance, you know, after we get to know each other, that you'll like me? I mean, can you see it happening?"

It didn't matter that he was pushing it —

whether he was sly or just awkward, she was defenseless against his Beta Male charm sans charisma, and she had her answer. "Not a chance," she lied.

"I miss her," Charlie said, and he looked away from his sister as if there was something in the sink that really, really needed studying. His shoulders shook with a sob and Jane went to him and held him as he slumped to his knees.

"I really miss her."

"I know you do."

"I hate this kitchen."

"Right there with you, kid."

The good sister, she was.

"I see this kitchen and I see her face and I can't handle it."

"Yes, you can. You will. It will get better."

"Maybe I should move or something."

"You do what you think you need to, but pain travels pretty well." Jane rubbed his shoulders and his neck, as if his grief was a knot in a muscle that could be worked out under direct pressure.

After a few minutes he was back, functioning, sitting at the counter between Sophie and Jane, drinking a cup of coffee. "You think I'm just imagining all this, then?"

Jane sighed. "Charlie, Rachel was the center of your universe. Anyone who saw you guys together knew that. Your life revolved around her. With Rachel gone, it's like you have no center, nothing to ground you, you're all wobbly and unstable, so things seem unreal. But you *do* have a center."

"I do?"

"It's you. I don't have a Rachel, or anyone like her on the horizon, but I'm not spinning out of control."

"So you're saying I need to be self-centered, like you?"

"I guess I am. Do you think that makes me a bad person?"

"Do you care?"

"Good point. Are you going to be okay? I need to go buy some yoga DVDs. I'm starting a class tomorrow."

"If you're going to take a class, then why do you need DVDs?"

"I have to look like I know what I'm doing or no one will go out with me. You going to be okay?"

"I'll be okay. I just can't go in the kitchen, or look at anything in the apartment, or listen to music, or watch TV."

"Okay then, have fun," Jane said, tweaking the baby's nose on the way out the door.

When she was gone, Charlie sat at the counter for a while looking at baby Sophie. Strangely enough, she was the only thing in the apartment that didn't remind him of Rachel. She was a stranger. She looked at him — those wide blue eyes — with sort of an odd, glazed look. Not with the adoration or wonder that you might expect, more like she'd been drinking and would be leaving as soon as she found her car keys.

"Sorry," Charlie said, averting his gaze to a stack of unpaid bills by the phone. He could feel the kid watching him, wondering, he thought, how many terry-cloth puppet people she'd have to blow to get a decent father over here. Still, he checked that she was securely strapped in her chair, then went off to grab the undone laundry, because he was, in fact, going to be a very good father.

Beta Males almost always make good fathers. They tend to be steady and responsible, the kind of guys a girl (if she was resolved to do without the seven-figure salary or the thirty-six-inch vertical leap) would want as a father for her children. Of course, she'd rather not have to sleep with him for that to happen, but after you've been kicked to the curb by a few Alpha Males, the idea of waking up in the arms of a guy who will adore you, if for no other reason than gratitude for sex, and will always be there, even past the point where you can stand to have him around, is a comfortable compromise.

For the Beta Male, if nothing else, is loyal. He makes a great husband as well as a great best friend. He will help you move and bring you soup when you are sick. Always considerate, the Beta Male thanks a woman after sex, and is often quick with an apology as well. He makes a great house sitter, especially if you aren't especially attached to your house pets. A Beta Male is trustworthy: your girlfriend is generally in safe hands with a Beta Male friend, unless, of course, she is a complete slut. (In fact, the *complete slut* through history may be exclusively responsible for the survival of the Beta Male gene, for loyal as he may be, the Beta Male is helpless in the face of charging, unimaginary bosoms.)

And while the Beta Male has the potential to be a great husband and father, the skills still need to be learned. So, for the next few weeks, Charlie did little but care for the tiny stranger in his house. She was an alien, really — a sort of eating, pooping, tantrum machine — and he didn't under-stand anything about her species. But as he tended to her, talked to her, lost a lot of sleep over her, bathed her, watched her nap, and admonished her for the dis-gusting substances that oozed and urped out of her, he started to fall in love. One morning, after a particularly active night of the feed-and-change parade, he awoke to find her staring goofily at the mobile over her crib, and when she saw him, she smiled. That did it. Like her mother before her, she set the course of his life with a smile. And as it had with Rachel, that wet morning in the bookstore, his soul lit up. The weirdness, the bizarre circumstances of Rachel's death, the red glowing items in the shop, the dark, winged thing above the street, all of it took a backseat to the new light of his life.

He didn't understand that she loved him unconditionally — so when he got up in the middle of the night to feed her, he put on a shirt and combed his hair and tested to see that his breath was free of funk. Within minutes of getting poleaxed with affection for his daughter, he started to de-velop a deep fear for her safety, which, over the course of a few days, blossomed into a whole new garden of paranoia.

"It looks like Nerf world in here," Jane said, one afternoon when she brought in the bills from the store and the checks for Charlie to sign. Charlie had padded every sharp corner or edge in the apartment with foam rubber and duct tape, put plastic covers on all of the electrical outlets, childproofed locks on all cabinets, installed new smoke, carbon monoxide, and radon detectors, and activated the V-Chip on the TV so that now he was incapable of watching anything that didn't feature baby animals or learning the alphabet.

"Accidents are the number one cause of death among children in America," Charlie said.

"But she can't even roll over on her stomach yet."

"I want to be ready. Everything I read says that one day you're breast-feeding them and the next day you wake up and they're dropping out of college." He was changing the baby on the coffee table and had used ten baby wipes so far, if Jane had the count right.

"I think that might be a metaphor. You know, for how fast they grow up."

"Well, it's done when she's ready to crawl."

"Why don't you just make a big foam-rubber suit for her, it's easier than padding the world. Charlie, it's scary-looking in here. You can't bring a woman here, she'd think you're nuts."

Charlie looked at his sister for a long second without saying anything, just frozen there, holding a disposable diaper in one hand and his daughter's ankles scissored between the fingers of the other.

"When you're ready," Jane stumbled on. "I mean, I'm not saying that you'd bring a woman here."

"Okay, because I'm not."

"Of course not. I'm not saying that. But you have to leave the apartment. For one thing, you need to go downstairs to the store. Ray has turned the point-of-sale computer into some kind of dating service and the truant officer has stopped by three times looking for Lily. And I can't keep doing the accounts and trying to run things and do my job, too, Charlie. Dad left you the business for a reason."

"But there's no one to watch Sophie."

"You have Mrs. Korjev and Mrs. Ling right here in the building, let one of them watch her. Hell, I'll watch her for a few hours in the evening, if that will help."

"I'm not going down there in the evening. That's when things are radioactive."

65

Jane set the stack of papers on the coffee table next to Sophie's head and backed away with her arms crossed. "Play what you just said back in your head, would you."

Charlie did, then shrugged. "Okay, that sounds a little crazy."

"Go make an appearance at the shop, Charlie. Just a few minutes to get your feet wet and put the fear of God in Ray and Lily, okay? I'll finish changing her."

Jane slid in between the couch and the coffee table, nudging her brother out of the way. In the process she knocked the dirty diaper to the floor, where it fell open.

"Oh my God!" She gagged and turned her head.

"Another reason not to eat brown mustard, huh?" Charlie said.

"You bastard!"

He backed away. "Okay, I'm going downstairs. You're sure you got this?"

"Go!" Jane said, waving him out of the room with one hand while holding her nose with the other.

5

Darkness Gets Uppity

"Hey, Ray," Charlie said as he came down the steps into the storeroom. He always tried to make a lot of noise on the steps and usually fired a loud and early "hello" to warn his employees that he was coming. He'd worked a number of jobs before coming back to take over the family business, and had learned from experience that nobody liked a sneaky boss.

"Hey, Charlie," Ray said. Ray was out front, sitting on a stool behind the counter. He was pushing forty, tall, balding, and moved through the world without ever turning his head. He couldn't. As a San Francisco policeman, he'd caught a gang-banger's bullet in the neck six years ago, and that was the last time he'd looked over his shoulder without using a mirror. Ray lived on a generous disability pension from the city and worked for Charlie in exchange for free rent on his fourth-floor apartment, thus keeping the transaction off both their books.

He spun around on the stool to face Charlie. "Hey — uh — I wanted to say that, you know, your situation, I mean, your loss. Everybody liked Rachel. You know, if I can do anything —"

It was the first time Charlie had seen Ray since the funeral, so the awkwardness of secondary condolences had yet to be forded. "You've done more than enough by picking up my shifts. Whatcha working on?" Charlie was trying desperately to not look at the various objects in the shop that were glowing dull red.

"Oh, this." Ray rotated and pushed back so that Charlie could see the computer screen, where there were displayed rows of portraits of smiling, young Asian women. "It's called Desperate Filipinas dot-com."

"Is this where you met Miss LoveYou LongTime?"

"That was not her name. Did Lily tell you that? That kid has problems."

"Yeah, well, kids," Charlie said, suddenly noticing a matronly woman in tweed who was browsing the curio shelves at the front of the store. She was carrying a porcelain frog that was glowing dull red.

Ray clicked on one of the pictures, which opened a profile. "Look at this one, boss. It says she's into *sculling*." He spun on his stool again and bounced his eyebrows at Charlie.

Charlie pulled his attention from the woman with the glowing frog and looked at the screen.

"That's rowing, Ray."

"No it's not. Look, it says she was a coxswain in college." Again with the eyebrow bounce, he offered a high five.

"Also rowing," Charlie said, leaving the ex-cop hanging. "The person at the back of the boat who yells at the rowers is called the coxswain."

"Really?" Ray said, disappointed. He'd been married three times, and been left by all three wives because of an inability to develop normal adult social skills. Ray reacted to the world as a cop, and while many women found that attractive initially, they expected him eventually to leave the attitude, along with his service weapon, in the coat closet when he arrived home. He didn't. When Ray had first come to work at Asher's Secondhand, it had taken two months for Charlie to get him to stop ordering customers to "move along, there's nothing to see here." Ray spent a lot of time being disappointed in himself and humanity in general.

"But, dude, rowing!" Charlie said, trying to make it all better. He liked the ex-cop in spite of his awkwardness. Ray was basically a good guy, kindhearted and loyal, hardworking and punctual, but most important, Ray was losing his hair faster than Charlie.

Ray sighed. "Maybe I should search for another Web site. What's a word that means that your standards are lower than the desperate?"

Charlie read down the page a little. "This woman has a master's degree in English lit from Cambridge, Ray. And look at her. She's gorgeous. And nineteen. Why is she desperate?"

"Hey, wait a minute. A master's degree at nineteen, this girl is too smart for me."

"No she's not. She's lying."

Ray spun on the stool as if Charlie had poked him in the ear with a pencil. "No!"

"Ray, look at her. She looks like one of those Asian models for Sour Apple Flavored Calamari Treats."

"They have that?"

Charlie pointed to the left side of the front window. "Ray, let me introduce you to Chinatown. Chinatown, this is Ray.

Ray, Chinatown."

Ray smiled, embarrassed. There was a store two blocks up that sold nothing but dried shark parts, the windows full of pictures of beautiful Chinese women holding shark spleens and eyeballs like they'd just received an Academy Award. "Well, the last woman I met through here did have a few errors and omissions in her profile."

"Like?" Charlie was watching the woman in tweed with the glowing frog, who was approaching the counter.

"Well, she said that she was twenty-three, five feet tall, a hundred five pounds, so I thought, 'Okay, I can have fun with a petite woman.' Turns out it was a hundred and five *kilos*."

"So, not what you expected?" Charlie said. He smiled at the approaching woman, feeling panic rise. She was going to buy the frog!

"Five foot — two-thirty. She was built like a mailbox. I might have gotten past that, but she wasn't even twenty-three, she was sixty-three. One of her grandsons tried to sell her to me."

"Ma'am, I'm sorry, you can't buy that," Charlie said to the woman.

"You hear the expression all the time," Ray went on, "but you hardly ever meet anyone really trying to sell his own grand-mother."

"Why not?" the woman asked.

"Fifty bucks," Ray said.

"That's outrageous," the woman said. "It's marked ten."

"No, it's fifty for the grandmother Ray is dating," Charlie said. "The frog is not for sale, ma'am, I'm sorry. It's defective."

"Then why do you have it on the shelf? Why is it marked for sale? I don't see any defect."

Evidently she couldn't see that the goofy porcelain frog was not only glowing in her hands, it had started to pulsate. Charlie reached across the counter and snatched it away from her.

"It's radioactive, ma'am. I'm sorry. You can't buy it."

"I wasn't dating her," Ray said. "I just flew to the Philippines to meet her."

"It is not radioactive," the woman said. "You're just trying to jack up the price. Fine, I'll give you twenty for it."

"No, ma'am, public safety," Charlie said, trying to look concerned, holding the frog to his chest as if shielding her from its dangerous energy. "And it's clearly ridiculous. You'll note that this frog is playing a banjo with only two strings. A travesty, really.

Why don't you let my colleague show you something in a cymbal-playing monkey. Ray, could you show this young woman something in a monkey, please." Charlie hoped that the "young woman" would win him points.

The woman backed away from the counter, holding her purse before her like a shield. "I'm not sure I want to buy anything from you wack jobs."

"Hey!" Ray protested, as if to say that there was only one wack job on duty and he wasn't it.

Then she did it, she quickstepped to a rack of shoes and picked up a pair of size-twelve, red Converse All Stars. They, too, were glowing. "I want these."

"No." Charlie tossed the frog over his shoulder to Ray, who fumbled it and almost dropped it. "Those aren't for sale either."

The tweed woman backed away toward the door, holding the sneakers behind her. Charlie stalked her down the aisle, taking the occasional grab at the All Stars. "Give them."

When the woman butt-bumped into the front door and the bell over the jamb jingled, she looked up and Charlie made his move, faking hard left, then going right, reaching around her and grabbing the laces of the sneakers, as well as a scoop of big, tweedy ass in the bargain. He quick-stepped back toward the counter, tossed the sneakers to Ray, and then turned and fell into a sumo stance to challenge the tweed woman.

She was still at the door, looking as if she couldn't decide to be terrified or disgusted. "You people need to be put away. I'm reporting you to the Better Business Bureau *and* the local merchants' association. And you, Mr. Asher, can tell Ms. Severo that I *will* be back." And with that, she was through the door and gone.

Charlie turned to Ray. "Ms. Severo? Lily? She was here to see Lily?"

"Truant officer," Ray said. "She's been in a couple of times."

"You might have said something."

"I didn't want to lose the sale."

"So, Lily —"

"Ducks out the back when she sees her coming. The woman also wanted to check with you that the notes for Lily's absences were legitimate. I vouched."

"Well, Lily is going back to school, and as of right now, I'm back to work."

"That's great. I took this call today — an estate in Pacific Heights. Lots of nice women's clothes." Ray tapped a piece of notepaper on the counter. "I'm not really qualified to handle it."

"I'll do it, but first we have a lot to catch up on. Flip the 'Closed' sign and lock the front door, would you, Ray?"

Ray didn't move. "Sure, but — Charlie, are you sure that you're ready to go back to work?" He nodded to the sneakers and frog on the counter.

"Oh, those, I think there's something wrong with them. You don't see anything unusual about those two items?"

Ray looked again. "Nope."

"Or that once I took the frog away from her, she went right for a pair of sneakers that are clearly not her size?"

Ray weighed the truth against the sweet deal he had here, with an apartment and under-the-table income and a boss that had really been a decent guy before he went 51/50, and he said, "Yeah, there was something strange about her."

"Aha!" said Charlie. "I just wish I knew where I could get a Geiger counter."

"I have a Geiger counter," Ray said.

"You do?"

"Sure, you want me to get it?"

"Maybe later," Charlie said. "Just lock up, and help me gather up some of the merchandise."

Over the next hour Ray watched as Charlie moved a set of what seemed randomly chosen items from the store to the back room, directing him to under no circumstances put them back out or sell them to anyone. Then he retrieved the Geiger counter that he'd obtained on a sweet trade for a stringless oversized tennis racket and tested each item as Charlie instructed. And, of course, they were as inert as dirt.

"And you don't see any glowing or pulsating or anything in this pile?" Charlie asked.

"Sorry." Ray shook his head, feeling a little embarrassed that he was witnessing this. "Good first day back to work, though," Ray said, trying to make it all better. "Maybe you should call it a day, go check on the baby, and make that estate call in the morning. I'll box this stuff up and mark it so Lily won't sell or trade it."

"Okay," Charlie said. "But don't throw it out, either. I'm going to figure this out."

"You betcha, boss. See you in the morning."

"Yeah, thanks, Ray. You can go home when you finish."

Charlie went back to his apartment, checking his hands the whole way to see if any of the red glow from the pile of objects had rubbed off on them, but they seemed normal. He sent Jane home, fed and bathed Sophie, and read her to sleep with a few pages from *Slaughterhouse-Five*, then went to bed early and slept fitfully. He awoke the next morning in a haze, then sat bolt upright in bed, eyes wide and heart pounding when he saw the note sitting on the nightstand. Another one. Then he noticed that this time it wasn't his handwriting, and the number was obviously a phone number, and he sighed. It was the estate appointment that Ray had made for him. He'd put it on the nightstand so he wouldn't forget. *Mr. Michael Mainheart*, it read; then *upscale women's clothing* and *furs,* with a double underline. The phone number had a local exchange. He picked up the note, and under it was a second piece of notepaper, this one with the same name, written in his own handwriting, and under it, the numeral 5. He didn't remember writing any of it. At that moment, something large and dark passed by the second-story bedroom window, but by the time he looked up, it was gone.

A blanket of fog lay over the Bay and from Pacific Heights the great orange towers of the Golden Gate Bridge jutted through the fog bank like carrots from the faces of sleeping conjoined twin snowmen. In the Heights, the morning sun had already opened the sky and workmen were scurrying about, tending yards and gardens around the mansions.

When he arrived at the home of Michael Mainheart the first thing Charlie noticed was that no one noticed him. There were two guys working in the yard, to whom Charlie waved as he passed, but they did not wave back. Then the mailman, who was coming off the big porch, drove him off the walkway into the dewy grass without so much as an "excuse me."

"Excuse me!" Charlie said, sarcastically, but the mailman was wearing headphones and listening to something that was inspiring him to bob his head like a pigeon feeding on amphetamines, and he bopped on. Charlie was going to shout something devastatingly clever, then thought better of it, for although it had been some years since he'd heard of a postal employee perpetrating a massacre, as long as the term "going postal" referred to anything besides choosing a shipping carrier, he felt he shouldn't press his luck.

Called a wack job by a complete stranger one day and shouldered off the sidewalk by a civil servant the next: this city was becoming a jungle.

Charlie rang the bell and waited to the side of the twelve-foot leaded-glass door. A minute later he heard light, shuffling steps approaching and a diminutive silhouette moved behind the glass. The door swung open slowly.

"Mr. Asher," said Michael Mainheart. "Thank you for coming." The old man was swimming in a houndstooth suit that he must have bought thirty years ago when he was a more robust fellow. When he shook Charlie's hand his skin felt like an old wonton wrapper, cool and a little powdery. Charlie tried not to shudder as the old man led him into a grand marble rotunda, with leaded-glass windows running to a vaulted, forty-foot ceiling and a circular staircase that swept up to a landing that led off to the upper wings of the house. Charlie had often wondered what it was like to have a house with wings. How would you ever find your car keys?

"Come this way," Mainheart said. "I'll show you where my wife kept her clothes."

"I'm sorry about your loss," Charlie said automatically. He'd been on scores of estate calls. *You don't want to come off as some kind of vulture,* his father used to say. *Always compliment the merchandise; it might be a piece of crap to you, but they might have a lot of their soul poured into it. Compliment but never covet. You can make a profit and preserve everyone's dignity in the process.*

"Holy shit," Charlie said as he followed the old man into a walk-in closet the size of his own apartment. "I mean — your wife had exquisite taste, Mr. Mainheart."

There was row upon row of designer couture clothing, everything from evening gowns to racks, two tiers high, of knit suits, arranged by color and level of formality — an opulent rainbow of silk and linen and wool. Cashmere sweaters, coats, capes, jackets, skirts, blouses, lingerie. The closet was shaped like a *T,* with a large vanity and mirror at the apex, and accessories on each wing (even the closet with wings!), shoes on one side, belts, scarves, and handbags on the other. A whole wing of shoes, Italian and French, handmade, from the skins of animals who had led happy, blemish-free lives. Full-length mirrors flanked the vanity at the end of the closet and Charlie caught the reflection of himself and Michael Mainheart in the mirror, he in his secondhand gray pinstripe and Mainheart in his ill-fitting houndstooth, studies in gray and black, stark and lifeless-looking in this vibrant garden.

The old man went to the chair at the vanity and sat down with a creak and a wheeze. "I expect it will take you some time to assess it," he said.

Charlie stood in the middle of the closet and looked around for a second before replying. "It depends, Mr. Mainheart, on what you want to part with."

"All of it. Every stitch. I can't stand the feel of her in here." His voice broke. "I want it gone." He looked away from Charlie at the shoe wing, trying not to show that he was tearing up.

"I understand," Charlie said, not sure what to say. This collection was completely out of his league.

"No, you don't understand, young man. You couldn't understand. Emily was my life. I got up in the morning for her, I went to work for her, I built a business for her. I couldn't wait to get home at night to tell her about my day. I went to bed with her and I dreamed about her when I slept. She was my passion, my wife, my best friend, the love of my life. And one day, without warning, she was gone and my life is a void. You couldn't possibly understand."

But Charlie did. "Do you have any children, Mr. Mainheart?"

"Two sons. They came back for the funeral, then they went home to their own families. They offer to do whatever they can, but . . ."

"They can't," Charlie finished for him. "No one can."

Now the old man looked up at him, his face as bereft and barren as a mummified basset hound. "I just want to die."

"Don't say that," Charlie said, because that's what you say. "That feeling will pass." Which he said because everyone had been saying it to him. As far as he knew, he was just slinging bullshit clichés.

"She was —" Mainheart's voice caught on the edge of a sob. A strong man, at once overcome by his grief and embarrassed that he was showing it.

"I know," Charlie said, thinking about how Rachel still occupied that place in his heart, and when he turned in the kitchen to say something to her, and she wasn't there, it took his breath.

"She was —"

"I know," Charlie interrupted, trying to give the old man a pass, because he knew what Mainheart was feeling. *She was meaning and order and light, and now that she's gone, chaos falls like a dark leaden cloud.*

"She was so phenomenally stupid."

"What?" Charlie looked up so quickly he heard a vertebra pop in his neck. Hadn't seen that coming.

"The dumb broad ate silica gel," Mainheart said, irritated as well as agonized.

"What?" Charlie was shaking his head, as if trying to rattle something loose.

"Silica gel."

"What?"

"Silica gel! Silica gel! Silica gel, you idiot!"

Charlie felt as if he should shout the name of some arcane stuff back at him: *Well, symethicone! Symethicone! Symethicone, you buttnugget!* Instead he said, "The stuff fake breasts are made of? She ate that?" The image of a well-dressed older woman macking on a goopish spoonful of artificial boob spooge was running across the lobes of his brain like a stuttering nightmare.

Mainheart pushed himself to his feet on the vanity. "No, the little packets of stuff they pack in with electronic equipment and cameras."

"The '*Do Not Eat*' stuff?"

"Exactly."

"But it says right on the packet — she ate that?"

"Yes. The furrier put packets of it in with her furs when he installed that cabinet." Mainheart pointed.

Charlie turned, and behind the large closet door where they had entered was a lighted glass cabinet — inside hung a dozen or so fur coats. The cabinet probably had its own air-conditioning unit to control the humidity, but that wasn't what Charlie was noticing. Even under the recessed fluorescent light inside the cabinet, one of the coats was clearly glowing red and pulsating. He turned back to Mainheart slowly, trying not to overreact, not sure, in fact, what would constitute an overreaction in this case, so he tried to sound calm, but not willing to take any shit.

"Mr. Mainheart, I appreciate your loss, but is there something more going on here than you've told me?"

"I'm sorry, I don't understand what you mean."

"I mean," Charlie said, "why, of all the used-clothing dealers in the Bay Area, did you decide to call me? There are people who are much more qualified to deal with a collection of this size and quality."

Charlie stormed over to the fur cabinet and pulled open the door. It made a *floof-tha* sound that the seal on a refrigerator door makes when opened. He grabbed the glowing jacket — fox fur, it appeared to be. "Or was it this? Did the call have something to do with this?" Charlie brandished the jacket like he was holding a murder weapon before the accused. *In short,* he thought about adding, *are you fucking with me?*

"You were the first used-clothing dealer in the phone book."

Charlie let the jacket drop. "Asher's Secondhand?"

"Starts with an *A,*" Mainheart said, slowly, carefully — obviously resisting the urge to call Charlie an idiot again.

"So it has nothing to do with this jacket?"

"Well, it has something to do with that jacket. I'd like you to take it away with all the rest of it."

"Oh," Charlie said, trying to recover. "Mr. Mainheart, I appreciate the call, and this is certainly a beautiful collection, amazing, really, but I'm not equipped to take on this kind of inventory. And I'll be honest with you, even though my father would be spinning in his grave for telling you this, there is probably a million dollars' worth of clothes in this closet. Maybe more. And given the time and space to resell it, it's probably worth a quarter of that. I just don't have that kind of money."

"We can work something out," Mainheart said. "Just to get it out of the house —"

"I could take some of it on consignment, I suppose —"

"Five hundred dollars."

"What?"

"Give me five hundred dollars and get it out of here by tomorrow and it's yours."

Charlie started to object, but he could feel what felt like the ghost of his father rising up to bonk him on the head with a spittoon if he didn't stop himself. *We provide a valuable service, son. We are like an orphanage to art and artifact, because we are willing to handle the unwanted, we give them value.*

"I couldn't do that, Mr. Mainheart, I feel as if I'd be taking advantage of your grief."

Oh for Christ's sake, you fucking loser, you are no son of mine. I have no son. Was that the ghost of Charlie's father, rattling chains in his head? Why, then, did it have the voice and vocabulary of Lily? Can a conscience be greedy?

"You would be doing me a favor, Mr. Asher. A huge favor. If you don't take it, my next call is to the Goodwill. I promised Emily that if something ever happened to her that I wouldn't just give her things away. Please."

And there was so much pain in the old man's voice that Charlie had to look away. Charlie felt for the old man because he *did* understand. He couldn't do anything to help, couldn't say, *It will get better,* like everyone kept saying to him. It wasn't getting better. Different, but not better. And this fellow had fifty more years in which to pack his hopes, or in his case, his history.

"Let me think about it. Check into storage. If I can handle it, I'll call you tomorrow, would that be all right?"

"I'd be grateful," Mainheart said.

Then, for no reason that he could think of, Charlie said, "May I take this jacket with me? As an example of the quality of the collection, in case I have to divide it among other dealers."

"That would be fine. Let me show you out."

As they passed into the rotunda, a shadow passed across the leaded-glass windows, three stories up. A large shadow. Charlie paused on the steps and waited for the old man to react, but he just tottered on down the staircase, leaning heavily on the railing as he went. When Mainheart reached the door he turned to Charlie, extending his hand. "I'm sorry about that, uh, outburst upstairs. I haven't been myself since —"

As the old man began to open the door a figure dropped outside, casting the silhouette of a bird as tall as a man through the glass.

"No!" Charlie dove forward, knocking the old man aside and slamming the door on the great bird's head, the heavy black beak stabbing through and snapping like hedge clippers, rattling an umbrella stand and scattering its contents across the marble floor. Charlie's face was only inches from the bird's eye, and he shoved the door with his shoulder, trying to keep the beak from snapping off one of his hands. The bird's claws raked against the glass, cracking one of the thick beveled panels as the animal thrashed to free itself.

Charlie threw his hip against the doorjamb then slid down it, dropped the fox jacket, and snatched one of the umbrellas from the floor. He stabbed up into the bird's neck feathers, but lost his purchase on the doorjamb — one of the black talons snaked through the opening and raked across his forearm, cutting through his jacket, his shirtsleeve, and into the flesh. Charlie shoved the umbrella with all he had, driving the bird's head back through the opening.

The raven let out a screech and took flight, its wings making a great whooshing noise as it went. Charlie lay on his back, out of breath, staring at the leaded-glass panels, as if any moment the shadow of the giant raven would come back, then he looked to Michael Mainheart, who lay crumpled on his side like a stringless marionette. Beside his head lay a cane with an ivory handle that had been carved into the shape of a polar bear that had fallen from the umbrella stand. The cane was glowing red. The old man was not breathing.

"Well that's fucked up," Charlie said.

6

Variable Speed Heroes

In the alley behind Asher's Secondhand, the Emperor of San Francisco hand-fed olive focaccia to the troops and tried to keep dog snot from fouling his breakfast.

"Patience, Bummer," the Emperor said to the Boston terrier, who was leaping at the day-old wheel of flat bread like a furry Super Ball, while Lazarus, the solemn golden retriever, stood by, waiting for his share. Bummer snorted an impatient reply (thus the dog snot). He'd worked up a furious appetite because breakfast was running late today. The Emperor had slept on a bench by the Maritime Museum, and during the night his arthritic knee had snaked out of his wool overcoat into the damp cold, making the walk to North Beach and the Italian bakery that gave them free day-old a slow and painful ordeal.

The Emperor groaned and sat down on an empty milk crate. He was a great rolling bear of a man, his shoulders broad but a little broken from carrying the weight of the city. A white tangle of hair and beard wreathed his face like a storm cloud. As far as he could remember, he and the troops had patrolled the city streets forever, but upon further consideration, it might have just been since Wednesday. He wasn't entirely sure.

The Emperor decided to make a proclamation to the troops about the importance of compassion in the face of the rising tide of heinous fuckery and political weaselocity in the nearby kingdom of the United States. (He found his audience was most attentive to his proclamations when the meat-laced focaccia were still nuzzled in the larder of his overcoat pockets, and presently a pepperoni and Parmesan reposed fragrant in the woolly depths, so the royal hounds were rapt.) But just as he cleared his throat to begin, a cargo van came screeching around the corner, went up on two wheels as it plowed through a row of garbage cans, and slid to a stop not fifty feet away. The driver's-side door flew open and a thin man in a suit leapt out, carrying a cane and a woman's fur coat, and made a beeline for the back door of Asher's. But before he got two steps the man fell to the concrete as if hit from behind, then rolled on his back and began flailing at the air with the cane and the coat. The Emperor, who knew most everyone, recognized Charlie Asher.

Bummer erupted into a fit of yapping, but the more levelheaded Lazarus growled once and took off toward Charlie.

"Lazarus!" the Emperor shouted, but the retriever charged on, followed now by his bug-eyed brother in arms.

Charlie was back on his feet and swinging the cane as if he was fencing with some phantom, using the coat like a shield. Living on the street, the Emperor had seen a lot of people battling with unseen demons, but Charlie Asher was apparently scoring some hits. The cane was making a thwacking noise against what appeared to be thin air — but no, there was something there, a shadow of some sort?

The Emperor climbed to his feet and limped into the fray, but before he got two steps Lazarus had leapt and appeared to be attacking Charlie, but he soared over the shopkeeper and snapped at a spot above his head — then hung there, his jaws sunk into the substantial neck of thin air.

Charlie took advantage of the distraction, stepped back, and swung the cane above the levitating golden retriever. There was a smack, and Lazarus let go, but now Bummer launched himself at the invisible foe. He missed whatever was there, and ended up performing a doggy swish shot into a garbage can.

Charlie made for the steel door of Asher's again, but found it locked, and as he reached for his keys, something caught him from behind.

"Let go, fuckface," the shade screeched.

The fur coat Charlie was holding appeared to be swept out of his hand and was pulled straight up, over the four-story building and out of sight.

Charlie turned and held the cane at ready, but whatever had been there seemed to be gone now.

"Aren't you just supposed to sit above the door and *nevermore* and be poetic and stuff?!" he shouted at the sky. Then, for good measure, added, "You evil fuck!"

Lazarus barked, then whined. A sharp and metallic yapping rose from Bummer's garbage can.

"Well, you don't see that every day," said the Emperor as he limped up to Charlie.

"You could see that?"

"Well, no, not really. Merely a shadow, but I could see that something was there. There *was* something there, wasn't there, Charlie?"

Charlie nodded, trying to catch his breath. "It will be back. It followed me across the city." He dug into his pocket for his keys. "You guys should duck into the store with me, Your Majesty." Of course Charlie knew the Emperor. Every San Franciscan knew the Emperor.

The Emperor smiled. "That's very kind of you, but we will be perfectly safe. For now I need to free my charge from his galvanized prison." The big man tipped the garbage can and Bummer emerged snorting and tossing his head as if ready to tear the ass out of any man or beast foolhardy enough to cross him (and he would have, as long as they were knee-high or shorter).

Charlie was still having trouble with the key. He knew he should have had the lock replaced, but it worked, if you finessed it a little, so he'd never made it a priority. Who the hell thought you'd ever have to get in quick to escape a giant bird? Then he heard a screech and turned to see not one, but two huge ravens coming over the roof and diving into the alley. The dogs arfed a frantic barking salvo at the avian intruders

94

and Charlie put so much body English into wiggling the key in the lock that he felt an atrophied dancing muscle tear in his hip.

"They're back. Cover me." Charlie threw the cane to the Emperor and braced himself for the impact, but as soon as the cane touched the old man's hand the birds were gone. You could almost hear the pop of the air replacing the space they had taken up. The dogs caught themselves in mid-ruff; Bummer whimpered.

"What?" the Emperor said. "What?"

"They're gone."

The Emperor looked at the sky. "You're sure?"

"For now."

"I saw two shadows. Really saw them this time," the Emperor said.

"Yes, there were two this time."

"What are they?"

"I have no idea, but when you took the cane they — well, they disappeared. You really saw them?"

"I'm sure of it. Like smoke with a purpose."

Finally the key turned in the lock and the door to Asher's back room swung open. "You should come in. Rest. I'll order something to eat."

"No, no, the men and I must be on our

rounds. I've decided to make a proclamation this morning and we need to see the printer. You'll be needing this." The Emperor presented the cane to Charlie like he was turning over a sword of the realm.

Charlie started to take it, then thought better of it. "Your Majesty, I think you'd better keep that. It looks as if you might be able to use it." Charlie nodded toward the Emperor's creaky knee.

The Emperor held the cane steady. "I am not a worshiper of the material, you know?"

"I understand that."

"I am a firm believer that desire is the source of most of human suffering, you're aware, and no culprit is more heinous than desire for material gain."

"I run my business based on those very principles. Still, I insist you keep the cane — as a favor to me, if you would?"

Charlie found himself affecting the Emperor's formal speech patterns, as if somehow he had been transported to a royal court where a nobleman was distinguished by bread crumbs in his beard and the royal guard were not above licking their balls.

"Well, as a favor, I will accept. It is a fine piece of craftsmanship."

"But more importantly, it will permit you to make your rounds in good time."

The Emperor now betrayed the desire in his heart as he let fly a wide grin and hugged the cane to his chest. "It is fine, indeed. Charlie, I must confess something to you, but I ask you to grant me the credulity due a man who has just shared witness, with a friend, of two giant, raven-shaped shades."

"Of course." Charlie smiled, when even a moment before he would have thought his smile lost somewhere in the months past.

"I hope you won't think me base, but the second I touched this, I felt as if I had been waiting for it my whole life."

Then, for no reason that he could think of, Charlie said, "I know."

A few minutes before, inside the store, Lily had been brooding. It wasn't her general brood, the reaction to a world where everyone was stupid and life was meaningless and the mere act of living was futile, especially if your mother forgot to get coffee at the store. This one was a more specific brood, that had started out when she arrived at work and Ray had pointed out that it was her turn to wear the vacuuming tiara, and insisted that if she wore the tiara, she actually vacuum the store. (In fact, she liked wearing the rhinestone tiara that Charlie, in a move of blatant bourgeois sneakiness, had designated be worn by whoever did the vacuuming and sweeping each day, and no other time. It was the vacuuming and sweeping she objected to. She felt manipulated, used, and generally taken advantage of, and not in the fun way.) But today, after she'd put the tiara and the vacuum away and had finally gotten a couple of cups of coffee in her system, the brooding had gone on, building to full-scale angst, when it began to dawn on her that she was going to have to figure out this college-career thing, because despite what *The Great Big Book of Death* said, she had not been chosen as a dark minion of destruction. Fuck!

She stood in the back room looking at all the items that Charlie had piled there the day before: shoes, lamps, umbrellas, porcelain figures, toys, a couple of books, and an old black-and-white television and a painting of a clown on black velvet.

"He said this stuff was glowing?" she asked Ray, who stood in the doorway to the store.

"Yes. He made me check it all with my Geiger counter."

"Ray, why the fuck do you have a Geiger counter?"

"Lily, why do you have a nose stud shaped like a bat?"

Lily ignored the question and picked up the ceramic frog from the night before, which now had a note taped to it that read DO NOT SELL OR DISPLAY in Charlie's meticulous block-letter printing. "This was one of the things? This?"

"That was the first one he freaked out about," said Ray matter-of-factly. "The truant officer tried to buy it. That started it all."

Lily was shaken. She backed over to Charlie's desk and sat in the squeaky oak swivel chair. "Do you see anything glowing or pulsating, Ray? Have you ever?"

Ray shook his head. "He's under a lot of stress, losing Rachel and taking care of the baby. I think maybe he needs to get some help. I know after I had to leave the force —" Ray paused.

There was a commotion going on out in the alley, dogs barking and people shouting, then someone was working a key in the lock of the back door. A second later, Charlie came in, a little breathless, his clothes smudged here and there with grime, one sleeve of his jacket torn and bloodstained.

"Asher," Lily said. "You're hurt." She quickly vacated his chair while Ray took Charlie by the shoulders and sat him down.

"I'm fine," Charlie said. "No big deal."

"I'll get the first-aid kit," Ray said. "Get that jacket off of him, Lily."

"I'm fine," Charlie said. "Quit talking about me like I'm not here."

"He's delirious," Lily said, trying to pry Charlie out of his jacket. "Do you have any painkillers, Ray?"

"I don't need painkillers," Charlie said.

"Shut up, Asher, they're not for you," Lily said, automatically, then she considered the book, Ray's story, the notes on all the items in the back room, and she shuddered. It appeared that Charlie Asher might not be the hapless geek she always thought him to be. "Sorry, boss. Let us help you."

Ray came back from the front with a small plastic first-aid kit. He peeled back Charlie's sleeve and began to clean the wounds with gauze and peroxide. "What happened?"

"Nothing," Charlie said. "I slipped and

fell in some gravel."

"The wound's pretty clean — no gravel in it. That must have been some fall."

"Long story." Charlie sighed. "Ouch!"

"What was all the noise in the alley?" Lily asked, needing badly to go smoke, but unable to pull herself away. She just couldn't imagine that Charlie Asher was the one. How could it be him? He was so, so, *unworthy*. He didn't understand the dark underbelly of life the way she did. Yet he was the one seeing the glowing objects. He was it. She was crestfallen.

"Just the Emperor's dogs after a seagull in the Dumpster. No big deal. I fell off a porch in Pacific Heights."

"The estate," Ray said. "How'd that go?"

"Not well. The husband was grief-stricken and had a heart attack while I was there."

"You're kidding."

"No, he just sort of became over-whelmed thinking about his wife and col-lapsed. I gave him CPR until the EMTs came and took him off to the hospital."

"So," Lily said, "did you get the — uh — did you get anything special?"

"What?" Charlie's eyes went wide. "What do you mean, special? There was nothing special."

"Chill, boss, I just meant will we get the grandma's clothes?" *He's it,* Lily thought. The fucker.

Charlie shook his head. "I don't know, it's so strange. The whole thing is so strange." He shuddered when he said it.

"Strange how?" Lily said. "Strange in a cool and dark way, or strange because you're Asher and you're out of it most of the time?"

"Lily!" Ray snapped. "Go out front. Dust something."

"You're not the boss of me, Ray. I'm just showing my concern."

"It's okay, Ray." Charlie looked like he was considering how, exactly, to define *strange,* and not coming up with anything that was working. Finally he said, "Well, for one thing, this woman's estate is way out of our league. The husband said he called me because we were the first secondhand store in the phone book, but he doesn't seem like the kind of man to do something like that."

"That's not that strange," Lily said. *Just confess,* she thought.

"You said that he was grief-stricken," Ray said, dabbing antibiotic ointment on Charlie's cuts. "Maybe he's doing things differently."

"Yes, and he was angry at his wife, too, for the way she died."

"How?" Lily asked.

"She ate silica gel," Charlie said.

Lily looked at Ray for an explanation, because silica gel sounded techno-geeky, which was Ray's particular field of geekdom. Ray said, "It's the antidesiccant that they pack with electronics and other things that are sensitive to humidity."

"The 'Do Not Eat' stuff?!" Lily said. "Oh my God, that's so stupid. Everyone knows you don't eat the 'Do Not Eat' stuff."

Charlie said, "Mr. Mainheart was pretty broken up."

"Well, I guess so," Lily said. "He married a complete fucktard."

Charlie cringed. "Lily, that's not appropriate."

Lily shrugged and rolled her eyes. She hated it when Charlie dropped into Dad mode. "Okay, okay. I'm going outside to smoke."

"No!" Charlie jumped out of the chair and put himself between Lily and the back door. "Out front. From now on if you have to smoke you go out front."

"But you said that I look like a child hooker when I smoke out front."

"I've reassessed. You've matured."

Lily closed one eye to see if she could better glimpse into his soul and thus figure out his true agenda. She smoothed over her black vinyl skirt, which made a tortured, squeaking noise at the touch. "You're trying to say I have a big butt, aren't you?"

"I absolutely am saying no such thing," Charlie insisted. "I am simply saying that your presence in front of the store is an asset and will probably attract business from the tourists on the cable car."

"Oh. Okay." Lily snatched her box of cloves off the desk and headed out past the counter and outside to brood, grieve really, because as much as she had hoped, she was not Death. The book was Charlie's.

That evening Charlie was watching the store, wondering why he had lied to his employees, when he saw a flash of red passing by the front window. A second later, a strikingly pale redhead came through the door. She was wearing a short, black cocktail dress and black fuck-me pumps. She strode up the aisle like she was auditioning for a music video. Her hair cascaded in long curls around her shoulders and down her back like a great auburn veil. Her eyes were emerald green, and when she saw him looking, she smiled, and stopped, some ten feet away.

Charlie felt an almost painful jolt that seemed to emanate from somewhere in the area of his groin, and after a second he recognized it as an autonomic lust response. He hadn't felt anything like that since Rachel had passed, and he felt vaguely ashamed.

She was examining him, looking him over like you would examine a used car. He was sure he must be blushing.

"Hi," Charlie said. "Can I help you?"

The redhead smiled again, just a little, and reached into a small black bag that he hadn't noticed she'd been carrying. "I found this," she said, holding up a silver cigarette case. Something Charlie didn't see very often anymore, even in the secondhand business. It was glowing, pulsating like the objects in the back room. "I was in the neighborhood and something made me think that this belonged here."

She moved to the counter opposite Charlie and set the cigarette case down in front of him.

Charlie could barely move. He stared at her, not even conscious that to avoid her eyes he was staring at her cleavage, and she appeared to be looking around his head and shoulders as if following the path of insects that were buzzing around him.

"Touch me," she said.

"Huh?" He looked up, saw she was serious. She held out her hand; her nails were manicured and painted the same deep red as her lipstick. He took her hand.

As soon as she touched him she pulled away. "You're warm."

"Thanks." In that moment he realized that she wasn't. Her fingers had been ice-cold.

"Then you're not one of us?"

He tried to think of what "us" might be? Irish? Low blood pressure? Nymphomaniac? Why did he even think that? "Us? What do you mean, 'us'?"

She backed away a step. "No. You don't just take the weak and the sick, do you? You take anyone."

"Take? What do you mean, 'take'?"

"You don't even know, do you?"

"Know what?" Charlie was getting very nervous. As a Beta Male, he found it difficult enough to function under the attention of a beautiful woman, but she was just plain spooky. "Wait. Can you see this thing glowing?" He held out the cigarette case.

"No glow. It just felt like it belonged

here," she said. "What's your name?"

"Charlie Asher. This is Asher's."

"Well, Charlie, you seem like a nice guy, and I don't know exactly what you are, and it doesn't seem like you know. You don't, do you?"

"I've been going through some changes," Charlie said, wondering why he felt compelled to share this at all.

The redhead nodded, as if confirming something to herself. "Okay. I know what it's like to, uh, to find yourself thrown into a situation where forces beyond your control are changing you into someone, something you don't have an owner's manual for. I understand what it is to not know. But someone, somewhere, does know. Someone can tell you what's going on."

"What are you talking about?" But he knew what she was talking about. What he didn't know was how she could possibly know.

"You make people die, don't you, Charlie?" She said it like she had worked up the courage to tell him that he had some spinach in his teeth. More of a service to him than an accusation.

"How do you — ?" How did she —

"Because it's what I do. Not like you, but

it's what I do. Find them, Charlie. Back-track and find whoever was there when your world changed."

Charlie looked at her, then at the cigarette case, then at the redhead again, who was no longer smiling, but was stepping backward toward the door. Trying to stay in touch with normal, he focused on the cigarette case and said, "I suppose I can do an appraisal —"

He heard the bell over the door jingle, and when he looked up she was gone.

He didn't see her moving by the windows on either side of the door; she was just gone. He ran to the front of the store and out the door onto the sidewalk. The Mason Street cable car was just topping the hill up by California Street and he could hear the bell, there was a thin fog coming up from the Bay that threw colorful halos around the neon signs of the other businesses, but there was no striking redhead on the street. He went to the corner and looked down Vallejo, but again no redhead, just the Emperor, sitting against the building with his dogs.

"Good evening, Charlie."

"Your Majesty, did you see a redhead go by here just now?"

"Oh yes. Spoke to her. I'm not sure you

have a chance there, Charlie, I believe she's spoken for. And she did warn me to stay away from you."

"Why? Did she say why?"

"She said that you were Death."

"I am?" Charlie said. "Am I?" His breath caught in his throat as the day played back in his head. "What if I am?"

"You know, son," the Emperor said, "I am not an expert in dealing with the fairer sex, but you might want to save that bit of information until the third date or so, after they've gotten to know you a little."

7

Thanatoast

While Charlie's Beta Male imagination may have often turned him toward timidity and even paranoia, when it came to accepting the unacceptable it served him like Kevlar toilet paper — bulletproof, if a tad disagreeable in application. The inability to believe the unbelievable would not be his downfall. Charlie Asher would never be a bug splattered on the smoky windscreen of dull imagination.

He knew that all the things that had happened to him in the last day were outside of the limits of possibility for most people, and since his only corroborating witness was a man who believed himself to be the Emperor of San Francisco, Charlie knew he would never be able to convince anyone that he had been pursued and attacked by giant foulmouthed ravens and then declared the tour guide to the undiscovered country by a sultry oracle in *fuck-me pumps*.

Not even Jane would give him that kind of quarter. Only one person would have, could have, and for the ten-thousandth time he felt Rachel's absence collapsing in his chest like a miniature black hole. Thus, Sophie became his co-conspirator.

The tiny kid, dressed in Elmo overalls and baby Doc Martens (courtesy of Aunt Jane), was propped up in her car seat on the breakfast bar next to the goldfish bowl. (Charlie had bought her six big goldfish about the time she'd started to notice moving objects. A girl needs pets. He'd named them after TV lawyers. Currently Matlock was tracking Perry Mason, trying to eat a long strand of fish doo that was trailing out of Perry's poop chute.)

Sophie was starting to show some of her mother's dark hair, and if Charlie saw it right, the same expression of bemused affection toward him (plus a drool slick).

"So I am Death," Charlie said as he tried to construct a tuna-fish sandwich. "Daddy is Death, sweetie." He checked the toast, not trusting the pop-up mechanism because the toaster people sometimes just liked to fuck with you.

"Death," Charlie said as the can opener

slipped and he barked his bandaged hand on the counter. "Dammit!"

Sophie gurgled and let loose a happy baby burble, which Charlie took to mean *Do tell, Daddy? Please go on, pray tell.*

"I can't even leave the house for fear of someone dropping dead at my feet. I'm Death, honey. Sure, you laugh now, but you'll never get into a good preschool with a father who puts people down for their dirt nap."

Sophie blew a spit bubble of sympathy. Charlie popped the toast up manually. It was a little rare, but if he pushed it down again it would burn, unless he watched it every second and popped it up manually again. So now he'd probably be infected with some rare and debilitating under-cooked toast pathogen. Mad toast disease! *Fucking toaster people.*

"This is the toast of Death, young lady." He showed her the toast. "Death's toast."

He put the toast on the counter and went back to attacking the tuna can.

"Maybe she was speaking figuratively? I mean, maybe the redhead just meant that I was, you know, deadly boring." Of course that didn't really explain all the other weird stuff that had been happening. "You think?" he asked Sophie.

He looked for an answer and the kid was wearing that Rachelesque smart-ass grin (minus teeth). She was enjoying his torment, and strangely enough, he felt better knowing that.

The can opener slipped again, spurting tuna juice on his shirt and sending his toast scooting to the floor, and now there was fuzz on it. Fuzz on his toast! Fuzz on the toast of Death. What the hell good was it to be the Lord of the Underworld if there was fuzz on your underdone toast. "Fuck!"

He snatched the toast from the floor and sent it sailing by Sophie into the living room. The baby followed it with her eyes, then looked back at her father with a delighted squeal, as if saying, *Do it again, Daddy. Do it again!*

Charlie picked her up out of the car seat and held her tight, smelling her sour-sweet baby smell, his tears squeezing out onto her overalls. He could do this if Rachel was here, but he couldn't, he wouldn't, without her.

He just wouldn't go out. That was the solution. The only way to keep the people of San Francisco safe was to stay in his apartment. So for the next four days he stayed in the apartment with Sophie, sending Mrs. Ling from upstairs out for groceries. (And he was accumulating a fairly large collection of vegetables for which he had no name nor any idea of how to prepare, as Mrs. Ling, regardless of what he put on the list, always did her shopping in the markets of Chinatown.) And after two days, when a new name appeared on the message pad next to his bed, Charlie responded by hiding the message pad under the phone book in a kitchen drawer.

It was on day five that he saw the shadow of a raven against the roof entrance of the building across the street. At first he wasn't sure whether it was a giant raven, or just a normal-sized raven projecting a shadow, but when he realized that it was noon and any normal shadow would be cast straight down, the tiny raven of denial vanished in a wisp. He pulled the blinds on that side of the apartment and sat in the locked bedroom with Sophie, a box of Pampers, a basket of produce, a six-pack each of baby formula and orange soda, and hid out until the phone rang.

"What do you think you're doing?" said a very deep man's voice on the other end of the line. "Are you insane?"

Charlie was taken aback; from the caller

ID, he'd expected a wrong number. "I'm eating this thing I think is either a melon or a squash." He looked at the green thing, which tasted like a melon but looked more like a squash, with spikes. (Mrs. Ling had called it "shut-up-and-eat-it-good-for-you.")

The man said, "You're screwing up. You have a job to do. Do what the book says or everything that means anything to you will be taken away. I mean it."

"What book? Who is this?" Charlie asked. He thought the voice sounded familiar, and it immediately sent him into alarm mode for some reason.

"I can't tell you that, I'm sorry," said the man. "I really am."

"I've got caller ID, you nit. I know where you're calling from."

"Oops," said the man.

"You should have thought of that. What kind of ominous power of darkness do you think you are if you don't even block caller ID?"

The little readout on the phone said *Fresh Music* and a number. Charlie called the number back but no one answered. He ran to the kitchen, dug the phone book out of the drawer, and looked up Fresh Music. It was a record store off upper Market in the Castro district.

The phone rang again and he grabbed the handset off the counter so violently he nearly chipped a tooth in answering.

"You merciless bastard!" Charlie screamed into the phone. "Do you have any idea what I've been going through, you heartless monster!"

"Well, fuck you, Asher!" Lily said. "Just because I'm a kid doesn't mean I don't have feelings." And she hung up.

Charlie called back.

"Asher's Secondhand," Lily answered, "family-owned by bourgeoisie douche waffles for over thirty years."

"Lily, I'm sorry, I thought you were someone else. What did you call about?"

"Moi?" Lily said. *"Je me fous de ta gueule, espèce de gaufre de douche."*

"Lily, stop speaking French. I said I was sorry."

"There's a cop down here to see you," she said.

Charlie had Sophie strapped to his chest like a terrorist baby bomb when he came down the back steps. She had just gotten to the point where she could hold up her head, so he had strapped her in face-out so she could look around. The way her arms

116

and legs waved around as Charlie walked, she looked as if she was skydiving and using a skinny nerd as a parachute.

The cop stood at the counter opposite Lily, looking like a cognac ad in an Italian-cut double-breasted suit in indigo raw silk with a buff linen shirt and yellow tie. He was about fifty, Hispanic, lean, with sharp facial features and the aspect of a predatory bird. His hair was combed straight back and the gray streaks at the temples made it appear that he was moving toward you even when he stood still.

"Inspector Alphonse Rivera," the cop said, extending his hand. "Thanks for coming down. The young lady said you were working last Monday night."

Monday. The day he'd battled the ravens back in the alley, the day the pale redhead had come into the store.

"You don't have to tell him anything, Asher," Lily said, obviously renewing her loyalty in spite of his douche wafflosity.

"Thanks, Lily, why don't you take a break and go see how things are going in the abyss."

She grumbled, then got something out of the drawer under the register, presumably her cigarettes, and retreated out the back door.

"Why isn't that kid in school?" Rivera asked.

"She's special," Charlie said. "You know, homeschooled."

"That what makes her so cheerful?"

"She's studying the Existentialists this month. Asked for a study day last week to kill an Arab on the beach."

Rivera smiled and Charlie relaxed a little. He produced a photograph from his breast pocket and held it out to Charlie. Sophie made as if to grab it. The photograph was of an older gentleman in his Sunday best standing on the steps of a church. Charlie recognized the Cathedral of Sts. Peter and Paul, which was just a few blocks away on Washington Square.

"Did you see this man Monday night? He was wearing a charcoal overcoat and a hat that night."

"No, I'm sorry. I didn't," Charlie said. And he hadn't. "I was here in the store until about ten. We had a few customers, but not this fellow."

"Are you sure? His name is James O'Malley. He isn't well. Cancer. His wife said he went out for a walk about dusk Monday night and he never came back."

"No, I'm sorry," Charlie said. "Did you ask the cable-car operator?"

"Already talked to the guys working this line that night. We think he may have collapsed somewhere and we haven't found him. It doesn't look good after this long."

Charlie nodded, trying to look thoughtful. He was so relieved that the cop wasn't here about anything connected with him that he was almost giddy. "Maybe you should ask the Emperor — you know him, right? He sees more of the nooks and crannies of the city than most of us."

Rivera cringed at the mention of the Emperor, but then relaxed into another smile. "That's a good idea, Mr. Asher. I'll see if I can track him down." He handed Charlie a card. "If you remember anything, give me a call, would you?"

"I will. Uh, Inspector," Charlie said, and Rivera paused a few steps from the counter, "isn't this sort of a routine case for an inspector to be investigating?"

"Yes, normally uniform personnel would handle something like this, but it may relate to something else I'm working on, so you get me instead."

"Oh, okay," Charlie said. "Beautiful suit, by the way. Couldn't help noticing. It's my business."

"Thanks," Rivera said, looking at his sleeves, a little wistful. "I had a short run of good fortune a while back."

"Good for you," Charlie said.

"It passed," Rivera said. "Cute baby. You two take care, huh?" And he was out the door.

Charlie turned to go back upstairs and nearly ran into Lily. She had her arms crossed under the "Hell Is Other People" logo on her T-shirt and was looking even more judgmental than usual. "So, Asher, you have something you want to tell me?"

"Lily, I don't have time for —"

She held out the silver cigarette case that the redhead had given him. It was still glowing red. Sophie was reaching for it.

"What?" Charlie said. Could Lily see it? Was she picking up on the weird glow?

Lily opened the case and pushed it into Charlie's face. "Read the engraving."

James O'Malley, read the ornate script.

Charlie took a step back. "Lily, I can't — I don't know anything about that old man. Look, I have to get Mrs. Ling to watch Sophie and get over to the Castro. I'll explain later, okay? I promise."

She thought about it for a second, staring at him accusingly, like she'd caught him feeding Froot Loops to her *bête noire,* and then relented. "Go," she said.

8

A Streetcar Named Confusion

Into the breach of the Castro district Charlie Asher charged, an antique sword-cane from the store on the van seat beside him, his jaw set like a bayonet, his visage a study in fearsome intensity. Half a block, half a block, half of a block onward — into the Valley of Overpriced Juice Bars and Outlandish Hair Highlights — rode the righteous Beta Male. And woe be unto the foolish ne'er-do-well who had dared to fuck with this secondhand death dealer, for his raggedy life would be fast for the bargain table. *There's going to be a showdown in Gay Town,* Charlie thought, *and I am gunning for justice.*

Well, not really *gunning* — since he had a sword concealed in a walking stick, not a gun — more of a *poking for justice* — which didn't really have the avenging angel connotation he was looking for — he was mad, and ready to kick ass, that's all. So, you know, just watch out. (Coincidentally, *Poking for Justice* was the title currently second in popularity at Castro Video Rentals, closely edging out *A Star Is Born: The Director's Cut*, and outranked only by *Cops Without Pants*, which was number one with a bullwhip.)

Charlie turned off Market Street and just around the corner on Noe Street he saw it: Fresh Music, the sign done in blocky, Craftsman-style stained glass, and he felt the hair at the back of his neck bristle and an urgency in his bladder. His body had gone into fight-or-flight mode, and for the second time in a week, he was going against his Beta Male nature and choosing to fight. Well, so be it, he thought. So be it. He would confront his tormentor and lay him low, as soon as he found a parking place — which he didn't.

He circled the block, cutting between cafés and bars, both of which were in abundance in the Castro. He drove up and down the side streets, lined with rows of immaculately kept (exorbitantly priced) Victorians and found no quarter for his trusty steed. After a half hour of orbiting the neighborhood, he headed back uptown and found a spot in a parking garage in the

Fillmore, then took the antique streetcar back down Market Street to the Castro. A cute little green, Italian-made antique streetcar, with oak benches, brass railings, and mahogany window frames — a charming brass bell and a top speed of about twenty miles per hour: this is how Charlie Asher charged into battle. He tried to imagine a horde of Huns hanging off the sides, waving wicked blades and firing arrows as they passed the murals in the Mission district, perhaps Viking raiders, shields fastened to the sides of the car, a great drum pounding as they rowed in to pillage the antique shops, the leather bars, the sushi bars, the leather sushi bars (don't ask), and the art galleries, in the Castro. And here, even Charlie's formidable imagination failed him. He got off the car at Castro and Market and walked back a block to Fresh Music, then paused outside the shop, wondering what in the hell he was going to do now.

What if the caller had just borrowed the phone? What if he stormed in screaming and threatening, and there was just some confused kid behind the counter? But then he looked in the door, and there, standing behind the counter, all alone, was an extraordinarily tall black man dressed com-

123

pletely in mint green, and at that point Charlie lost his mind.

"You killed her," Charlie screamed as he stormed by the racks of CDs toward the man in mint. He drew the sword as he ran, or tried to, hoping to bring it out in a single fluid movement from the cane sheath and across the throat of Rachel's killer. But the sword-cane had been in the back of Charlie's shop for a long time, and except for three times when Lily's friend Abby tried to leave with it (once trying to buy it, when Charlie refused to sell it to her, then twice trying to steal it), the sword hadn't been drawn in years. The little brass stud that you pushed to release the blade had stuck, so when Charlie delivered the deathblow, he swung the entire cane, which was heavier — and slower — than the sword would have been. The man in mint green — quick for his size — ducked, and Charlie took out an entire row of Judy Garland CDs, lost his balance, bounced off the counter, spun around, and again tried for the single draw-and-cut move that he had seen so many times in samurai movies, and had practiced so many times in his head on the way here. This time the sword came free of the scabbard and slashed a deadly arch three feet in front of the man in mint, completely decapitating a life-sized cutout of Barbra Streisand.

"That is un-unfucking called for!" thundered the tall man.

As Charlie recovered his balance for a backhand slash, he saw something large and dark coming down over him and recognized it at the last instant, as the antique cash register slammed down on his head. There was a flash, a ding, and everything got dark and gooey.

When Charlie came to, he was tied to a chair in the back room of the record store, which looked remarkably like the back room of his own store, except all the stacked boxes were full of records and CDs instead of all variety of used jetsam. The tall black man was standing over him, and Charlie thought at first that he might be turning to mist or smoke, but then he realized it was just that his vision was going wavy, and then pain lit up the inside of his head like a strobe light.

"Ouch."

"How's your neck?" asked the tall man. "Does your neck feel broken? Can you feel your feet?"

"Go ahead, kill me, you fucking coward," said Charlie, bucking around in the chair, trying to lunge at his captor and feeling a little like the Black Knight in *Monty Python's Holy Grail* after his arms and legs had been hacked off. If this guy took one step closer, Charlie could head-butt him in the nads, he was sure of it.

The tall man stomped on Charlie's toes, a size-eighteen glove-leather loafer driven by two hundred and seventy pounds of death and used-record dealer.

"Ouch!" Charlie hopped his chair in a little circle of pain. "Goddammit! Ouch!"

"So you do have feeling in your feet?"

"Get it over with. Go ahead." Charlie stretched his neck as if offering his throat to be cut — his strategy was to lure his captor into range, then sever the tall man's femoral artery with his teeth, then gloat as the blood coursed all over his mint-green slacks onto the floor. Charlie would laugh long and sinister as he watched the life drain out of the evil bastard, then he would hop his chair out to the street and onto the streetcar at Market, transfer to the number forty-one bus at Van Ness, hop off at Columbus, and hop the two blocks home, where someone would untie him. He had a plan — and a bus pass with four more days left on it — so this son of a bitch had picked the wrong guy to fuck with.

"I have no intention of killing you, Charlie," said the tall man, keeping a safe distance. "I'm sorry I had to hit you with the register. You didn't really leave me any options."

"You could have tasted the fatal sting of my blade!" Charlie glanced around for his sword-cane, just in case the guy had left it within reach.

"Yeah, sure, there was that one, but I thought I'd go with the one without the stains and the funeral."

Charlie strained against his bonds, which he realized now were plastic shopping bags. "You're messing with Death, you know? I am Death."

"Yeah, I know."

"You do?"

"Sure." The tall man spun another wooden chair around and sat on it reversed, facing Charlie. His knees were up at the level of his elbows and he looked like a great green tree frog, crouched to pounce on an insect. Charlie noticed for the first time that he had golden eyes, stark and striking in contrast to his dark skin. "So am I," said the evil mint-green frog guy.

"You? You're Death?"

"*A* Death, not *THE* Death. I don't think

there is a *THE* Death. Not anymore, anyway."

Charlie couldn't grasp it, so he struggled and wobbled until the tall man had to reach out and steady him to keep him from toppling over.

"You killed Rachel."

"I did not."

"I saw you there."

"Yes, you did. That's a problem. Will you please stop thrashing around?" He shook Charlie's chair. "But I wasn't instrumental in Rachel's death. That's not what we do, not anymore, anyway. Didn't you even look at the book?"

"What book? You said something about a book on the phone."

"*The Great Big Book of Death*. I sent it to your shop. I told a woman at the counter that I was sending it, and I got delivery confirmation, so I know it got there."

"What woman — Lily? She's not a woman, she's a kid."

"No, this was a woman about your age, with New Wave hair."

"Jane? No. She didn't say anything, and I didn't get any book."

"Oh, shit. That explains why they've been showing up. You didn't even know."

"Who? What? They?"

Mint Green Death sighed heavily. "I guess we're going to be here awhile. I'm going to make some coffee. Do you want some?"

"Sure, try to lull me into a false sense of security, then spring."

"You're tied the fuck up, motherfucker, I don't need to lull you into shit. You've been fucking with the fabric of human existence and someone needed to shut your ass down."

"Oh, sure, go *black* on me. Play the ethnic card."

Mint Green climbed to his feet and headed toward the door to the shop. "You want cream?"

"And two sugars, please," Charlie said.

"This is really cool, why are you giving it back?" said Abby Normal. Abby was Lily's best friend, and they were sitting on the floor in the back room of Asher's Secondhand, looking through *The Great Big Book of Death*. Abby's real name was Alison, but she would no longer tolerate the ignominy of what she called her "daylight-slave name." Everyone had been much more responsive to calling her by her chosen name than they had been to Lily's, Darquewillow

Elventhing, which you always had to spell for people.

"Turns out it's Asher, not me," Lily said. "He'll be really pissed if he finds out I took it. And he's Death now, I guess, so I could get in trouble."

"Are you going to tell him you had the book?" Abby scratched the silver spider stud in her eyebrow; it was a fresh piercing and still healing and she couldn't stop messing with it. Abby, like Lily, was dressed all in black, boots to hair, the difference being that she had a black-widow's red hourglass on the front of her black T-shirt and she was thinner and more waiflike in her affected creepiness.

"No. I'll just say it got misfiled. That happens a lot here."

"How long did you think it was you?"

"Like a month."

"What about the dreams and the names and stuff it talks about, you didn't have any of that, right?"

"I thought I was just growing into my powers. I made a lot of lists of people I wanted gone."

"Yeah, I do that. And you just found out yesterday that it was Asher?"

"Yeah," said Lily.

"That sucks," said Abby.

"Life sucks," said Lily.

"So, what now?" asked Abby. "Junior college?"

They both nodded, woefully, and looked into the depths of their respective nail polishes to avoid sharing the humiliation of one of them having gone from dark demigod to local loser in an instant. They lived their lives hoping for something grand and dark and supernatural to happen, so when it had, they took it more in stride than was probably healthy. Fear, after all, is a survival mechanism.

"So all these things are soul objects?" asked Abby, as cheerfully as her integrity would allow. She waved to the piles of stuff Charlie had marked with "Do Not Sell" signs. "There's like a person's soul in there?"

"According to the book," said Lily. "Asher says he can see them glow."

"I like the red Converse All Stars."

"Take them, they're yours," said Lily.

"Really?"

"Yeah," Lily said. She took the All Stars off the shelf and held them out. "He'll never miss them."

"Cool. I have the perfect pair of red fishnets I can wear with them."

"They probably have the soul of some

131

sweaty jock in them," Lily said.

"He may worship at my feet," said Abby, doing a pirouette and an arabesque (remnants, along with an eating disorder, of ten years of ballet lessons).

"So I'm like a Santa's Helper of Death?!" Charlie said, waving his coffee cup. The tall man had untied his one arm so he could drink his coffee, and Charlie was baptizing the stockroom floor with French roast with every gesture. Mr. Fresh frowned.

"What in the hell are you talking about, Asher?" Fresh felt bad about hitting Charlie Asher with a cash register and tying him up, and now he was wondering if the blow hadn't caused some sort of brain damage.

"I'm talking about the Santa at Macy's, Fresh. When you're a kid, and you notice that the Santa Claus at Macy's has a fake beard, and that there are at least six Salvation Army Santas working Union Square, you ask your parents about it and they tell you that the real Santa is in the North Pole, and he's really busy, so all these other guys are Santa's helpers, who are out helping him with his work. That's what you're saying, that we're Santa's helpers to Death?"

Mr. Fresh had been standing by his desk, but now he sat down again across from Charlie so he could look him in the eye. Very softly he said, "Charlie, you know that that's not true now, right? I mean about Santa's helpers and all?"

"Of course I know that there's no Santa Claus. I'm using it as a metaphor, you tool."

Mr. Fresh took this opportunity to reach out and smack Charlie upside the head. Then immediately regretted it.

"Hey!" Charlie put down his cup and rubbed one of his receding-hairline inlets, which was going red from the blow.

"Rude," said Mr. Fresh. "Let's not be rude."

"So you're saying that there *is* a Santa?" Charlie said, cringing in anticipation of another smack. "Oh my God, how deep does this conspiracy go?"

"No, there's no goddamn Santa. I'm just saying that I don't know what we are. I don't know if there is a big Death with a capital *D,* although the book hints that there used to be. I'm just saying that there are many of us, a dozen that I know of right here in the city — all of us picking up soul vessels and seeing that they get into the right hands."

"And that's based on someone randomly coming into your shop and buying a record?" Then Charlie's eyes went wide as it hit him. "Rachel's Sarah McLachlan CD. *You* took it?"

"Yes." Fresh looked at the floor, not because he was ashamed, but to avoid seeing the pain in Charlie Asher's eyes.

"Where is it? I want to see it," said Charlie.

"I sold it."

"To who? Find it. I want Rachel back."

"I don't know. To a woman. I didn't get her name, but I'm sure it was meant for her. You'll be able to tell."

"I will? Why will I?" he asked. "Why me? I don't want to kill people."

"We don't kill people, Mr. Asher. That's a misconception. We simply facilitate the ascendance of the soul."

"Well, one guy died because I said something to him, and another had a heart attack because of something I did. A death that results from your actions is basically killing someone, unless you're a politician, right? So why me? I'm not that highly skilled at bullshit. So why me?"

Mr. Fresh considered what Charlie was saying, and felt like something sinister had crawled up his spine. In all his years, he didn't remember ever having his actions directly result in someone's death, nor had he heard of it happening with the other Death Merchants. Of course you occasionally showed up at the time when the person was passing, but not often, and never as a cause.

"Well?" Charlie said.

Mr. Fresh shrugged. "Because you saw me. Surely you've noticed that no one sees you when you're out to get a soul vessel."

"I've never gone out to get a soul vessel."

"Yes, you have, and you will, at least you should be. You need to get with the program, Mr. Asher."

"Yeah, so you said. So you're — uh — we're invisible when we're out getting these soul vessels?"

"Not invisible, so to speak, it's just that no one sees us. You can go right into people's homes and they'll never notice you standing right beside them, but if you speak to someone on the street they'll see you, waitresses will take your order, cabs will stop for you — well, not me, I'm black, but, you know, they would. It's sort of a will thing, I think. I've tested it. Animals can see us, by the way. You'll want to watch out for dogs when you're retrieving a vessel."

135

"So that's how you got to be a — what do they call us?"

"Death Merchants."

"Get out. Really?"

"It's not in the book. I came up with it."

"It's very cool."

"Thanks." Mr. Fresh smiled, relieved for a moment not to be thinking about the gravity of Charlie's unique transition to Death Merchant. "Actually, I think it's a character from an album cover, guy behind a cash register, eyes glowing red, but I didn't know that when I came up with it."

"Well, it makes perfect sense."

"Yeah, I thought so," said Mr. Fresh. "More coffee?"

"Please." Charlie held out his empty cup. "So, someone saw you. That's how you became a Death Merchant?"

"No, that's how *you* became one. I think that you may, uh —" Fresh didn't want to mislead this poor guy, but on the other hand he didn't actually know what had happened. "I think you may be different from the rest of us. No one saw me. I was working security for a casino in Vegas when that went sour for me — I have a problem with authority, I'm told — so I came to San Francisco and opened this shop, started dealing in used records and

CDs, mostly jazz at first. After a while it just started happening: the glowing soul vessels, people coming in with them, finding them at estate sales. I don't know why or how, it just did, and I didn't say anything about it to anyone. Then the book came in the mail."

"The book again. Don't you have a copy around?"

"There's only one copy. At least that I know of."

"And you just mailed it out?"

"I sent it certified mail!" Fresh boomed. "Someone at your store signed for it. I think I did my part."

"Okay, sorry, go on."

"Anyway, when I got to the Castro it was a very sad place. The only guys you saw on the street were very old or very young, all the ones in the middle were either dead or sick with HIV, walking with canes, towing oxygen cylinders. Death was everywhere. It's like there needed to be a soul way station, and I was here, trading records. Then the book showed up in the mail. There were a lot of souls coming in. For those first few years I was picking up vessels every day, sometimes two or three times a day. You'd be surprised how many gay men have their souls in their music."

"Have you sold them all?"

"No. They come in, they go out. There's always some inventory."

"But how can you be sure the right person gets the right soul?"

"Not my problem, is it?" Mr. Fresh shrugged. He'd worried about it at first, but it seemed to all happen as it should, and he'd gotten into the rhythm of trusting whatever mechanism or power was behind all of this.

"Well, if that's your attitude, why do it at all? I don't want this job. I have a job, and a kid."

"You have to do it. Believe me, after I got the book, I tried not doing it. We all did. At least the ones I've talked to did. I'm guessing you've already seen what happens if you don't. You'll start hearing the voices, then the shades start coming. The book calls them Underworlders."

"The giant ravens? Them?"

"They were just indistinct shadows and voices until you showed up. There's something going on. Starting with you, and continuing with you. You let them get a soul vessel, didn't you?"

"Me? You said there's a bunch of Death Merchants."

"The others know better. It was you.

You fucked up. I thought I saw one flying over earlier in the week. Then today, I was out walking, and the voices were bad. Really bad. That's when I called you. It was you, wasn't it?"

Charlie nodded. "I didn't know. How could I know?"

"So they got one?"

"Two," Charlie said. "A hand came out of the sewer. It was my first day."

"Well, that's it," said Fresh, cradling his head in his hands. "We are most certainly fucked now."

"You don't know that," Charlie said, trying to look on the bright side. "We could have been fucked before. I mean, we run secondhand stores for dead people, that's sort of a definition of *fucked*."

Mr. Fresh looked up. "The book says if we don't do our jobs everything could go dark, become like the Underworld. I don't know what the Underworld is like, Mr. Asher, but I've caught some of the road show from there a couple of times, and I'm not interested in finding out. How 'bout you?"

"Maybe it's Oakland," Charlie said.

"What's Oakland?"

"The Underworld."

"Oakland is not the Underworld!" Mr.

Fresh leapt to his feet; he was not a violent man, you really didn't have to be when you were his size, but —

"The Tenderloin?" Charlie suggested.

"Don't make me smack you. Neither of us wants that, do we, Mr. Asher?"

Charlie shook his head. "I've seen the ravens," Charlie said, "but I haven't heard any voices. What voices?"

"They talk to you when you're on the street. Sometimes you'll hear a voice coming out of a heating vent, a downspout, sometimes a storm drain. It's them, all right. Female voices, taunting. I've gone years without hearing them, I'll almost forget, then I'll be going to pick up a vessel, and one will call to me. I used to phone the other merchants, ask them if they'd done something, but we stopped that right away."

"Why?"

"Because that's part of what we think brings them up. We're not supposed to have any contact. It took us a while to figure that out. I had only found six of the merchants in the city back then, and we were having lunch once a week, talking about what we knew, comparing notes — that's when we saw the first of the shades. In fact, just to be safe, this will be the last time that you and I have contact." Mr.

Fresh shrugged again and began to untie Charlie's bonds, thinking: *It all changed that day at the hospital. This guy has changed everything, and I'm sending him out like a lamb to the slaughter — or maybe he's the one to do the slaughtering. This guy might be the one —*

"Wait, I don't know anything," Charlie pleaded. "You can't just send me out to do this without more background. What about my daughter? How do I know who to sell the souls to?" He was panicked and trying to ask all the questions before he was set free. "What are the numbers after the names? Do you get the names like that? How long do I have to do this before I can retire. Why are you always dressed in mint green?" As Mr. Fresh untied one ankle, Charlie was trying to tie the other back to the chair.

"My name," said Mr. Fresh.

"Pardon?" Charlie stopped tying himself up.

"I dress in mint green because of my first name. It's Minty."

Charlie completely forgot what he was worried about. "Minty? Your name is Minty Fresh?"

Charlie appeared to be trying to stifle a sneeze, but then snorted an explosive laugh. Then ducked.

141

9

The Dragon, the Bear, and the Fish

In the hallway of the third floor of Charlie's building, a meeting was going on between the great powers of Asia: Mrs. Ling and Mrs. Korjev. Mrs. Ling, by holding Sophie, had the strategic advantage, while Mrs. Korjev, who was fully twice the size of Mrs. Ling, possessed the threat of massive retaliatory force. What they had in common, besides being widows and immigrants, was a deep love for little Sophie, a precarious grasp on the English language, and a passionate lack of confidence in Charlie Asher's ability to raise his daughter alone.

"He is angry when he leave today. Like bear," said Mrs. Korjev, who was possessed of an atavistic compulsion toward ursine simile.

"He say no poke," said Mrs. Ling, who

limited herself to English verbs in the present tense only, as a devotion to her Chan Buddhist beliefs, or so she claimed. "Who give poke to baby?"

"Pork is good for child. Make her grow strong," said Mrs. Korjev, who then quickly added, "like bear."

"He say it turn her into shih tzu. Shih tzu is dog. What kind father think little girl turn into dog?" Mrs. Ling was especially protective of little girls, as she had grown up in a province of China where each morning a man with a cart came around to collect the bodies of baby girls who had been born during the night and hurled into the street. She was lucky that her own mother had spirited her away to the fields and refused to come home until the new daughter was accepted as part of the family.

"Not shih tzu," corrected Mrs. Korjev. "Shiksa."

"Okay, shiksa. Dog is dog," said Mrs. Ling. "Is irresponsible." Not once was the letter *r* heard in Mrs. Ling's pronunciation of *irresponsible*.

"Is Yiddish word for not a Jew girl. Rachel is Jew, you know." Mrs. Korjev, unlike most of the Russian immigrants left in the neighborhood, was not a Jew. Her people had come from the steppes of Russia, and she was, in fact, descended from Cossacks — not generally considered a Hebrew-friendly race. She atoned for the sins of her ancestors by being ferociously protective (not unlike a mother bear) of Rachel, and now Sophie.

"The flowers need water today," said Mrs. Korjev.

At the end of the hallway was a large bay window that looked out on the building across the street and a window box full of red geraniums. On afternoons, the two great Asian powers would stand in the hallway, admire the flowers, talk of the cost of things, and complain about the increasing discomfort of their shoes. Neither dared start her own window box of geraniums, lest it appear that she had stolen the idea from across the street, and in the process set off an escalating window-box competition that could ultimately end in bloodshed. They agreed, tacitly, to admire — but not covet — the red flowers.

Mrs. Korjev liked the very redness of them. She had always been angry that the Communists had co-opted that color, for otherwise it would have evoked an unbridled happiness in her. Then again, the Russian soul, conditioned by a thousand years of angst, really wasn't equipped for unbridled happiness, so it was probably for the best.

Mrs. Ling was also taken with the red of the geraniums, for in her cosmology that color represented good fortune, prosperity, and long life. The very gates of the temples were painted that same color red, and so the red flowers represented one of the many paths to *wu* — eternity, enlightenment — essentially, the universe in a flower. She also thought that they would taste pretty good in soup.

Sophie had only recently discovered color, and the red splashes against the gray shiplap was enough to put a toothless smile on her little face.

So the three were staring into the joy of red flowers when the black bird hit the window, throwing a great spiderweb crack around it. But rather than fall away, the bird seemed to leak into the very crack, and spread, like black ink, across the window and in, onto the walls of the hallway.

And the great powers of Asia fled to the stairway.

Charlie was rubbing his left wrist where the plastic bag had been tied around it.

145

"What, did your mother name you after a mouthwash ad?"

Mr. Fresh, looking somewhat vulnerable for a man of his size, said, "Toothpaste, actually."

"Really?"

"Yeah."

"Sorry, I didn't know," Charlie said. "You could have changed it, right?"

"Mr. Asher, you can resist who you are for only so long. Finally you decide to just go with fate. For me that has involved being black, being seven feet tall — yet not in the NBA — being named Minty Fresh, and being recruited as a Death Merchant." He raised an eyebrow as if accusing Charlie. "I have learned to accept and embrace all of those things."

"I thought you were going to say gay," Charlie said.

"What? A man doesn't have to be gay to dress in mint green."

Charlie considered Mr. Fresh's mint-green suit — made from seersucker and entirely too light for the season — and felt a strange affinity for the refreshingly-named Death Merchant. Although he didn't know it, Charlie was recognizing the signs of another Beta Male. (Of course there are gay Betas: the Beta Male boy-

146

friend is highly prized in the gay community because you can teach him how to dress yet you can remain relatively certain that he will never develop a fashion sense or be more fabulous than you.) Charlie said, "I suppose you're right, Mr. Fresh. I'm sorry if I made assumptions. My apologies."

"That's okay," said Mr. Fresh. "But you really should go."

"No, I still don't understand, how do I know who the souls go to? I mean, after this happened, there were all kinds of soul vessels in my store I hadn't even known about. How do I know I didn't sell them to someone who already had one? What if someone has a set?"

"That can't happen. At least as far as we know. Look, you'll just know. Take my word for it. When people are ready to receive the soul, they get it. Have you ever studied any of the Eastern religions?"

"I live in Chinatown," said Charlie, and although that was technically kinda-sorta true, he knew how to say exactly three things in Mandarin: *Good day; light starch, please;* and *I am an ignorant white devil,* all taught to him by Mrs. Ling. He believed the last to translate to "top of the morning to you."

"Let me rephrase that, then," said Mr. Fresh. "Have you ever studied any of the Eastern religions?"

"Oh, Eastern religions," Charlie said, pretending he had just misinterpreted the question before. "Just Discovery Channel stuff — you know, Buddha, Shiva, Gandalf — the biggies."

"You understand the concept of karma? How unresolved lessons are re-presented to you in another life."

"Yes, of course. Duh." Charlie rolled his eyes.

"Well, think of yourself as a soul re-assignment agent. We are agents of karma."

"Secret agents," Charlie said wistfully.

"Well, I hope it goes without saying," said Mr. Fresh, "that you can't tell anyone what you are, so yes, I suppose we *are* secret agents of karma. We hold a soul until a person is ready to receive it."

Charlie shook his head as if trying to clear water from his ears. "So if someone walks into my store and buys a soul vessel, until then they've been going through life without a soul? That's awful."

"Really?" said Minty Fresh. "Do you know if you have a soul?"

"Of course I do."

"Why do you say that?"

"Because I'm me." Charlie tapped his chest. "Here I am."

"That's just a personality," said Minty, "and barely one. You could be an empty vessel, and you'd never know the difference. You may not have reached a point in life where you are ready to receive your soul."

"Huh?"

"Your soul may be more evolved than you are right now. If a kid fails tenth grade, do you make him repeat grades K through nine?"

"No, I guess not."

"No, you just make him start over at the beginning of tenth grade. Well, it's the same with souls. They only ascend. A person gets a soul when they can carry it to the next level, when they are ready to learn the next lesson."

"So if I sell one of those glowing objects to someone, they've been going through life without a soul?"

"That's my theory," said Minty Fresh. "I've read a lot on this subject over the years. Texts from every culture and religion, and this explains it better than anything else I can come up with."

"Then it's not all in the book you sent."

"That's just the practical instructions. There's no explanations. It's Dick-and-Jane simple. It says to get a calendar and put it next to your bed and the names will come to you. It doesn't tell you how you will find them, or what the object is, just that you have to find them. Get a day planner. That's what I use."

"But what about the number? When I would find a name written next to the bed, there was always a number next to it."

Mr. Fresh nodded and grinned a little sheepishly. "That's how many days you'll have to retrieve the soul vessel."

"You mean it's how long before the person dies? I don't want to know that."

"No, not how long before the person dies, how long you have to retrieve the vessel, how many days are left. I've been looking at this for a long time, and the number is never above forty-nine. I thought that might be significant, so I started looking for it in literature about death and dying. Forty-nine days just happens to be the number of days of *bardo,* the term used in the Tibetan *Book of the Dead* for the transition between life and death. Somehow, we Death Merchants are the medium for moving these souls, but we have to get there within the forty-nine days, that's my theory, anyway. Don't be surprised sometimes if the person has been dead for weeks before you get his name. You still have the number of days left in *bardo* to get the soul vessel."

"And if I don't make it in time?" Charlie asked.

Minty Fresh shook his head dolefully. "Shades, ravens, dark shit rising from the Underworld — who knows? Thing is, you have to find it in time. And you will."

"How, if there's no address or instructions, like 'it's under the mat.' "

"Sometimes — most of the time, in fact — they come to you. Circumstances line up."

Charlie thought about the stunning red-head bringing him the silver cigarette case. "You said sometimes?"

Fresh shrugged. "Sometimes you have to really search, find the person, go to their house — once I even hired a detective to help me find someone, but that started to bring the voices. You can tell if you're getting close by checking to see if people notice you."

"But I have to make a living. I have a kid —"

"You'll do that, too, Charlie. The money comes as part of the job. You'll see."

Charlie did see. He had seen already: the Mainheart estate clothing — he'd make tens of thousands on it if he got it.

"Now you have to go," said Minty Fresh. He held out his hand to shake and a grin cut his face like a crescent moon in the night sky. Charlie took the tall man's hand, his own hand disappearing into the Death Merchant's grip.

"I'm still sure I have questions. Can I call you?"

"No," said the mint one.

"Okay, then, I'm going now," Charlie said, not really moving. "Completely at the mercy of forces of the Underworld and stuff."

"You take care," said Minty Fresh.

"No idea what the hell I'm doing," Charlie went on, taking tentative baby steps toward the door. "The weight of all of humanity on my shoulders."

"Yeah, make sure you stretch in the morning," said the big man.

"By the way," Charlie said, out of rhythm with his whining, "are you gay?"

"What I am," said Minty Fresh, "is alone. Completely and entirely."

"Okay," Charlie said. "I'm sorry."

"It's okay. I'm sorry I smacked you in the head."

Charlie nodded, grabbed his sword-cane from behind the counter, and walked out of Fresh Music into an overcast San Francisco day.

Well, he wasn't exactly Death, but he wasn't Santa's helper, either. It didn't really matter that no one would believe him even if he told them. Death Merchant seemed a little dire, but he liked the idea of being a secret agent. An agent of KARMA — Karma Assessment Reassignment Murder and Ass — okay, he could work on the acronym later, but a secret agent nevertheless.

Actually, although he didn't know it, Charlie was well suited to be a secret agent. Because they function below the radar, Beta Males make excellent spies. Not the "James Bond, Aston Martin with missiles, boning the beautiful Russian rocket scientist on an ermine-skin bedspread" sort of spy — more the "bad comb-over, deep-cover bureaucrat fishing coffee-sodden documents out of a Dumpster" spy. His overt nonthreateningness allows him access to places and people that are closed to the Alpha Male, wearing his testosterone on his sleeve. The Beta male can, in fact, be dangerous, not so much in the "Jet Li entire body is a deadly weapon" way but more in the "drunk on the riding mower making a Luke Skywalker assault on the toolshed" sort of way.

So, as Charlie headed for the streetcar stop on Market Street, he mentally tried on his new persona as a secret agent, and was feeling pretty good about it, when, as he passed a storm drain, he heard a female voice whisper harshly, "We'll get the little one. You'll see, fresh Meat. We'll have her soon."

As soon as Charlie walked into his store from the alley, Lily bolted into the back room to meet him.

"That cop was here again. That guy died. Did you kill him?" To the machine-gun update she added, "Uh, sir?" Then she saluted, curtsied, then did a praying-hands Japanese bow thing.

Charlie was thrown by all of it, coming as it did when he was in a panic about his daughter and had just driven across town like a madman. He was sure the gestures of respect were just some dark cover-up for a favor or a misdeed, or, as often was the case, the teenager was messing with him. So he sat down on one of the high hardwood stools near the desk and said, "Cop? Guy? 'Splain, please. And I didn't kill anyone."

Lily took a deep breath. "That cop that was by here the other day came back. Turns out that guy you went up to see in Pacific Heights last week" — she looked at something she had written on her arm in red ink — "Michael Mainheart, killed himself. And he left a note to you. Saying that you were to take his and his wife's clothes and sell them at the market rate. And then he wrote" — and here she again referred to her ink-stained arm — " 'What about "I just want to die" did you not understand?' " Lily looked up.

"That's what he said after I gave him CPR the other day," Charlie said.

"So, did you kill him? Or whatever you call it. You can tell me." She curtsied again, which disturbed Charlie more than somewhat. He'd long ago defined his relationship with Lily as being built on a strong base of affectionate contempt, and this was throwing everything off.

"No, I did not kill him. What kind of question is that?"

"Did you kill the guy with the cigarette case?"

"No! I never even saw that guy."

"You realize that I am your trusted minion," Lily said, this time adding another bow.

"Lily, what the hell is wrong with you?"

"Nothing. There's nothing wrong at all, Mr. Asher — uh, Charles. Do you prefer Charles or Charlie?"

"You're asking now? What else did the cop say?"

"He wanted to talk to you. I guess they found that Mainheart guy dressed in his wife's clothing. He hadn't been home from the hospital for an hour before he sent the nurse away, got all cross-dressed up, then took a handful of painkillers."

Charlie nodded, thinking about how adamant Mainheart had been about having his wife's clothes out of the house. He was using any way he could to feel close to her, and it wasn't working. And when wearing her clothes didn't put him closer, he'd gone after her the only way he knew how, by joining her in death. Charlie understood. If it hadn't been for Sophie, he might have tried to join Rachel.

"Pretty kinky, huh?" Lily said.

"No!" Charlie barked. "No it's not, Lily. It's not like that at all. Don't even think that. Mr. Mainheart died of grief. It might look like something else, but that's what it was."

"Sorry," Lily said. "You're the expert."

Charlie was staring at the floor, trying to

156

put some sense to it all, wondering if his losing the fur coat that was Mrs. Mainheart's soul vessel meant that the couple would never be together again. Because of him.

"Oh yeah," Lily added. "Mrs. Ling called down all freaked out and yelling all Chinesey about a black bird smashing the window —"

Charlie was off the stool and taking the stairs two at a time.

"She's in your apartment," Lily called after him.

There was an orange slick of TV attorneys floating on the top of the fishbowl when Charlie got to his apartment. The Asian powers were standing in his kitchen, Mrs. Korjev was holding Sophie tight to her chest, and the infant was virtually swimming, trying to escape the giant marshmallowy canyon of protection between the massive Cossack fun bags. Charlie snatched his daughter as she was sinking into the cleavage for the third time and held her tight.

"What happened?" he asked.

There followed a barrage of Chinese and Russian mixed with the odd English word: *bird, window, broken, black, and make shit on myself.*

157

"Stop!" Charlie held up a free hand. "Mrs. Ling, what happened?"

Mrs. Ling had recovered from the bird hitting the window and the mad dash down the steps, but she was now showing an uncharacteristic shyness, afraid that Charlie might notice the damp spot in the pocket of her frock where the recently deceased Barnaby Jones lay orangely awaiting introduction to some wonton, green onions, a pinch of five spices, and her soup pot. "Fish is fish," she said to herself when she squirreled that rascal away. There were, after all, five more dead attorneys in the bowl, who would miss one?

"Oh, nothing," said Mrs. Ling. "Bird break window and scare us. Not so bad now."

Charlie looked to Mrs. Korjev. "Where?"

"On our floor. We are talking in hall. Speaking of what is best for Sophie, when *boom,* bird hits window and black ink run through window. We run here and lock door." Both the widows had keys to Charlie's apartment.

"I'll have it fixed tomorrow," Charlie said. "But that's all. Nothing — no one came in?"

"Is third floor, Charlie. No one comes in."

Charlie looked to the fishbowl. "What happened there?"

Mrs. Ling's eyes went wide. "I have to go. Mah-jongg night at temple."

"We come in, lock door," explained Mrs. Korjev. "Fish are fine. Put Sophie in car seat like always we are doing, then go look in hallway for coast to be clear. When Mrs. Ling look back, fish are dead."

"Not me! Is Russian who see dead fish," said Mrs. Ling.

"It's okay," Charlie said. "Did you see any birds, anything dark in the apartment?"

The two women shook their heads. "Only upstairs," Mrs. Ling said.

"Let's go look," Charlie said, moving Sophie to his hip and picking up his sword-cane. He led the two women to the little elevator, did a quick assessment of Mrs. Korjev's size versus the cubic footage, and led them up the stairs. When he saw the broken bay window he felt a little weak in the knees. It wasn't so much the window, it was what was on the roof across the street. Refracted a thousand times in the spiderwebbed safety glass was the shadow of a woman that was cast on the building. He handed the baby to Mrs. Korjev, approached the window, and knocked a hole in the glass to see better. As he did, the shadow slid down the side of the building, across the sidewalk, and into the storm drain next to where a dozen tourists had just disembarked from a cable car. None of them appeared to have seen anything. It was just past one and the sun was casting shadows nearly straight down. He looked back at the two windows.

"Did you see that?"

"You mean break window?" Mrs. Ling said, slowly approaching the window and peering through the hole Charlie had made. "Oh no."

"What? What?"

Mrs. Ling looked back at Mrs. Korjev. "You are right. Flowers need water."

Charlie looked through the hole in the window and saw that Mrs. Ling was referring to a window box full of dead, black geraniums.

"Safety bars on all the windows. Tomorrow," Charlie said.

Not far away, as the crow flies, under Columbus Avenue, in a wide pipe junction where several storm sewers met, Orcus, the Ancient One, paced, bent over like a hunchback, the heavy spikes that jutted from his shoulders scraping the sides of the pipe, throwing off sparks and the smell of smoldering peat.

"You're going to fuck up your spikes if you keep pacing like that," said Babd.

She was crouched in one of the smaller pipes to the side, next to her sisters, Nemain and Macha. Except for Nemain, who was beginning to show a gunmetal relief of bird feathers over her body, they were devoid of depth; flat absences of light, absolute black even in the gloom filtering down through the storm grates — shadows, silhouettes, really — the darker ancestors of the modern mud-flap girls. Shades: delicate and female and fierce.

"Sit. Have a snack. What good to take the Above if you look like hell in the end?"

Orcus growled and spun on the Morrigan, the three. "Too long out of the air! Too long." From the basket on his belt he hooked a human skull on one of his claws, popped it in his mouth, and crunched down on it.

The Morrigan laughed, sounding like wind through the pipes, pleased that he was enjoying their gift. They'd spent much of the day under San Francisco's graveyards digging out the skulls (Orcus liked them decoffinated) and polishing off the dirt and detritus until they shone like bone china.

"We flew," said Nemain. She took a moment to admire the blue-black feather shapes on her surface. "Above," she added unnecessarily. "They are everywhere, like cherries waiting to be stolen."

"Not stolen," said Orcus. "You think like a crow. They are ours for the taking."

"Oh yeah, well, where were you? I got these." The shade held up William Creek's umbrella in one hand and the fur jacket she'd ripped away from Charlie Asher in the other. They still glowed red, but were rapidly dimming. "Because of these, I was Above. I flew." When no one reacted, Nemain added, "Above."

"I flew, too," said Babd timidly. "A little." She was a tad self-conscious that she'd manifested no feather patterns or dimension.

Orcus hung his great head. The Morrigan moved to his side and began stroking the long spikes that had once been wings. "We will all be Above, soon," said Macha. "This new one doesn't know what he is doing. He will make it so we can all be Above. Look how far we've come — and we are so close now. Two Above in such a short time. This New Meat, this ignorant one, he may be all we need."

Orcus lifted his bull-like head and grinned, revealing a sawmill of teeth. "They will be like fruit for the picking."

"See," said Nemain. "Like I said. Did you know that Above you can see really far? Miles. And the wonderful smells. I never realized how damp and musty it is down here. Is there any reason that we can't have a window?"

"Shut up!" growled Orcus.

"Jeez, bite my head off, why don't you."

"Don't tease," said the bullheaded Death. He rose and led the other Deaths, the Morrigan, down the pipe toward the financial district, to the buried Gold Rush ship where they made their home.

PART TWO

Secondhand Souls

Do not seek death. Death will find
   you.
But seek the road which makes death
   a fulfillment.

— *Dag Hammarskjöld*

10

Death Takes a Walk

Mornings, Charlie walked. At six, after an early breakfast, he would turn the care of Sophie over to Mrs. Korjev or Mrs. Ling (whoever's turn it was) for the workday and walk — stroll really, pacing out the city with the sword-cane, which had become part of his daily regalia, wearing soft, black-leather walking shoes and an expensive, second-hand suit that had been retailored at his cleaner's in Chinatown. Although he pretended to have a purpose, Charlie walked to give himself time to think, to try on the size of being Death, and to look at all the people out and about in the morning. He wondered if the girl at the flower stand, from whom he often bought a carnation for his lapel, had a soul, or would give hers up while he watched her die. He watched the guy in North Beach make cappuccinos with faces and fern leaves drawn in the foam, and wondered if a guy like that could actually function without a soul, or was his soul collecting dust in Charlie's back room? There were a lot of people to see, and a lot of thinking to be done.

Being out among the people of the city, when they were just starting to move, greeting the day, making ready, he started to feel not just the responsibility of his new role, but the power, and finally, the specialness. It didn't matter that he had no idea what he was doing, or that he might have lost the love of his life for it to happen; he had been chosen. And realizing that, one day as he walked down California Street, down Nob Hill into the financial district, where he'd always felt inferior and out of touch with the world, as the brokers and bankers quickstepped around him, barking into their cell phones to Hong Kong or London or New York and never making eye contact, he started to not so much stroll, as strut. That day Charlie Asher climbed onto the California Street cable car for the first time since he was a kid, and hung off the bar, out over the street, holding out the sword-cane as if charging, with Hondas and Mercedes zooming along the street beside him, passing under his armpit just inches away. He got off at the end of the line, bought a Wall Street Journal from a machine, then walked to the nearest storm drain, spread out the Journal to protect his trousers against oil stains, then got down on his hands and knees and screamed into the drain grate, "I have been chosen, so don't fuck with me!" When he stood up again, a dozen people were standing there, waiting for the light to change. Looking at him.

"Had to be done," Charlie said, not apologizing, just explaining.

The bankers and the brokers, the executive assistants and the human-resource people and the woman on her way to serve up clam chowder in a sourdough bowl at the Boudin Bakery, all nodded, not sure exactly why, except that they worked in the financial district, and they all understood being fucked with, and in their souls if not in their minds, they knew that Charlie had been yelling in the right direction. He folded his paper, tucked it under his arm, then turned and crossed the street with them when the light changed.

Sometimes Charlie walked whole blocks when he thought only of Rachel, and would become so engrossed in the memory of her eyes, her smile, her touch, that he ran straight into people. Other times people would bump into him, and not even lift his wallet or say "excuse me," which might be a matter of course in New York, but in San Francisco meant that he was close to a soul vessel that needed to be retrieved. He found one, a bronze fireplace poker, set out by the curb with the trash on Russian Hill. Another time, he spotted a glowing vase displayed in the bay window of a Victorian in North Beach. He screwed up his courage and knocked on the door, and when a young woman answered, and came out on the porch to look for her visitor, and was bewildered because she didn't see anyone there, Charlie slipped past her, grabbed the vase, and was out the side door before she came back in, his heart pounding like a war drum, adrenaline sizzling through his veins like a hormonal tilt-a-whirl. As he headed back to the shop that particular morning, he realized, with no little sense of irony, that until he became Death, he'd never felt so alive.

Every morning, Charlie tried to walk in a different direction. On Mondays he liked to go up into Chinatown just after dawn, when all the deliveries were being made — crates of produce, carrots, lettuce, broccoli, cauliflower, melons, and a dozen varieties of cabbage, tended by Latinos in the Central Valley and consumed by Chinese in Chinatown, having passed through Anglo hands just long enough to extract the nourishing money. On Mondays the fishing companies delivered their fresh catches — usually strong Italian men whose families had been in the business for five generations, handing off their catch to inscrutable Chinese merchants whose ancestors had bought fish from the Italians off horse-drawn wagons a hundred years before. All sorts of live and recently live fish were moved across the sidewalk: snapper and halibut and mackerel, sea bass and ling cod and yellowtail, clawless Pacific lobster, Dungeness crab, ghastly monkfish, with their long saberlike teeth and a single spine that jutted from their head, bracing a luminous lure they used to draw in prey, so deep in the ocean that the sun never shone. Charlie was fascinated by the creatures from the very deep sea, the big-eyed squid, cuttlefish, the blind sharks that located prey with electromagnetic impulses — creatures who never saw light. They made him think of what might be facing him from the Underworld, because even as he fell into a rhythm of finding names at his bedside, and soul vessels in all manner of places, and the appearance of the ravens and the shades subsided, he could feel them under the street whenever he passed a storm sewer. Sometimes he could hear them whispering to one another, hushing quickly in the rare moments when the street went quiet.

To walk through Chinatown at dawn was to become part of a dangerous dance, because there were no back doors or alleys for loading, and all the wares went across the sidewalk, and although Charlie had enjoyed neither danger nor dancing up till now, he enjoyed playing dance partner to the thousand tiny Chinese grandmothers in black slippers or jelly-colored plastic shoes who scampered from merchant to merchant, squeezing and smelling and thumping, looking for the freshest and the best for their families, twanging orders and questions to the merchants in Mandarin, all the while just a second or a slip away from being run over by sides of beef, great racks of fresh duck, or hand trucks stacked high with crates of live turtles. Charlie was yet to retrieve a soul vessel on one of his Chinatown walks, but he stayed ready, because the swirl of time and motion forecast that one foggy morning someone's granny was going to get knocked out of her moo shoes.

One Monday, just for sport, Charlie grabbed an eggplant that a spectacularly wizened granny was going for, but instead of twisting it out of his hand with some mystic kung fu move as he expected, she looked him in the eye and shook her head — just a jog, barely perceptible really — it might have been a tic, but it was the most eloquent of gestures. Charlie read it as saying: *O White Devil, you do not want to purloin that purple fruit, for I have four thousand years of ancestors and civilization on you; my grandparents built the railroads and dug the silver mines, and my parents survived the earthquake, the fire, and a society that outlawed even being Chinese; I am mother to a dozen, grandmother to a hundred, and great-grandmother to a legion; I have birthed babies and washed the dead; I am history and suffering and wisdom; I am a Buddha and a dragon; so get your fucking hand off my eggplant before you lose it.*

And Charlie let go.

And she grinned, just a little. Three teeth.

And he wondered if it ever did fall to him to retrieve the soul vessel of one of

173

these crones of Chronos, if he'd even be able to lift it. And he grinned back.

And asked for her phone number, which he gave to Ray. "She seemed nice," Charlie told him. "Mature."

Sometimes Charlie's walks took him through Japantown, where he passed the most enigmatic shop in the city, Invisible Shoe Repair. He really intended to stop in one day, but he was still coming to terms with giant ravens, adversaries from the Underworld, and being a Merchant of Death, and he wasn't sure he was ready for invisible shoes, let alone invisible shoes that needed repair! He often tried to look past the Japanese characters into the shop window as he passed, but saw nothing, which, of course, didn't mean a thing. He just wasn't ready. But there was a pet shop in Japantown (House of Pleasant Fish and Gerbil), where he had originally gone to buy Sophie's fish, and where he returned to replace the TV attorneys with six TV detectives, who also simultaneously took the big Ambien a week later. Charlie had been distraught to find his baby daughter drooling away in front of a bowl floating more dead detectives than a film noir festival, and after flushing all six at once and having to use the plunger to dislodge Magnum and Mannix, he vowed that next time he would find more resilient pals for his little girl. He was coming out of House of PF&G one afternoon, with a Habitrail pod containing a pair of sturdy hamsters, when he ran into Lily, who was making her way to a coffeehouse up on Van Ness, where she was planning to meet her friend Abby for some latte-fueled speed brooding.

"Hey, Lily, how are you doing?" Charlie was trying to appear matter-of-fact, but he found that the awkwardness between him and Lily over the last few months was not mitigated by her seeing him on the street carrying a plastic box full of rodents.

"Nice gerbils," Lily said. She wore a Catholic schoolgirl's plaid skirt over black tights and Doc Martens, with a tight black PVC bustier that was squishing pale Lily-bits out the top, like a can of biscuit dough that's been smacked on the edge of the counter. The hair color du jour was fuchsia, over violet eye shadow, which matched her violet, elbow-length lace gloves. She looked up and down the street and, when she didn't see anyone she knew, fell into step next to Charlie.

"They're not gerbils, they're hamsters," Charlie said.

"Asher, do you have something you've been keeping from me?" She tilted her head a little, but didn't look at him when she asked, just kept her eyes forward, scanning the street for someone who might recognize her walking next to Charlie, thus forcing her to commit seppuku.

"Jeez, Lily, these are for Sophie!" Charlie said. "Her fish died, so I'm bringing her some new pets. Besides, that whole gerbil thing is an urban myth —"

"I meant that you're Death," Lily said.

Charlie nearly dropped his hamsters. "Huh?"

"It's so wrong —" Lily continued, walking on after Charlie had stopped in his tracks, so now he had to scurry to catch up to her. "Just so wrong, that you would be chosen. Of all of life's many disappointments, I'd have to say that this is the crowning disappointment."

"You're sixteen," Charlie said, still stumbling a little at the matter-of-fact way she was discussing this.

"Oh, throw that in my face, Asher. I'm only sixteen for two more months, then what? In the blink of an eye my beauty becomes but a feast for worms, and I, a forgotten sigh in a sea of nothingness."

"Your birthday is in two months? Well,

we'll have to get you a nice cake," Charlie said.

"Don't change the subject, Asher. I know all about you, and your Death persona."

Charlie stopped again and turned to look at her. This time, she stopped as well. "Lily, I know I've been acting a little strangely since Rachel died, and I'm sorry you got in trouble at school because of me, but it's just been trying to deal with it all, with the baby, with the business. The stress of it all has —"

"I have *The Great Big Book of Death*," Lily said. She steadied Charlie's hamsters when he lost his grip. "I know about the soul vessels, about the dark forces rising if you fuck up, all that stuff — all of it. I've known longer than you have, I think."

Charlie didn't know what to say. He was feeling panic and relief at the same time — panic because Lily knew, but relief because at least someone knew, and believed it, and had actually seen the book. The book!

"Lily, do you still have the book?"

"It's in the store. I hid it in the back of the glass cabinet where you keep the valuable stuff that no one will ever buy."

"No one ever looks in that cabinet."

"No kidding? I thought if you ever found

177

it, I'd say it had always been there."

"I have to go." He turned and started walking the other direction, but then realized that they had already been heading toward his neighborhood and turned around again. "Where are you going?"

"To get some coffee."

"I'll walk with you."

"You will not." Lily looked around again, wary that someone might see them.

"But, Lily, I'm Death. That should at least have given me some level of cool."

"Yeah, you'd think, but it turns out that you have managed to suck the cool out of being Death."

"Wow, that's harsh."

"Welcome to my world, Asher."

"You can't tell anyone about this, you know that?"

"Like anyone cares what you do with your gerbils."

"Hamsters! That's not —"

"Chill, Asher." Lily giggled. "I know what you mean. I'm not going to tell anyone — except Abby knows — but she doesn't care. She says she's met some guy who's her dark lord. She's in that stage where she thinks a dick is some kind of mystical magic wand."

Charlie adjusted his hamster box uncomfortably. "Girls go through a stage like that?" Why was he just hearing about this now? Even the hamsters looked uncomfortable.

Lily turned on a heel and started up the street. "I'm not having this conversation with you."

Charlie stood there, watching her go, balancing the hamsters and his completely useless sword-cane while trying to dig his cell phone out of his jacket pocket. He needed to see that book, and he needed to see it sooner than the hour it would take him to get home. "Lily, wait!" he called. "I'm calling a cab, I'll give you a ride."

She waved him off without looking and kept walking. As he was waiting for the cab company to answer, he heard it, the voice, and he realized that he was standing right over a storm drain. It had been over a month since he'd heard them, and he thought maybe they'd gone. "We'll have her, too, Meat. She's ours now."

He felt the fear rise in his throat like bile. He snapped the phone shut and ran after Lily, cane rattling and hamsters bouncing as he went. "Lily, wait! Wait!"

She spun around quickly and her fuchsia wig only did the quarter turn instead of the half, so her face was covered with hair when she said, "One of those ice-cream cakes from Thirty-one Flavors, okay? After that, despair and nothingness."

"We'll put that on the cake," Charlie said.

11

The Girls Can Get a Little Dark at Times

The Great Big Book of Death, as it turned out, wasn't that big, and certainly wasn't that comprehensive. Charlie read through it a dozen times, took notes, made copies, ran searches trying to find some reference to any of the stuff covered, but all of the material in the twenty-eight lavishly illustrated pages boiled down to this:

1. Congratulations, you have been chosen to act as Death. It's a dirty job, but someone has to do it. It is your duty to retrieve soul vessels from the dead and dying and see them on to their next body. If you fail, Darkness will cover the world and Chaos will reign.

2. Some time ago, the Luminatus, or the

Great Death, who kept balance between light and darkness, ceased to be. Since then, Forces of Darkness have been trying to rise from below. You are all that stands between them and destruction of the collective soul of humanity.

3. In order to hold off the Forces of Darkness, you will need a number two pencil and a calendar, preferably one without pictures of kitties on it.

4. Names and numbers will come to you. The number is how many days you have to retrieve the soul vessel. You will know the vessels by their crimson glow.

5. Don't tell anyone what you do, or dark forces, etc. etc. etc.

6. People may not see you when you are performing your Death duties, so be careful crossing the street. You are not immortal.

7. Do not seek others. Do not waver in your duties or the Forces of Darkness will destroy all that you care about.

8. You do not cause death, you do not prevent death, you are a servant of Destiny, not its agent. Get over yourself.

9. Do not, under any circumstances, let

a soul vessel fall into the hands of those from below — because that would be bad.

A few months passed before Charlie worked the shop again alone with Lily. She asked him, "Well, did you get a number two pencil?"

"No, I got a number one pencil."

"You rogue! Asher, hello, Forces of Darkness —"

"If the world without this Luminatus is so precariously balanced that my buying a pencil with one-grade-harder lead is going to cast us all into the abyss, then maybe it's time."

"Whoa, whoa, whoa, whoa, whoa," Lily chanted like she was trying to bring a spooked horse under control. "It's one thing for me to be all nihilistic and stuff, for me it's a fashion statement, I have the outfits for it. You can't be all horny for the grave wearing your stupid Savile Row suits."

Charlie was proud of her for recognizing that he was wearing one of his expensive secondhand Savile Rows. She was learning the trade in spite of herself.

"I'm tired of being afraid," he said. "I've dealt with the Forces of Darkness or whatever, Lily, and you know what, we're one and one."

"Should you be telling me this? I mean, the book said —"

"I think I'm different than what the book says, Lily. The book says that I don't cause death, but there have been two now that have died more or less because of my actions."

"And I repeat, should you be telling me this? As you have pointed out many times, I am a kid, and wildly irresponsible. It's *wildly* irresponsible, right? I'm never listening that closely."

"You're the only one who knows," Charlie said. "And you're seventeen now, not a kid, you're a young woman now."

"Don't fuck with me, Asher. If you keep talking like that I'll get another piercing, take X until I'm dehydrated like a mummy, talk on my cell phone until the battery is dead, then find some skinny, pale guy and suck him until he cries."

"So, it will be like a Friday?" Charlie said.

"What I do with my weekends is my own business."

"I know!"

"Well, then shut up!"

"I'm tired of being afraid, Lily!"

"Well, then stop being afraid, Charlie!"

They both looked away, embarrassed. Lily pretended to shuffle through the day's receipts while Charlie pretended to be looking for something in what he called his walking satchel and Jane called his man purse.

"Sorry," Lily said, without looking up from the receipts.

"S'okay," Charlie said. "Me, too."

Still not looking up, Lily said, "But really, should you be telling me any of this?"

"Probably not," Charlie said. "It's sort of a big burden to carry. Sort of —"

"A dirty job?" Lily looked up now and grinned.

"Yeah," Charlie smiled, relieved. "I won't bring it up again."

"That's okay. It's kind of cool."

"Really?" Charlie couldn't remember anyone ever referring to him as cool. He was touched.

"Not you. The whole Death thing."

"Yeah, right," Charlie said. Yes! Still batting a thousand on the zero-cool quotient. "But you're right, it's not safe. No more talk about my, uh, avocation."

"And I'll never call you Charlie again," Lily said. "Ever."

"That would be fine," Charlie said.

"We'll act like this never happened. Excellent. Good talk. Resume your thinly veiled contempt."

"Fuck off, Asher."

"Atta girl."

They were waiting for him the next morning when he took his walk. He expected it, and he wasn't disappointed. He'd stopped in the shop to pick up an Italian suit he'd just taken in, as well as a cigar lighter that had languished in a curio case in the back for two years, which he stuffed in his satchel with the glowing porcelain bear that was the soul vessel of someone who had passed long ago. Then he stepped outside and stood just above the opening of the storm drain — waved at the tourists on the cable car as it clanked by.

"Good morning," he said cheerily. Anyone watching him might have thought he was greeting the day, since there was no one around.

"We'll peck out her eyes like ripe plums," hissed a female voice out of the drain. "Bring us up, Meat. Bring us up so we can lap your blood from the gaping wound we tear in your chest."

"And crunch your bones in our jaws like

candy," added a different voice, also female.

"Yeah," agreed the first voice, "like candy."

"Yeah," said a third.

Charlie felt his entire body go to gooseflesh, but he shook it off and tried to keep his voice steady.

"Well, today would be a good day for it," Charlie said. "I'm well rested from sleeping in my comfy bed with the down comforter. Not like I spent the night in a sewer or anything."

"Bastard!" A hissing female chorus.

"Well, talk to you on the next block."

Strolled up the block into Chinatown, pacing out the sidewalk jauntily with his sword-cane, the suit inside a light garment bag thrown over his shoulder. He tried whistling, but thought that might be a little too cliché. They were already under the next corner when he got there.

"I'm going to suck the baby's soul out through her soft spot while you watch, Meat."

"Oh, nice!" Charlie said, gritting his teeth and trying not to sound as horrified as he was. "She's starting to crawl around pretty well now, so don't miss breakfast that day, because if she has her little rubber spoon, she'll probably kick your ass."

There was a screech of anger from the sewers and a harsh, hissing chatter. "He can't say that? Can he say that? Does he know who we are?"

"Taking a left at the next block. See you there."

There was a young Chinese man dressed in hip-hop wear who looked at Charlie and took a quick step to the side so as not to catch whatever kind of crazy this well-dressed *Lo pak** was carrying. Charlie tapped his ear and said, "Sorry, wireless headset."

The hip-hop guy nodded curtly, like he knew that, and despite appearances to the contrary, he had not been trippin', but had, in fact, been chillin' like a mo-fuckin' villain, so step the fuck off, wigga. He crossed against the light, limping slightly under the weight of the subtext.

Charlie entered Golden Dragon Cleaners and the man at the counter, Mr. Hu, whom Charlie had known since he was eight, greeted him with an expansive and warm twitch of the left eyebrow, which was his usual greeting, and a good indi-

*white man

188

cator to Charlie that the old man was still alive. A cigarette streamed at the end of a long black holder clinched in Hu's dentures.

"Good morning, Mr. Hu," Charlie said. "Beautiful day, isn't it?"

"Suit?" said Mr. Hu, looking at the suit Charlie had slung over his shoulder.

"Yes, just the one today," Charlie said. Charlie brought all of his finer merchandise to Golden Dragon to be cleaned, and he'd been giving them a lot of business the last few months, with all the estate clothes he'd been taking in. He also had them do his alterations, and Mr. Hu was considered to be the best three-fingered tailor on the West Coast, and perhaps, the world. Three Fingered Hu, he was known as in Chinatown, although to be fair, he was actually possessed of eight fingers, and was only missing the two smaller fingers from his right hand.

"Tailor?" Hu asked.

"No, thank you," Charlie said. "This one's for resale, not for me."

Hu snatched the suit out of Charlie's hand, tagged it, then called, "One suit for the White Devil!" in Mandarin, and one of his granddaughters came speeding out of the back, grabbed the suit, and was gone

189

through the curtain before Charlie could see her face. "One suit for the White Devil," she repeated for someone in the back.

"Wednesday," said Three Fingered Hu. He handed Charlie the ticket.

"There's something else," Charlie said.

"Okay, Tuesday," said Hu, "but no discount."

"No, Mr. Hu, I know it's been a long time since I needed it, but I wonder if you still have your other business?"

Mr. Hu closed one eye and looked at Charlie for a full minute before he replied. When he did, he said, "Come," then disappeared behind the curtain leaving a cloud of cigarette smoke.

Charlie followed him into the back, through a noisy, steaming hell of cleaning fluids, mangle irons, and a dozen scurrying employees to a tiny plywood-walled office in the back, where Hu closed the door and locked them in as they did their business, something they'd first done over twenty years ago.

The first time Three Fingered Hu had led Charlie Asher through the stygian back room of Golden Dragon Cleaners, the ten-year-old Beta Male was sure that he was going to be kidnapped and sold into dry-cleaning slavery, butchered and turned into dim sum, or forced to smoke opium and fight fifty kung fu fighters at once while still in his pj's (Charlie had a very tenuous grasp of his neighbors' culture at age ten), but despite his fear, he was driven by a passion that had been embedded in his very genes millions of years ago: a quest for fire. Yes, it was a crafty Beta Male who first discovered fire, and true, it was almost immediately taken away from him by an Alpha Male. (Alphas missed out on the discovery of fire, but because they did not understand about grabbing the hot, orangey end of the stick, they are credited with inventing the third-degree burn.) Still, the original spark burns bright in every Beta's veins. When Alpha boys have long since moved on to girls and sports, Betas will still be pursuing pyrotechnics well into adolescence and sometimes beyond. Alpha Males may lead the armies of the world, but it's the Betas who actually get the shit blowed up.

And what better testimonial for a purveyor of fireworks than to be missing critical digits? Three Fingered Hu. When Hu opened his thick, trifold case across the desk, revealing his wares, young Charlie felt he had passed through the fires of hell to arrive, at last, in paradise, and he gladly handed over his wad of crumpled, sweaty dollar bills. And even as long silver ashes from Hu's cigarette fell over the fuses like deadly snow, Charlie picked his pleasure. He was so excited he nearly peed himself.

The death-dealing Charlie who walked out of Golden Dragon Cleaners that morning with a compact paper parcel tucked under his arm felt a similar excitement, for as much as it was against his nature, he was rushing, once again, into the breach. He headed to the storm sewer grate and, waving the glowing porcelain bear from his satchel at the street, shouted, "I'm going over one block and up four, bitches. Join me?"

"The White Devil has finally gone around the bend," said Three Fingered Hu's eleventh grandchild, Cindy Lou Hu, who stood at the counter next to her venerated and digitally challenged ancestor.

"His money not crazy," said Three.

Charlie had noticed the alley on one of his walks to the financial district. It lay between Montgomery and Kearney Streets and had all the things a good alley should have: fire escapes, Dumpsters, various steel doors tagged with graffiti, a rat, two seagulls, assorted filth, a guy passed out under some cardboard, and a half-dozen "No Parking" signs, three with bullet holes. It was the Platonic ideal of an alley, but what distinguished it from other alleys in the area was that it had two openings into the storm-drain system, spaced not fifty yards apart, one on the street end and one in the middle, concealed between two Dumpsters. Having recently developed an eye for storm drains, Charlie couldn't help but notice.

He chose the drain that was hidden from the street, crouched down about four feet away, and opened the parcel from Three Fingered Hu. He removed eight M-80s and trimmed the two-inch-long waterproof fuses to about a half inch with a pair of nail clippers he kept on his key chain. (An M-80 is a very large firecracker, purported to have the explosive power of a quarter of a stick of dynamite. Rural children use them to blow up mailboxes or school plumbing, but in the city they have largely been replaced by the 9 mm Glock pistol as the preferred instrument of mischievous fun.)

"Kids!" Charlie called into the drain. "You with me? Sorry I didn't get your names." He drew the sword from his cane, set it by his knee, then dug the porcelain bear out of his satchel and sat it by his other knee. "There you go," he called.

There was a vicious hiss from the drain, and even as he thought it was completely dark, it got even darker. He could see silver disk shapes moving in the blackness, like coins tumbling through a dark ocean, but these were paired up — eyes.

"Give it, Meat. Give it," whispered a female voice.

"Come and get it," Charlie said, trying to fight down the greatest case of the willies he'd ever felt. It was like dry ice was being applied to his spine and it was all he could do not to shiver.

The shadow in the drain started to leak out across the pavement, just an inch or so, but he could see it, like the light had changed. But it hadn't. The shadow took the shape of a female hand and moved another six inches toward the glowing bear. That's when Charlie grabbed the sword and snapped it down on the shadow. It didn't hit pavement, but connected with something softer, and there was a deafening screech.

"You piece of shit!" screamed the voice — now in anger, not pain. "You worthless little — you —"

"Quick and the dead, ladies," Charlie said. "Quick and the dead. C'mon, give it another shot."

A second hand-shaped shadow snaked out of the drain on the left, then another on the right. Charlie pushed the bear away from the drain as he pulled the cigar lighter from his pocket. He lit the short fuses of four of the M-80s and tossed them into the drain, even as the shadows were reaching out.

"What was that?"

"What did he throw?"

"Move, I can't —"

Charlie put his fingers in his ears. The M-80s exploded and Charlie grinned. He sheathed the sword in the cane, gathered up his stuff, and sprinted for the other drain. Inside an enclosed space the noise would be punishing, brutal even. He kept grinning.

He could hear a chorus of screaming and cursing, in half a dozen dead languages, some of them running over others, like someone was spinning the dial on a shortwave radio that spanned both time and space. He dropped to his knees and listened at the drain, careful to stay an arm's length away. He could hear them coming, tracking him under the street. He hoped he was right that they couldn't come out, but even if they did, he had the sword, and the sunlight was his turf. He lit four more M-80s, these with longer fuses, and tossed them one by one into the drain.

"Who's New Meat now?" he said.

"What? What did he say?" said a sewer voice.

"I can't hear shit."

Charlie waved the porcelain bear in front of the drain. "You want this?" He tossed in another M-80.

"You like that, do you?" Charlie shouted, throwing in the third firecracker. "That'll teach you to use your beak on my arm, you fucking harpies!"

"Mr. Asher," came a voice from behind him.

Charlie looked around to see Alphonse Rivera, the police inspector, standing over him.

"Oh, hi," Charlie said, then realizing that he was holding a lit M-80, he said, "Excuse me a second." He tossed the firecracker in the drain. At that moment they all started going off.

Rivera had retreated a few steps and had his hand in his jacket, presumably on his gun. Charlie put the porcelain bear in his satchel and climbed to his feet. He could hear the voices shrieking at him, cursing.

"You fucking loser," screeched one of the dark ones. "I'll weave a basket of your guts and carry your severed head in it."

"Yeah," said another voice. "A basket."

"I think you threatened that already," said a third.

"I did not," said the first.

"Shut the fuck up!" Charlie yelled at the drain, then he looked at Rivera, who had drawn his weapon and was holding it at his side.

"So," Rivera said, "problems with, uh, someone in the drain?"

Charlie grinned. "You can't hear that, can you?" The cursing was ongoing, but now in some language that sounded as if it required a lot of mucus to speak properly, Gaelic or German or something.

"I can hear a distinct ringing in my ears, Mr. Asher, from the report of your distinctly illegal fireworks, but beyond that, nothing, no."

"Rats," Charlie said, unconsciously raising an eyebrow in a *so are you gonna buy that load of horseshit?* way. "Hate the rats."

"Uh-huh," Rivera said flatly. "The rats, they used their beak on your arm and evidently you feel that they have a secret desire for cheap animal curios?"

197

"So *that* you heard?" Charlie asked.

"Yep."

"That's gotta make you wonder, then, huh?"

"Yep," said the cop. "Nice suit, though. Armani?"

"Canali, actually," Charlie said. "But thanks."

"Not what I'd pick for bombing storm drains, but to each his own." Rivera hadn't moved. He was standing just off the curb, about ten feet away from Charlie, his weapon still at his side. A jogger ran by them and used the opportunity to quicken his pace. Charlie and Rivera both nodded politely as he passed.

"So," Charlie said, "you're a professional, where would you go with this?"

Rivera shrugged. "Not on any prescriptions you might have taken too many of, are you?"

"I wish," Charlie said.

"Up all night drinking, thrown out by the wife, out of your mind with remorse?"

"My wife passed away."

"I'm sorry. How long?"

"Going on a year now."

"Well, that's not going to work," said Rivera. "Do you have any history of mental illness?"

"Nope."

"Well, you do now. Congratulations, Mr. Asher. You can use that next time."

"Do I have to do the perp walk?" Charlie asked, thinking about how he'd explain this to child services. Poor Sophie, her dad an ex con *and* Death, school was going to be tough. "This jacket is tailored, I don't think I can get it over my head for the perp walk. Am I going to jail?"

"Not with me, you're not. You think this would be any easier for me to explain? I'm an inspector, I don't arrest guys for throwing firecrackers and yelling into storm drains."

"Then why do you have your weapon drawn?"

"Makes me feel more secure."

"I can see that," Charlie said. "I probably appeared a little unstable."

"Ya think?"

"So where's that leave us?"

"That the rest of your stash?" Rivera nodded toward the paper bag of firecrackers under Charlie's arm.

Charlie nodded.

"How about you toss that down the storm drain and we'll call it a day."

"No way. I have no idea what they'll do if they get their hands on fireworks."

Now it was Rivera's turn to raise an eyebrow. "The rats?"

Charlie threw the bag in the storm sewer. He could hear whispering from below, but tried not to show Rivera that he was listening.

Rivera holstered his weapon and shot his lapels. "So, do you take suits like that into your shop very often?" he asked.

"More now than I used to. I've been doing a lot of estate work," Charlie said.

"You still have my card, give me a call if you get a forty long, anything Italian, medium- to lightweight wool, oh, or raw silk, too."

"Yeah, silk's perfect for our weather. Sure, I'll be happy to save you something. By the way, Inspector, how did you happen to be in a back alley, off a side street, in the middle of a Tuesday morning?"

"I don't have to tell you that," said Rivera with a smile.

"You don't?"

"No. You have a nice day, Mr. Asher."

"You, too," said Charlie. So now he was being followed both above *and* below the street? Why else would a homicide detective be here? Neither the *Great Big Book* nor Minty Fresh had said a word about the cops. How were you supposed to keep this whole death-dealing thing a secret when a cop was watching you? His elation at having taken the battle to the enemy, something that was deeply against his nature, evaporated. He wasn't sure why, but something was telling him that he had just fucked up.

Below the street the Morrigan looked at one another in amazement.

"He doesn't know," said Macha, examining her claws, which shone like brushed stainless steel in the dim light coming from above. Her body was beginning to show the gunmetal-blue relief of feathers, and her eyes were no longer just silver disks, but now had the full awareness of a predatory bird's. She had once flown over the battlefields of the North, landing on those soldiers who were dying of their wounds, pecking out their souls in her bird form of a hooded crow. The Celts had called the severed heads of their enemies Macha's Acorn Crop, but they had no idea that she cared nothing for their tributes or their tribes, only for their blood and their souls. It had been a thousand years since she had seen her woman claws like this.

"I still can't hear," said her sister Nemain, who groomed the blue-black feather shapes on her own body, hissing with the pleasure as she ran the dagger points over her breasts. She was showing fangs as well, which dented her delicate jet lips. It had been her lot to drip venom on those she would mark for death. There was no fiercer warrior than one who had been touched by the venom of Nemain, for with nothing to lose, he took the field without fear, in a frenzy that gave him the strength of ten, and dragged others to their doom with him.

Babd raked her rediscovered claws across the side of the culvert, cutting deep gouges into the concrete. "I love these. I forgot I even had these. I'll bet we can go Above. Want to go Above? I feel like I could go Above. Tonight we can go Above. We could tear his legs off and watch him drag himself around in his own blood, that would be fun." Babd was the screamer — her shriek on the battlefield said to send armies into retreat — ranks of soldiers a hundred deep would die of fright. She was all that was fierce, furious, and not particularly bright.

"The Meat doesn't know," repeated Macha. "Why would we give away our advantage in an early attack."

"Because it would be fun," said Babd. "Above? Fun? I know, instead of a basket, you can weave a hat from his entrails."

Nemain slung some venom off her claws and it hissed in a steaming line across the concrete. "We should tell Orcus. He'll have a plan."

"About the hat?" asked Babd. "You have to tell him it was my idea. He loves hats."

"We have to tell him that New Meat doesn't know."

The three moved like smoke down the pipes toward the great ship, to share the news that their newest enemy, among other things, did not know what he was, or what he had wrought on the world.

12

The Bay City Book of the Dead

Charlie named the hamsters Parmesan and Romano (or Parm and Romy, for short) because when the time came for thinking up names, he just happened to be reading the label on a jar of Alfredo sauce. That was all the thought that went into it and that was enough. In fact, Charlie thought he might have even gone overboard, considering that when he returned home the day of the great firecracker/sewer debacle, he found his daughter gleefully pounding away on the tray of her high chair with a stiff hamster.

Romano was the poundee, Charlie could tell because he'd put a dot of nail polish between his little ears so he could tell it apart from its companion, Parmesan, who was equally stiff inside the plastic Habitrail box. In the bottom of the exercise wheel, actually. Dead at the wheel.

"Mrs. Ling!" Charlie called. He pried

the expired rodent from his darling daughter's little hand and dropped it in the cage.

"Is Vladlena, Mr. Asher," came a giant voice from the bathroom. There was a flush and Mrs. Korjev emerged from the bathroom pulling at the clasps of her overalls. "I'm sorry, I am having to crap like bear. Sophie was safe in chair."

"She was playing with a dead hamster, Mrs. Korjev."

Mrs. Korjev looked at the two hamsters in the plastic Habitrail box — gave it a little tap, shook it back and forth. "They sleep."

"They are not sleeping, they're dead."

"They are fine when I go in bathroom. Playing, running on wheel, having laugh."

"They were not having a laugh. They were dead. Sophie had one in her hand." Charlie looked more closely at the rodent that Sophie had been tenderizing. Its head looked extremely wet. "In her mouth. She had it in her mouth." He grabbed a paper towel from the roll on the counter and started wiping out the inside of Sophie's mouth. She made a la-la-la sound as she tried to eat the towel, which she thought was part of the game.

"Where is Mrs. Ling, anyway?"

"She have to go pick up prescription, so

I watch Sophie for short time. And tiny bears are happy when I go in bathroom."

"Hamsters, Mrs. Korjev, not bears. How long were you in there?"

"Maybe five minute. I am thinking I am now having a strain in my poop chute, so hard I am pushing."

"Aiiiiieeeee," came the cry from the doorway as Mrs. Ling returned, and scampered to Sophie. "Is past time for nap," Mrs. Ling snapped at Mrs. Korjev.

"I've got her now," Charlie said. "One of you stay with her while I get rid of the H-A-M-S-T-E-R-S."

"He mean the tiny bears," said Mrs. Korjev.

"I get rid, Mr. Asher," said Mrs. Ling. "No problem. What happen them?"

"Sleeping," said Mrs. Korjev.

"Ladies, go. Please. I'll see one of you in the morning."

"Is my turn," said Mrs. Korjev sadly. "Am I banish? Is no Sophie for Vladlena, yes?"

"No. Uh, yes. It's fine, Mrs. Korjev. I'll see you in the morning."

Mrs. Ling was shaking the Habitrail cage. They certainly were sound little sleepers, these hamsters. She liked ham. "I take care," she said. She tucked the cage under her arm and backed toward the door, waving. "Bye-bye, Sophie. Bye-bye."

"Bye-bye, bubeleh," said Mrs. Korjev.

"Bye-bye," Sophie said, with a baby wave.

"When did you learn *bye-bye?*" Charlie said to his daughter. "I can't leave you for a second."

But he did leave her the very next day, to find replacements for the hamsters. He took the cargo van to the pet store this time. Whatever courage or hubris he'd rallied in order to attack the sewer harpies had melted away, and he didn't even want to go near a storm drain. At the pet store he picked out two painted turtles, each about as big around as a mayonnaise-jar lid. He bought them a large kidney-shaped dish that had its own little island, a plastic palm tree, some aquatic plants, and a snail. The snail, presumably, to bolster the self-esteem of the turtles: "You think we're slow? Look at that guy." To shore up the snail's morale in the same way, there was a rock. Everyone is happier if they have someone to look down on, as well as someone to look up to, especially if they resent both. This is not only the Beta Male strategy for survival, but the basis for capitalism, democracy, and most religions.

After he grilled the clerk for fifteen minutes on the vitality of the turtles, and was assured that they could probably survive a nuclear attack as long as there were some bugs left to eat, Charlie wrote a check and started tearing up over his turtles.

"Are you okay, Mr. Asher?" asked the pet-shop guy.

"I'm sorry," Charlie said. "It's just that this is the last entry in the register."

"And your bank didn't give you a new one?"

"No, I have a new one, but this is the last one that my wife wrote in. Now that this one is used up, I'll never see her handwriting in the check register again."

"I'm sorry," said the pet-shop guy, who, until that moment, had thought the rough patch that day was going to be consoling a guy over a couple of dead hamsters.

"It's not your problem," Charlie said. "I'll just take my turtles and go."

And he did, squeezing the check register in his hand as he drove. She was slipping away, every day a little more.

A week ago Jane had come down to borrow some honey and found the plum jelly that Rachel liked in the back of the refrigerator, covered in green fuzz.

"Little brother, this has got to go," Jane said, making a face.

"No. It was Rachel's."

"I know, kid, and she's not coming back for it. What else do you — oh my God!" She dove away from the fridge. "What was that?"

"Lasagna. Rachel made it."

"This has been in here for over a year?"

"I couldn't make myself throw it out."

"Look, I'm coming over Saturday and cleaning out this apartment. I'm going to get rid of all the stuff of Rachel's that you don't want."

"I want it all."

Jane paused while moving the green-and-purple lasagna to the trash bin, pan and all. "No you don't, Charlie. This kind of stuff doesn't help you remember Rachel, it just hurts you. You need to focus on Sophie and the rest of both of your lives. You're a young guy, you can't give up. We all loved Rachel, but you have to think about moving on, maybe going out."

"I'm not ready. And you can't come over this Saturday, that's my day in the shop."

"I know," Jane said. "It's better if you're not here."

"But you can't be trusted, Jane," Charlie said, as if that was as obvious as the fact that Jane was irritating. "You'll throw out all the pieces of Rachel, and you'll steal my clothes." Jane *had* been swiping Charlie's suits pretty regularly since he'd started dressing more upscale. She was wearing a tailored, double-breasted jacket that he'd just gotten back from Three Fingered Hu a few days ago. Charlie hadn't even worn it yet. "Why are you still wearing suits, anyway? Isn't your new girlfriend a yoga instructor? Shouldn't you be wearing those baggy pants made out of hemp and tofu fibers like she does? You look like David Bowie, Jane. There, I've said it. I'm sorry, but it had to be said."

Jane put her arm around his shoulder and kissed him on the cheek. "You are so sweet. Bowie is the only man I've ever found attractive. Let me clean out your apartment. I'll watch Sophie that day — give the widows a day to do battle down at the Everything for a Dollar Store."

"Okay, but just clothes and stuff, no pictures. And just put it in the basement in boxes, no throwing anything away."

"Even food items? Chuck, the lasagna, I mean —"

"Okay, food items can go. But don't let Sophie know what you're doing. And leave Rachel's perfume, and her hairbrush. I

210

want Sophie to know what her mother smelled like."

That night, when he finished at the shop, he went down to the basement to the little gated storage area for his apartment and visited the boxes of all of the things that Jane had packed up. When that didn't work, he opened them and said good-bye to every single item — pieces of Rachel. Seemed like he was always saying good-bye to pieces of Rachel.

On his way home from the pet shop he had stopped at A Clean, Well-Lighted Place for Books because it, too, was a piece of Rachel and he needed a touchstone, but also because he needed to research what he was doing. He'd scoured the Internet for information on death, and while he'd found that there were a lot of people who wanted to dress like death, get naked with the dead, look at pictures of the naked and the dead, or sell pills to give erections to the dead, there just wasn't anything on how to go about being dead, or Death. No one had ever heard of Death Merchants or sewer harpies or anything of the sort. He left the store with a two-foot-high stack of books on Death and Dying, figuring, as a Beta Male typically does, that before he tried to take the battle to the enemy again, he'd better find out something about what he was dealing with.

That evening he settled in on the couch next to his baby daughter and read while the new turtles, Bruiser and Jeep (so named in hope of instilling durability in them), ate freeze-dried bugs and watched *CSI Safari-land* on cable.

"Well, honey, according to this Kübler-Ross lady, the five stages of death are anger, denial, bargaining, depression, and acceptance. Well, we went through all of those stages when we lost Mommy, didn't we?"

"Mama," Sophie said.

The first time she had said "Mama" had brought Charlie to tears. He had been looking over her little shoulder at a picture of Rachel. The second time she said it, it was less emotional. She was in her high chair at the breakfast bar and was talking to the toaster.

"That's not Mommy, Soph, that's the toaster."

"Mama," Sophie insisted, reaching out for the toaster.

"You're just trying to fuck with me, aren't you?" Charlie said.

"Mama," Sophie said to the fridge.

"Swell," Charlie said.

He read on, realizing that Dr. Kübler-Ross had been exactly right. Every morning when he woke up to find another name and number in the day planner at his bedside, he went through the entire five-step process before he finished breakfast. But now that the steps had a name — he started to recognize the stages as experienced by the family members of his clients. That's how he referred to the people whose souls he retrieved: clients.

Then he read a book, called *The Last Sack*, about how to kill yourself with a plastic bag, but it must not have been a very effective book, because he saw on the back cover that there had been two sequels. He imagined the fan mail:

Dear *Last Sack* Author:
I was almost dead, but then my sack got all steamed up and I couldn't see the TV, so I poked an eyehole. I hope to try again with your next book.

The book really didn't help Charlie much, except to instill in him a new paranoia about plastic bags.

Over the next few months he read: *The Egyptian Book of the Dead*, from which he learned how to pull someone's brain out through his nostril with a buttonhook, which he was sure would come in handy someday; a dozen books on dealing with death, grief, burial rituals, and myths of the Underworld, from which he learned that there had been personifications of Death since the dawn of time, and none of them looked like him; and the Tibetan *Book of the Dead*, from which he learned that *bardo,* the transition between this life and the next, was forty-nine days long, and that during the process you would be met by about thirty thousand demons, all of which were described in intricate detail, none of which looked like the sewer harpies, and all of which you were supposed to ignore and not be afraid of because they weren't real because they were of the material world.

"Strange," Charlie said to Sophie, "how all of these books talk about how the material world isn't significant, yet I have to retrieve people's souls, which are attached to material objects. It would appear that death, if nothing else, is ironic, don't you think?"

"No," Sophie said.

At eighteen months Sophie answered all questions either "No," "Cookie," or "like Bear" — the last Charlie attributed to leaving his daughter too often in the care of Mrs. Korjev. After the turtles, two more hamsters, a hermit crab, an iguana, and two widemouthed frogs passed on to the great wok in the sky (or, more accurately, on the third floor), Charlie finally acquiesced and brought home a three-inch-long Madagascar hissing cockroach that he named Bear, just so his daughter wouldn't go through life talking total nonsense.

"Like Bear," Sophie said.

"She's talking about the bug," Charlie said, one night when Jane stopped by.

"She's not talking about the bug," Jane said. "What kind of father buys a cockroach for a little girl anyway? That's disgusting."

"Nothing's supposed to be able to kill them. They've been around for like a hundred million years. It was that or a white shark, and they're supposed to be hard to keep."

"Why don't you give up, Charlie? Just let her get by with stuffed animals."

"A little kid should have a pet. Especially a little kid growing up in the city."

"We grew up in the city and we didn't have any pets."

"I know, and look how we turned out," Charlie said, gesturing back and forth between the two of them, one who dealt in death and had a giant cockroach named Bear, and the other who was on her third yoga-instructor girlfriend in six months and was wearing his newest Harris tweed suit.

"We turned out great, or at least one of us did," Jane said, gesturing to the splendor of her suit, like she was a game-show model giving the big prize package on *Let's Get Androgynous*. "You have *got* to gain some weight. This is tailored way too tight in the butt," she said, lapsing once again into self-obsession. "Am I camel-toeing?"

"I am not looking, not looking, not looking," Charlie chanted.

"She wouldn't need pets if she ever saw the outside of this apartment," Jane said, pulling down on the crotch of her trousers to counteract the dreaded dromedary-digit effect. "Take her to the zoo, Charlie. Let her see something besides this apartment. Take her out."

"I will, tomorrow. I'll take her out and show her the city," Charlie said. And he would have, too, except he woke to find the name Madeline Alby written on his day planner, and next to her name, the number one.

Oh yeah, and the cockroach was dead.

"I will take you out," Charlie said as he put Sophie in her high chair for breakfast. "I will, honey. I promise. Can you believe that they'd only give me one day?"

"No," Sophie said. "Juice," she added, because she was in her chair and this was juice time.

"I'm sorry about Bear, honey," Charlie said, brushing her hair this way, then that, then giving up. "He was a good bug, but he is no more. Mrs. Ling will bury him. That window box of hers must be getting pretty crowded." He didn't remember there being a window box in Mrs. Ling's window, but who was he to question?

Charlie threw open the phone book and, mercifully, found an M. Alby with an address on Telegraph Hill — not ten minutes' walk away. No client had ever been this close, and with almost six months without a peep or a shade from the sewer harpies, he was starting to feel like he had this whole Death Merchant thing under control. He'd even placed most of the soul vessels that he'd collected. The short notice felt bad. Really bad.

The house was an Italianate Victorian on the hill just below the Coit Tower, the great granite column built in honor of the San Francisco firemen who had lost their lives in the line of duty. Although it's said to have been designed with a fire-hose nozzle in mind, almost no one who sees the tower can resist the urge to comment on its resemblance to a giant penis. Madeline Alby's house, a flat-roofed white rectangle with ornate scrolling trim and a crowning cornice of carved cherubs, looked like a wedding cake balanced on the tower's scrotum.

So as Charlie trudged up the nut sack of San Francisco, he wondered exactly how he was going to get inside the house. Usually he had time, he could wait and follow someone in, or construct some kind of ruse to gain entrance, but this time he had only one day to get inside, find the soul vessel, and get out. He hoped that Madeline Alby had already died. He really didn't like being around sick people. When he saw the car parked out front with the small green hospice sticker, his hopes for a dead client were smashed like a cupcake with a sledgehammer.

He walked up the front porch steps at the left of the house and waited by the door. Could he open it himself? Would people be able to see it, or did his special "unnoticeability" extend to objects he moved as well? He didn't think so. But then the door opened and a woman about Charlie's age stepped out onto the porch. "I'm just having a smoke," she called back into the house, and before she could close the door behind her, Charlie slipped inside.

The front door opened into a foyer; to his right Charlie saw what had originally been the parlor. There was a stairway in front of him, and another door beyond that that he guessed led to the kitchen. He could hear voices in the parlor and peeked around the corner to see four elderly women sitting on two couches that faced each other. They were in dresses and hats, and they might have just come from church, but Charlie guessed they had come to see their friend off.

"You'd think she'd give up the smoking, with her mother upstairs dying of cancer," said one of the ladies, wearing a gray skirt and jacket with matching hat, and a large enameled pin in the shape of a Holstein cow.

"Well, she always was a hardheaded girl," said another, wearing a dress that looked as if it had been made from the same floral material as the couch. "You know she used to meet with my son Jimmy up in Pioneer Park when they were little."

"She said she was going to marry him," said another woman, who looked like a sister of the first.

The ladies laughed, whimsy and sadness mixed in their tones.

"Well, I don't know what she was thinking, he's as flighty as can be," said Mom.

"Yeah, and brain damaged," added the sister.

"Well, yes, he is now."

"Since the car ran over him," said Sis.

"Didn't he run right in front of a car?" asked one of the ladies who had been silent until now.

"No, he ran right into it," said Mom. "He was on the drugs then." She sighed. "I always said I had one of each — a boy, a girl, and a Jimmy."

They all nodded. This was not the first time this group had done this, Charlie guessed. They were the type that bought sympathy cards in bulk, and every time they heard an ambulance go by they made a note to pick up their black dress from the cleaner's.

"You know Maddy looked bad," said the lady in gray.

"Well, she's dying, sweetheart, that's what happens."

"I guess." Another sigh.

The tinkle of ice in glasses.

They were all nursing neat little cocktails. Charlie guessed they'd been mixed by the younger woman who was outside smoking. He looked around the room for something that was glowing red. There was an oak rolltop desk in the corner that he'd like to get a look in, but that would have to wait until later. He ducked out of the doorway and into the kitchen, where two men in their late thirties, maybe early forties, were sitting at an oak table, playing Scrabble.

"Is Jenny coming back? It's her turn."

"She might have gone up to see Mom with one of the ladies. The hospice nurse is letting them go up one at a time."

"I just wish it was over. I can't stand this waiting. I have a family I need to get back to. I'm about to crawl out of my fucking skin."

The older of the two reached across the table and set two tiny blue pills by his brother's tiles.

"These help."

"What are they?"

"Time-released morphine."

"Really?" The younger brother looked alarmed.

"You hardly even feel them, they just sort of take the edge off. Jenny's been taking them for two weeks."

"That's why you guys are taking this so well and I'm a wreck? You guys are stoned on Mom's pain medication?"

"Yep."

"I don't take drugs. Those are drugs. You don't take drugs."

The older brother sat back in his chair. "Pain medication, Bill. What are you feeling?"

"No, I'm not taking Mom's pain meds."

"Suit yourself."

"What if she needs them?"

"There's enough morphine in that room to bring down a Kodiak bear, and if she needs more, then hospice will bring more."

Charlie wanted to shake the younger brother and yell, *Take the drugs, you idiot.* Maybe it was the benefit of experience. Having now seen this situation happen again and again, families on deathwatch, out of their minds with grief and exhaustion, friends moving in and out of the house like ghosts, saying good-bye or just covering some sort of base so they could say they had been there, so perhaps they wouldn't have to die alone themselves. Why was none of this in the books of the dead? Why didn't the instructions tell him about all the pain and confusion he was going to see?

"I'm going to go find Jenny," said the older brother, "see if she wants to get something to eat. We can finish the game later if you want."

"That's okay, I was losing anyway." The younger brother gathered up the tiles and put the board away. "I'm going to go upstairs and see if I can catch a nap, tonight's my night watching Mom."

The older brother walked out and Charlie watched the younger brother drop the blue pills into his shirt pocket and leave the kitchen, leaving the Death Dealer to ransack the pantry and the cabinets looking for the soul vessel. But he felt before he even started that it wouldn't be there. He was going to have to go upstairs.

He really, really hated being around sick people.

Madeline Alby was propped up and tucked into bed with a down comforter up around her neck. She was so slight that her body barely showed under the covers. Charlie guessed that she might weigh seventy or eighty pounds max. Her face was drawn and he could see the outlines of her eye sockets and her jawbone jutting through her skin, which had gone yellow. Charlie guessed liver cancer. One of her friends from downstairs was sitting at her bedside, the hospice-care worker, a big woman in scrubs, sat in a chair across the room, reading. A small dog, a Yorkshire terrier, Charlie thought, was snuggled up between Madeline's shoulder and her neck, sleeping.

When Charlie stepped into the room, Madeline said, "Hey there, kid."

He froze in his steps. She was looking right at him — crystal-blue eyes, and a smile. Had the floor squeaked? Had he bumped something?

"What are you doing there, kid?" She giggled.

"Who do you see, Maddy?" asked the friend. She followed Madeline's gaze but looked right through Charlie.

"A kid over there."

"Okay, Maddy. Do you want some water?" The friend reached for a child's sippy cup with a built-in straw from the nightstand.

"No. Tell that kid to come in here, though. Come in here, kid." Madeline worked her arms out of the covers and started moving her hands in sewing motions, like she was embroidering a tapestry in the air before her.

"Well, I'd better go," said the friend. "Let you get some rest." The friend glanced at the hospice woman, who looked over her reading glasses and smiled with her eyes. The only expert in the house, giving permission.

The friend stood and kissed Madeline Alby on the forehead. Madeline stopped sewing for a second, closed her eyes, and leaned into the kiss, like a young girl. Her friend squeezed her hand and said, "Good-bye, Maddy."

Charlie stepped aside and let the woman pass. He watched her shoulders heave with a sob as she went through the door.

"Hey, kid," Madeline said. "Come over here and sit down." She paused in her sewing long enough to look Charlie in the eye, which freaked him out more than a little. He glanced at the hospice worker, who glanced up from her book, then went back to reading. Charlie pointed to himself.

"Yeah, you," Madeline said.

Charlie was going into a panic. She could see him, but the hospice nurse could not, or so it seemed.

An alarm beeped on the nurse's watch

and Madeline picked up the little dog and held it to her ear. "Hello? Hi, how are you?" She looked up at Charlie. "It's my oldest daughter." The little dog looked at Charlie, too, with a distinct "save me" look in its eyes.

"Time for some medicine, Madeline," the nurse said.

"Can't you see I'm on the phone, Sally," Madeline said. "Hang on a second."

"Okay, I'll wait," the nurse said. She picked up a brown bottle with an eye-dropper in it, filled the dropper, and checked the dosage and held.

"Bye. Love you, too," Madeline said. She held the tiny dog out to Charlie. "Hang that up, would you?" The nurse snatched the dog out of the air and set it down on the bed next to Madeline.

"Open up, Madeline," the nurse said. Madeline opened wide and the nurse squirted the eyedropper into the old woman's mouth.

"Mmm, strawberry," Madeline said.

"That's right, strawberry. Would you like to wash it down with some water?" The nurse held the sippy cup.

"No. Cheese. I'd like some cheese."

"I can get you some cheese," said the nurse.

"Cheddar cheese."

"Cheddar it is," said the nurse. "I'll be right back." She tucked the covers around Madeline and left the room.

The old woman looked at Charlie again. "Can you talk, now that she's gone?"

Charlie shrugged and looked in every direction, his hand over his mouth, like someone looking for an emergency spot to spit out a mouthful of bad seafood.

"Don't mime, honey," Madeline said. "No one likes a mime."

Charlie sighed heavily, what was there to lose now? She could see him. "Hello, Madeline. I'm Charlie."

"I always liked the name Charlie," Madeline said. "How come Sally can't see you?"

"Only you can see me right now," Charlie said.

"Because I'm dying?"

"I think so."

"Okay. You're a nice-looking kid, you know that?"

"Thanks. You're not bad yourself."

"I'm scared, Charlie. It doesn't hurt. I used to be afraid that it would hurt, but now I'm afraid of what happens next."

Charlie sat down on the chair next to the bed. "I think that's why I'm here, Madeline, you don't need to be afraid."

"I drank a lot of brandy, Charlie. That's why this happened."

"Maddy — can I call you Maddy?"

"Sure, kid, we're friends."

"Yes, we are. Maddy, this was always going to happen. You didn't do anything to cause it."

"Well, that's good."

"Maddy, do you have something for me?"

"Like a present?"

"Like a present you would give to yourself. Something I can keep for you and give you back later, when it will be a surprise."

"My pincushion," Madeline said. "I'd like you to have that. It was my grandmother's."

"I'd be honored to keep that for you, Maddy. Where can I find it?"

"In my sewing box, on the top shelf of that closet." She pointed to an old-style single closet across the room. "Oh, excuse me, phone."

Madeline talked to her oldest daughter on the edge of the comforter while Charlie got the sewing box from the top shelf of the closet. It was made of wicker and he could see the red glow of the soul vessel inside. He removed a pincushion fashioned from red velvet wrapped with bands of real silver and held it up for Madeline to see. She smiled and gave him the thumbs-up, just as the nurse returned with a small plate of cheese and crackers.

"It's my oldest daughter," Madeline explained to the nurse, holding the edge of the comforter to her chest so her daughter didn't hear. "Oh my, is that cheese?"

The nurse nodded. "And crackers."

"I'll call you back, honey, Sally has brought cheese and I don't want to be rude." She hung up the sheet and allowed Sally to feed her bites of cheese and crackers.

"I believe this is the best cheese I've ever tasted," Madeline said.

Charlie could tell from the expression on her face that it was, indeed, the best cheese she had ever tasted. Every ounce of her being was going into tasting those slivers of cheddar, and she let loose little moans of pleasure as she chewed.

"You want some cheese, Charlie?" Madeline asked, spraying cracker shrapnel all over the nurse, who turned to look at the corner where Charlie was standing with the pincushion tucked safely in his jacket pocket.

"Oh, you can't see him, Sally," Madeline

13

Cry Havoc, and Let Slip the Gogs of War!

Watching Madeline Alby die had shaken Charlie. It wasn't her death so much, it was the life he'd seen in her minutes before she passed. He thought: *If you have to stare Death in the eye to be able to take the life out of your moments, then who better to do it than the man who shaves Death's face?*

"Cheese wasn't in the book," Charlie said to Sophie as he walked her out of the shop in her new runner's stroller — which looked like someone had crossbred a carbon-fiber bicycle and a baby carriage and ended up with a vehicle you could use to take a day trip to Thunderdome — but it was strong, easy to push, and kept Sophie safely wrapped in an aluminum frame. Because of the cheese, he didn't make her wear her helmet. He wanted her to be able to look around, see the world around her, and be in it. It was watching Madeline Alby eat cheese with every ounce of her being, like it was the first and best time, that made him realize that he had never really tasted cheese, or crackers, or life. And he didn't want his daughter to live that way. He'd moved her into her own room the night before, the bedroom that Rachel had decorated for her with clouds painted on the ceiling and a happy balloon carrying a happy bunch of animal friends across the sky in its basket. He hadn't slept well, and had gotten up five times during the night to check on her, only to find her sleeping peacefully, but he could lose a little sleep if Sophie could go through life without his fears and limitations. He wanted her to experience all the glorious cheese of life.

They strolled through North Beach. He stopped and bought a coffee for himself and some apple juice for Sophie. They shared a giant peanut-butter cookie, and a crowd of pigeons followed them down the sidewalk feasting on the river of crumbs that flowed from Sophie's stroller. The World Cup soccer championships was playing on televisions in bars and cafés, and people spilled out onto the sidewalks and out into the street, watching the game, cheering, jeering, hugging, swearing, and generally acting out waves of elation and dejection in the company of new companions who were visiting this Italian-American neighborhood from all around the world. Sophie cheered with the soccer fans and shrieked with joy because they were happy. When the crowd was disappointed — a kick blocked, a play foiled — Sophie was distressed, and would look to her daddy to fix it and make everyone happy again. And Daddy did, because a few seconds later, they were all cheering again. A tall German man taught Sophie to sing "Goooooooooooooooooooooooal!" the way the announcer did, practicing with her until she got the full five-second sustain, and she was still practicing three blocks away, when Charlie had to shrug at confused onlookers as if to say, *The kid's a soccer fan, what can you do?*

As naptime approached, Charlie looped through the neighborhood and headed up through Washington Square Park, where people were reading and lounging in the shade, a guy played guitar and sang Dylan songs for change, two white Rasta boys kicked a Hacky Sack around, and people were generally settling in for a pleasant and windless summer day. Charlie spied a black kitten sneaking out of a hedge near busy Columbus Avenue, stalking a wild McMuffin wrapper, it appeared, and he pointed it out to Sophie.

"Look, Sophie, kitty." Charlie felt bad about the demise of Bear, the cockroach. Maybe this afternoon he'd go to the pet shop and get a new friend for Sophie.

Sophie screamed with glee and pointed to the little cat.

"Can you say 'kitty'?" Charlie said.

Sophie pointed, and gave a drooly grin.

"Would you like a kitty? Can you say 'kitty,' Sophie?"

Sophie pointed to the cat. "Kitty," she said.

The little cat dropped on the spot, dead.

"Fresh Music," Minty Fresh answered the phone, his voice a bass-sax sketch of cool jazz.

"What the fuck is this? You didn't say anything about this? The book didn't say anything about this? What the fuck is going on?"

"You'll be wanting the library or a church," Minty said. "This is a record store, we don't answer general questions."

"This is Charlie Asher. What the fuck

did you do? What have you done to my little girl?"

Minty frowned and ran his hand over his scalp. He'd forgotten to shave this morning. He should have known something was going to go wrong. "Charlie, you can't call me. I told you that. I'm sorry if something has happened to your little girl, but I promise you that I —"

"She pointed at a kitten and said 'kitty' and it fell over, stone dead."

"Well, that is an unfortunate coincidence, Charlie, but kittens do have a pretty high mortality rate."

"Yeah, well, then she pointed to an old guy feeding the pigeons and said 'kitty' and he dropped over dead, too."

Minty Fresh was glad that there was no one in the store right then to see the look on his face, because he was sure that the full impact of the willies dancing up and down his spine was blowing his appearance of unflappable chill. "That child has a speech disorder, Charlie. You should have her looked at."

"A speech disorder! A speech disorder! A cute lisp is a speech disorder. My daughter *kills* people with the word *kitty*. I had to keep my hand over her mouth all the way home. There's probably video somewhere. People thought I was one of those people who beats their kid in department stores."

"Don't be ridiculous, Charlie, people love the parents who beat their kids in department stores. It's the ones who just let their kids wreak havoc that everybody hates."

"Can we stay on point, Fresh, please? What do you know about this? What have you figured out in all your years as a Death Merchant?"

Minty Fresh sat down on the stool behind the counter and stared into the eyes of the cardboard cutout of Cher, hoping to find answers there. But the bitch was holding out. "Charlie, I got nothin'. The kid was in the room when you saw me, and you saw what it did to you. Who knows what it did to her. I told you I thought you were in a different league than the rest of us, well, maybe the kid is something else, too. I've never heard of a Death Merchant who could just 'kitty' someone to death, or cause anyone to die outside of normal, mortal means. Have you tried having her use other words? Like *puppy?*"

"Yeah, I was going to do that, but I thought it might fuck up property values if everyone in my neighborhood suddenly fell over dead! No, I didn't try any other words. I don't even want to make her eat her green beans for fear she'll *kitty* me."

"I'm sure you have some kind of immunity."

"The *Great Big Book* says that we're not immune to death ourselves. I'd say the next time a kitten comes on the Discovery Channel my sister could be picking out caskets."

"I'm sorry, Charlie, I don't know what to tell you. I'll check out my library at home, but it sounds like the kid is a lot closer than we are to how all the legends portray Death. Things tend to balance, however, maybe there's some positive side to this, uh, disorder she has. In the meantime, maybe you should head over to Berkeley, see if you can find anything at the library there. It's a repository library — every book that's printed goes there."

"Haven't you tried that?"

"Yes, but I wasn't looking for something specific like this. Look, just be careful going over. Don't take the BART tunnel."

"You think the sewer harpies are in the BART tunnels?" Charlie asked.

"Sewer harpies? What's that?"

"It's what I call them," Charlie said.

"Oh. I don't know. It's underground,

and I've been on a train when the power goes out. I don't think you want to risk it. It feels like their territory. Speaking of that, from my end they've been conspicuously silent for the last six months or so. Not a peep."

"Yeah, the same here," Charlie said. "But I suppose this phone call might change that."

"Yeah, it probably will. But with your daughter's condition, we might be in a whole new game, too. You watch your ass, Charlie Asher."

"You, too, Minty."

"Mr. Fresh."

"I meant Mr. Fresh."

"Good-bye, Charlie."

In his cabin on the great ship, Orcus picked his teeth with the splintered femur of an infant. Babd combed his black mane with her claws as the bullheaded death pondered what the Morrigan had seen from the drain on Columbus Avenue: Charlie and Sophie in the park.

"It is time," said Nemain. "Haven't we waited long enough?" She clacked her claws like castanets, flinging drops of venom on the walls and floor.

"Would you be careful," Macha said.

"That shit stains. I just put new carpet in here."

Nemain stuck out a black tongue. "Washerwoman," she said.

"Whore," Macha replied.

"I don't like this," Orcus said. "This child disturbs me."

"Nemain is right. Look how strong we've become," Babd said, stroking the webbing that was growing back between the spikes on Orcus's shoulders — it looked as if he had fans mounted there, like some ornate samurai armor. "Let us go. The child's sacrifice might give you your full wings back."

"You think you can?"

"We can, once it's dark," said Macha. "We're stronger than we've been in a thousand years."

"Just one of you go, and go in stealth," said Orcus. "Hers is a very old talent, even in this new body. If she masters it, our chance may have passed for another thousand years. Kill the child and bring its corpse to me. Don't let her see you until you strike."

"And her father? Kill him?"

"You're not that strong. But if he wakes to find his child gone, then maybe his grief will destroy him."

"You don't have any idea what you're

doing, do you?" said Nemain.

"You stay here tonight," said Orcus.

"Dammit," said Nemain, slinging steaming venom across the wall. "Oh, pardon me for questioning the exalted one. Hey, head of the bull, I wonder what comes out of the other end?"

"Ha," said Babd. "Ha. Good one."

"And what kind of brain do you find under the feathers?" said Orcus.

"Oh! He got you, Nemain. Think about how bad he got you when I'm killing the child tonight."

"I was talking to you," Orcus said. "Macha goes."

She came in through the roof, tearing up the bubble skylight over the fourth floor and dropping into the hallway. She moved as silent as a shadow down the hall to the stairs, then appeared to float down, her feet barely touching the steps. On the second floor she paused at the door and examined the locks. There were two strong dead bolts in addition to the one in the main plate. She looked up and saw a stained-glass transom, latched with a tiny brass latch. A claw slipped quickly through the gap, and with a twist of the wrist the brass lock popped off and clattered on the hardwood floor inside. She slithered up and through the transom and flattened herself against the floor inside, waiting like a pool of shadow.

She could smell the child, hear the gentle snoring coming from across the apartment. She moved to the middle of the great room, and paused. New Meat was there, too, she could sense him, sleeping in the room across from the child. If he interfered she'd tear his head from his body and take it back to the ship as proof to Orcus that he should never underestimate her. She was tempted to take him anyway, but not until she had the child.

A night-light in the child's room sent a soft pink band of light across the living room. Macha waved a taloned hand and the light went out. She trilled a small purr of self-satisfaction. There had been a time when she could extinguish a human life in the same way, and maybe that time was coming again.

She slid into the child's room and paused. By the moonlight streaming through the window she could see that the child lay curled on her side in her crib, hugging a plush rabbit. But she couldn't see into the corners of the room — the shadows so dark and liquid that even her night-creature eyes couldn't penetrate them. She moved to the crib and leaned over it. The child was sleeping with her mouth wide open. Macha decided to drive a single claw through the roof of her mouth into her brain. It would be silent, leave plenty of blood for the father to find, and she could carry the child's corpse that way, hooked on her claw like a fish for the market. She reached down slowly and leaned into the crib so she'd have maximum leverage for the plunge. The moonlight sparkled off the three-inch talon and she drew back, and she was distracted for an instant by its pretty shininess when the jaws locked down on her arm.

"Motherfu—" she screeched as she was whipped around and slammed against the wall. Another set of jaws clamped onto her ankle. She twisted herself into a half-dozen forms, which did nothing to free her, and she was tossed around like a rag doll into the dresser, the crib, the wall again. She raked at her attacker with her claws, found purchase, then felt as if her claws were being ripped out by the root, so she let go. She could see nothing, just felt wild, disorienting movement, then impact. She kicked hard at whatever had her ankle and it released her, but the attacker on her arm whipped her through the window and against the security bars outside. She heard glass hitting the street below, pushed with all her might, shape-shifting at a furious rate until she was through the bars and falling to the pavement.

"Ouch. Fuck!" came the shout from out on the street, a female voice. "Ouch."

Charlie flipped on the light to see Sophie sitting up in her crib holding her bunny and laughing. The window behind her had been shattered, and the glass was gone. Every piece of furniture except the crib had been overturned and there were basketball-sized holes in the plaster of two walls, the wooden lath behind it splintered as well. All over the floor there were black feathers, and what looked like blood, but even as Charlie watched, the feathers started to evaporate into smoke.

"Goggy, Daddy," Sophie said. "Goggy." Then she giggled.

Sophie slept the rest of the night in Daddy's bed while Daddy sat up in a chair next to her, watching the locked door, his sword-cane at his side. There was no window in Charlie's bedroom, so the door was the only way in or out. When Sophie awoke just after dawn, Charlie changed her, bathed her, and dressed her for the day. Then he called Jane to make her breakfast while he cleaned up the glass and plaster in Sophie's room and went downstairs to find some plywood to nail over the broken window.

He hated that he couldn't call the police, couldn't call someone, but if this is what one phone call to another Death Merchant was going to cause, he couldn't risk it. And what would the police say anyway, about black feathers and blood that dissolved to smoke as you watched?

"Someone threw a brick through Sophie's window last night," he told Jane.

"Wow, on the second floor, too. I thought you were crazy when you put security bars all the way up the building, but I guess not so much, now. You should replace the window with that glass with the wire running through it, just to be safe."

"I will," Charlie said. Safe? He had no idea what had happened in Sophie's room, but the fact that she was safe amid all the destruction scared the hell out of him. He'd replace the window, but the kid was sleeping in his room from now until she was thirty and married to a huge guy with ninja skills.

When Charlie returned from the basement with the sheet of plywood and hammer and nails, he found Jane sitting at the breakfast counter, smoking a cigarette.

"Jane, I thought you quit."

"Yeah, I did. A month ago. Found this one in my purse."

"Why are you smoking in my house?"

"I went into Sophie's room to get her bunny for her."

"Yeah? Where's Sophie? There might still be some glass on the floor in there, you didn't —"

"Yeah, she's in there. And you're not funny, Asher. Your thing with the pets has gone completely overboard. I'm going to have to do three yoga classes, get a massage, and smoke a joint the size of a thermos bottle to take the adrenaline edge off. They scared me so bad I peed myself a little."

"What in the hell are you talking about, Jane?"

"Funny," she said, smirking. "That's really funny. I'm talking about the goggies, Daddy."

Charlie shrugged at his sister as if to say, *Could you be any more incoherent or incomprehensible?* — a gesture he had perfected over thirty-two years, then ran to

Sophie's room and threw the door open.

There, on either side of his darling daughter, were the two biggest, blackest dogs he had ever seen. Sophie was sitting, leaning against one, while hitting the other in the head with her stuffed bunny. Charlie took a step toward rescuing Sophie when one of the dogs leapt across the room and knocked Charlie to the floor, pinning him there. The other put itself between Charlie and the baby.

"Sophie, Daddy's coming to get you, don't be afraid." Charlie tried to squirm out from under the dog, but it just lowered its head and growled at him. It didn't budge. Charlie figured that it could take the better part of one of his legs and some of his torso off in one bite. The thing's head was bigger than the Bengal tigers' at the San Francisco zoo.

"Jane, help me. Get this thing off of me."

The big dog looked up, keeping its paws on Charlie's shoulders.

Jane swiveled on her bar stool and took a deep drag on her cigarette. "No, I don't think so, little brother. You're on your own after springing this on me."

"I didn't. I've never seen these things before. No one's ever seen these things before."

"You know, we dykes have very high dog tolerance, but that doesn't give you the right to do this. Well, I'll leave you to it," Jane said, gathering up her purse and keys from the breakfast bar. "You enjoy your little canine pals. I'm going to go call in freaked out to work."

"Jane, wait."

But she was gone. He heard the front door slam.

The big dog didn't seem to be interested in eating Charlie, just holding him there. Every time he tried to slither out from under it, the thing growled and pushed harder.

"Down. Heel. Off." Charlie tried commands he'd heard dog trainers shout on TV. "Fetch. Roll over. Get the fuck off me, you beast." (He ad-libbed that last one.)

The animal barked in Charlie's left ear, so loud that he lost hearing and there was just a ringing on that side. In his other ear he heard a little-girl giggle from across the room. "Sophie, honey, it's okay."

"Goggie, Daddy," Sophie said. "Goggie." She stumbled over and looked down at Charlie. The big dog licked her face, nearly knocking her over. (At eighteen months, Sophie moved like a small drunk most of the time.) "Goggie," Sophie said again.

She grabbed the giant hound by its ear and dragged it off Charlie. Or more accurately, it let her lead it by the ear off of him. Charlie leapt to his feet and started to reach for Sophie, but the other hound jumped in front of him and growled. The thing's head came up to Charlie's chest, even with its feet flat on the ground.

He figured the hounds must weigh four or five hundred pounds apiece. They were easily twice the size of the biggest dog he'd seen before, a Newfoundland that he'd seen swimming in the Aquatic Park down by the Maritime museum. They had the short fur of a Doberman, the broad shoulders and chest of a rottweiler, but the wide square head and upturned ears of a Great Dane. They were so black that they appeared to actually absorb light, and Charlie had only ever seen one type of creature that did that: the ravens from the Underworld. It was clear that wherever these hounds had come from, it wasn't from around here. But it was also clear that they were not here to hurt Sophie. She wouldn't even make a good meal for animals this size, and they certainly could have snapped her in two long before now if they'd meant her harm.

The damage in Sophie's room the night

before might have been caused by the hounds, but they had not been the aggressors. Something had come here to hurt her, and they had protected her, even as they were now. Charlie didn't care why, he was just grateful that they were on his side. Where they'd been when he first rushed into the room after the window broke, he didn't know, but it appeared that now that they were here, they were not going to go away.

"Okay, I'm not going to hurt her," Charlie said. The dog relaxed and backed off a few steps. "She's going to need to go potty," Charlie said, feeling a little stupid. He just noticed that they were both wearing wide silver collars, which, strangely, disturbed him more than their size. After the stretching it had gotten over the last year and a half, his Beta Male imagination fit easily around two giant hounds showing up in his little girl's bedroom, but the idea that someone had put collars on them was throwing him.

There was a knock at the front door and Charlie backed out of the room. "Honey, Daddy will be right back."

14

Barking Mad

Charlie opened the door and Lily breezed by. "Jane said you have two huge black dogs up here. I need to see."

"Lily, wait," Charlie called, but she was across the living room and into Sophie's room before he could stop her. There was a low growl and she came backing out.

"Oh my fucking God, dude," she said around a huge grin. "They are so cool. Where did you get them?"

"I didn't *get* them anywhere. They were just here."

Charlie joined Lily just outside the door to Sophie's room. She turned and grabbed his arm. "Are they, like, instruments of your death dealing or something?"

"Lily, I thought we agreed that we wouldn't talk about that."

And they had. In fact, Lily had been great about it. Since she'd first found out about him being a Death Merchant, she'd hardly brought it up at all. She'd also gone on to graduate from high school without getting a major criminal record and enroll in the Culinary Institute, the upside of which was that she actually wore her white chef's coat, checked pants, and rubber clogs to work, which tended to soften her makeup and hair, which remained severe, dark, and a little scary.

Sophie giggled and rolled over against one of the hounds. They had been licking her and she was covered with hellish dog spit. Her hair was plastered into a dozen unlikely spikes, making her appear a little like a wide-eyed Animé character.

Sophie saw Lily in the doorway and waved. "Goggie, 'Ily. Goggie," she said.

"Hi, Sophie. Yes, those are nice doggies," Lily said, then to Charlie: "What are you going to do?"

"I don't know what to do. They won't let me near her."

"That's good, then. They're here to protect her."

Charlie nodded. "I think they are. Something happened last night. You know how the *Great Big Book* talks about the *others?* I think one of them came after her last night, and these guys showed up."

252

"I'm impressed. I'd think you'd be more freaked out."

Charlie didn't want to tell her that he was worn out from freaking out the day before about his little girl killing an old man with the word *kitty*. Lily already knew too much, and it was obvious now that whatever lay below was dangerous. "I guess I should be, but they aren't here to hurt her. I need to go check the library in Berkeley, see if there's anything about them there. I need to get Sophie away from them."

Lily laughed. "Yeah, that's going to happen. Look, I have work and school today, but I'll go do your research for you tomorrow. In the meantime you can try to make friends with them."

"I don't want to make friends with them."

Lily looked at the hounds, one of whom Sophie was pounding on with her little fists as she laughed gleefully, then looked back at Charlie. "Yes, you do."

"Yeah, I guess I do," Charlie said. "Have you ever seen a dog that size before?"

"There are no dogs that size."

"What do you call those, then?"

"Those aren't dogs, Asher, those are hellhounds."

"How do you know that?"

"I know that because before I started

learning about herbs and reductions and stuff, I spent my free time reading about the dark side, and those guys come up from time to time."

"If we know that, then what are you going to do research on?"

"I'm going to try to find out what sent them." She patted his shoulder. "I have to go open the shop. You go make nice with the goggies."

"What do I feed them?"

"Purina Hellhound Chow."

"They make that?"

"What do you think?"

" 'Kay," Charlie said.

It took a couple of hours, but after Sophie started smelling like diaper surprise, one of the giant dogs nosed her toward Charlie as if to say, *Clean her up and bring her back*. Charlie could feel them watching him as he changed his daughter, grateful that disposable diapers didn't require pins. If he'd accidentally poked Sophie with a pin, he was sure one of the hellhounds would have bitten his head off. They watched him carefully as he moved her to the breakfast bar, and sat on either side of her high chair as he gave her breakfast.

As an experiment, he made an extra piece of toast and tossed it to one of the hounds. It snapped it out of the air and licked its chops once, eyes now locked on Charlie and the loaf of bread. So Charlie toasted four more slices and the hounds alternately snapped each out of the air so swiftly that Charlie wasn't sure he didn't see some sort of vapor from the pressure of their jaws clamping down.

"So, you're hellish beasts from another dimension, and you like toast. Okay."

Then, as Charlie started to toast four more slices, he stopped, feeling stupid. "You don't really care if it's toasted, do you?" He flipped a slice of bread to the closest of the dogs, who snapped it out of the air. "Okay, that will speed things up." Charlie fed them the remainder of the loaf of bread. He spread a few slices with a thick coat of peanut butter, which did nothing whatsoever, then a half dozen more he spread with lemon dishwasher gel, which appeared to have no ill effect except that it made them burp neat, aquamarine-colored bubbles.

"Go walk, Daddy," Sophie said.

"No walk today, sweetie. I think we'll just stay right here in the apartment and try to figure out our new pals."

Charlie got Sophie out of her chair, wiped the jelly off her face and out of her hair, then sat down with her on the couch to read to her from the *Chronicle*'s classified ads, which was where he plied a large part of his business, other than the Death stuff. But no sooner had he settled into a rhythm than one of the hellhounds came over, took his arm in its mouth, and dragged him into his bedroom, even as he protested, swore, and smacked it in the head with a brass table lamp. The big dog let him go, then stood staring at Charlie's date book like it had been sprayed with beef gravy.

"What?" Charlie said, but then he saw. Somehow, in all the excitement, he hadn't noticed a new name in the book. "Look, the number is thirty. I have a whole month to find this one. Leave me alone." Charlie also noticed in passing that engraved on the hellhound's great silver collar was the name ALVIN.

"Alvin? That's the stupidest name I've ever heard."

Charlie went back to the couch, and the dog dragged him back into the bedroom, this time by the foot. As they went through the door Charlie reached for his sword-cane. When Alvin dropped him Charlie leapt to his feet and drew the blade. The big dog rolled over on his back and whimpered. His companion appeared at the door, panting. (Mohammed was the hound's name, according to the plate on the collar.) Charlie considered his options. He had always felt the sword-cane a pretty formidable weapon, had even been willing to take on the sewer harpies with it, but it occurred to him that these animals had obviously wiped the floor with one of those other creatures of darkness and had no problem sitting down and eating a loaf of soapy toast a couple of hours later. In short, he was out of his league. They wanted him to go retrieve the soul vessel, he would retrieve the soul vessel. But he wasn't leaving his darling daughter alone with them. "Alvin is still a stupid name," he said, sheathing the sword.

When Mrs. Korjev arrived, Charlie had put Sophie down for her nap, and a dark pile of hellhounds was napping by her crib — snoring great clouds of lemony-fresh dog breath into the air. It was probably part of Charlie's rising rascal nature, but he let Mrs. Korjev enter Sophie's room with only the warning that the little girl had a couple of new pets. He suppressed a snicker as the great Cossack grandmother backed out of the room swearing in Russian.

"Is giant dogs in there."

"Yes, there are."

"But not like normal giant dog. They are like extra-giant, black animal, they are —"

"Like bear?" Charlie suggested.

"No, I wasn't going to say 'bear,' Mr. Smart-Alec. Not like bear. Like volf, only bigger, stronger —"

"Like bear?" Charlie ventured.

"You make your mother ashamed when you are mean, Charlie Asher."

"Not like bear?" Charlie asked.

"Is not important now. I am just surprised. Vladlena is old woman with weak heart, but you go have good laugh and I will sit with Sophie and huge dogs."

"Thank you, Mrs. Korjev, their names are Alvin and Mohammed. It's on their collars."

"You have food for them?"

"There are some steaks in the freezer. Just give each one of them a couple and stand back."

"How they like steaks done?"

"I think frozen will be fine, they eat like —"

Mrs. Korjev raised a finger in warning; it

lined it up with a large mole on the side of her nose and looked as if she was sighting down a weapon.

"— like horses. They eat like horses," Charlie said.

Mrs. Ling did not take her introduction to Alvin and Mohammed with quite the composure of her Russian neighbor. "Aiiiiieeeeeeeeee! Giant shiksas shitting," exclaimed Mrs. Ling as she ran down the hall after Charlie. "Come back! Shiksas shitting!"

Indeed, Charlie returned to the apartment to find great steaming baguettes of poo strewn about the living room. Alvin and Mohammed were flanking the door to Sophie's room like massive Chinese foo dogs at the temple gates, looking not so fierce as shamefaced and contrite.

"Bad dogs," Charlie said. "Scaring Mrs. Ling. Bad dogs." He considered for a moment trying to rub their noses in their offense, but short of bringing in a backhoe and chaining them to it, he wasn't sure that he could make that happen. "I mean it, you guys," he added, in an especially stern voice.

"I'm sorry, Mrs. Ling," Charlie said to the diminutive matron. "These are Alvin and Mohammed. I should have been more specific when I said I'd gotten new pets for Sophie." Actually, he had been vague on purpose, hoping for some sort of hysterical reaction. Not that he really wanted to frighten the old lady, it's just that Beta Males are seldom ever in a position to frighten anyone physically, so when they get the opportunity, they sometimes lose their sense of judgment.

"Is okay," said Mrs. Ling, staring at the hellhounds. She seemed distracted, mainly because she was. Having recovered from the initial shock, she was doing the math in her head — a rapid-fire abacus clicking off the weight and volume of each pony-sized canine, and dividing him into chops, steaks, ribs, and packages of stew meat.

"You'll be all right, then?" Charlie asked.

"You not be late, okay?" said Mrs. Ling. "I want to go to Sears and look at chest freezer today. You have power saw I can borrow."

"Power saw? Well, no, but I'm sure Ray has one he can lend you. I'll be back in a couple of hours," Charlie said. "But let me clean this up first." He headed to the basement in hopes of finding the coal shovel that his father had once kept there.

As they parted ways that day, both Charlie and Mrs. Ling were counting on

Sophie's history of high pet mortality to quickly solve their respective poop and soup problems. Such, however, was not to be the case.

When several weeks passed with no ill effects on the hellhounds, Charlie accepted the possibility that these might, indeed, be the only pets that could survive Sophie's attention. He was tempted, many times, to call Minty Fresh and ask his advice, but since his last call might have caused the hellhounds to appear in the first place, he resisted the urge.

Lily's research trips yielded little more:

"They talk about them all through time," Lily said, calling from the Berkeley library on her cell phone. "Mostly it's about how they like to chase blues singers, and evidently there's a German robot soccer team called the Hellhounds, but I don't think that's relevant. The thing that comes up again and again, in a dozen cultures, is that they guard the passage between the living and the dead."

"Well, that makes sense," Charlie said. "I guess. It doesn't say where that passage is, does it? What BART station?"

"No, Asher, it doesn't. But I found this book by a nun who had been excommunicated in the 1890s, isn't that cool? This library is amazing. They have like nine million books."

"Yes, that's great, Lily, what did the ex-nun say?"

"She had found all the references for hellhounds, and the thing they all seemed to agree on was they serve directly the ruler of the Underworld."

"She was Catholic and she called it the Underworld?"

"Well, they threw her out of the Church for writing this book, but yeah, that's what she said."

"She didn't have a number we could call in case they got lost."

"I'm over here on my day off, Asher, trying to do you a favor. Are you going to keep being a smart-ass about it?"

"No, I'm sorry, Lily. Go on."

"That's it. It's not like there's a care-and-feeding guide. Mostly, the research implies that having hellhounds around is a bad thing."

"What's the title of this book, *The Complete Guide to the Fucking Obvious*?"

"You're paying me for this, you know? Time and travel."

"Sorry. Yes. So I should try to get rid of them."

"They eat people, Asher. Who's riding the duh train now?"

So, with that, Charlie decided that he needed to take an active role in ridding himself of the monstrous canines.

Since the only thing about the hellhounds that he could be sure of was that they would go anywhere he took Sophie, he brought them along on their trip to the San Francisco Zoo, and left them locked in the van with the engine running and a shop-vac hose run from the exhaust pipe through the vent window. After what he considered to be an extraordinarily successful tour of the zoo, in which not a single animal shuffled off the mortal coil under the delighted eye of his daughter, Charlie returned to the van to find two very stoned, but otherwise unharmed hellhounds who were burping a burnt plastic vapor after having eaten his seat covers.

Various experiments revealed that Alvin and Mohammed were not only immune to most poisons, but they rather liked the taste of bug spray and consequently licked all the paint off the baseboards in Charlie's apartment in the week following the exterminator's quarterly service.

As time wore on, Charlie tried to measure the danger of having the giant canines around against the damage that would be done to Sophie's psyche from witnessing their demise, as she was obviously becoming attached to them, so he backed off the more direct attacks on them and stopped throwing Snausages in front of the number 90 crosstown express bus. (This decision was also made easy when the city of San Francisco threatened to sue Charlie if his dogs wrecked another bus.)

Direct attacks, in fact, were difficult for Charlie (as the only true Beta Male martial art was based entirely on the kindness of strangers), so he turned on the hellhounds the awesome power of the Beta Male kung fu of passive aggression.

He started conservatively, taking them for a ride over to the East Bay in the van, luring them onto the Oakland mudflats with a rack of beef ribs, then driving away quickly, only to find them waiting in the apartment when he returned, having covered the entire living room with a patina of drying mud. He then tried an even more indirect approach: crating up the hounds and air-freighting them to Korea in the hope they would find themselves in an entrée, only to find that they actually made it back to the shop before he had time to sweep the dog hair out of his apartment.

He thought that perhaps he might use their own natural instincts to chase them away, after he read on the Internet that the essence of cougar urine was sometimes sprinkled on shrubs and flowers to keep dogs from urinating on them. After a fairly exhaustive search through the phone book, he finally found the number of an outdoorsman's supply store in South San Francisco that was a certified mountain-lion whizz dealer.

"Sure, we carry cougar urine," the guy said. He sounded like he was wearing a buckskin jacket and had a big beard, but Charlie might have just been projecting.

"And that's supposed to keep dogs away?" Charlie asked.

"Works like a charm. Dogs, deer, and rabbits. How much do you need?"

"I don't know, maybe ten gallons."

There was a pause, and Charlie was sure he could hear the guy picking flecks of elk meat out of his beard. "We sell it in one-, two-, and five-ounce bottles."

"Well, that's not going to do it," Charlie said. "Can't you get me like a large economy size — preferably from a cougar that's been fed nothing but dog for a couple of months? I assume that this is domesticated cougar pee, right? I mean you don't go out in the wild and collect it your-self."

"No, sir, I believe they get it from zoos."

"The wild stuff is probably better, huh?" Charlie asked. "If you can get it, I mean? I don't mean you personally. I wasn't im-plying that you were out in the wild fol-lowing a mountain lion around with a measuring cup. I meant a professional — hello?" The bearded buckskin-sounding guy had hung up.

So Charlie sent Ray over to South San Francisco in the van to buy up all the cougar whizz they had, but in the end it achieved nothing other than making the whole second floor of Charlie's building smell like a cat box.

When it appeared that even the most passive-aggressive attempts would not work, Charlie resorted to the ultimate Beta Male attack, which was to tolerate Alvin and Mohammed's presence, but to resent the hell out of them and drop snide re-marks whenever he had the chance.

Feeding the hellhounds was like shov-eling coal into two ravenous steam engines — Charlie started having fifty pounds of dog food delivered every two days to keep up with them, which they, in turn, con-

266

verted to massive torpedoes of poo that they dropped in the streets and alleys around Asher's Secondhand like they were staging their own doggie blitzkrieg on the neighborhood.

The upside of their presence was that Charlie went for months on end without hearing a peep from the storm drains or seeing an ominous raven shadow on a wall when he was retrieving a soul vessel. And to that end, the death dealing, the hounds served their purpose as well, for whenever a new name appeared in his date book, the hounds would drag Charlie to the calendar every morning until he returned with the soul object, so he went two years without missing or being late for a retrieval. The big dogs, of course, accompanied Charlie and Sophie on their walks, which had resumed once Charlie was sure that Sophie had her "special" language skill under control. The hounds, while certainly the largest dogs that anyone had ever seen, were not so large as to be unbelievable, and everywhere they went, Charlie was asked what breed they were. Tired of trying to explain, he would simply say, "They're hellhounds," and when asked where he got them, he would reply, "They just showed up in my daughter's room one night and wouldn't go away," after which people not only thought him a liar, but an ass as well. So he modified his response to "They're Irish hellhounds," which for some reason, people accepted immediately (except for one Irish football fan in a North Beach restaurant who said, "I'm Irish and those things aren't bloody Irish." To which Charlie replied, "Black Irish." The football fan nodded as if he knew that all along and added to the waitress, "Can I get another fookin' pint o' here before I dry up and blow away, lass?")

In a way, Charlie started to enjoy the notoriety of being the guy with the cute little girl and the two giant dogs. When you have to maintain a secret identity, you can't help but relish a little public attention. And Charlie did, until the day he and Sophie were stopped on a side street on Russian Hill by a bearded man in a long cotton caftan and a woven hat. Sophie was old enough by then to do a lot of her own walking, although Charlie kept a piggyback kid sling with him so he could carry her when she got tired (but more often he would just balance her while she rode on the back of Alvin or Mohammed).

The bearded man passed a little too closely to Sophie and Mohammed growled and imposed himself between the man and the child.

"Mohammed, get back here," Charlie said. It turned out the hellhounds *could* be trained, especially if you only told them to do things they were going to do anyway. ("Eat, Alvin. Good boy. Poop now. Excellent.")

"Why do you call this dog Mohammed?" asked the bearded man.

"Because that's his name."

"You should not have called this dog Mohammed."

"I didn't call the dog Mohammed," Charlie said. "His name was Mohammed when I got him. It was on his collar."

"It is blasphemy to call a dog Mohammed."

"I tried calling him something else, but he doesn't listen. Watch. Steve, bite this man's leg? See, nothing. Spot, bite off this man's leg. Nothing. I might as well be speaking Farsi. You see where I'm going with this?"

"Well, I have named my dog Jesus. How do you feel about that?"

"Well, then I'm sorry, I didn't realize you'd lost your dog."

"I have not lost my dog."

"Really? I saw these flyers all over town

with 'Have You Found Jesus?' on them. It must be another dog named Jesus. Was there a reward? A reward helps, you know." Charlie noted that more and more lately, he had a hard time resisting the urge to fuck with people, especially when they insisted upon behaving like idiots.

"I do not have a dog named Jesus and that doesn't bother you because you are a godless infidel."

"No, really, you can *not* name your dog anything you want and it won't bother me. But, yes, I am a godless infidel. At least that's how I voted in the last election." Charlie grinned at him.

"Death to the infidel! Death to the infidel!" said the bearded man in response to Charlie's irresistible charm. He danced around shaking his fist in the Death Merchant's face, which scared Sophie so that she covered her eyes and started to cry.

"Stop that, you're scaring my daughter."

"Death to the infidel! Death to the infidel!"

Mohammed and Alvin quickly got bored watching the dance and sat down to wait for someone to tell them to eat the guy in the nightshirt.

"I mean it," Charlie said. "You need to stop." He looked around, feeling embarrassed, but there was no one else on the street.

"Death to the infidel. Death to the infidel," chanted the beard.

"Have you seen the size of these dogs, Mohammed?"

"Death to — hey, how did you know my name was Mohammed? Doesn't matter. Never mind. Death to the infidel. Death to the —"

"Wow, you certainly are brave," Charlie said, "but she's a little girl and you're scaring her and you really need to stop that now."

"Death to the infidel! Death to the infidel!"

"Kitty!" Sophie said, uncovering her eyes and pointing at the man.

"Oh, honey," Charlie said. "I thought we weren't going to do that."

Charlie slung Sophie up on his shoulders and walked on, leading the hellhounds away from the bearded dead man who lay in a peaceful heap on the sidewalk. He had stuffed the man's little woven hat in his pocket. It was glowing a dull red. Strangely, the bearded man's name wouldn't appear in Charlie's date book until the next day.

"See, a sense of humor is important,"

Charlie said, making a goofy face over his shoulder at his daughter.

"Silly Daddy," Sophie said.

Later, Charlie felt bad about his daughter using the "kitty" word as a weapon, and he felt that a decent father would try to give some sort of meaning to the experience — teach some sort of lesson, so he sat Sophie down with a pair of stuffed bears, some tiny cups of invisible tea, a plate of imaginary cookies, and two giant hounds from hell, and had his first, heart-to-heart, father-daughter talk.

"Honey, you understand why Daddy told you not to ever do that again, right? Why people can't know that you can do that?"

"We're different than other people?" Sophie said.

"That's right, honey, because we're different than other people," he said to the smartest, prettiest little girl in the world. "And you know why that is, right?"

"Because we're Chinese and the White Devils can't be trusted?"

"No, not because we're Chinese."

"Because we are Russian, and in our hearts are much sorrow?"

"No, there is not much sorrow in our hearts."

"Because we are strong, like bear?"

"Yes, sweetie, that's it. We're different because we're strong, like bear."

"I knew it. More tea, Daddy?"

"Yes, I'd love some more tea, Sophie."

"So," said the Emperor, "I see you have experienced the multifarious ways in which a man's life is enriched by the company of a good brace of hounds."

Charlie was sitting on the back step of the shop, pulling whole frozen chickens from a crate and tossing them to Alvin and Mohammed one at a time. Each chicken was snapped out of the air with so much force that the Emperor, and Bummer and Lazarus, who were crouched across the alley suspiciously eyeing the hellhounds, flinched as if a pistol was being fired nearby.

"Multifarious enrichment," Charlie said, tossing another chicken. "That is exactly how I'd describe it."

"There is no better, nor more loyal, friend than a good hound," said the Emperor.

Charlie paused, having pulled not a chicken from the box, but a portable electric mixer. "A friend indeed," he said, "a friend indeed." Mohammed snapped down the mixer without even chewing — two feet of cord hung from the side of his mouth.

"That doesn't hurt him?" said the Emperor.

"Roughage," Charlie explained, throwing a frozen chicken chaser to Mohammed, who gulped it down with the rest of the mixer cord. "They're not really my dogs. They belong to Sophie."

"A child needs a pet," said the Emperor. "A companion to grow up with — although these fellows seem to have done most of their growing."

Charlie nodded, tossing the alternator from an eighty-three Buick into Alvin's eager jaws. There was a clanking and the dog belched, but his tail thumped against the Dumpster asking for more. "Well, they have been her constant companions," Charlie said. "At least now we have them trained so they'll just guard whatever building she's in. For a while they wouldn't leave her side. Bath time was a challenge."

The Emperor said, "I believe it was the poet Billy Collins who wrote, *'No one here likes a wet dog.'*"

"Yes, and he probably never had to get a squirming toddler and two four-hundred-pound dogs out of a bubble bath, either."

"But they've mellowed, you say?"

"They had to. Sophie started school. The teacher frowned on giant dogs in class." Charlie flipped an answering machine to Alvin, who crunched it up like a dog biscuit, shards of dog-spit-covered plastic raining down from his jaws.

"So what did you do?"

"It took us a few days, and a lot of explaining, but I trained them to just sit outside the front door of the school."

"And the faculty relented?"

"Well, I spray-paint them with that granite-texture spray paint every morning, then tell them to sit absolutely still on either side of the door. No one seems to notice them."

"And they obey? All day?"

"Well, it's just a half day right now, she's only in kindergarten. And you have to promise them a cookie."

"There's always a price to be paid." The Emperor pulled a frozen chicken out of the box. "May I?"

"Please." Charlie waved him on.

The Emperor tossed the chicken to Mohammed, who chomped it down in a single bite.

"My, that *is* satisfying," said the Emperor.

"That's nothing," Charlie said. "If you feed them mini–propane cylinders they burp fire."

15

The Call of Booty

"Fuck puppets," Ray said out of nowhere.

He was on the stair-climbing machine next to Charlie and they were both sweating and staring at a row of six, perfectly tuned female bottoms aimed at them from the machines in front of them.

"What was that?" Charlie said.

"Fuck puppets," Ray said. "That's what they are."

Ray had talked Charlie into coming to his health club with him under the pretense of getting him into the flow of being single. Actually, because Ray was an ex-cop, watched people more closely than really was healthy, had too much time on his hands, and didn't get out much himself, the real reason he asked Charlie to come work out with him was so he could get to know him outside of the shop. He'd noticed a strange pattern that had developed since Rachel's death, of Charlie showing up with people's property shortly after their obituary appeared in the paper. Because Charlie kept to himself socially and was secretive about what he did when he was out of the shop, not to mention all the little animals that ended up dead in Charlie's apartment, Ray suspected that he might be a serial killer. Ray decided to try to get close to his boss and find out for sure.

"Keep your voice down, Ray," Charlie said. "Jeez." Since Ray couldn't turn his head, he was talking right at the women's butts.

"They can't hear me; look, every single one has on a headset." He was right, every one of them was talking on a cell phone. "You and I are invisible to them."

Having actually been invisible to people, or nearly so, Charlie did a double take. It was midmorning and the gym was full of lean spandex-clad women in their twenties with disproportionately large breasts, perfect skin, and expensive hair, who seemed to have the ability to look right through him the way that everyone did when he was in pursuit of a soul vessel. In fact, when he and Ray had first come into the gym, Charlie had actually looked around for some object, pulsing red, thinking that he might have missed a name on his date book that morning.

"After I was shot I dated a physical therapist that worked here for a while," Ray said. "She called them that: *fuck puppets*. Every one of them has an apartment that some older executive guy is paying for — just like he paid for the health-club membership and the fake tits. They spend their days getting facials and manicures, and their nights under some suit out of his suit."

Charlie was wildly uncomfortable with Ray's litany, talking about these women who were only a couple of feet away. Like any Beta Male, he would have been wildly uncomfortable in the presence of so many beautiful women anyway, but this made it worse.

"So like they're like trophy wives?" Charlie said.

"Nuh-uh, like wannabe trophy wives. They don't get the guy, the house, whatever. They just exist to be his perfect piece of ass."

"Fuck puppets?" Charlie said.

"Fuck puppets," said Ray. "But forget them, they're not why you're here."

Ray was right, of course. They weren't why Charlie was there. Five years had passed since Rachel's death, and everyone had been telling him he needed to get back in the game, but that's not why he agreed to accompany the ex-cop to the gym. Because Charlie spent too much time on his own, especially since Sophie had started school, and because he'd been hiding a secret identity and avocation, he'd started to suspect that everyone might have one. And since Ray kept to himself, talked a lot about people in the neighborhood who had died, and because he really didn't seem to have a social life beyond the Filipino women he contacted online, Charlie suspected Ray might be a serial killer. Charlie thought he'd try to get closer to Ray and find out.

"So they're like mistresses?" Charlie said. "Like in Europe?"

"I suppose," Ray said. "But did you ever get the impression that mistresses worked this hard to look good? I think fuck puppet is more accurate, because when they get too old to hold the attention of their guy, they've got nothing more going. They'll be done, like marionettes with no one at the strings."

"Jeez, Ray, that's harsh." *Maybe Ray is stalking one of these women,* Charlie thought.

Ray shrugged.

Charlie looked up and down the line of perfect derrieres, then felt the weight of his years alone or in the company of a child and two giant dogs, and said, "I want a fuck puppet."

Aha! thought Ray. *He's picking a victim.* "Me, too," he said. "But guys like us don't get fuck puppets, Charlie. We just get ignored by them."

Aha! Charlie thought. *The bitter sociopath comes out.* "So that's why you brought me here, so I could show I was out of shape in front of gorgeous women who wouldn't notice?"

"No, the fuck puppets are fun to look at, but there's some normal women who come here, too." *Who won't talk to me either,* Ray thought.

"Who won't talk to you either," Charlie said. *Because they can tell that you are a psychokiller.*

"We'll see in the juice bar after our workout," Ray said. *Where I'll sit at an angle so I can watch you pick your victim.*

You sick fuck, they thought.

Charlie awoke to find not one, but three new names in his date book, and the last one, a Madison McKerny, had only three days for him to retrieve her soul vessel.

Charlie kept a stack of newspapers in the house and, typically, would go back for a month looking for an obituary of his new client. More often, if the hellhounds would give him some peace, he would simply wait for the name to appear in the obituary section, then go find the soul vessel when it was easy to get into the house, with mourners or posing as an estate buyer. But this time he had only three days, and Madison McKerny hadn't appeared in the obituaries, so that meant she was probably still alive, and he couldn't find her in the phone book either, so he was going to need to get moving quickly. Mrs. Ling and Mrs. Korjev liked to do their marketing on Saturdays, so he called his sister, Jane, and asked her to come watch Sophie.

"I want a baby brother," Sophie announced to her Auntie Jane.

"Oh, sweetie, I'm sorry, you can't have a baby brother, because that would mean that Daddy had sex, and that's never going to happen again."

"Jane, don't talk to her that way," Charlie said. He was making sandwiches for them and wondering why he always got stuck making the sandwiches. To Sophie, he said, "Honey, why don't you go in your room and play with Alvin and Mohammed, Daddy needs to talk with Auntie Jane."

"Okay," Sophie said, skipping off to her room.

"And don't change clothes again, those are fine," Charlie said. "That's the fourth outfit she's had on today," he said to Jane. "She changes clothes like you change girl-friends."

"Ouch. Be gentle, Chuck, I'm sensitive and I can still kick your ass."

Charlie spanked some mayonnaise onto a whole wheat slice to show he was serious. "Jane, I'm not sure it's healthy for her to have all these different aunties around. She's already had a hard time losing her mother, and now you've moved away — I just don't think she should keep getting at-tached to these women only to have them yanked out of her life. She needs a consis-tent female influence."

"First, I have not moved *away,* I've moved across town, and I see her every bit as often as when I lived in the building. Second, it's not like I'm promiscuous, I'm just shitty at relationships. Third, Cassie and I have been together for three months, and we're doing fine so far, which is *why* I've moved out. And fourth, Sophie did not lose her mother, she never had her mother, she had you, and if you're going to be a decent human being, you need to get laid."

"That's what I mean, you can't talk like that in front of Sophie."

"Charlie, it's true! Even Sophie can see it. She doesn't even know what it is and she can tell that you're not getting any."

Charlie stopped constructing sandwiches and came over to the counter. "It's not sex, Jane. It's human contact. I was getting my hair cut the other day and the hairdresser's breast rubbed against my shoulder and I almost came. Then I almost cried."

"Sounds like sex to me, little brother. Have you been with anyone since Rachel died?"

"You know I haven't."

"That's wrong. Rachel wouldn't want that for you. You have to know that. I mean she took pity on you and hooked up with you, and that couldn't have been easy for her, knowing she could do so much better."

"Took pity on me?"

"That's what I'm saying. She was a sweet woman, and you're much more pitiful now than you were then. You had more hair then, and you didn't have a kid and two dogs the size of Volvos. Hell, there's probably some order of nuns that would do you now, just as a holy act of mercy. Or penance."

"Stop it, Jane."

"The Sisters of Perpetual Nookiless Suffering."

"I'm not that bad," Charlie said.

"The Holy Order of Saint Bonny of the BJ, patron saint of Web porn and incurable wankers."

"Okay, Jane, I'm sorry I said that about you changing girlfriends. I was out of line."

Jane leaned back on her bar stool and crossed her arms, looking satisfied but skeptical. "But the problem remains."

"I'm fine. I have Sophie and I have the business, I don't need a girlfriend."

"A girlfriend? A girlfriend is too ambitious for you. You just need someone to have sex with."

"I do not."

"Yes, you do."

"Yes, I do," Charlie said, defeated. "But I have to go. Are you okay to watch Sophie?"

"Sure, I'm going to take her to my place. I have an obnoxious neighbor up the street that I'd like to introduce to the puppies. Will they poop on command?"

"They will if Sophie tells them."

"Perfect. We'll see you tonight. Promise me you'll ask someone out. Or at least look for someone to ask out."

"I promise."

"Good. Did you get that new blue pin-stripe tailored yet?"

"Stay out of my closet."

"Don't you need to get going?"

Ray figured that it had probably started when Charlie murdered all those little animals he brought home for his daughter. Maybe buying the big black dogs was a cry for help — pets that someone would really notice being gone. According to the movies, they all started out that way — with the little animals, then before long they moved up to hitchhikers, hookers, and pretty soon they were mummifying a whole flock of counselors at some remote summer camp and posing the crusty remains around a card table in their mountain lair. The mountain lair didn't fit the profile for Charlie, since he had allergies, but that might just be an indication of his diabolical genius. (Ray had been a street cop, so it hadn't really been necessary for him to study criminal profiling, and his theories tended toward the colorful, a side effect of his Beta Male imagination and large DVD collection.)

But Charlie had asked Ray to use his contacts on the force and at the DMV a half-dozen times to locate people, all of whom ended up dead a few weeks later. But not murders. And while a lot of items belonging to the recently deceased had turned up in the shop in the last few years (Ray had found antitheft numbers etched on a dozen items and called them in to a friend on the force who identified the owners), none of them had been murdered either. There were a few accidents, but mostly it was natural causes. Either Charlie was devious to an extraordinary degree, or Ray was out of his mind, a possibility that he didn't discount completely, if for no other reason than he had three ex-wives who would testify to it. Thus, he'd devised the workout ruse to draw Charlie out. Then again, Charlie had always treated him really well, and if it turned out he *didn't* have a mountain lair full of mummified camp counselors, Ray knew he'd feel bad about tricking him.

What if there was nothing wrong with Charlie except that he needed to get laid?

Ray was chatting with Eduardo, his new girlfriend at *DesperateFilipina.com*, when Charlie came down the back steps.

"Ray, I need you to find someone for me."

"Hang on a second, I have to sign off. Charlie, check out my new squeeze." Ray pulled up a photo on the screen of a heavily made-up but attractive Asian woman.

"She's pretty, Ray. I can't give you any time off right now to go to the Philippines, though. Not until we hire someone to take Lily's shifts." Charlie leaned into the screen. "Dude, her name is *Eduardo*."

"I know. It's a Filipino thing, like Edwina."

"She has a five-o'clock shadow."

"You're just being a racist. Some races have more facial hair than others. I don't care about that, I just want someone who is honest and caring and attractive."

"She has an Adam's apple."

Ray squinted at the screen, then quickly clicked off the monitor and spun around on the stool. "So who do you need me to find?"

"It's okay, Ray," Charlie said. "An Adam's apple doesn't preclude someone from being honest, caring, and attractive, it just makes it less likely."

"Right. It was just bad lighting, I think. Anyway, who do you need to find?"

"All I have is the name Madison McKerny. I know he or she lives in the city, but that's all I know."

"It's a she."

"Pardon me?"

"Madison, it's a stripper's name."

Charlie shook his head. "You know this woman?"

"I don't know her, although the name seems familiar. But Madison is a new-generation stripper name. Like Reagan and Morgan."

"Lost me, Ray."

"I've spent some time in strip joints, Charlie. I'm not proud of it, but it's sort of what you do when you're a cop. And you pick up on the pattern of stripper names."

"Didn't know that."

"Yeah, and there's sort of a progression going back to the fifties: Bubbles, Boom Boom, and Blaze begat Bambi, Candy, and Jewel, who begat Sunshine, Brandy, and Cinnamon, who begat Amber, Brittany, and Brie, who begat Reagan, Morgan, and Madison. Madison is a stripper name."

"Ray, you weren't even alive in the fifties."

"No, I wasn't alive during the forties either, but I know about World War Two and big-band music. I'm into history."

"Right. So, I need to look for a stripper?

Doesn't help. I don't even know where to start."

"I'll go through the DMV and the tax records. If she's in town we'll have an address on her by this afternoon. Why do you need to find her?"

There was a pause while Charlie pretended to find a smudge on the glass of the counter display case, wiped it away, then said, "Uh, it's an estate thing. One of the estates we got recently had some items that were left to her."

"Shouldn't the executor of the estate take care of that, or his lawyer?"

"It's minutiae, not named in the will. The executor asked me to handle it. There's fifty bucks in it for you."

Ray grinned. "That's okay, I was going to help anyway, but if she turns out to be a stripper I get to go with you, okay?"

"Deal," Charlie said.

Three hours later Ray gave the address to Charlie and watched as his boss bolted out of the shop and grabbed a cab. Why a cab? Why not take the van? Ray wanted to follow, *needed* to follow, but he had to find someone to cover the store. He should have anticipated this, but he'd been distracted.

Ray had been distracted since talking to Charlie, not just by the search for Madison McKerny, but also because he was trying to figure out how to work "Do you have a penis?" casually into the conversation with his sweetheart, Eduardo. After a couple of teasing e-mails, he could stand it no longer and had just typed out, *Eduardo, not that it makes any difference, but I'm thinking of sending you some sexy lingerie as a friendship present, and I wondered if I should make any special accommodations for the panties.*

Then he waited. And waited. And granted that it was five in the morning in Manila, he was second-guessing himself. Had he been too vague, or had he not been vague enough? And now he had to go. He knew where Charlie was going, but he had to get there before anything happened. He dialed Lily's cell phone, hoping that she wouldn't be working at her other job and would do him a favor.

"Speak, ingrate," Lily answered.

"How did you know it was me?" Ray asked.

"Ray?"

"Yeah, how did you know it was me?"

"I didn't," Lily said. "What do you want?"

291

"Can you come cover the store for me for a couple of hours?" Then, as he heard her take a deep breath that he was pretty sure would be propellant for verbal abuse, he added, "There's fifty bucks extra in it for you." Ray heard her exhale. Yes! After graduating from the Culinary Institute, Lily had gotten a job as a sous chef at a bistro in North Beach, but she didn't make enough to move out of her mother's apartment yet, so she let Charlie talk her into keeping a couple of shifts at Asher's Secondhand, at least until he could find a replacement.

"Okay, Ray, I'll come in for a couple of hours, but I have to be at the restaurant by five, so be back or I'm closing up early."

"Thanks, Lily."

Charlie sincerely hoped that Ray wasn't a serial killer, despite all the indications to the contrary. He would never have found this woman without Ray's police contacts, and what would he do in the future if he needed to find someone and Ray was in jail? Then again, Ray's experience as a cop could account for his never leaving any evidence. But why, then, would he continue to pursue the Filipino women over the Internet if he was just looking to kill people? Maybe that's what he did when he went to the Philippines to visit his paramours. Maybe he killed desperate Filipinas. Maybe Ray was a tourist serial killer. *Deal with it later,* Charlie thought. *For now, there's a soul vessel to retrieve.*

Charlie got out of the cab outside of the Fontana, an apartment building just a block up from Ghirardelli Square, the waterfront chocolate factory turned tourist mall. The Fontana was a great, curved, concrete-and-glass building that commanded views of Alcatraz and the Golden Gate Bridge, and that had drawn the disdain of San Franciscans since it had been built in the 1960s. It wasn't that it was an ugly building, although no one would argue that it wasn't, but with the Victorian and Edwardian structures all around it, it looked very much like a giant air conditioner from outer space attacking a nineteenth-century neighborhood. However, the views from the apartments were exquisite, there was a doorman, underground parking, and a pool on the roof, so if you could handle the stigma of residing in an architectural pariah, it was a great place to live.

The address Ray had given him for

Madison was on the twenty-second floor, and so, presumably, was her soul vessel. Charlie wasn't sure of the exact range of his unnoticeability (he refused to think of it as invisibility, because it wasn't), but he hoped that it reached twenty-two floors. He was going to have to get past the doorman and into an elevator, and posing as an estate buyer wasn't going to work.

Ah, well, nothing ventured, nothing gained. If he got caught, he'd just have to find another way in. He waited by the door until a young woman in business attire went in, then followed her into the lobby. The doorman didn't even look at him.

Ray saw Charlie get out of the cab and told his own driver to stop a block away, where he hopped out, threw the driver a five and told him to keep the change, then dug in his pocket for the rest of the fare while the driver pounded on the wheel impatiently and cursed under his breath in Urdu.

"Sorry, it's been a while since I took a cab," Ray said. Ray had a car, a nice little Toyota, but the only parking place he could find was eight blocks away from his apartment in the parking lot of a hotel managed by a friend of his, and when you got a parking place in San Francisco, you kept it, so Ray mostly used public transportation and only drove the car on his days off to keep the battery charged. He'd jumped in a taxi outside Charlie's shop and shouted, "Follow that cab!" thus completely terrifying the Japanese family in the back.

"Sorry," Ray said. "*Konichiwa*. It's been a while since I took a cab." Then he jumped back out and caught a cab that didn't have a fare.

He sneaked quickly up the street, going from light post, to newspaper machine, to ad kiosk, ducking behind each, staying in his stealth-crouch, and achieving nothing whatsoever except to look like a complete loon to the kid standing at the bus stop across the street. He reached the underground parking entrance of the Fontana just as Charlie was making for the door. Ray crouched behind the key-card pillar.

He wasn't sure what he was going to do if Charlie went for the building. Fortunately, he'd memorized Madison McKerny's phone number, and he could warn her that Charlie was coming. In the cab on the way down here he'd remembered where he'd seen her name: on the register at his health club. Madison McKerny was one of the midmorning fuck puppets from the gym, and as Ray suspected, Charlie was stalking her.

He watched Charlie fall in behind a young woman in business dress who was heading up the walk into the Fontana, then Charlie was gone. Just gone.

Ray came out onto the sidewalk to get a better angle. The woman was still there, she'd gone only a couple of steps, but he couldn't see Charlie. There were no bushes, no walls, the whole damn lobby was glass, where the hell had he gone? Ray was sure he hadn't looked away, he didn't even think he had blinked, and he would have seen any sudden move Charlie might have made.

Reverting to the Beta Male's tendency to blame himself, Ray wondered if maybe he'd had some kind of petit mal seizure that had made him black out for a second. Whether he did or not, he had to warn Madison McKerny. He reached to his belt and felt the empty cell-phone clip, then remembered putting his phone under the register when he'd gotten to work that morning.

Charlie found the right apartment and rang the bell. If he could get Madison

McKerny to come out into the hallway, he could slip in behind her and look through her apartment for her soul vessel. Just down the hall there was a table with an artificial flower arrangement. He'd tipped it over, hoping she was compulsive or curious enough to come out of her apartment to get a closer look. If she wasn't home, well, he'd have to break in. Odds were that with a doorman downstairs, she didn't have an alarm system. But what if she could see him? Sometimes they could, the clients. Not often, but it happened, and —

She opened the door.

Charlie was stunned. She was stunning. Charlie stopped breathing and stared at her breasts.

It wasn't that she was a young and gorgeous brunette, with perfect hair and perfect skin. Nor was it that she was wearing a thin, white silk robe that just barely concealed her swimsuit-model figure. Nor was it because she had disproportionately large but alert breasts that were straining against the robe and peeking out of the plunging neckline as she leaned out the door, although that would have been enough to render the hapless Beta breathless under any circumstances. It was that her breasts were glowing red, right through the silk robe, glowing right out of the décolletage like twin rising suns, pulsating like the lightbulb boobies of a kitschy Hawaiian hula girl lamp. Madison McKerny's soul was residing in her breast implants.

"I've got to get my hands on those," Charlie said, forgetting that he wasn't exactly alone and he wasn't exactly thinking to himself.

Then Madison McKerny noticed that Charlie was there and the screaming started.

16

The Call of Booty II: Requiem for a Fuck Puppet

Ray threw the door open so hard that the little bell went flying off its holder and tinkled across the floor.

"Oh, jeez," Ray said. "You won't believe it. I can't believe it myself."

Lily looked at Ray over her half-frame reading glasses and set down the French cookbook she'd been looking at. She didn't really need reading glasses, but looking over the top of them conveyed instant condescension and disdain, a look that she felt flattered her.

"I have something I need to tell you, too," Lily said.

"No," Ray said, looking around to make sure there were no customers in the store. "What I have to tell you is really important."

"Okay," Lily said. "Mine's not that important to me. You go first."

"Okay." Ray took a deep breath and launched. "I think Charlie may be a serial killer with ninja powers."

"Wow, that is good," Lily said. "Okay, my turn. A Miss Me-So-Horny called for you. She wanted you to know that she's packing eight inches of luscious man-meat." Lily held up Ray's cell phone, which he'd left under the register.

"Oh my God, not again!" Ray cradled his head in his hands and fell against the counter.

"She said she was eager to share it with you." Lily examined her nails. "So, Asher's a ninja, huh?"

Ray looked up. "Yes, and he's stalking a fuck puppet from my gym."

"Think you're living a rich enough fantasy life, Ray?"

"Shut up, Lily, this is a disaster. My job and my apartment depend on Charlie, not to mention that he has a kid, and the new light of my life is a guy."

"No, she's not." Lily wondered about herself, giving in so early — she didn't enjoy torturing Ray the way she used to.

"Huh? What?"

"I'm just fuckin' with you, Ray. She

didn't call. I read all of your e-mail and IMs."

"That stuff is private."

"Which is why you have it all here on the store's computer?"

"I spend a lot of time here, with the time difference . . ."

"And speaking of privacy, what's the deal with Asher being a ninja and a serial killer? I mean, both? At the same time?"

Ray moved in close, and talked into his collar, as if revealing a huge conspiracy. "I've been watching him. Charlie's been taking in a lot of stuff from dead people. It's gone on for years. But he's always having to take off on a moment's notice, having me cover his shifts, and he never explains where he's going, except soon after that happens, one of the dead people's things shows up in the shop. So today I followed him, and he was after a woman who goes to my gym, who we might have seen the other day."

Lily stepped back, crossed her arms, and looked disgusted with Ray, which was fairly easy, since she'd had years of practice. "Ray, did it occur to you that Asher handles estates, and that we've been doing much better business since he started doing more estates — that the quality of the merchandise is much higher? Probably because he gets there early?"

"I know, but that's not it. You're not around as much now, Lily. I was a cop, I notice these things. For one thing, did you know that there was a homicide detective keeping track of Charlie? That's right. Gave me his card, told me to call if anything unusual happened."

"No, Ray, you didn't."

"Charlie disappeared, Lily. I was watching him, and he just blinked out of existence, right before my eyes. And last I saw him he was going into the fuck puppet's building."

Lily wanted to grab the stapler off the counter and rapidly drive about a hundred staples into Ray's shiny forehead. "You ungrateful fucktard! You called the cops on Asher? The guy who has given you a job and a place to live for what, ten years?"

"I didn't call the black-and-whites, just this Inspector Rivera. I know him from when I was on the force. He'll keep it on the down low."

"Go get your checkbook and your car," Lily barked. "We're going to bail him out."

"He probably hasn't even been processed yet," Ray said.

"Ray, you pathetic toss-beast. Go. I'll

close up the store and wait for you out front."

"Lily, you can't talk to me that way. I don't have to put up with it."

Because he couldn't turn his head, Ray wasn't able to avoid the first two staples Lily put in his forehead, but by then he had decided it was best to go get his checkbook and his car, and backed away.

"What's a fuck puppet, anyway?" Lily shouted after him, somewhat surprised at the violent intensity of her loyalty to Charlie.

The policewoman fingerprinted Charlie nine times before she looked up at Inspector Alphonse Rivera and said, "This motherfucker got no fingerprints."

Rivera took Charlie's hand and turned it palm up, and looked at his fingers. "I can see the ridges, right there. He's got completely normal fingerprints."

"Well, you do it, then," said the woman. " 'Cause alls I got on the card is smooth."

"Fine, then," Rivera said. "Come with me."

He led Charlie over to a wall that had a big ruler painted on it and told him to face a camera.

"How's my hair?" Charlie said.

"Don't smile."

Charlie frowned.

"Don't make a face. Just look straight ahead and — your hair is fine, though now you've got ink on your forehead. This is not that hard, Mr. Asher, criminals do this all the time."

"I'm not a criminal," Charlie said.

"You broke into a security building and harassed a young woman, that makes you a criminal."

"I didn't break into anything and I didn't harass anyone."

"We'll see. Ms. McKerny said you threatened her life. She's definitely going to press charges, and if you ask me, you're both lucky I showed up when I did."

Charlie wondered about that. The fuck puppet had started screaming and backed into her apartment, and he had followed her, trying to explain, trying to figure out how this was going to work, and at the same time paying way too much attention to her breasts.

"I didn't threaten her."

"You said she was going to die. Today."

Well, they had him there. Charlie had, in all the confusion and screaming, mentioned that he had to get hold of her breasts because she was going to die today.

In retrospect, he felt he probably should have kept that information to himself.

Rivera led him upstairs and into a small room with a table and two chairs. Just like on TV, Charlie looked for a one-way mirror but was disappointed to see only concrete-block walls painted in easy-clean moss-green enamel. Rivera had him sit, but then went to the door.

"I'm going to leave you here for a few minutes, until Miss McKerny comes down to file charges. It's more hospitable here than the holding cell. You want something to drink?"

Charlie shook his head. "Should I call an attorney?"

"It's up to you, Mr. Asher. That's certainly your right, but I can't advise you one way or another. I'll be back in five. You can make your call then if you'd like."

Rivera left the room and Charlie saw the inspector's partner, a gruff, bald-headed bull of a guy named Cavuto, standing outside the door waiting for him. That guy actually scared Charlie. Not as much as the prospect of having to retrieve Madison McKerny's breast implants, or what would happen if he didn't, but still scary.

"Cut him loose," Cavuto said.

"What, cut him loose? I just got him processed, the McKerny woman —"

"Is dead. Boyfriend shot her, then, when our guys responded to the shots-fired call, did himself."

"What?"

"Boyfriend was married, McKerny wanted more security and was going to tell the wife. He flipped out."

"You know all that already?"

"Her neighbor told the uniforms as soon as they arrived. Come on, it's our case. We need to roll. Cut this guy loose. Ray Macy and some Goth-chef chick are waiting for him downstairs."

"Ray Macy is the one who called me, he thought Asher was going to kill her."

"I know. Right crime, wrong guy. Let's go."

"We still have him on the concealed-weapon charge."

"A cane with a sword in it? What, you want to go before a judge and tell him that you arrested this guy on suspicion of being a serial killer but he plea-bargained it down to being a huge fucking nerd?"

"Okay, I'll cut him loose, but I'm telling you, Nick, this guy told McKerny that she was going to die today. There's some weird shit going on here."

"And we don't have enough weird shit to deal with already?"

"Good point," Rivera said.

Madison McKerny looked beautiful in her beige silk dress, her hair and makeup perfect, as usual, her diamond-stud earrings and a platinum-diamond solitaire necklace complemented the silver handles of her walnut-burl casket. For someone who wasn't breathing, she was breathtaking, especially for Charlie, who was the only one who could see her hooters pulsing red in the casket.

Charlie hadn't been to a lot of funerals, but Madison McKerny's seemed nice, and fairly well attended for someone who had been only twenty-six. It turned out that Madison had grown up in Mill Valley, just outside San Francisco, so a lot of people had known her. Evidently, except for her family, most of them had lost touch and seemed somewhat surprised that she had been gunned down by her married boyfriend who had kept her in an expensive apartment in the city.

"Not like you vote 'most likely' for that in the yearbook," Charlie said, trying to make conversation with one of her classmates, a guy he'd ended up standing next to at the urinals in the men's room.

"How did you know Madison?" said the guy, a condescending tone in his voice. He looked like he'd been voted "most likely to piss everyone off by being rich and having nice hair."

"Oh, me? Friend of the groom," Charlie said. He zipped up and headed to the sink before hair guy could think of something to say.

Charlie was surprised to see a few people at the funeral whom he knew, and each time he walked away from one, he'd run into another.

First Inspector Rivera, who lied. "Had to come. It's our case. I've gotten to know the family a little."

Then Ray, who lied. "She went to my gym. I just thought I should pay my respects."

Then Rivera's partner, Cavuto, who didn't lie. "I still think you're kinky, and that goes for your ex-cop friend, too."

And Lily, who was also honest. "I wanted to see a dead fuck puppet."

"Who's running the store?" Charlie asked.

"Closed. Death in the family. You know Ray called the cops on you, right?"

They hadn't had a chance to talk since

Charlie had been released. "I should've figured," Charlie said.

"He said he saw you go into the dead chick's building and just disappear. He thinks you have ninja powers. That part of the thing?" She bounced her eyebrows — a Groucho Marx conspiracy bounce — made less effective by the fact that her eyebrows were pencil thin and drawn on in magenta.

"Yeah, it's kind of part of the thing. Ray doesn't suspect about the thing, does he?"

"No, I covered for you. But he still thinks you might be a serial killer."

"I thought *he* might be a serial killer."

Lily shuddered. "God, you guys need to get laid."

"True, but right now I'm here to do a thing regarding the thing."

"You still haven't gotten her thing thing?"

"I can't even figure out how to get it. Her thing is still in the thing." He nodded to the casket.

"You're fucked," Lily said.

"We have to go sit now," Charlie said. He led her into the chapel, where the service was beginning.

Behind him Nick Cavuto, who had been

standing three feet away with his back to Charlie, made a beeline for his partner and said, "Can we just shoot Asher and find cause later? I'm sure the fucker's done something to deserve it."

Charlie didn't know what he was going to do, how he was going to retrieve the soul implants, but he really thought something would occur to him. Some supernatural ability would manifest itself at the last minute. He thought that all through the ceremony. He thought that when they closed the casket, during the funeral procession to the cemetery, and all through the graveside ceremony. He began to lose hope as the mourners dispersed and the casket was lowered, and by the time the ground crew started throwing dirt down the hole with a backhoe, he'd pretty much given up on having an idea.

There was grave robbing, but that really wasn't an idea, was it? And even with his years of experience in the death-dealing business, Charlie didn't think he was up for breaking into a cemetery, spending all night digging up a casket, then cutting the implants out of a dead woman's body. It wasn't the same as swiping a vase off the mantel. Why couldn't Madison McKerny's soul be in a vase on the mantel?

"Didn't get the thing, then," said a voice beside him.

Charlie turned to see Inspector Rivera standing not a foot away. He hadn't even seen him since they'd left the funeral home.

"What thing?"

"Yeah, what thing?" Rivera said. "They didn't bury her with those diamonds you saw, you know that, right?"

"That would have been a shame," Charlie said.

"Sisters got them," Rivera said. "You know, Charlie, most people don't stay to watch them actually cover the box."

"Really?" Charlie said. "I was just curious. See if they used shovels or what. How about you?"

"Me? I'm watching you. You ever get over that thing with the storm sewers?"

"Oh, that? I just needed a little adjustment in my medication." It was an expression that Charlie had picked up from Jane. She wasn't actually on medication, but the excuse seemed to work for her.

"Well, you keep an eye on that, Charlie. And I'll keep an eye on you. Adios." Rivera walked off.

"Adios, Inspector," Charlie said. "Hey,

by the way, nice suit."

"Thanks, I bought it from your store," Rivera said without turning around.

When was he in my store? Charlie thought.

For the next couple of weeks Charlie felt as if someone had dialed his nervous system up past the recommended voltage and he was nearly vibrating with anxiety. He thought that perhaps he should call Minty Fresh, warn him of his failure to retrieve Madison McKerney's soul vessel, but if the sewer harpies weren't rising because of that, maybe the contact with another Death Merchant would put them over the top. Instead he kept Sophie home and made sure that she was never out of sight of the hellhounds. In fact, he kept the hellhounds locked in her room most of the time; otherwise they kept dragging him to his day planner, which had no new names. Only the overdue Madison McKerny and the two women — Esther Johnson and Irena Posokovanovich — who had appeared on the same day, but still had some time left before expiration — or whatever you called it.

So he started his walks again, listening as he passed storm drains and manhole covers, but the darkness didn't appear to be rising.

Charlie felt naked walking the street without his sword-cane, which Rivera had kept, so he set out to replace it, and in the process found two more Death Merchants in the city. He found the first at a used-book store in the Mission, Book 'em Danno. Well, it wasn't really a bookstore anymore — it still had a couple of tall cases of books, but the rest of the store was a bricolage of bric-a-brac, from plumbing fittings to football helmets. Charlie understood completely how it happened. You started with a bookstore, then you made a single innocent trade, a set of bookends for a first edition maybe, then another, you picked up a grab-all box at a yard sale to get one item — pretty soon you had a whole section of unmatched crutches and obsolete radio tubes, and couldn't for the life of you remember how you'd acquired a bear trap, yet there it was, next to the lime-green tutu and the Armadrillo penis pump: secondhand out of hand. In the back of the store, by the counter, stood a bookcase in which every volume was pulsing with a dull red light.

Charlie tripped over a spittoon and caught himself on an elk-antler coatrack.

"You okay?" asked the proprietor, looking up from the book he was reading. He was maybe sixty, skin spotted from too much sun, but he hadn't seen any in a while and he'd gone pasty. He had long, thinning gray hair and wore oversized bifocals that gave him the look of an educated turtle.

"No, I'm fine," Charlie said, ripping his gaze off the soul-vessel books.

"I know it's a little cluttered in here," the turtle guy said. "I've been meaning to clear it out, but then, I've been meaning to clear it out for thirty years and I haven't managed it yet."

"It's okay, I like your store," Charlie said. "Great selection."

The owner looked at Charlie's expensive suit and shoes and squinted. It was clear he recognized the worth of the clothes and was qualifying Charlie as a rich collector or antiques hunter. "You looking for anything special?" he asked.

"Sword-cane," Charlie said. "Doesn't have to be antique." He wanted to buy this guy a coffee and share stories of snatching soul objects, of confronting the Underworlders, of being a Death Merchant. This guy was a kindred spirit, and from the size of his collection of soul objects, all of them books, he'd been doing this longer than Minty Fresh.

Turtle guy shook his head. "Haven't seen one for years. If you want to give me a card, I'll put out feelers for you."

"Thanks," Charlie said. "I'll keep looking. That's part of the fun." He started backing down the aisle, but he couldn't leave without saying something else, getting some kind of information. "Hey, how is it, doing business in this neighborhood?"

"Better now than it used to be," said the guy. "The gangs have settled down some, this part of the Mission has turned into the edgy, artsy-fartsy neighborhood. That's been good for business. You from the City?"

"Born and raised," Charlie said. "Just haven't been to this neighborhood much. You haven't had any weird stuff on the street last couple of weeks, then?"

The turtle guy looked fully at Charlie now, even took off his giant glasses. "Except for the thumper sound systems going by, quiet as a mouse. What's your name?"

"Charlie. Charlie Asher. I live over in the North Beach–Chinatown area."

"I'm Anton, Charlie. Anton Dubois. Nice meeting you."

"Okay," Charlie said. "I have to go now."

"Charlie. There's a pawnshop off Fillmore Street. Fulton and Fillmore, I think. The owner carries a lot of edged weapons. She might have your cane."

"Thanks," Charlie said. "You watch yourself, Anton. Okay?"

"Always do," said Anton Dubois, and he looked back to his book.

Charlie left the store feeling even more anxious, but not quite as alone as he had five minutes before. The next day, he found a new sword-cane at the pawnshop in the Fillmore, and he also found a case of cutlery and kitchen utensils that pulsated with red light. The owner was younger than Anton Dubois, late thirties maybe, and wore a .38 revolver in a shoulder holster, which shocked Charlie less than the fact that she was a woman. He'd envisioned all the Death Merchants as being men, but of course there was no reason to think that. She wore jeans and a plain chambray shirt, but was dripping with mismatched jewelry that Charlie guessed was a self-indulgence she justified for being "in the business" the same way he justified his expensive suits. She was pretty in a lady-cop sort of way, with a nice smile, and Charlie found himself wondering if he should maybe ask her out, then heard an audible pop in his head as that bubble of self-destructive stupidity exploded. Sure, dinner and a movie, and release the Forces of Darkness on the world. Great first date. Everyone was right, he really needed to get laid.

He bought the sword-cane for cash, without quibbling, and left the store without engaging the owner in conversation, but he took a business card from the holder on the counter as he left. Her name was Carrie Lang. It was all he could do to not warn her, tell her to be careful of what might be coming from below, but he realized that every second he was there, he was probably increasing the danger to all of them.

Watch yourself, Carrie, he whispered to himself as he walked away.

That evening he decided to take action to ease some of the tension in his life. Or at least it was decided for him when Jane and her girlfriend Cassandra showed up at the apartment and offered to watch Sophie.

"Go, find a woman," Jane said. "I got the kid."

"It doesn't work that way," Charlie said. "I was gone all day, I haven't spent any quality time with my daughter."

Jane and Cassandra — an athletic, attractive redhead in her midthirties, who Charlie promised himself he would have asked out if she hadn't been living with his sister — pushed him out the door, slammed it in his face, and locked it.

"Don't come home until you've gotten some," Jane shouted over the transom.

"Does that work for you?" Charlie shouted back. "Just go find someone to do you, like a scavenger hunt?"

"Here's five hundred dollars. Five hundred dollars works for anyone." A wad of bills came flying over the transom, followed by his cane, a sport coat, and his wallet.

"This is my money, isn't it?" Charlie shouted.

"It's you that needs to get laid," Jane shouted back. "Go. Don't come back until you've done the dance of the beast with two backs."

"I could just lie."

"No, you can't," Cassie said. She had a sweet voice, like you'd want her to tell you a bedtime story. "The desperation will still show in your eyes. And I mean that in a nice way, Charlie."

"Sure, how else could I take it?"

"Bye, Daddy," Sophie said from the other side of the door. "Have fun."

"Jane!"

"Relax, she just came in. Go."

So Charlie, thrown out of his own home, by his own sister, said good-bye to the daughter he adored and went out to find a total stranger with whom to be intimate.

"Just a massage," Charlie said.

"Okay," said the girl as she arranged oils and lotions on a shelf. She was Asian, but Charlie couldn't tell from where in Asia, maybe Thailand. She was petite and had black hair that hung down past her waist. She wore a red silk kimono with a chrysanthemum design. She never looked him in the eye.

"Really, I'm just tense. I don't want anything but a completely ethical and hygienic massage, just like it says on the sign." Charlie stood at the end of a narrow cubicle, fully dressed, with a massage table on one side of him and the masseuse and her shelf of oils on the other.

"Okay," said the girl.

Charlie just looked at her, unsure of what to do next.

"Clothes off," said the girl. She placed a clean white towel on the massage table near Charlie, nodded to it, then turned her back. "Okay?"

"Okay," Charlie said, feeling now that he

319

was here, he needed to go through with it. He'd paid the woman at the door fifty dollars for the massage, after which she made him sign a release that stated that all he was getting was a massage, that tipping was encouraged, but did not imply any services beyond a massage, and that if he thought that he was getting anything but a massage he was going to be one disappointed White Devil. She made him initial each of the six languages it was printed in, then she winked, a long slow wink, exaggerated by very long false eyelashes, and performed the internationally accepted blow-job mime, with round mouth and rhythmic tongue pushing out the cheek. "Lotus Flower make you bery relax, Mr. Macy."

Charlie had signed Ray's name, not so much as a small revenge for calling the cops on him, but because he thought the management might recognize Ray's name and give him a discount.

He kept his boxers on and climbed on the table, but Lotus Flower slipped them off him as deftly as a magician pulling a scarf from his sleeve. She draped a towel over his bottom and dropped her kimono. Charlie saw it fall and glanced back to see a tiny, seminaked woman rubbing oil on her palms to warm it. He looked away and slammed his forehead into the table several times even as he felt his erection struggling for freedom beneath him.

"My sister made me come here," he said. "I didn't want to come."

"Okay," she said.

She rubbed the oil into his shoulders. It smelled of almonds and sandalwood. There must have been menthol or lavender or something in it, because he felt it tingle on his skin. Every place she touched hurt. Like he'd dug a ditch to Ecuador the day before, or pulled a barge across the Bay with a rope. It was like she had special sensory powers, she could find the exact spot where he carried his pain, then touch it, release it. He moaned, just a little.

"*Bery* tense," she said, working her fingers up his spine.

"I haven't slept well in two weeks," he said.

"That nice." She reached across to work his rib cage and he felt her small breasts press against his back. He stopped breathing for a second and she giggled.

"*Bery* tense," she said.

"I had this thing happen at work. Well, not at work, but I'm afraid I did something that could put everyone I know in danger,

321

and I can't make myself do what needs to be done to fix it. People could die."

"That nice," said Lotus Flower, kneading his biceps.

"You don't speak English, do you?"

"Oh. Little. No worries. You want happy ending?"

Charlie smiled. "Can you just keep rubbing?"

"No happy ending? Okay. Twenty dollar, fifteen minute."

So Charlie paid her, and talked to her, and she rubbed his back, and he paid her again, and he told her all the things that he couldn't share with other people: all the worries, all the fears, all the regrets. He told her of how he missed Rachel, yet how sometimes he would forget what she looked like and would run to the dresser in the middle of the night to look at her photo. He paid her for two hours in advance and dozed off, feeling her hands on his skin, and he dreamed of Rachel and sex, and when he woke up Lotus Flower was massaging his temples and tears were running into his ears. He told her it was the menthol in the oil, but it was the lonely coming up in him, like the pain in his back that he hadn't known he'd had until it was touched.

She massaged his chest, reaching over his head and letting her breasts rub against his face as she worked, and when he rose again under the towel, she asked, "You want happy ending now?"

"Nah," he said. "Happy endings are so Hollywood." Then he caught her wrists, sat up, kissed the back of her hands, and thanked her. He tipped her a hundred dollars. She smiled, put on her kimono, and left the cubicle.

Charlie dressed and left the Happy Relax Good Time Oriental Massage Parlor, which he had walked by a thousand times during his life, always wondering what was behind the red door with brown paper taped over the window. Now he knew: the pathetic puddle of lonely frustration that was Charlie Asher, for whom there would be no happy ending.

He made his way up to Broadway and headed up the hill into North Beach. He was only a few blocks from home when he sensed someone behind him. He turned, but all he saw was a guy a couple of blocks back buying a newspaper from a machine. He walked another half block and could see the activity on the street up ahead: tourists out walking, waiting for tables in

Italian restaurants, barkers trying to lure tourists into strip clubs, sailors barhopping, hipsters smoking outside of City Lights bookstore, looking cool and literary before the next poetry slam, which would go off in a bar across the street.

"Hey, soldier," a voice at his side. A woman's voice, soft and sexy. Charlie turned and looked down the alley he was passing. He could see a woman in the shadows, leaning against the wall. She was wearing an iridescent body stocking or something and a mercury light at the other end of the alley was drawing a silver outline of her figure. The hair rose on his neck, but he felt something twinge in his loins as well. This was his neighborhood, and the hookers had been calling to him since he was twelve, but this was the first time he'd ever stopped and paid more attention than a wave and a smile.

"Hey," Charlie said. He felt dizzy — drunk or stoned — maybe all the toxins had broken loose from the long massage, but he had to lean on his cane to steady himself.

She stepped away from the wall and the light silhouetted her, highlighting outlandish curves. Charlie realized he was grinding his teeth and his right kneecap began to bounce. This was not the street-worn body of a junkie — a dancer maybe, a goddess.

"Sometimes," she said, hissing the last s, "a rough fuck down a dark alley is the best medicine for a weary warrior."

Charlie looked around: the party a block ahead, the guy reading his newspaper under the streetlamp two blocks back. No one down the alley waiting to ambush him.

"How much?" he asked. He couldn't even remember what sex felt like, but all he could think about right now was release — a rough fuck down a dark alley with this . . . this goddess. He couldn't see her face, just the line of a cheekbone, but that was exquisite.

"The pleasure of your company," she said.

"Why me?" Charlie said, he couldn't help himself — it was his Beta nature.

"Come find out," she said. She cupped her breasts, fell back against the wall, and propped one heel up on the bricks. "Come."

He walked into the alley and leaned the cane on the wall, then took her uplifted knee in one hand, a breast in the other, and pulled her against him for a kiss. She felt like she was wearing velvet, her mouth was warm and tasted base, gamy, like venison or liver. He didn't even feel her undo his jeans, just a strong hand on his erection.

"Ah, strong meat," she hissed.

"Thanks, I've been going to the gym."

She bit his neck, hard, and he squeezed her breast and thrust against her hand. She threw her uplifted leg around his back and pulled him hard against her. He felt something sharp, painful digging into his scrotum and he tried to pull away. She pulled him tighter with her leg. She was incredibly strong.

"New Meat," she said. "Don't fight me or I'll tear them off."

Charlie felt the claw on his balls and the breath caught in his throat. Her face was an inch from his now, and he looked for her eyes, but could see only an obsidian blackness reflecting the highlights from the streetlight.

She held her free hand in front of his face and he watched as claws began to grow out of her fingertips, reflecting the streetlight like brushed chrome, until they were three inches long. She poised them over his eyes and he reached for his sword-cane against the wall. She knocked it away, and the claws were at his face again.

"Oh no, Meat. Not this time." She hooked a claw into his nostril. "Shall I drive it into your brain? That would be quickest, but I don't want quick. I've waited so long for this."

She released the pressure on his balls, and to his horror, he realized that he was still hard. She started rubbing his erection, pushing the claw deeper into his nose to hold him steady. "I know, I know — when you come, I'll put it in your ear and yank. I've taken off a half a man's head that way. You'll like it. You're lucky, if Nemain had been sent you'd be dead already."

"Bitch," Charlie managed to say.

She was stroking him harder and he was cursing his body for betraying him this way. He tried to pull away and her leg wrapped behind him crushed the breath out of him. "No, you come, *then* I'll kill you."

She pulled the claw from his nose and put it next to his ear. "Don't make me leave unsatisfied, Meat," she said, but in that instant her claw caught the side of his scalp and he hit her as hard as he could in the ribs with both of his fists.

"You fuckface!" she shrieked. She let her leg fall; yanked him aside by his penis, and reared back for a full slash of her claws to his head. Charlie tried to raise his forearm to take the blow, but then there was an explosion and a piece of her shoulder splattered on the wall, spinning her around.

Charlie felt her release his penis, and he threw himself across the alley. She rebounded off the wall with both claws aimed at his face. There was another explosion and she was knocked back again. This time she came up facing the street, and before she could brace to leap, two more shots hit her in the chest and she screeched, the sound like a thousand angry ravens set afire.

Five more quick shots and she was danced backward by the impacts; even as she went she was changing, her arms getting wider, her shoulders smoothing. Two more shots, and the next screech wasn't even remotely human, but that of a huge raven. She rose into the night sky trailing feathers and spattering a liquid that might have been blood, except that it was black.

Charlie climbed to his feet and staggered out of the alley to where Inspector Alphonse Rivera was still in shooting stance, holding a 9mm Beretta aimed at the dark sky.

"Do I even want to know what the fuck that was?" Rivera said.

"Probably not," Charlie said.

"Tie your coat around your waist," said the cop.

Charlie looked down and saw that the front of his jeans had been shredded as if by razors.

"Thanks," Charlie said.

"You know," Rivera said, "this could have all been avoided if you'd just taken the happy ending like everybody else."

17

Was It Good for You?

The next morning, Jane's girlfriend Cassie heard someone in the hall and opened the door. Charlie stood there, covered in blood, black goo, and smelling of sandalwood and almond oil; he had a cut over his ear, blood crusted in his nose, the front of his pants were in shreds, and there were tiny black feathers stuck to him everywhere.

"Why, Charlie," she said, somewhat surprised, "it appears that I underestimated you. When you decide to get your freak on, you do not mess around."

"Shower," Charlie said.

"Daddy!" Sophie called from her bedroom. She came running out with arms thrown wide, followed by two giant dogs and a lesbian aunt in Brooks Brothers. Halfway across the living room she saw her father, turned, and went squealing out of the room in terror.

Jane pulled up by the couch and stared. "Jesus, Chuck, what'd you do, try to fuck a leopard?"

"Something like that," Charlie said. He stumbled by her and went through his bedroom to the master bath.

Jane looked at Cassandra, who was trying to keep her smile from breaking into laughter. "You wanted him to get out more."

"You tell him about Mom?" Jane said.

"Thought that news should come from you," said Cassandra.

"Well, guns suck, I can tell you that," said Babd, the most recent of the three death divas to make an appearance Above. "Sure, they look great from down here, but up close — noisy, impersonal — give me a battle-ax or a cudgel any day."

"I like to cudgel," said Macha, who had her claws up inside Madison McKerny's severed head and was working the mouth like a hand puppet.

"It's your own fault," scolded Nemain. She had one of Madison McKerny's silicone implants — bits of fuck-puppet gore still clinging to it — and was pressing it to Babd's wounds to heal them. Even as the black flesh regenerated, the red glow in the implant dimmed. "We're wasting the power in these. And after waiting years to get another soul?"

Babd sighed. "I suppose in retrospect the hand job wasn't such a great idea."

"I suppose the hand job wasn't such a great idea," mocked Macha's hand puppet.

"I did that on the battlefields of the North, what, ten thousand times?" said Babd. "A final wank for the dying warrior — just seemed like the least I could do. I'm especially good at it, you know. It takes a powerful touch to keep a soldier hard when his guts are running between his fingers."

"She *is* good at it," said Orcus. "I'll vouch for that." He leaned back on his throne to display three feet of black, bull death-wood to show his enthusiasm.

"Not now, I just did my lipstick," puppeted Macha with the head, making its eyes bug out with her claws so it appeared that the dead girl was impressed by Orcus's prodigious unit.

They all snickered. She'd had Orcus and her Morrigan sisters giggling all morning with her puppet show, putting the implants on a shelf and working the head above them. *"Of course they're real, he really paid for them, didn't he?"*

They'd been giddy since pulling the soul vessels out of the fuck puppet's grave, that victory even overshadowing Babd's failure to kill the Death Merchant. But as the light ebbed out of the implants, their mood darkened. Nemain threw the useless implant against the bulkhead of the ship and it exploded and spattered the room with clear goo.

"What a waste," she growled. "We will take the Above, and I will eat his liver while he watches."

"What is it with you and eating livers?" Babd said. "I hate liver."

"Patience, Princesses," said Orcus as he weighed the remaining implant in his talon. "We were a thousand years coming to this place, for this battle, a few more to gather our force will but make the victory sweeter." He snatched the head away from Macha and took a bite out of it as if it were a crisp, ripe plum. "You really could have passed on the hand job, though," he said, spraying bits of brain at Babd.

"I've got us on a flight to Phoenix at two," Jane said. "We connect there to a commuter and we're in Sedona by suppertime."

Charlie had just come out of the shower

and wore only a pair of fresh jeans. He was drying his hair with a beige towel, leaving red streaks on it from his still-bleeding scalp. He sat down on the bed.

"Wait, wait, wait. How long has she known?"

"They diagnosed her six months ago. It had already spread from her colon to her other organs."

"And she waited until now to tell us."

"She didn't tell us. A guy named Buddy called. Evidently they've been living together. He said she didn't want us to worry. He broke down on the phone."

"Mom's living with a guy?" Charlie was staring at the red stripes on the towel. He'd been up all night, trying to explain to Inspector Rivera what had happened in the alley, without actually telling him anything. He was bleeding, battered, exhausted, and his mother was dying. "I can't believe her. She flipped when Rachel moved in before we were married."

"Yeah, well, you can yell at her for being a hypocrite when you see her tonight."

"I can't go, Jane. I have the store, and Sophie — she's too little for something like this."

"I called Ray and Lily, they've got the shop covered. Cassandra will watch Sophie overnight and the Communist-bloc ladies can watch her until Cassie gets home from work."

"Cassie's not coming with you?"

"Charlie, Mom still refers to me as her tomboy."

"Oh yeah, sorry." Charlie sighed. He was nostalgic for the days when Jane was the freak in the family and he was the normal one. "You going to try to reconcile that with her?"

"I don't know. I don't really have a plan. I don't even know if she's lucid. I've been on autopilot since I heard. I was waiting for you to get home so I could fall apart."

Charlie stood up, went to his sister, and put his arms around her. "You did great. I'm back, I got it from here. What do you need?"

She hugged him back, then pushed back with tears in her eyes. "I need to go home and pack. I'll come by at noon with a cab to get you, okay?"

"I'll be ready." He shook his head. "I can't believe Mom is living with a guy."

"A guy named Buddy," Jane said.

"The slut," Charlie said.

Jane laughed, which is all that Charlie wanted right then.

Lois Asher was sleeping when Charlie

and Jane arrived at her home in Sedona. A potbellied sunburned man wearing Bermuda shorts and a safari shirt let them in: Buddy. He sat at the kitchen table with Charlie and Jane, and professed his love for their mother, told them about his own life as an aircraft mechanic in Illinois before he retired, then recited a play-by-play of what they had done since Lois had been diagnosed. She'd gone through three courses of chemotherapy, then, sick and hairless, she had given in. Charlie and Jane looked at each other, feeling guilty that they hadn't been there to help.

"She didn't want to bother you two," Buddy said. "She's been acting like dying was something she could do in her spare time, between hair appointments."

Charlie snapped to attention. That was the kind of thing he'd thought to himself several times when he was retrieving a soul vessel and had seen people who were so far in denial about what was happening to them that they were still buying five-year calendars.

"Women, what are you gonna do with 'em," Buddy said, winking at Jane.

Charlie suddenly felt a great wave of affection for this sunburned little bald guy who his mother was shacked up with.

"We want to thank you for being here for her, Buddy."

"Yeah." Jane nodded, still looking a little dazed.

"Well, I'm here for the whole shebang, and then some, if you need me."

"Thanks," Charlie said. "We will." And they would, because it was immediately evident to Charlie that Buddy was going to hang on himself only as long as he felt he was needed.

"Buddy," said a soft female voice from behind Charlie. He turned to see a big, thirtyish woman in scrubs: another hospice worker — another of the amazing women that Charlie had seen in the homes of the dying, helping to deliver them into the next world with as much comfort and dignity and even joy as they could gather — benevolent Valkyries, midwives of the final light, they were — and as Charlie watched them at work, he saw that rather than become detached from, or callous to their job, they became involved with every patient and every family. They were *present*. He'd seen them grieve with a hundred different families, taking part in an intensity of emotion that most people would feel only a few times in their lives. Watching them over the years had made Charlie feel more reverent toward his task of being a Death Merchant. It might be a curse on him, but ultimately, it wasn't about him, it was about serving, and the transcendence in serving, and the hospice workers had taught him that.

The woman's name tag read GRACE. Charlie smiled.

"Buddy," she said. "She's awake and she's asking for you."

Charlie stood. "Grace, I'm Charlie, Lois's son. This is my sister, Jane."

"Oh, she talks about you two all the time."

"She does?" said Jane, a tad surprised.

"Oh yes. She tells me you were quite the tomboy," Grace said. "And you —" she said to Charlie. "You used to be nice but then something happened."

"I learned to talk," Charlie said.

"That's when I stopped liking him," Jane said.

Lois Asher was propped in a nest of pillows, wearing a perfectly coiffed gray wig tied back in the style she had always worn her real hair, a silver squash-blossom necklace and matching earrings and rings, a mauve silk nightgown that blended so well with the Southwestern

338

decor of the bedroom that it looked as if Lois might be trying to disappear into her surroundings. And she did, except the space she'd made for herself in the world was a little bigger than she now required. There was a gap between the wig and her scalp, her nightgown hung almost empty, and her rings jangled on her fingers like bangles. It was clear to Charlie that she hadn't actually been sleeping when they'd arrived, but had sent Buddy out with the excuse to give Grace time to dress and arrange her for presentation to her children.

Charlie noticed that the squash-blossom necklace was glowing dull red against Lois's nightgown and he felt a long, sad sigh rise in his chest. He hugged his mother and could feel the bones in her back and shoulders, as delicate and fragile as a bird's. Jane tried to fight down a sob as soon as she saw her mother, but managed only to produce what sounded like a painful snort. She fell to her knees at her mother's bedside.

Charlie knew it was perhaps the stupidest question one could ask the dying, yet he asked: "How are you doing, Mom?"

She patted his hand. "I could use an old-fashioned. Buddy won't let me have any alcohol, since I can't keep it down. You met Buddy?"

"He seems like a nice man," Jane said.

"Oh, he is. He's been good to me. We're just friends, you know."

Charlie looked across the bed at Jane, who raised her eyebrows.

"It's okay, we know you guys are living together," Charlie said.

"Living together? Me? What do you take me for?"

"Never mind, Mom."

His mother waved off the thought as if she was shooing a fly. "And how is that little Jewish girl of yours, Charlie?"

"Sophie? She's doing great, Mom."

"No, that's not it."

"What's not it?"

"It wasn't Sophie, it was something else. Pretty girl — too good for you, really."

"You're thinking of Rachel, Mom. She passed on five years ago, remember?"

"Well, you can't blame her, can you? You were such a sweet little boy, then I don't know what happened to you. Do you remember?"

"Yeah, Mom, I was sweet."

Lois looked at her daughter. "And what about you, Jane, have you found yourself a

340

nice man? I hate the idea of you being alone."

"Still looking for Mr. Right," Jane said, giving Charlie the *"we've got to get away and have an emergency meeting"* head toss that she had practiced around their mother since she was eight.

"Mom, Jane and I will be right back. We can call Sophie and talk to her then, okay?"

"Who's Sophie?" Lois asked.

"She's your granddaughter, Mom. You remember, beautiful little Sophie?"

"Don't be silly, Charles, I'm not old enough to be a grandmother."

Outside the bedroom Jane fumbled around and in her purse and produced a pack of cigarettes, but couldn't figure out whether to smoke one or not. "Holy Motown Jesus with Pips, what the fuck is going on in there?"

"She's got a lot of morphine in her, Jane. Did you smell that acrid smell? That's her sweat glands trying to take the poisons out of her body that her kidneys and liver would normally filter. Her organs are starting to shut down, it means that there's a lot of toxins going to her brain."

"How do you know that?"

"I've read about it. Look, she never lived

in reality completely, you know that? She hated the shop and hated Dad's work, even though it supported her. She hated his collecting, even though she was just as bad. And the thing with Buddy not living here — she's trying to reconcile who she's always thought she was with who she really is."

"Is that why I still want to punch her lights out?" Jane said. "That's wrong, isn't it?"

"Well, I suppose —"

"I'm a horrible person. My mother is dying of cancer and I want to punch her lights out."

Charlie put his arm around his sister's shoulder and started walking her toward the front door so she could go outside and smoke. "Don't be so hard on yourself," he said. "You're doing the same thing, trying to reconcile all the moms that Mom ever was — the one you wanted, the one she was when you needed her and she was there, the one she was when she didn't understand. Most of us don't live our lives with one, integrated self that meets the world, we're a whole bunch of selves. When someone dies, they all integrate into the soul — the essence of who we are, beyond the different faces we wear throughout our lives. You're just hating the selves you've always hated, and loving the ones you've always loved. It's bound to mess you up."

Jane stopped and stepped back from him. "Then how come it's not messing you up?"

"I don't know. Maybe because of what I went through with Rachel."

"So you think that when someone dies suddenly like that, that this face-reconciliation thing happens?"

"I don't know. I don't think it's a conscious process. Maybe more for you than for Mom, you know what I mean? You feel like you have to put things right before she's gone, and it's frustrating."

"So what happens if she doesn't integrate all that before she dies. What happens if I don't?"

"I think you get another chance."

"Really? Like reincarnation? What about Jesus and stuff?"

"I think that there's a lot of stuff that's not in the book. In any of the books."

"Where's this coming from? I never got the impression you were spiritual. You wouldn't even go to yoga with me."

"I wouldn't go to yoga with you because I'm not bendy, not because I'm not spiritual."

They'd gotten to the door, and when Charlie pulled it open it made the same sound a refrigerator door makes. When they stepped out onto the front porch he realized why, as a wave of hundred-and-ten-degree heat hit them.

"Jeez, did you accidentally open the door to hell?" Jane said. "I don't need to smoke this badly. Get inside, get inside, get inside." She shoved him inside and closed the door. "That's heinous. Why would someone live in this climate?"

"I'm confused," Charlie said. "Did you start smoking again or not?"

"I didn't really," Jane said. "I just have one when I'm really stressed out. It's like thumbing your nose at Death. Haven't you ever felt like doing that?"

"You have no idea," Charlie said.

With Charlie and Jane there, they sent the hospice nurse home at night and watched Lois in four-hour shifts. Charlie gave his mother her medication, wiped her mouth, fed her what little she would take in, but by now she was mostly having sips of water or apple juice, and he listened as she lamented losing her looks and her things, as she remembered being a great beauty, the belle of the ball at parties before he was born, an object of desire, which clearly she loved more than being a wife or a mother or any of the dozen other faces she had worn in her life. Sometimes she would actually turn her attention to her son . . .

"I loved you as a little boy. I would take you to cafés in North Beach and everyone would just dote on you. You were so sweet. Beautiful. Both of us were."

"I know."

"Remember when we dumped all of the cereal out of the boxes so you could get the prize out? A little submarine, I think? Do you remember?"

"I remember, Mom."

"We were close then."

"Yeah, we were."

Charlie would take her hand then and let her remember great times that they had never really had. The time had long passed for correcting facts and changing impressions.

When she exhausted herself he let her sleep, and read by a flashlight sitting in the chair at her bedside. He was there, in the middle of the night, reading a crime novel, when the door opened and a slight man of about fifty crept into the room, stopped by the door, and looked around. He wore sneakers and black jeans, a long-sleeved black T-shirt — but for the oversized wire-frame glasses, he was just short a hand grenade and a survival knife from looking like someone on a commando mission.

"Just be quiet," Charlie said softly. "She's sleeping."

The little man jumped straight up about two feet and came down in a crouch. He was breathing hard and Charlie was afraid he might faint if he didn't relax.

"It's okay. It's in the top drawer of that dresser over there — it's a squash-blossom necklace. Take it."

The little man ducked behind the door, then peeked around the edge. "You can see me?"

"Yes." Charlie put his book down and got up from the chair, and went to the dresser.

"Oh, this is bad. This is really, really bad."

"It's not that bad," Charlie said.

The little man shook his head violently. "No, it's really bad. Look away. Look over there. I'm not here. I'm not here. You can't see me."

"Here it is," Charlie said. He took the squash-blossom necklace from its velvet case in the drawer and held it up.

"What is?"

"What you're looking for."

"How did you know?"

"Because I do what you do. I'm a Death Merchant."

"A what?"

Then Charlie remembered that Minty Fresh said he had coined the term, so maybe only the Death Merchants in San Francisco knew it. "I collect soul vessels."

"No, you don't. You can't see me. You can't see me. Sleep. Sleep." The little man was waving his hands up and down in the air like he was drawing a curtain of deception before him, or possibly clearing spiderwebs out of the room.

"These are not the droids you seek," Charlie said, grinning.

"What?"

"You don't have Jedi powers, you git. Just take the necklace."

"I don't understand."

"Come with me," Charlie said. "It's time for my sister to watch her anyway." He led the little guy out of his mother's room into the living room. They stood by the front window, looking at the sun coming up and casting shadows of the broken teeth of the red rock mountains around them. "What's your name?"

"Vern. Vern Glover."

"I'm Charlie. Nice to meet you. How long does she have, Vern?"

"What do you mean?"

"How long on your calendar. How many days were left?"

"How do you know about that?"

"I told you. I do what you do. I can see you. I can see that necklace glowing red. I know what you are."

"But you can't. The *Great Big Book* says that horrible Forces of Darkness will rise if I talk to you."

"See this cut over my ear, Vern?"

Vern nodded.

"Forces of Darkness. Fuck 'em. Fuck the Forces of Darkness, Vern. How long does my mother have?"

"It's your mother? I'm sorry, Charlie. She has two more days."

"Okay," Charlie said, nodding. "Then we'd better go get a doughnut."

"Pardon?"

"Doughnut! Doughnut! You like doughnuts, don't you?"

"Yes, but why?"

"Because the continuance of human existence as we know it depends on us having doughnuts together."

"Really?" Vern's eyes went wide.

"No, not really. I'm just fucking with

you." Charlie put his arm around Vern's shoulder. "But let's go get one anyway. I'll wake my sister for her watch."

Charlie called home from his mobile phone to check on Sophie. Then, satisfied she was safe, he returned to the booth at Dunkin' Donuts, where Vern and a cruller were waiting for him. Vern had taken off his stocking cap and had a wild mop of silver gray hair over large, aviator-frame glasses that made him look like a tan and wiry mad scientist.

"So like she was really hot?"

"Vern, you wouldn't believe. I'm telling you, body of a goddess. Covered with really fine feathers, soft as down." Charlie innately recognized another Beta Male like he recognized another Death Merchant, so he nearly stumbled over himself to tell the story of his adventure with the sexy sewer harpy, knowing he had a sympathetic audience.

"But she was going to put her claw through your brain, right?"

"Yeah, she said she was, but you know something, I think there was some chemistry there."

"You don't think it was just that she had your crank in her hand at the time, because that can cloud a guy's judgment."

"Yeah, there's that, but still, you have to think, of all the Death Merchants in all of the cities on the planet, she chose me to share the death wank. I think she had a thing for me."

"Well, you're in the City of Two Bridges," said Vern, brushing a little maple glaze from the corner of his mouth. "That's where it's supposed to happen."

"Where what's supposed to happen?" Charlie had really enjoyed being the senior Death Merchant, acting as the elder statesman to Vern, who had been called to recruit souls only six months ago. Now he was thrown.

"In *The Great Big Book of Death*, it says that we can't talk about what we do, or try to find each other, or the Forces of Darkness will rise up in the City of Two Bridges and there will be a horrible battle and the Underworld will rise and cover the land if we lose. You guys have two bridges in San Francisco, right?"

Charlie tried to hide his surprise. Vern had obviously gotten a different version of the *Great Big Book* than they got in San Francisco. "Well, two main ones, yes. Sorry, it's been a long time since I read the book. Remind me why the City of Two

350

Bridges is so important?"

Vern gave Charlie the big "duh" look. "Because that is where the new Luminatus, the Great Death, will take power."

"Oh yeah, of course, the Luminatus." Charlie thumped himself in the side of the head. He had no idea what Vern was talking about.

"You think that they won't need us anymore, after the Great Death takes power?" Vern asked. "I mean, will there be layoffs? Because the Big Book makes it sound like the Luminatus rising is a good thing, but I've been making a ton of money since I got this gig."

Yeah, that's going to be our problem, layoffs, Charlie thought. "I think we'll be fine. Like the book says, it's a dirty job, but someone has to do it."

"Right, right, right. So this cop that shot the sexy-goddess babe, he didn't do anything?"

"No, not nothing. First he put me in the back of his cop car and tried to get me to tell him what had been going on when he showed up, and what had been going on for these last few years he's been checking on me."

"And what did you tell him?"

"I told him that it was as much a mystery to me as it was to him."

"And he believed that?"

"No. He didn't. But he did believe it when I told him that if I told him more it would get worse, so we came up with a story that justified his firing his weapon. A guy with a gun taking a shot at me, then at him — descriptions, everything. Then when he was sure we had it straight, he took me to the station and I wrote out my statement."

"That's it, he let you go."

"No, then he told me stories about his career, and the weird stuff he's encountered, and why because of that, he was going to let me go. The guy is a complete nut job. He believes in vampires and demons and giant owls — he said that he once handled a call for a polar-bear attack in Santa Barbara."

"Wow," said Vern. "You lucked out."

"I called him before we left the city. He's going to check on my building until I get home, make sure my daughter is okay." Charlie hadn't told Vern about the hellhounds.

"You must be worried sick about her," Vern said. "I have a kid, she's a junior in high school, lives with my ex-wife in Phoenix."

"Yeah, so you know," Charlie said. "So, Vern, you've never seen any of these dark creatures? Never heard voices coming out of the storm drains? Nothing like that?"

"Nope. Not like you're talking about. We don't have storm drains in Sedona. We have a desert with rivers through it."

"Right, but have you ever missed getting a soul vessel?"

"Yeah, at first, when I got the *Great Big Book*, I thought it was a joke. I skipped three or four of them."

"And nothing happened?"

"Well, I wouldn't say that. I'd wake up early, and look up at the mountain above my house, and there'd be a shadow there, looked like a big oil slick."

"So?"

"So, it would be on the wrong side of the mountain. It would be on the same side as the sun. And during the course of the day, it moved down the mountain. Oh, if you didn't look at it, watch it, you'd look right by it, but it was coming down into the city, hour by hour. I drove out to where I saw it going, and waited for it."

"And?"

"You could hear crows calling. I waited until it got a half a block from me, moving so slow you could barely see it, but it got louder and louder, like a huge flock of crows. Scared the bejesus out of me. I went home, looked up the name I'd written down during the night, and they lived in the neighborhood I'd been in. The shadow was coming out of the mountain for the soul vessel."

"Did it get it?"

"I guess. I didn't."

"And nothing happened?"

"Oh yeah, something happened. The next time the shadow moved faster, like a cloud blowing over. And I followed it, and sure enough, it was heading right for a woman's house whose name was on my calendar. That's when I realized that the *Great Big Book* wasn't bullshitting."

"But the shadow thing, it never came for you?"

"Third time," Vern said.

"There was a third time?"

"Oh yeah, like you didn't think this was all a load of crap when it first started happening to you?"

"Okay, good point," Charlie said. "Sorry. Go on."

"So, the third time, the shadow comes down off a mountain on the other side of town, at night, during a full moon, and this time, you can see the crows flying in it.

Not like really see them, but like shadows of them. Some people noticed it that time. I got in my car again, took my dog, Scottie, with me. I already knew where the thing was going. I pulled up a couple of doors down from the guy's house — to warn him, you know. I didn't realize yet what the book was saying about us not being seen, otherwise I would have just gone for the soul vessel. Anyway, I'm at the door, and the shadow is coming across the street, all the edges shaped like crows, and Scottie starts barking like mad, and runs at it. Brave little guy. Anyway, as soon as the shadow touches him he yelps and drops over dead. Meantime, a woman comes to the door, and I look in and see a statue, like a fake Remington bronze on the table in the foyer behind her, and it's glowing red, like red-hot. And I blow by her and grab it. And the shadow evaporates. Just like that, it's gone. That's the last time I was late getting a soul vessel."

"Sorry about your dog," Charlie said. "What did you tell the woman?"

"That's the funny thing, I didn't tell her anything. She was talking to her husband in the next room, and he wasn't answering her, and she runs back to see what happened to him. Didn't even look at me.

Turns out the guy was having a heart attack. I took the statue, went and picked up Scottie's body, and left."

"That had to be tough."

"I thought I was Death for a while, you know, special. Because the guy croaked with me there, but it was just coincidence."

"Yeah, that happened to me, too," Charlie said. But he was still disturbed by the whole "great battle" revelation. "Vern, would you mind if I took a look at your *Great Big Book*?"

"I don't think so, Charlie. In fact, I think we'd better say good-bye. I mean, if the *Great Big Book* is right, and I don't have any reason to believe it's not, then we shouldn't even be talking."

"But it's a different version than I have."

"You don't think there's a reason for that?" Vern said. His eyes magnified in his big glasses made him look like a madman for a second.

"Okay, then," Charlie said. "But e-mail me, okay? That shouldn't hurt."

Vern looked in his coffee cup like he was thinking, as if by telling the story of the shadow that came down out of the mountains, he'd frightened himself. Finally he looked up and smiled. "You know, I'd like that. I could use some pointers, and if something weird starts to happen, we'll stop."

"Deal," Charlie said. He drove Vern back to his car, which was parked around the block from his mother's house, and they said good-bye.

Jane met Charlie at the door. "Where have you been? I need the car to go get her floss."

"I brought doughnuts," Charlie said, holding up the box, maybe a little too proud.

"Well, that's not the same, is it?"

"As floss?"

"Dental floss. Can you believe it? Charlie, if I'm still flossing on my deathbed, you have my permission to garrote me with it. No, I'm leaving you *instructions* to garrote me with it."

"Okay," Charlie said. "So other than that, she's okay?"

Jane was digging in her purse, had found her cigarettes and was looking for her lighter. "Like gum disease is the big danger at this point. Goddammit! Did they take my lighter at the airport?"

"You still don't smoke, Jane," Charlie said.

She looked up. "So what's your point?"

"Nothing." He handed her the keys to the rental car. "Can you grab me some toothpaste while you're out?"

She gave up searching for the lighter and threw the cigarettes back into her purse. "What is it with this family and the compulsive dental hygiene?"

"I forgot to bring any."

"Okay." Jane braced the keys in her hand, ready to go in the ignition, and tucked her purse under her arm like a football. She dropped into a crouch and pulled down her mirrored, wraparound sunglasses that, with her short platinum blond hair and Charlie's black pinstripe suit, made her look a little like a cyborg assassin from the future getting ready to dash out into the poisonous atmosphere of planet Duran Duran. "It's fucking hot out there, isn't it?"

Charlie nodded and held up the doughnut box again. "The glazed have suffered."

"Oh," Jane said, lifting her glasses again. "Cassandra called. After you called this morning she noticed your date book on the nightstand. Well actually, she said that Alvin and Mohammed dragged her in there and pushed it at her. She wondered if you needed it."

"What about Sophie, is she okay?"

"No, she's been abducted by aliens, but I wanted you to digest the bad news about forgetting your date book first."

"You know, that right there is why Mom is ashamed of you," Charlie said.

Jane laughed. "Guess what? She's not."

"She's not?"

"No, this morning she told me that she always knew who I was, always knew what I was, and that she has always loved me, just the way I am."

"Did you card her? There's an impostor in our mom's bed."

"Shut up, it was nice. Important."

"She was probably just saying that because she's dying."

"She did say that she wished I wouldn't wear men's suits all the time."

"She's not alone on that one," Charlie said.

Jane fell back into assault mode. "I'm off on the floss mission. Call Cassandra."

"Done," Charlie said.

"And Buddy needs a doughnut." Jane threw open the door and ran out into the heat screaming like a berserker charging the enemy.

Charlie closed the door behind her so as not to let the air-conditioning out, and watched through the glass as his sister ran across the zero-scaped yard like she was on fire. He looked beyond her to the red rock mesa rising out of the desert. There seemed to be a deep crevasse in it that he hadn't seen there before. He looked again, and saw that it wasn't a crevasse at all, just a long, sharp shadow.

Then he ran out into the driveway and looked at the position of the sun, then at the shadow. It was on the wrong side of the mesa. There couldn't be a shadow on this side — the sun was also on this side. He shaded his eyes and watched the shadow until he thought his brains were cooking in the sun. It was moving, slowly, but moving, and not the way a shadow moves. It was moving with purpose, against the sun, toward his mother's house.

"My date book," he said to himself. "Oh, shit."

18

Yo Momma So Dead That . . .

On her last day, Lois Asher rallied. After not having even been able to get up to go to the breakfast table, or into the living room to sit and watch TV for three weeks, got up and danced with Buddy to an old Ink Spots song. She was playful and full of laughter, she teased her children and hugged them, she ate a chocolate-marshmallow sundae, and she brushed and flossed afterward. She put on her favorite silver jewelry and wore it to the dinner table, and when she couldn't find her squash-blossom necklace she shrugged it off like it was a minor thing — she must have misplaced it. Oh, well.

Charlie knew what was happening because he had seen it before, and Buddy and Jane knew because Grace, the hospice nurse, explained it to them. "It happens again and again. I've seen people come out of a coma and sing their favorite songs, and all I can tell you is to enjoy it. People see the light come back into eyes that have been dull for months, and they start to place hope on it. It's not a sign of getting well, it's an opportunity to say good-bye. It's a gift."

Charlie had also learned by observing that it really helped everyone to let go if they were at least mildly medicated, so he and Jane took some antianxiety pills that Jane's therapist had prescribed and Buddy washed down a time-released morphine pill with some scotch. Medication and forgiveness can make for joyous moments with the dying — it's like they get to return to childhood — and because nothing in the future matters, because you don't have to train them for life, teach lessons, forge applicable and practical memories, all the joy can be wicked from those last moments and stored in the heart. It was the best and closest time Charlie had ever had with his mother and his sister, and Buddy, in the sharing, became family as well.

Lois Asher went to bed at nine and died at midnight.

"I can't stay for the funeral," Charlie said to his sister the next morning.

"What do you mean you can't stay for the funeral?"

Charlie looked out the window at the giant ice pick of a shadow that had made its way down the mountain toward his mother's house. Charlie could see it churning at the edges, like flocks of birds or swarming insects. The point was less than a half mile away.

"I have something I have to do at home, Jane. I mean, I forgot to do it and I really, really can't stay."

"Don't be mysterious. What the hell do you need to do that you can't attend your own mother's funeral?"

Charlie was pressing his Beta Male imagination to the breaking point to come up with something credible on the spot. Then a light went on. "The other night, when you sent me out to get laid?"

"Yeah?"

"Well, it was an adventure, to be sure, but when I went to get my scalp sewed up, I also had a test. I talked to the doctor today, and I have to go get treatment. Right now."

"You moron, I didn't send you out to have unsafe sex. What were you thinking?"

"It *was* safe sex." *Right, sure,* he thought, he almost scoffed at himself. "It's the wounds they're worried about. But if I get on these drugs right away, there's a good chance that I'll be okay."

"They're putting you on the cocktail? As a preventative?"

Sure, that's it, the cocktail! Charlie thought. He nodded gravely.

"Okay, then, go." Jane turned and hid her face.

"Maybe I can get back in time for the funeral," Charlie said. Could he? He had to retrieve two overdue soul vessels in less than a week, and hope that no new names had appeared in his date book.

"We'll do it a week from today," Jane said, turning back around, tears blinked away. "You go home, get treated, come back. Buddy and I will handle the arrangements."

"I'm sorry," Charlie said. He put his arms around his sister.

"Don't you die on me, too, you fucker," Jane said.

"I'll be fine. I'll be back as soon as I can."

"Bring back that charcoal Armani of yours for me to wear to the funeral, and Cassie's strappy black pumps, okay?"

"You? In strappy black pumps?"

"It's what Mom would have wanted," Jane said.

★ ★ ★

When Charlie landed in San Francisco there were four frantic messages on his cell phone from Cassandra. She had always seemed so calm, composed — a stable counterpoint to his sister's flights of fancy. She sounded a wreck on the phone.

"Charlie, she's got him trapped and they're going to eat him and I don't know what to do. I don't want to call the cops. Call me when you land."

Charlie did call, all the way into the city in the shuttle van he called, but kept getting transferred to voice messaging. When he got out of the van in front of his store he heard a hiss coming out of the storm drain at the corner.

"I missed finishing with you, lover," came the voice.

"No time," Charlie said, hopping over the curb and running into the store.

"You never called," purred the Morrigan.

Ray was behind the counter mousing through Asian cuties when Charlie came storming through.

"You'd better get upstairs," Ray said. "They're freaking out up there."

"No kidding," Charlie said as he passed. He took the stairs two at a time.

365

He was fumbling his key into the lock when Cassandra threw the door open and pulled him into his apartment.

"She won't let him go. I'm afraid they're going to eat him."

"Who, what? That's what you said on my voice mail. Where is Sophie?"

Cassandra dragged him to Sophie's room, where he was met in the doorway by a growling Mohammed.

"Daddy!" Sophie shrieked. She ran across the room and leapt into his arms. She gave him a big hug and a sloppy kiss that left a chocolate Sophie-print on his cheek. "Down," she said. "Down, down." Charlie put her down and she ran back into her room, but Mohammed prevented Charlie from entering, pushed his nose into Charlie's shirt, leaving a giant dog-nose print in chocolate. Evidently there had been a chocolate orgy going on in his absence.

"His mother is supposed to pick him up at one," Cassandra said. "I don't know what to do."

Charlie strained to see around the hell-hound and saw Sophie standing with her hand on Alvin's collar while he menaced a little boy who was crouched in the corner. The little boy was a little wide-eyed, but otherwise unhurt, and he didn't seem that frightened. In fact, he was hugging a box of Crunchy Cheese Newts, and was eating one, then feeding the next one to Alvin, who was dripping hellish dog drool onto the kid's shoes in anticipation of the next newt.

"I love him," Sophie said. She went to the little boy and kissed him on the cheek, leaving a chocolate smear. Not the first. It appeared that this little guy had been suffering Sophie's affections for quite some time, for he was covered with chocolaty goodness and orange Cheese-Newt dust. "I want to keep him."

The little boy grinned.

"He came over for a playdate. I guess you scheduled it before you left," Cassandra said. "I thought it would be okay. I tried to get him out of there, but the dogs won't let me by. What are we going to tell his mother?"

"I want to keep him," Sophie said. Big kiss.

"His name is Matthew," Cassie said.

"I know his name. He goes to Sophie's school."

Charlie started into the room. Mohammed blocked the doorway.

"Matty, are you all right?" Charlie said.

"Uh-huh," said the chocolate-, cheese-, and dog-drool-sodden kid.

"I want him to stay, Dad," Sophie said. "Alvin and Mohammed want him to stay, too."

Charlie thought that perhaps he had not been strict enough in setting limits for his daughter. Maybe after losing her mother, he just hadn't had the heart to say no to her, and now she was taking hostages.

"Honey, Matty has to get cleaned up. His mommy is coming to get him so he can go be traumatized in his own house."

"No! He's mine."

"Honey, tell Mohammed to let me in. If we don't get Matty cleaned up, he won't be able to come back."

"He can sleep in your room," Sophie said. "I'll take care of him."

"No, young lady, you tell Mohammed to get —"

"I have to pee," Matthew said. He climbed to his feet and skipped by Alvin, who followed him, then under Mohammed and past Charlie and Cassandra to the bathroom. "Hi," he said as he went by. He closed the door and they could hear the sound of tinkle. Alvin and Mohammed bullied their way through the doorway and waited outside the bathroom.

Sophie sat down hard, her feet splayed out, her lower lip pushed out like the cowcatcher on a steam engine. Her shoulders started heaving before he could hear the sob — like she was saving up breath — then the wailing and the tears. Charlie went to her and picked her up.

"I — I — I — I, he — he — he — he —"

"It's okay, honey. It's okay."

"But I love him."

"I know you do, honey. It'll be okay. He'll go to his house and you can still love him."

"Nooooooooooooooooooooooooo —"

She buried her face in his jacket, and as much as his heart was breaking for his daughter, he was also thinking about how much Three Fingered Wu was going to ding him for getting the chocolate stain out of his jacket.

"They just let him go pee," Cassandra said, staring at the hellhounds. "Just like that. I thought they were going to eat him. They wouldn't let me near him."

"It's okay," Charlie said. "You didn't know."

"Know what?"

"They love the Crunchy Cheese Newts."

"You're kidding?"

"Sorry. Look, Cassie, can you clean up

Sophie and Matty and take care of this? I have some stuff in my date book I have to take care of right away."

"Sure, but —"

"Sophie will be fine. Won't you, honey?"

Sophie nodded sadly and wiped her eyes on his coat. "I missed you, Daddy."

"I missed you, too, sweetie. I'll be home tonight."

He kissed her, got his date book from the bedroom, and ran around the apartment collecting his keys, cane, hat, and man purse. "Thanks, Cassie. You have no idea how grateful I am."

"Sorry about your mother, Charlie," Cassandra said as he passed.

"Yeah, thanks," Charlie said, quickly checking the edge of the sword in his cane as he went by.

"Charlie, your life is out of control," Cassandra said, now slipping back into the unflappable persona that they were all used to.

"Okay, I'll need to borrow your strappy black pumps, too," Charlie said as he headed out the door.

"I think I've made my point," Cassie called after him.

Ray stopped Charlie at the bottom of the

stairs. "You got a minute, boss?"

"Not really, Ray. I'm in a hurry."

"Well, I just wanted to apologize."

"For what?"

"Well, it seems silly now, but I kind of suspected you of being a serial killer."

Charlie nodded as if he were considering the grave consequences of Ray's confession, when, in fact, he was trying to remember if there was any gas in the van. "Well, Ray, I accept your apology, and I'm sorry I ever gave you that impression."

"I think all those years on the force made me suspicious, but Inspector Rivera stopped by and set me straight."

"He did, did he? What exactly did he say?"

"He said that you had been checking some stuff out for him, getting into places he couldn't get without a warrant and so forth, stuff that you'd both get in a lot of trouble for if anyone found out, but was helping to put the bad guys away. He said that's why you're so secretive."

"Yes," Charlie said solemnly, "I have been fighting crime in my spare time, Ray. I'm sorry I couldn't tell you."

"I understand," Ray said, backing away from the stairway. "Again, I'm sorry. I feel like a traitor."

"It's okay, Ray. But I really have to go. You know, fighting the Forces of Darkness and all." Charlie held his cane out as if it were a sword and he was charging into action, which, bizarrely, it was and he was.

Charlie had six days to retrieve three soul vessels if he was going to get caught up before he returned to Arizona for his mother's funeral. Two, the names that had appeared in his date book the same day as Madison McKerny were seriously overdue. The last had appeared in the book only a couple of days ago, when he was in Arizona — yet it was in his own handwriting. He'd always thought that he had been doing some kind of sleep writing, but now, this was a whole new twist. He promised himself he would freak out about it as soon as he had some time.

Meanwhile, with the near-death hand job and the dead-mom thing, he hadn't even done the preliminary research on the first of the two, Esther Johnson and Irena Posokovanovich, and both were now past their pickup date — one by three days. What if the sewer harpies had already gotten there? As strong as they'd become already, he didn't even want to think about what they could do if they got hold of another soul. He considered calling Rivera to watch his back when he went to the house, but what would he say he was doing? The sharp-faced cop knew there was something supernatural going on, and he'd taken Charlie's word that he was one of the good guys (not a hard sell when he'd seen the sewer harpy driving a three-inch claw up his nostril only to survive nine rounds of 9mm in the torso and still fly away).

Charlie was driving with no destination, heading into Pacific Heights just because the traffic was lighter in that direction. He pulled over to the curb and called information.

"I need a number and address for an Esther Johnson."

"There's no Esther Johnson, sir, but I have three E. Johnsons."

"Can you give me the addresses?"

She gave him the two who had addresses. A recording offered to dial the number for him for an additional charge of fifty cents.

"Yeah, how much to drive me there?" Charlie asked the computer voice. Then he hung up and dialed the E. Johnson with no address.

"Hi, could I speak with Esther Johnson," Charlie said cheerfully.

"There's no Esther Johnson here," said a man's voice. "I'm afraid you have the wrong number."

"Wait. Was there an Esther Johnson there, until maybe three days ago?" Charlie asked. "I saw the E. Johnson in the phone book."

"That's me," said the man, "I'm Ed Johnson."

"Sorry to bother you, Mr. Johnson." Charlie disconnected and dialed the next E. Johnson.

"Hello," a woman's voice.

"Hi, could I speak to Esther Johnson, please?"

A deep breath. "Who is calling?"

Charlie used a ruse that had worked a dozen times before. "This is Charlie Asher, of Asher's Secondhand. We've taken in some merchandise that has Esther Johnson's name on it and we wanted to make sure it's not stolen."

"Well, Mr. Asher, I'm sorry to tell you that my aunt passed away three days ago."

"Bingo!" Charlie said.

"Pardon?"

"Sorry," Charlie said. "My associate is playing a scratch-off lotto ticket here in the shop, and he's just won ten thousand dollars."

"Mr. Asher, this isn't really a good time. Is this merchandise you have valuable?"

"No, just some old clothes."

"Another time, then?" The woman sounded not so much bereaved as harried. "If you don't mind."

"No, I'm sorry for your loss," Charlie said. He disconnected, checked the address, and headed up toward Golden Gate Park and the Haight.

The Haight: mecca for the Free Love movement of the sixties, where the Beat Generation begat the Flower Children, where kids from all over the country had come to tune in, turn on, and drop out — and had kept coming, even as the neighborhood went through alternating waves of renewal and decline. Now, as Charlie drove down Haight Street, amid the head shops, vegetarian restaurants, hippie boutiques, music stores, and coffeehouses, he saw hippies that ranged in age from fifteen to seventy. Grizzled oldsters panhandling or passing out pamphlets, and young, white-Rastafarian dreadlocked teenagers in flowing skirts or hemp drawstring trousers, with shining piercings and vacant pot-blissed stares. He passed brown-toothed crackheads barking at cars as they passed, a spiky holdover here and there from the punk movement, old guys in berets and wayfarers who might have stepped out of a jazz club in 1953. It wasn't so much like the hands of time had stood still here, more like they'd been thrown in the air in exasperation, the clock declaring, "Whatever! I'm outta here."

Esther Johnson's house was just a couple of blocks off Haight, and Charlie was lucky enough to find parking in a twenty-minute green zone nearby. (If the time came that he ever got to talk to someone in charge, he was going to make a case for special parking privileges for Death Merchants, for while it was nice that no one could see him when he was retrieving a soul vessel, some cool Death plates or "black" parking zones would be even better.)

The house was a small bungalow, unusual for this neighborhood, where most everything was three stories tall and painted in whatever color would contrast most with the house next to it. Charlie had taught Sophie her colors here, using grand Victorians as color swatches.

"Orange, Daddy. Orange."

"Yes, honey, the man barfed up orange. Look at that house, Sophie, it's purple."

The block did have its share of transients, so he knew the doors of the Johnson house would be locked. *Ring the bell and try to sneak through, or wait?* He really couldn't afford to wait — the sewer harpies had hissed at him from a grate as he approached the house. He rang the bell, then quickstepped to the side.

A pretty, dark-haired woman of about thirty, wearing jeans and a peasant blouse, opened the door, looked around, and said, "Hello, can I help you?"

Charlie nearly fell through a window. He looked behind his back, then back at the woman. No, she was looking right at him.

"Yes, you rang the bell?"

"Oh, me? Yes," Charlie said. "I'm, uh — you meant me, right?"

The woman stepped back into the house. "What can I do for you?" she said, a bit stern now.

"Oh, sorry — Charlie Asher — I own a secondhand store over in North Beach, I just talked to you on the phone, I think."

"Yes. But I told you that it wasn't important."

"Right, right, right. You did, but I was in the neighborhood, and I thought, well, I'd just drop by."

"I got the impression you were calling from your shop. You got all the way across town in five minutes?"

"Oh, right, well, the van is like a mobile shop to me."

"So the person who won the lotto is with you?"

"Right, no, he quit. I had to kick him out of the van. New money, you know? All full of himself. Will probably buy a big rock of cocaine and a half-dozen hookers and he'll be broke by the weekend. Good riddance, I say."

The woman backed another step into the house and pulled the door partway shut. "Well, if you have the clothes with you, I suppose I can take a look at them."

"Clothes?" Charlie couldn't believe she could see him. He was completely screwed now. He'd never get the soul vessel and then — well, he didn't want to think of what would happen then.

"The clothes you said you thought might belong to my aunt. I could look at them."

"Oh, I don't have those with me."

Now she had the door closed to the point where he could see just one blue eye, the embroidery around the neckline of her blouse, the button on her jeans, and two toes. (She was barefoot.) "Maybe you'd better check another time. I'm trying to get my aunt's things together, and I'm doing it all by myself, so it's a little hectic. She was in this house for forty-two years. I'm overwhelmed."

"That's why I'm here," Charlie said, thinking, *What the hell am I talking about?* "I do this all the time, uh, Ms. —"

"Mrs., actually. Mrs. Elizabeth Sarkoff."

"Well, Mrs. Sarkoff, I do this sort of thing a lot, and sometimes it can get overwhelming going through the possessions of a loved one, especially if they've been in one place for a long time like your aunt. It helps to have someone who doesn't have an emotional attachment to help sort things out. Plus, I have a pretty good eye for what's valuable and what's not."

Charlie wanted to give himself a high five for coming up with that on the spur of the moment.

"And do you charge for this service?"

"No, no, no, but I may make an offer to buy items you'd like to get rid of, or you can place them in my shop on consignment if you'd prefer."

Elizabeth Sarkoff sighed heavily and hung her head. "Are you sure? I wouldn't want to take advantage."

"It would be my pleasure," he said.

Mrs. Sarkoff swung the door wide. "Thank God you showed up, Mr. Asher. I just spent an hour trying to figure out which set of elephant salt-and-pepper shakers to keep and which to throw away. She has ten pairs! Ten! Please come in."

Charlie sauntered through the door feeling very proud of himself. Six hours later, when he was waist deep in porcelain-cow figurines, and he still hadn't located the soul vessel, he lost all sense of accomplishment.

"So she had a special connection to Holsteins?" Charlie called to Mrs. Sarkoff, who was in the next room, inside a walk-in closet, sorting through yet another huge pile of collectible crap.

"No, I don't think so. Lived her whole life here in the City. I'm not sure if she ever saw a cow outside of those talking ones that sell cheese on TV."

"Swell," Charlie said. He'd been through every inch of the house except the closet where Elizabeth Sarkoff was working and he hadn't found the soul vessel. He'd peeked into the closet a couple of times, taking a fast inventory of the contents, and didn't see anything glowing red. He was starting to suspect that either he was too late, and the Underworlders had gotten the soul vessel, or it had been buried with Esther Johnson.

He was heading down toward the basement again when his cell phone rang.

"Charlie Asher's phone," Charlie said.

"Charlie, it's Cassie. Sophie wants to know if you're going to come home in time to tell her a story and tuck her in. I gave her dinner and her bath."

Charlie ran up the stairs and looked out the front windows. It had gotten dark and he hadn't even noticed. "Crap, Cassie, I'm sorry. I didn't realize it was so late. I'm with an estate client. Tell her I'll be home to tuck her in."

"Okay, I will," Cassandra said, sounding exhausted. "And, Charlie, you can clean up the bathroom floor. You've got to do something about those dogs getting in the tub with her. There are drifts of Mr. Bubble suds all over your apartment."

"They do enjoy their bath."

"That's cute, Charlie. If I didn't love your sister I'd hire someone to break your legs."

"My mom just died, Cassie."

"You're playing the dead-mom card? Now? Charlie Asher, you —"

"Gotta go," Charlie said. "Be home soon." Charlie pushed the disconnect button four times, then one more time, just to be sure. Cassandra had been such a sweet woman, only days ago. What happened to people?

Charlie bounded into the bedroom. "Mrs. Sarkoff?"

"Yes, still in here," came a voice from the closet.

"I'm going to have to be going. My daughter needs me."

"I hope everything is all right."

"Yes, not an emergency, I've just been gone for a couple of days. Look, if you need any more help —"

"No, I wouldn't think of it. Why don't you give me a few days to sort things out and I'll bring some items by your shop."

"I don't mind, really." Charlie felt silly yelling to someone who was in a closet.

"No, I'll be in touch, I promise."

Charlie couldn't think of any way of pressing the situation right now, and he needed to get home.

"Okay, then. I'll be going."

"Thank you, Mr. Asher. You've been a lifesaver."

"You're welcome. Bye." Charlie let himself out and the front door locked behind him with a click. He could hear stirring below the street — the rustling of feathers, the distant calls of ravens — as he made his way back to where he had parked his van. And when he got there, of course, it had been towed.

When she heard the front door lock, Audrey went to the back of the closet and moved the big cardboard wardrobe box aside to reveal an elderly woman who was sitting calmly in a folding lawn chair, knitting.

"He's gone, Esther. You can come out now."

"Well, help me up, dear, I think I'm stuck like this," Esther said.

"I'm sorry," Audrey said. "I had no idea he'd stay that long."

"I don't understand why you let him in in the first place," Esther said, creaky but on her feet now.

"So he could satisfy his curiosity. See for himself."

"And where did you get that Elizabeth Sarkoff name?"

"My second-grade teacher. It was the first thing I could think of."

"Well, I guess you fooled him. I don't know how to thank you."

"He'll be back. You know that, right?" Audrey said.

"I hope not too soon," Esther said. "I really need to visit the powder room."

★ ★ ★

"Where is it, lover?" hissed the Morrigan from the grate on Haight Street, near where Charlie was trying to flag down a cab. "You're slipping, Meat," said the hellish chorus.

Charlie looked around to see if anyone else had heard, but passersby seemed very intent on their own conversations, or if alone, were staring intently at a point only twelve feet in front of them on the sidewalk, both strategies to avoid eye contact with the panhandlers and crazy people who lined the sidewalk. Not even the crazy people seemed to notice.

"Fuck off," Charlie said, in a furious whisper at the curb. "Fucking harpies."

"Oh, lover, this teasing is so delicious. The little one's blood will be so delicious!"

The young homeless guy sitting just down the curb looked up at Charlie. "Dude, get the clinic to up your lithium and they'll go away. It worked for me."

Charlie nodded and gave the guy a dollar. "Thanks, I'll look into that."

He'd have to call Jane in Arizona in the morning and find out how far the shadow had moved down the mesa, if it had moved. Why would what he did or didn't do in San Francisco affect what was happening in Sedona? All this time he'd been trying to convince himself that it wasn't about him, and now it appeared that it very much *was* about him. *The Luminatus will rise in the City of Two Bridges,* Vern had said. What kind of dependable prophecy can you get from a guy named Vern, anyway? (*Come on down to Vern's Discount Prophecy — The Nostradamus with the Low-Price Promise.*) It was absurd. He had to keep going forward, doing his part, and doing his best to collect the soul vessels that came to him. And if he didn't, well, the Forces of Darkness would rise and rule over the world. So what. Bring it on, sewer hoes! Big deal.

But his inner Beta Male, the gene that had kept his kind alive for three million years, spoke up: *Forces of Darkness ruling the world? Okay, that would be bad,* it said.

"She so loved the smell of Pine-Sol," said the third woman that day to claim to have been Charlie's mother's best friend. The funeral hadn't been so bad, but now there was a potluck in the clubhouse of a nearby gated senior community where Buddy had lived before he moved in with Charlie's mom. The couple had returned there often to play cards and socialize with Buddy's old crew.

"Did you get some sloppy joe?" asked best friend number three. Despite the hundred-degree heat, she wore a pink sweatsuit emblazoned with rhinestone poodles and carried a nervous little black poodle under her arm everywhere she went. The dog licked her potato salad while she was distracted by talking to Charlie. "I don't know if your mother ever ate sloppy joe. Only thing I ever saw her take in was an old-fashioned. She did enjoy her cocktails."

"Yes, she did," Charlie said. "And I think I'm going to go enjoy one myself, right now."

Charlie had flown into Sedona that morning after spending the night in San Francisco trying to find the two overdue soul vessels. Although he couldn't find a burial notice for Esther Johnson, the pretty brunette woman at her house had told him that she had been interred the day after he'd first gone to the house in the Haight, and he assumed that the soul vessel had been, once again, buried with her. (Was the brunette's name Elizabeth? Of course it was Elizabeth, he was fooling himself to even pretend to forget. Beta Males do not forget the names of pretty women. Charlie could remember the name of the centerfold of the first *Playboy* he'd ever swiped from the shelves in his dad's shop. He even remembered that her turnoffs were bad breath, mean people, and genocide, and resolved that he would never have, be, or commit any of those things, just in case he ran into her sometime when she was casually sunning her breasts on the hood of a car.) There was no trace of the other woman, Irena Posokovanovich, who was supposed to have died days ago. No notice, no records at hospitals, no one living in her house. It was as if she'd evaporated, and taken her soul vessel with her. He had a couple more weeks to get to the third name in his date book, but he wasn't sure what he was going to have to deal with to get to it. Darkness was rising.

Someone beside him said, "Small talk doesn't really get any smaller than when you've lost a loved one, huh?"

Charlie turned toward the voice, surprised to see Vern Glover, diminutive Death Merchant, munching some coleslaw and ranch beans.

"Thanks for coming," Charlie said automatically.

Vern waved off the thanks with his

plastic fork. "You saw the shadow?"

Charlie nodded. When he'd gotten to his mother's house this morning, the shadow of the mesa had reached his mother's front yard, and the calls of the carrion birds that churned in its edges were deafening. "You didn't tell me that no one else could see it. I called my sister from San Francisco to check the progress, but she didn't see anything."

"Sorry, they can't see it — at least as far as I've ever been able to tell they can't. It was gone for five days. It came back this morning."

"When I came back?"

"I guess. Did we cause this? Doughnuts and coffee and it's the end of the world?"

"I missed two souls back home," Charlie said, smiling at a gentleman in burgundy golf wear who held his hand to his heart in sympathy as he passed them.

"Missed? Did the — what did you call them — the *sewer harpies* get them?"

"Could be," Charlie said. "But whatever is happening, it seems to be following me."

"Sorry," Vern said. "I'm glad we talked, though. I don't feel so alone."

"Yeah," Charlie said.

"And sorry about your mother," Vern added quickly. "You okay?"

"Hasn't even hit me yet," Charlie said. "I guess I'm an orphan."

"I'll make sure and check out whoever gets her necklace," Vern said. "I'll be careful with it."

"Thanks," Charlie said. "You think we have any control over who gets the soul next? I mean really. The *Great Big Book* says it will move on as it should."

"I guess," Vern said. "Every time I've sold one the glow has gone out right away. If it wasn't the right person, that wouldn't happen, right?"

"Yeah, I guess so," Charlie said. "So there is some order to this."

"You're the expert," Vern said — then he dropped his fork. "Who is that? She's so hot."

"That's my sister," Charlie said. Jane was coming across the room toward them. She was wearing Charlie's charcoal double-breasted Armani and the strappy black pumps; her platinum hair was lacquered into thirties finger waves, which flowed out from under a small black hat with a veil that covered her face down to her lips, which shone like red Ferraris. To Charlie, she looked, as usual, like the cross between a robot assassin and a Dr. Seuss character, but if he tried to squint past the fact that she was his sister, and a lesbian, and his sister, then he could possibly see how the hair, lips, and sheer linear altitude of her might strike someone as hot. Especially someone like Vern, who would require climbing equipment and oxygen to scale a woman Jane's height.

"Vern, I'd like you to meet my incredibly hot sister, Jane. Jane, this is Vern."

"Hi, Vern." Jane took Vern's hand and the Death Merchant winced at her grip.

"Sorry for your loss," Vern said.

"Thanks," Jane said. "Did you know our mother?"

"Vern knew her very well," Charlie said. "In fact, it was one of Mom's dying wishes that you let Vern buy you a doughnut. Wasn't it, Vern?"

Vern nodded so hard that Charlie thought he could hear vertebrae cracking.

"Her dying wish," Vern said.

Jane didn't move, or say anything. Because her eyes were covered, Charlie couldn't see her expression, but he guessed that she might be trying to burn holes in his aorta with her laser-beam vision.

"You know, Vern, that would be lovely, but could I take a rain check? We just buried my mother and I have some things to go over with my brother."

"That's fine," Vern said. "And it doesn't have to be a doughnut, if you're watching your figure. You know, a salad, coffee, anything."

"Sure," Jane said. "Since it's what Mom wanted. I'll give you a call. Charlie told you I'm a lesbian, though, right?"

"Oh my God," Vern said. He almost doubled over with excitement before he remembered that he was at a postfuneral potluck and he was openly imagining a ménage à trois with the deceased's daughter. "Sorry," he squealed.

"See you, Vern," Charlie said as his sister hustled him toward the kitchen cubicle of the clubhouse. "I'll e-mail you about that other thing."

As soon as they rounded the corner into the kitchen Jane punched Charlie in the solar plexus, knocking the wind out of him.

"What were you thinking?" Jane hissed. She flipped back her veil so he could see just how pissed off she was, just in case the punch in the breadbasket hadn't conveyed the message.

Charlie was gasping and laughing at the same time. "It's what Mom would have wanted."

"My mom just died, Charlie."

"Yeah," Charlie said. "But you have no idea what you've just done for that guy in there."

"Really?" Jane raised an eyebrow.

"He will remember this day always," Charlie said. "That guy will never again have a sexual fantasy in which you do not walk through, probably wearing borrowed shoes."

"And you don't find that creepy?"

"Well, yes, you're my sister, but it's a seminal moment for Vern."

Jane nodded. "You're a pretty good guy, Charlie, looking out for a tiny stranger like that."

"Yeah, well, you know —"

"For an ass bag!" Jane said as she sank a fist into Charlie's solar plexus.

Strangely, as he gasped for breath, Charlie felt that wherever his mother was right now, she was pleased with him.

Bye, Mom, he thought.

PART THREE

Battleground

Tomorrow we shall meet,
Death and I —
And he shall thrust his sword
Into one who is wide awake.
                    — *Dag Hammarskjöld*

19

We're Okay, as Long as Things Don't Get Weird

ALVIN AND MOHAMMED

When Charlie arrived home from his mother's funeral, he was met at the door by two very large, very enthusiastic canines, who, undistracted by keeping watch over Sophie's love hostage, were now able to visit the full measure of their affection and joy upon their returning master. It is generally agreed, and in fact stated in the bylaws of the American Kennel Club, that you have not been truly dog-humped until you have been double-dog-humped by a pair of four-hundred-pound hounds from hell (Section 5, paragraph 7: Standards of Humping and Ass-dragging). And despite having used an extra-strength antiperspirant that very morning before leaving

Sedona, Charlie found that getting poked repeatedly in the armpits by two damp devil-dog dicks was leaving him feeling less than fresh.

"Sophie, call them off. Call them off."

"The puppies are dancing with Daddy." Sophie giggled. "Dance, Daddy!"

Mrs. Ling covered Sophie's eyes to shield her from the abomination of her father's unwilling journey into bestiality. "Go wash hands, Sophie. Have lunch while you daddy make nasty with shiksas." Mrs. Ling couldn't help but do a quick appraisal of the monetary value of the slippery red dogwoods currently pummeling her landlord's oxford-cloth shirt like piston-driven leviathan lipsticks. The herbalist in Chinatown would pay a fortune for a powder made from the desiccated members of Alvin and Mohammed. (The men of her homeland would go to any length to enhance their virility, including grinding up endangered species and brewing them in tea, not unlike certain American presidents, who believe there is no stiffy like the one you get from bombing a few thousand foreigners.) Yet it appeared that the desiccated-dog-dick fortune would remain unclaimed. Mrs. Ling had long ago given up on collecting hellhound bits, when after trying to dispatch Alvin with a sharp and ringing blow to the cranium from her cast-iron skillet, he bit the skillet off its handle, crunched it down in a slurry of dog drool and iron filings, and then sat up and begged for seconds.

"Throw some water on them!" Charlie cried. "Down, doggies. Good doggies. Oh, yuck."

Mrs. Ling was galvanized into action by Charlie's distress call, and timing her move with the oscillating pyramid of man and dog meat in the doorway, dashed by Charlie, into the hallway, and down the steps.

LILY

Lily came up the stairs and skidded to a stop on the hallway carpet when she saw the hellhounds pounding away at Charlie. "Oh, Asher, you sick bastard!"

"Help," Charlie said.

Lily pulled the fire extinguisher off the wall, dragged it to the doorway, pulled the pin, and proceeded to unload on the bouncing trio. Two minutes later Charlie was collapsed in a frosty heap on the threshold and Alvin and Mohammed were locked in

Charlie's bedroom, where they were joyfully chewing away on the expended fire extinguisher. Lily had lured them in there when they had tried to bite the CO_2 stream, seeming to enjoy the freezing novelty of it over the welcome-home humping they were giving Charlie.

"You okay?" Lily said. She was wearing one of her chef coats over a red leather skirt and knee-high platform boots.

"It's been kind of a rough week," Charlie said.

She helped him to his feet, trying to avoid touching the damp spots on his shirt. Charlie did a controlled fall toward the couch. Lily helped him land, ending with one arm pinned awkwardly under his back.

"Thanks," Charlie said. There was still frost in his hair and eyelashes from the fire extinguisher.

"Asher," Lily said, trying not to look him in the eye. "I'm not comfortable with this, but I think, given the situation, that it's time I said something."

"Okay, Lily. You want some coffee?"

"No. Please shut up. Thank you." She paused and took a deep breath, but did not extricate her arm from behind Charlie's back. "You have been good to me over the years, and although I would not admit this to anyone else, I probably wouldn't have finished school or turned out as well as I have if it hadn't been for your influence."

Charlie was still trying to see, blinking away ice crystals on his eyelids, thinking that maybe his eyeballs were frostbitten. "It was nothing," he said.

"Please, please, shut up," Lily said. Another deep breath. "You have always been decent to me, despite what I would call some of my bitchier moments, and in spite of the fact that you are some dark death dude, and probably had other things to worry about — sorry about your mom, by the way."

"Thanks," Charlie said.

"Well, given what I've heard about your night out before your mom died and whatnot, and what I've seen here today, I think — that it's only right — that I do you."

"Do me?"

"Yes," she said, "for the greater good, even though you are a complete tool."

Charlie squirmed away from her on the couch. He looked at her for a second, trying to figure out if she was putting him on, then, deciding that she wasn't, he said, "That's very sweet of you, Lily, and —"

"Nothing weird, Asher. You need to understand that I'm only doing this out of basic human decency and pity. You can just take it to the hoes on Broadway if you need to get your freak on."

"Lily, I don't know what —"

"And not in the butt," Lily added.

There was a high-pitched little-girl giggle from behind the couch. "Hi, Daddy," Sophie said, popping up behind him. "I missed you."

Charlie swung her up over the back of the couch and gave her a big kiss. "I missed you, too, sweetie."

Sophie pushed him away. "How come you have frosting on your hair?"

"Oh, that — Lily had to spray some frost on Alvin and Mohammed to settle them down and it got on me."

"They missed you, too."

"I could tell," Charlie said. "Honey, could you go play in your room for a bit while I talk to Lily about business?"

"Where are the puppies?" Sophie asked.

"They're having a T.O. in Daddy's room. Can you go play and we'll have some Cheese Newts in a little while?"

"Okay," Sophie said, sliding to the floor. "Bye, Lily." She waved to Lily.

"Bye, Sophie," Lily said, looking even

more pale than usual.

Sophie marched away in rhythm to her new chant, "Not in the butt — not in the butt — not in the butt."

Charlie turned to face Lily. "Well, that ought to liven up Mrs. Magnussen's first-grade class."

"Sure, it's embarrassing now," Lily said, without missing a beat, "but someday she'll thank me."

Charlie tried to look at his shirt buttons as if he were deep in thought, but instead started to giggle, tried to stop, and ended up snorting a little. "Jeez, Lily, you're like a little sister to me, I could never —"

"Oh, fine. I offer you a gift, out of the goodness of my heart, and you —"

"Coffee, Lily," Charlie said with a sigh. "Could I just get you to make me a cup of coffee instead of doing me — and sit and talk to me while I drink it? You're the only one who knows what's going on with Sophie and me, and I need to try to sort things out."

"Well, that will probably take longer than doing you," Lily said, looking at her watch. "Let me call down to the store and tell Ray that I'll be a while."

"That would be great," Charlie said.

"I was only going to do you in exchange

for information about your Death Merchant thing, anyway," Lily said, picking up the phone on the breakfast bar.

Charlie sighed again. "That's what I need to sort out."

"Either way," Lily said, "I'm unbending on the butt issue."

Charlie tried to nod gravely, but started giggling again. Lily chucked the San Francisco Yellow Pages at him.

THE MORRIGAN

"This soul smells like ham," said Nemain, wrinkling her nose at a lump of meat she had impaled on one long claw.

"I want some," said Babd. "Gimme." She slashed at the carrion with her own talons, snagging a fist-sized hunk of flesh in the process.

The three were in a forgotten subbasement beneath Chinatown, lounging on timbers that had been burned black in the great fire of 1906. Macha, who was starting to manifest the pearl headdress she wore in her woman form, studied the skull of a small animal by the light of a candle she'd made from the fat of dead babies. (Macha was ever the artsy-craftsy one, and the other two were jealous of her skills.) "I don't understand why the soul is in the meat, but not in a man."

"Tastes like ham, too, I think," Nemain said, spitting glowing red bits of soul when she talked. "Macha, do you remember ham? Do we like it?"

Babd ate her bit of meat and wiped her claws on her breast feathers. "I think ham is new," she said, "like cell phones."

"Ham is not new," Macha said. "It's smoked pork."

"No," said Babd, aghast.

"Yes," said Macha.

"Not human flesh? Then how is there a soul in it?"

"Thank you," Macha said. "That's what I've been trying to say."

"I've decided that we like ham," said Nemain.

"There's something wrong," Macha said. "It shouldn't be this easy."

"Easy?" said Babd. "Easy? It's taken hundreds — no, thousands of years to get this far. How many thousands of years, Nemain?" Babd looked to the poison sister.

"Many," said Nemain.

"Many," said Babd. "Many thousands of years. That's not easy."

"Souls coming to us, without bodies, without the soul stealers, that seems too easy."

"I like it," Nemain said.

They were quiet for a moment, Nemain nibbled at the glowing soul, Babd preened, and Macha studied the animal skull, turning it over in her talons.

"I think it's a woodchuck," Macha said.

"Can you make ham from woodchuck?" Nemain asked.

"Don't know," said Macha.

"I don't remember woodchuck," Nemain said.

Babd sighed heavily. "Things are going so well. Do you two ever think about when we are Above all the time, and Darkness rules all, about, you know, what then?"

"What do you mean, what then?" Macha asked. "We will hold dominion over all souls, and visit death as we wish until we consume all the light of humanity."

"Yeah, I know," Babd said, "but then what? I mean, you know, dominion and all that is nice, but will Orcus always have to be around, snorting and growling?"

Macha put down her skull and sat up on a blackened beam. "What's this about?"

Nemain smiled, her teeth perfectly even, the canines just a little too long. "She's pining about that skinny soul stealer with the sword."

"New Meat?" Macha couldn't believe her ears, which had become visible only a few days ago when the first of the *gift souls* had wandered into their claws, so they hadn't been tested in a while. "You like New Meat?"

"*Like* is a little strong," Babd said. "I just think he's interesting."

"Interesting in that you'd like to arrange his entrails in interesting patterns in the dirt?" Macha said.

"Well, no, I'm not talented that way like you."

Macha looked at Nemain, who grinned and shrugged. "We could probably try to kill Orcus once Darkness rises," Nemain said.

"I am a little tired of his preaching, and he'll be impossible if the Luminatus doesn't appear." Macha shrugged a surrender. "Sure, why not."

THE EMPEROR

The Emperor of San Francisco was troubled. He sensed that something very wrong was going on in the City, yet he was at a loss as to what to do. He didn't want to alarm the people unduly, but he did not

405

want them to be unprepared for whatever danger they might face. He believed that a just and benevolent ruler would not use fear to manipulate his people, and until he had some sort of proof that there was an actual threat, it would be criminal to call for any action.

"Sometimes," he said to Lazarus, the steadfast golden retriever, "a man must muster all of his courage to simply sit still. How much humanity has been spoiled for the confusion of movement with progress, my friend? How much?"

Still, he'd been seeing things, strange things. One late night in Chinatown he'd seen a dragon made of fog snaking through the streets. Then, early one morning, down by the Boudin Bakery at Ghirardelli Square, he saw what looked like a nude woman covered in motor oil crawl out of a storm sewer and grab a tall, half-full latte cup out of the trash, then dive right back in the sewer as a policeman on a bicycle rounded the corner. He knew that he saw these things because he was more sensitive than other people, and because he lived on the streets and could sense the slightest nuance of change there, and largely because he was completely barking-at-the-moon batshit. But none of that relieved him of the responsibility to his people, nor did it ease his mind about the disturbing nature of what he was seeing.

The squirrel in the hoop skirt was really bothering the Emperor, but he couldn't exactly say why. He liked squirrels — often took the men to Golden Gate Park to chase them, in fact — but a squirrel walking upright and digging through the trash behind the Empanada Emporium while wearing a pink ball gown from the eighteenth century — well — it was off-putting. He was sure that Bummer, who was curled up sleeping in the oversized pocket of his coat, would agree. (Bummer, being a rat dog at heart, had a less than enlightened outlook upon coexistence with any rodent, no less one dressed for the court of Louis XVI.)

"Not to be critical," said the Emperor, "but shoes would be a welcome complement to the ensemble, don't you think, Lazarus?"

Lazarus, normally tolerant of all non-cookie creatures great and small, growled at the squirrel, who appeared to have the feet of a chicken sticking out from under her skirt, which — you know — was weird.

With the growl, Bummer squirmed awake and emerged from the woolen bed-chamber like Grendel from his lair. He immediately erupted into an apoplectic barking fit, as if to say, *You guys, in case you didn't notice, there's a squirrel in a ball gown going through the trash over there and you're just sitting here like a couple of concrete library lions!* The message thus barked, off he went, a furry squirrel-seeking missile, bent on single-minded annihilation of all things rodent.

"Bummer," called the Emperor. "Wait."

Too late. The squirrel had tried to take off up the side of the brick building, but snagged her skirt on a gutter and fell back to the alley, just as Bummer was hitting full stride. Then the squirrel snatched up a small board from a broken pallet and swung it at his pursuer, who leapt just in time to miss taking a nail in one of his bug eyes.

Growling ensued.

The Emperor noticed at that point that the squirrel's hands were reptilian in nature, the fingernails painted a pleasant pink to match her gown.

"You don't see that every day," the Emperor said. Lazarus barked in agreement.

The squirrel dropped the board and took off toward the street, moving nicely on her chicken feet, her skirt held up in her lizard hands. Bummer had recovered from the initial shock of a weapon-wielding squirrel (something he had encountered before only in doggie nightmares brought on by the late-night gift of chorizo pizza from a charitable Domino's guy) and took off after the squirrel, followed closely by the Emperor and Lazarus.

"No, Bummer," the Emperor called. "She's not a normal squirrel."

Lazarus, because he did not know how to say "well, duh," stopped in his tracks and looked at the Emperor.

The squirrel rocketed out of the alley and took a quick turn down the gutter, falling now to all fours as she went.

Just as he reached the corner, the Emperor saw the trail of the tiny pink dress disappear down a storm sewer, followed closely by the intrepid Bummer. The Emperor could hear the terrier's bark echoing out of the grate, fading as Bummer pursued his prey into the darkness.

RIVERA

Nick Cavuto sat down across from Rivera with a plate of buffalo stew roughly the size of a garbage-can lid. They were having lunch at Tommy's Joynt, an old-school eatery on Van Ness that served home-style food like meat loaf, roasted turkey and stuffing, and buffalo stew every day of the year, and featured San Francisco sports teams on the TV over the bar whenever anyone was playing.

"What?" said the big cop, when he saw his partner roll his eyes. "Fucking what?"

"Buffalo almost went extinct once," Rivera said. "You have ancestors on the Great Plains?"

"Special law enforcement portions — protecting and serving and stuff requires protein."

"A whole bison?"

"Do I criticize your hobbies?"

Rivera looked at his half a turkey sandwich and cup of bean soup, then at Cavuto's stew, then at his runt of a sandwich, then at his partner's colossus of a stew. "My lunch is embarrassed," he said.

"Serves you right. Revenge for the Italian suits. I love going to every call with people thinking I'm the victim."

"You could buy a steamer, or I could have my guy find you some nice clothes."

"Your guy the serial-killing thrift-store owner? No thanks."

"He's not a serial killer. He's got some

weird shit going on, but he's not a killer."

"Just what we need, more weird shit. What was he really doing when you had that shots-fired report?"

"Just like it said, I was going by and a guy tried to rob him at gunpoint. I drew my weapon and told the perp to halt, he drew down on me, and I fired."

"Your ass. You never fired eleven shots in your life you didn't hit the ten X ring with nine of them. The fuck happened?"

Rivera looked down the long table, made sure the three guys sitting down at the other end were engaged in the game showing on the TV over the bar. "I hit her with every shot."

"Her? Perp was a woman?"

"I didn't say that."

Cavuto dropped his spoon. "Partner? Don't tell me you shot the redhead? I thought that was over."

"No. This was a new thing — like — Nick, you know me, I'm not going to fire unless it's justified."

"Just say what happened. I got your back."

"It was like this bird woman or something. All black. I mean fucking black as tar. Had claws that looked like — I don't know, like three-inch-long silver ice picks or something. My shots took chunks out of her — feathers and black goo and shit everywhere. She took nine in the torso and flew away."

"Flew?"

Rivera sipped his coffee, eyeing his partner's reaction over the edge of the cup. They had been through some extraordinary things working together, but if the situation had been reversed, he wasn't sure he'd believe this story either. "Yeah, flew."

Cavuto nodded. "Okay, I can see why you wouldn't put that in the report."

"Yeah."

"So this bird woman," Cavuto said, like that was settled, he totally believed it, now what? "She was robbing the Asher guy from the thrift shop?"

"Giving him a hand job."

Cavuto nodded, picked up his spoon, and took a huge bite of stew and rice, still nodding as he chewed. He looked as if he were going to say something, then quickly took another bite, as if to stop himself. He appeared to be distracted by the game on television, and finished his lunch without another word.

Rivera ate his soup and sandwich in silence as well.

As they were leaving, Cavuto grabbed

two toothpicks from the dispenser by the register and gave one to Rivera as they walked out into a beautiful San Francisco day.

"So you were following Asher?"

"I've been trying to keep an eye on him. Just in case."

"And you shot her nine times for giving the guy a hand job," Cavuto finally asked.

"I guess," Rivera said.

"You know, Alphonse, that right there is why I don't hang out with you socially. Your values are fucked up."

"She wasn't human, Nick."

"Still. A hand job? Deadly force? I don't know —"

"It wasn't deadly force. I didn't kill her."

"Nine to the chest?"

"I saw her — it — last night. On my street. Watching me from a storm sewer."

"Ever think to ask Asher how he happened to know the flying bulletproof bird woman in the first place?"

"Yeah, I did, but I can't tell you what he said. It's too weird."

Cavuto threw his arms in the air. "Well, sweet Tidy Bowl Jesus skipping on the blue toilet water, we wouldn't want it to get fucking weird, would we?"

LILY

They were on their second cup of coffee and Charlie had told Lily about not getting the two soul vessels, about the encounter with the sewer harpy, about the shadow coming out of the mountains in Sedona and the other version of *The Great Big Book of Death*, and his suspicions that there was a frightening problem with his little girl, the symptoms of which were two giant dogs and an ability to kill with the word *kitty*. To Charlie's thinking, Lily was reacting to the wrong story.

"You hooked up with a demon from the Underworld and I'm not good enough for you?"

"It's not a competition, Lily. Can we not talk about that? I knew I shouldn't have told you. I'm worried about other stuff."

"I want details, Asher."

"Lily, a gentleman doesn't share the details of his amorous encounters."

Lily crossed her arms and assumed a pose of disgusted incredulity, an eloquent pose, because before she said it, Charlie knew what was coming: "Bullshit. That cop shot pieces off her, but you're worried about protecting her honor?"

Charlie smiled wistfully. "You know, we

shared a moment —"

"Oh my God, you complete man-whore!"

"Lily, you can't possibly be hurt by my — by my response to your generous — and let me say right here — extraordinarily tempting offer. Gee whiz."

"It's because I'm too perky, isn't it? Not dark enough for you? You being Mr. Death and all."

"Lily, the shadow in Sedona was coming for *me*. When I left town, it went away. The sewer harpy came for *me*. The other Death Merchant said that I was different. They never had deaths happen as a result of their presence like I have."

"Did you just say 'gee whiz' to me? What am I, nine? I am a woman —"

"I think I might be the Luminatus, Lily."

Lily shut up.

She raised her eyebrows. As if *"no."*

Charlie nodded. As if *"yes."*

"The Big Death?"

"With a capital *D*," Charlie said.

"Well, you're totally not qualified for that," Lily said.

"Thanks, I feel better now."

Being two hundred feet under the sea always made Minty uneasy, especially if he'd been drinking sake and listening to jazz all night, which he had. He was in the last car on the last train out of Oakland, and he had the car to himself, like his own private submarine, cruising under the Bay with the echo of a tenor sax in his ear like sonar, and a half-dozen sake-sodden spicy tuna rolls sitting in his stomach like depth charges.

He'd spent his evening at Sato's on the Embarcadero, Japanese restaurant and jazz club. Sushi and jazz, strange bedfellows, shacked up by opportunity and oppression. It began in the Fillmore district, which had been a Japanese neighborhood before World War II. When the Japanese were shipped off to internment camps, and their homes and belongings sold off, the blacks, who came to the city to work in the shipyards building battleships and destroyers, moved into the vacant buildings. Jazz came close behind.

For years, the Fillmore was the center of the San Francisco jazz scene, and Bop City on Post Street the premier jazz club. When the war ended and the Japanese returned, many a late night might find Japanese kids standing under the windows of Bop City, listening to the likes of Billie Holiday, Oscar Peterson, or Charles Mingus, listening to art happen and dissipate into the San Francisco nights. Sato was one of those kids.

It wasn't just historical happenstance — Sato had explained to Minty, late one night after the music had ended and the sake was making him wax eloquent — it was philosophical alignment: jazz was a Zen art, dig? Controlled spontaneity. Like *sumi-e* ink painting, like haiku, like archery, like kendo fencing — jazz wasn't something you planned, it was something you did. You practiced, you played your scales, you learned your chops, then you brought all your knowledge, your conditioning, to the moment. "And in jazz, every moment is a crisis," Sato quoted Wynton Marsalis, "and you bring all your skill to bear on that crisis." Like the swordsman, the archer, the poet, and the painter — it's all right there — no future, no past, just that moment and how you deal with it. Art happens.

And Minty, taken by the need to escape his life as Death, had taken the train to Oakland to find a moment he could hide in, without the regret of the past or the anxiety of the future, just a pure *right now* resting in the bell of a tenor sax. But the sake, too much future looming ahead, and too much water overhead had brought on the blues, the moment melted, and Minty was uneasy. Things were going badly. He'd been unable to retrieve his last two soul vessels — a first in his career — and he was starting to see, or hear, the effects. Voices out of the storm sewers — louder and more numerous than ever — taunting him. Things moving in the shadows, on the periphery of his vision, shuffling, scuffling dark things that disappeared when you looked right at them.

He'd even sold three discs off the soul-vessels rack to the same person, another first. He hadn't noticed it was the same woman right away, but when things started to go wrong, the faces played back and he realized. She'd been a monk the first time, a Buddhist monk of some kind, wearing gold-and-maroon robes, her hair very short, as if her head had been shaved and was growing out. What he remembered was that her eyes were a crystal blue, unusual in someone with such dark hair and skin. And there was a smile deep in those eyes that made him feel as if a soul had found its rightful place, a good home at a higher level. The next time he'd seen her was six months later and she was in jeans and leather jacket, her hair sort of out of control. She'd taken a CD from the "One Per Customer" rack, a Sarah McLachlan, which is what he'd have chosen for her if asked, and he barely noticed the crystal-blue eyes other than to think that he'd seen that smile before. Then, last week, it was her again, with hair down around her shoulders, wearing a long skirt and a belted muslin poet's shirt — like an escapee from a Renaissance fair, not unusual for the Haight, but not quite common in the Castro — still, he thought nothing of it, until she had paid him and glanced over the top of her sunglasses to count the cash out of her wallet. The blue eyes again, electric and not quite smiling this time. He didn't know what to do. He had no proof she was the monk, the chick in the leather jacket, but he knew it was her. He brought all his skills to bear on the situation, and essentially, he folded.

"So you like Mozart?" he asked her.

"It's for a friend" was all she said.

He rationalized not confronting her by that simple statement. A soul vessel was supposed to find its rightful owner, right?

419

It didn't say he had to sell it *directly* to them. That had been a week ago, and since then the voices, the scuffling noises in the shadows, the general creepiness, had been nearly constant. Minty Fresh had spent most of his adult life alone, but never before had he felt the loneliness so profoundly. A dozen times in the last few weeks he'd been tempted to call one of the other Death Merchants under the pretense of warning them about his screwup, but mainly just to talk to someone who had a clue about what his life was like.

He stretched his long legs out over three train seats and into the aisle, then closed his eyes and laid his head back against the window, feeling the rhythm of the rattling train coming through the cool glass against his shaved scalp. Oh no, that wasn't going to work. Too much sake and something akin to *bed spins*. He jerked his head forward and opened his eyes, then noticed through the doors that the train had gone dark two cars up. He sat upright and watched as the lights went out in the next car — no, that's not what happened. Darkness moved through the car like a flowing gas, taking the energy out of the lights as it went.

"Oh, shit," Minty said to the empty car.

He couldn't even stand up inside the train, but stand up he did, staying slumped a little, his head against the ceiling, but facing the flowing darkness.

The door at the end of the car opened and someone stepped through. A woman. Well, not exactly a woman. What looked like the shadow of a woman.

"Hey, lover," it said. A low voice, smoky.

He'd heard this voice before, or a voice like it.

The darkness flowed around the two floor lights at the far end of the car, leaving the woman illuminated in outline only, a gunmetal reflection against pure blackness. Since he was first tapped as a Death Merchant, Minty had never remembered feeling afraid, but he was afraid now.

"I'm not your lover," Minty said, his voice as smooth and steady as a bass sax, not giving up a note of fear. *A crisis in every moment,* he thought.

"Once you've had black, you never go back," she said, taking a step toward him, her blue-black outline the only thing visible in any direction now.

He knew there was a door a few feet behind him that was held shut with powerful hydraulics, and that led to a dark tunnel two hundred feet under the Bay, lined with a deadly electric rail — but for some reason, that sounded like a really friendly place to be right now.

"I've had black," said Minty.

"No, you haven't, lover. You've had shades of brown, dark cocoa and coffee maybe, but I promise you, you've never had black. Because once you do, you *never ever* come back."

He watched as she moved toward him — flowed toward him — and long silver claws sprouted from her fingertips, playing in the dim glow from the safety lights, dripping something that steamed when it hit the floor. There were scurrying sounds on either side of him, things moving in the darkness, low and quick.

"Okay, good point," Minty said.

20

Attack of the Crocodile Guy

It was a brutally hot night in the City, and everyone had their windows open. From the roof across the alley, the spy could see the little girl happily splashing away in a tub full of suds, the two giant hounds sitting just outside the tub licking shampoo from her hand and belching bubbles as she screeched with glee.

"Sophie, don't feed the puppies soap, okay?" The shopkeeper's voice from another room.

"Okay, Dad. I won't. I'm not a kid, you know," she said, pouring more strawberry-kiwi shampoo into her palm and holding it out for one of the dogs to lick. A cloud of fragrant bubbles burped out of the beast, through the bars of the window, and out into the still air over the alley.

The hounds were the problem, but if the spy had his timing right, he'd be able to take care of them and get to the child without interference.

In the past he'd been an assassin, a bodyguard, a kickboxer, and most recently a certified fiberglass-insulation installer — skills that could serve him well in his current mission. He had the face of a crocodile — sixty-eight spiked teeth and eyes that gleamed like black glass beads. His hands were the claws of a raptor, the wicked black nails encrusted with dried blood. He wore a black silk tuxedo, but no shoes — his feet were webbed like those of a waterbird, with claws for digging prey from the mud.

He rolled the large Persian rug to the edge of the roof and waited; then, just as he had planned, he heard, "Sweetie, I'm going to take the trash out, I'll be right back."

"Okay, Dad."

Funny how the illusion of security can make us careless, the spy thought. No one would leave a young child alone in the bath unattended, but the company of two canine bodyguards wouldn't make her unattended, would it?

He waited, and the shopkeeper emerged from the steel door downstairs carrying two trash bags. He seemed momentarily thrown off by the fact that the Dumpster, which was normally right outside the door, had been moved down the alley twenty feet or so, but shrugged, kicked the door wide, and while it hissed slowly shut on its pneumatic cylinder, he dashed for the Dumpster. That's when the spy sent the rug off the roof. The rug unrolled as it fell the four stories. Unfurled, it hit the shopkeeper with a substantial thud and drove him to the ground.

In the bathroom, the huge dogs perked up. One let out a woof of caution.

The spy already had the first bolt in his crossbow. Now he let it fly — nylon line hissed out and the bolt hit the rug with a thump, penetrating the rug and probably the shopkeeper's calf, effectively pinning him under the rug, perhaps even to the ground. The shopkeeper screamed. The great hounds dashed out of the bathroom.

The spy loaded another bolt, attached it to the free end of the nylon line attached to the first bolt, then fired it through another section of the rug below. The shopkeeper continued to shout, but with the heavy rug pinned over him, he couldn't move. As the spy loaded his third bolt the hounds burst through the doorway into the alley.

The third bolt wasn't attached to a line,

but had a wicked titanium-spiked tip. The spy aimed at the pneumatic cylinder on the door, hit it, and the door slammed shut, locking the hounds in the alley. He'd practiced this a dozen times in his mind, and it was all going exactly as planned. The front doors to the shop and the apartment building had been Super Glued shut before he'd come up on the roof — no easy job getting that done without being seen.

His fourth shot put a bolt in the window frame over the hall window. The bars on the bathroom were too narrow, but he knew that the shopkeeper would have left the door to the apartment open. He attached a carabiner to the nylon line and slid silently down the line to the window ledge. He unclipped, then squeezed through the bars and dropped to the floor in the hallway.

He kept close to the hall walls, taking careful, exaggerated steps to keep his toenails from catching on the carpet. He could smell onions cooking in a nearby apartment and hear the child's voice coming from the door down the hall, which he could see was open, if only a crack.

"Dad, I'm ready to get out! Dad, I'm ready to get out!"

He paused at the doorway, peeked into the apartment. He knew the child would scream when she saw him — his jagged teeth, the claws, his cold black eyes. He would see to it that her screams were short-lived, but nobody could remain calm in the face of his fearsomeness. Of course, the fearsome effect was somewhat reduced by the fact that he was only fourteen inches tall.

He pushed the door open, but as he stepped into the apartment something grabbed him from behind, yanking him off his feet, and in spite of his training and stealth skills, he screamed like a flaming wood duck.

Someone had Super Glued the key slot in the back door and Charlie had snapped his key off trying to get it open. There was some kind of arrow stuck on a string through the back of his leg and it hurt like hell — blood was filling up his shoe. He didn't know what had happened, but he knew it wasn't good that the hellhounds were bouncing around him whimpering.

He pounded the door with both fists. "Open the goddamn door, Ray!"

Ray opened the door. "What?"

The hellhounds knocked them both

down going through the door. Charlie jumped to his feet and limped after them, up the steps. Ray followed.

"Charlie, you're bleeding."

"I know."

"Wait, you're dragging some kind of line. Let me cut it."

"Ray, I've got to go —"

Before Charlie could finish his sentence, Ray had pulled a knife from his back pocket, flicked it open, and cut the nylon line. "Used to carry this on the job to cut seat belts and stuff."

Charlie nodded and headed up the steps. Sophie was standing in the kitchen, wrapped in a mint-green bath towel, shampoo horns still protruding from her head — she looked like a small, soapy version of the Statue of Liberty. "Dad, where were you? I wanted to get out."

"Are you okay, honey?" He knelt in front of her and smoothed down her towel.

"I needed help on the rinse. That's your responsibility, Dad."

"I know, honey. I'm a horrible father."

"Okay —" Sophie said. "Hi, Ray."

Ray was topping the steps, holding a bloody arrow on the end of a string. "Charlie, this went through your leg."

Charlie turned and looked at his calf for

the first time, then sat on the floor, sure that he was going to pass out.

"Can I have it?" Sophie said, picking up the arrow.

Ray grabbed a dish towel from the counter and pressed it on Charlie's wound. "Hold this on it. I'll call 911."

"No, I'm okay," Charlie said, pretty sure now he was going to throw up.

"What happened out there?" Ray said.

"I don't know, I was —"

Someone in the building started screaming like they were being deep-fried. Ray's eyes went wide.

"Help me up," Charlie said.

They ran through the apartment and out into the hall — the screaming was coming from the stairwell.

"Can you make it?" Ray said.

"Go. Go. I'm with you." Charlie steadied himself against Ray's shoulder and hopped up the stairs behind him.

The harsh screaming coming from Mrs. Ling's apartment had dwindled to pleas for help in English, peppered with swearing in Mandarin. "No! Shiksas! Help! Back! Help!"

Charlie and Ray found the diminutive Chinese matron backed against her stove by Alvin and Mohammed, swinging a

429

cleaver at them to keep them at bay while they barked salvos of strawberry-kiwi-flavored bubbles at her.

"Help! Shiksas try to take supper," said Mrs. Ling.

Charlie saw the stockpot steaming on the stove, a pair of duck feet sticking out of it. "Mrs. Ling, is that duck wearing trousers?"

She looked quickly, then turned and took a swipe at the hellhounds with the cleaver. "Could be," she said.

"Down, Alvin. Down, Mohammed," Charlie commanded, which the hellhounds ignored completely. He turned to Ray. "Ray, would you go get Sophie?"

The ex-cop, who felt himself the master of all situations chaotic, said, "Huh?"

"They won't back off unless she tells them to. Go get her, okay." Charlie turned to Mrs. Ling. "Sophie will call them off, Mrs. Ling. I'm sorry."

Mrs. Ling had been considering her dinner. She tried to shove the duck feet under the broth with her cleaver, but to little effect. "Is ancient Chinese recipe. We don't tell White Devils about it so you don't ruin it. You hear of paper-wrap chicken? This duck in pants."

The hellhounds growled.

"Well, I'm sure it's delicious," Charlie said, leaning against her fridge so he didn't fall over.

"You bleeding, Mr. Asher."

"Yes, I am," Charlie said.

Ray arrived, carrying the towel-wrapped Sophie. He set her down.

"Hi, Mrs. Ling," Sophie said, then she stepped out of her towel, went to the hellhounds, and grabbed them by their collars. "You guys didn't rinse," she said. Then, buck naked, her hair still in shampoo spikes, Sophie led the hellhounds out of Mrs. Ling's apartment.

"Uh, someone shot you, boss," Ray said.

"Yes, they did," said Charlie.

"You should get medical attention."

"Yes, I should," Charlie said. His eyes rolled back in his head and he slid down the front of Mrs. Ling's refrigerator.

Charlie spent the entire night in the emergency room of St. Francis Memorial waiting for treatment. Ray Macy stayed with him the whole time. While Charlie enjoyed the screaming and whimpering from the other patients waiting for treatment, the retching and pervasive barf smell began to wear on him after a while. When he started to turn green, Ray tried to use

431

his ex-cop status to gain favor with the head ER nurse, whom he had known in that old life.

"He's hurt bad. Can't you sneak him in somewhere? He's a good guy, Betsy."

Nurse Betsy grinned (which was the expression she used in lieu of telling people to fuck off) and scanned the waiting room to make sure that no one seemed particularly attentive. "Can you get him to the window?"

"Sure," Ray said. He helped Charlie out of his chair and got him to the little bulletproof window. "This is Charlie Asher," Ray said. "My friend."

Charlie looked at Ray.

"I mean my boss," Ray added quickly.

"Mr. Asher, are you going to die on me?"

"Hope not," Charlie said. "But you might want to ask someone with more medical experience than me."

Nurse Betsy grinned.

"He's been shot," Ray said, ever the advocate.

"I didn't see who shot me," Charlie said. "It's a mystery."

Nurse Betsy leaned into the window. "You know we have to report all gunshot wounds to the authorities. Are you sure you don't want to take a veterinarian hostage and have him sew you up?"

"I don't think my insurance will cover that," Charlie said.

"Besides, it wasn't a gunshot," Ray added. "It was an arrow."

Nurse Betsy nodded. "Let me see?"

Charlie started to roll up his pant leg and lift his leg up on the little counter. Nurse Betsy reached through the little window and knocked his foot off the shelf. "For Christ's sakes, don't let the others see I'm looking."

"Ouch, sorry."

"Is it still bleeding?"

"No, I don't think so."

"Hurt?"

"Like a bitch."

"Big bitch or little bitch?"

"Extra large," Charlie said.

"You allergic to any painkillers?"

"Nope."

"Antibiotics?"

"Nope."

Nurse Betsy reached into her uniform pocket and pulled out a handful of pills, picked out two round ones and one long one, and slid them through the little window. "By the power invested in me by Saint Francis of Assisi, I now pronounce you painless. The round ones are Percocet, the oval one is Cipro. I'll put it on your chart." She looked at Ray. "Fill out his papers for him, he's going to be too fucked up to do it in a few minutes."

"Thanks, Betsy."

"You get any Prada or Gucci bags in that store where you work — they're mine."

"No problem," Ray said. "Charlie owns the store."

"Really?"

Charlie nodded.

"Free," Betsy added. She slid another round pill across the counter. "For you, Ray."

"I'm not hurt."

"It's a long wait. Anything could happen." She grinned in lieu of telling him to fuck off.

An hour later the paperwork was done and Charlie was heaped in a fiberglass chair in a posture that seemed possible only if his bones had turned to marshmallow.

"They killed Rachel here," Charlie said.

"Yeah, I know," Ray said. "I'm sorry."

"I still miss her."

"Yeah, I know," Ray said. "How's your leg?"

"But they gave me Sophie," Charlie said, ignoring the question. "So, you know, that was good."

"Yeah, I know," Ray said. "How are you feeling now?"

"I'm a little concerned that growing up without a mother, Sophie won't be sensitive enough."

"You're doing a great job with her. I meant how are you feeling physically?"

"Like that thing where she kills people, just by looking at them. That can't be good for a little girl. My fault, all my fault."

"Charlie, does your leg hurt?" Ray had opted not to take the painkiller Nurse Betsy had given him, and now he was regretting it.

"And the thing with the hellhounds — what kid has to deal with that? That can't be healthy."

"Charlie, how do you feel?"

"I'm a little sleepy," Charlie said.

"Well, you lost a lot of blood."

"I'm relaxed, though. You know, blood loss relaxes you. You suppose that's why they did leeches in the Middle Ages? They could use them instead of tranquilizers. *'Yes, Bob, I'll be right in to the meeting, but let me stick a leech on, I'm feeling a little anxious.'* Like that."

"Great idea, Charlie. You want some water?"

"You're a good guy, Ray. Did I ever tell you that? Even if you are serial-killing desperate Filipinas on your vacation."

"What?"

Nurse Betsy came to the window. "Asher!" she called.

Ray looked pleadingly at her through the window — a few seconds later she was coming through the door with a wheelchair.

"How's Painless doing?" she said.

"Oh my God, he's incredibly irritating," Ray said.

"You didn't take your medicine, did you?"

"I don't like drugs."

"Who's the nurse here, Ray? It's the circle of meds, not just the patient, but everyone around him. Haven't you seen The Lion King?"

"That's not in *The Lion King*. That's the *circle of life*."

"Really? I've been singing that song wrong the whole time? Wow, I guess I don't like that movie after all. Help me get Painless into the chair. We'll have him home by breakfast."

"We got here at dinnertime," Ray said.

"See how you are when you're off your meds?"

Charlie had a foam walking cast and crutches when he got home from the hospital. The painkillers had worn off to a level where he was no longer painless. His head was throbbing like tiny twin aliens were going to burst out of his temples. Mrs. Korjev came out of his apartment and cornered him in the hallway.

"Charlie Asher, I am having bone to pick with you. Last night am I seeing my little Sophie run by my apartment naked and soapy like bear, pulling giant black dogs around singing 'not in butt'? In old country we have word for that, Charlie Asher. Word is *nasty.* I still have number for child service from days when my boys were boys."

"Soapy like bear?"

"Don't change subject. Is nasty."

"Yes, it is. I'm sorry. It won't happen again. I was shot and wasn't thinking straight."

"You are shot?"

"In the leg. It's only a flesh wound." Charlie had waited his entire life to say those words and he felt very macho at that moment. "I don't know who shot me. It's a

mystery. They dropped a rug on me, too."
The rug diminished the machismo somewhat. He vowed not to mention it hence-
forth.

"You come in. Have breakfast. Sophie
will not eat toast Vladlena make. She say is
raw and have toast germs."

"That's my girl," Charlie said.

Charlie was no sooner in the door and
on his way to rescue his daughter from
toast-borne pathogens, when Mohammed
grabbed the tip of one of his crutches in
his mouth and dragged a hopping Charlie
into the bedroom.

"Hi, Daddy," Sophie said as her father
went hopping by. "No skipping in the
house," she added.

Mohammed head-butted the hapless
Beta Male to his date book. There were
two names there under today's date, which
wasn't that unusual. What was unusual
was that they were the names that had appeared before: Esther Johnson and Irena
Posokovanovich — the two soul vessels
he'd missed.

He sat down on the bed and tried to rub
the pain aliens back into his temples. How
to even start? Would these names keep
coming back until he got the soul vessels?
That hadn't happened with the fuck pup-

pet. What was different here? Things were obviously getting worse — now they were shooting at him.

Charlie picked up the phone and dialed Ray Macy's number.

It took Ray four days to come back to Charlie with the report. He had the information in three, but he'd wanted to be absolutely sure that all the painkillers had worn off and Charlie wasn't going to be crazy anymore — going on all night about being the big death, "with a capital *D*." Ray also felt a little guilty because he'd been holding out on Charlie about breaking some rules in the store.

They met in the back room on a Wednesday morning, before the store opened. Charlie had made coffee and taken a seat at the desk so he could prop his foot up. Ray sat on some boxes of books.

"Okay, shoot," Charlie said.

"Well, first, I found three more crossbow bolts. Two had barbed-steel tips like the one that went through your leg, and one had a titanium spike. That one was stuck in the pneumatic closer on the back door."

"Don't care, Ray. What about the two women?"

"Charlie, someone shot you with a deadly weapon. You don't care?"

"Correct. Don't care. It's a mystery. Know what I like about mysteries? They're mysterious."

Ray was wearing a Giants cap and he flipped it around backwards for emphasis. If he'd been wearing glasses he would have whipped those off, but he wasn't, so he squinted like he had. "I'm sorry, Charlie, but someone wanted you and the dogs out of the house at the same time. They threw that rug on you from the rooftop across the alley, then, when you were pinned down and the dogs were outside, they shot the closer on the door so it would slam shut. They sabotaged the back door's lock and glued the front doors shut, probably before they even started with the rug, then they slid down a line to the hall window, slipped between the bars, and — well, then it's un-clear."

Charlie sighed. "You're not going to tell me about the two women until you finish this, are you?"

"It was highly organized. This wasn't a random assault."

"The hall window upstairs has bars on it, Ray. No one can get in. No one got in."

"Well, that's where it gets a little crazy.

You see, I don't think it was a human intruder."

"You don't?" Charlie actually seemed to be paying attention now.

"In order to get through those bars, an intruder would have to be under two feet tall, and less than, say, thirty pounds. I'm thinking a monkey."

Charlie put down his coffee so hard that a java geyser jumped out of the cup onto some papers on the desk. "You think that I was shot by a highly organized monkey?"

"Don't be that way —"

"Who then slid down a wire, broke into the building, and did what? Made off with fruit?"

"You should have heard some of the stupid shit you were saying the other night at the hospital, and did I make fun of you?"

"I was on drugs, Ray."

"Well, there's no other explanation." To Ray's Beta Male imagination, the monkey explanation seemed completely reasonable — except for lack of motive. *But you know monkeys, they'll fling poo at you just for the hell of it, so who's to say —*

"The explanation is that it's a mystery," Charlie said. "I appreciate your trying to bring this . . . this furry bastard to justice,

Ray, but I need to know about the two women."

Ray nodded, defeated. He should have just shut up until he'd figured out why someone would want to get a monkey into Charlie's apartment. "People can train monkeys, you know. Do you have any valuable jewelry in your apartment?"

"You know," Charlie said, scratching his chin and looking at the ceiling as if remembering. "There was a small car parked across from the shop all day on Vallejo. And when I looked the next day, there was a pile of banana peels, like someone had been staking the place out. Someone who ate bananas."

"What kind of car was it?" Ray said, his notepad ready.

"I'm not sure, but it was red, and definitely monkey size."

Ray looked up from his notes. "Really?"

Charlie paused, as if thinking carefully about his answer. "Yes," he said, very sincerely. "Monkey size."

Ray flipped his notebook back to the pages in the front. "There is no need to be that way, Charlie. I'm just trying to help."

"It might have been bigger," Charlie said, remembering. "Like a monkey SUV — like what you might drive if you were

442

transporting — I don't know — a barrel of monkeys."

Ray cringed, then read from the pages. "I went to the Johnson woman's house. No one is living there, but the house isn't on the market. I didn't see the niece you talked about. Funny thing is, the neighbors knew she'd been sick, but no one had heard that she'd died. In fact, one guy said he thought he saw her getting into a U-Haul truck with a couple of movers last week."

"Last week? Her niece said that she died two weeks ago."

"No niece."

"What?"

"Esther Johnson doesn't have a niece. She was an only child. Didn't have brothers or sisters, and no nieces on her late husband's side of the family."

"So she's alive?"

"Apparently." Ray handed Charlie a photograph. "That's her latest driver's-license photo. This changes things. Now we're looking for a missing person, someone who will leave a trail. But the other one — Irena — is even better." He handed Charlie another picture.

"She's not dead either?"

"Oh, there was a death notice in the

paper three weeks ago, but here's the giveaway — all of her bills are still being paid, by personal check. Checks *she* signed." Ray sat back on his stool, smiling, feeling the sweetness of righteous indignation over the monkey theory, and a little guilt alleviation for not telling Charlie about the special transactions.

"Well?" Charlie finally asked.

"She's at her sister's house in the Sunset. Here's the address." Ray tore a page out of his notebook and handed it to Charlie.

21

Common Courtesy

Charlie was torn — he really wanted to take his sword-cane, but he couldn't carry it while using the crutches. He considered duct-taping it to one of the crutches, but he thought that might attract attention.

"You want me to go with you?" Ray asked. "I mean, you okay to drive, with your leg and all?"

"I'll be fine," Charlie said. "Someone needs to watch the store."

"Charlie, before you go, can I ask you something?"

"Sure." *Don't ask, don't ask, don't ask,* Charlie thought.

"Why did you need me to find these two women?"

You robot-necked bastard, you had to ask. "I told you, estate stuff." Charlie shrugged. *No big deal, let it go, nothing to see here.*

"Yeah, I know you told me that, and normally that would make sense, but I found out a lot about these two while looking for them — no one in either of their families has died recently."

"Funny thing," Charlie said, juggling his keys, the cane, his date book, and his crutches by the back door. "Both bequests were from nonrelatives. Old friends." *No wonder women don't like you, you just won't leave things alone.*

"Uh-huh," Ray said, unconvinced. "You know, when people run, when they go as far as faking their own death to get away, they are usually running *from* something. Are you that something, Charlie?"

"Ray, listen to yourself. Are you back on your serial-killer thing? I thought Rivera explained that."

"So this is for Rivera?"

"Let's say he's interested," Charlie said.

"Why didn't you just say so?"

Charlie sighed. "Ray, I'm not supposed to talk about this stuff, you know that. Fourth Amendment and all. I came to you because you're good, and you have contacts. I depend on you and I trust you. I think you know that you can depend on me and trust me, right? I mean, in all these years, I've never put your disability pension in jeopardy by being careless about our arrangement, have I?"

It was a threat, however subtle, and Charlie felt bad for doing it, but he just couldn't let Ray continue to push on this, particularly since he was in unexplored territory himself — he didn't even know what kind of bluff he was covering.

"So Mrs. Johnson isn't going to end up dead if I find her for you?"

"I will not lay a hand on Mrs. Johnson or Mrs. Pojo . . . Mrs. Pokojo — or that other woman either. You have my word on it." Charlie raised his hand as if swearing on a Bible and dropped one of his crutches.

"Why don't you just use the cane?" Ray said.

"Right," Charlie said. He leaned the crutches on the door and tried his weight on the bad leg and the cane. The doctors had, indeed, said that it was just a flesh wound, so there was no tendon damage, just muscle, but it hurt like hell to put any weight on that foot. The cane would work, he decided. "I should be back to relieve you before five." He limped out the door.

Ray didn't like being lied to. He'd had quite enough of that from his desperate Filipinas and was becoming sensitive about being taken for a fool. Who did Charlie Asher think he was fooling? As soon as he got the store squared away, he'd give Rivera a call and see for himself.

He went out into the store and did a little dusting, then went to Charlie's "special" rack, where he kept the weird estate items that he made such a fuss about. You were only supposed to sell one to each customer, but Ray had sold five of them to the same woman in the last two weeks. He knew he should have said something to Charlie, but really, why? Charlie wasn't being open with him about anything, it seemed.

Besides, the woman who bought the stuff was cute, and she'd smiled at Ray. She had nice hair, a cute figure, and really striking light blue eyes. Plus there was something about her voice — she seemed so, what? Peaceful, maybe. Like she knew that everything was going to be okay and no one needed to worry. Maybe he was projecting. And she didn't have an Adam's apple, which was a big plus in Ray's book lately. He'd tried to get her name, even get a look at something in her wallet, but she'd paid in cash and had been as careful as a poker player covering her cards. If she'd driven, she'd parked too far away for him to see her get into her car from the store, so there was no license number to trace.

He resolved to ask her name if she came in today. And she was due to come in. She only came in when he was working alone. He'd seen her check through the window once when he was working with Lily, and only came into the store later when Lily was gone. He really hoped she'd come in.

He tried to calm himself down for his call to Rivera. He didn't want to seem like a rube to a guy who was still on the job. He used his own cell phone for the call so Rivera would see it was him calling.

Charlie didn't like leaving Sophie for this long, given what had happened a few days ago, but on the other hand, whatever might be threatening her was obviously being caused by his missing these two soul vessels. The quicker he fixed the problem, the quicker the threat would be diminished. Besides, the hellhounds were her best defense, and he'd given express instructions to Mrs. Ling that the dogs and Sophie were not to be separated for any amount of time, for any reason.

He took Presidio Boulevard through Golden Gate Park into the Sunset, reminding himself to take Sophie to the Japanese Tea Garden to feed the koi, now that her plague on pets seemed to have subsided.

The Sunset district lay just south of Golden Gate Park, bordered by the American Highway and Ocean Beach on the west, and Twin Peaks and the University of San Francisco on the east. It had once been a suburb, until the city expanded to include it, and many of its houses were modest, single-story family dwellings, built en masse in the 1940s and '50s. They were like the mosaics of little boxes that peppered neighborhoods across the entire country in that postwar period, but in San Francisco, where so much had been built after the quake and fire of '06, then again in the economic boom of the late twentieth century, they seemed like anachronisms from both ends of time. Charlie felt like he was driving through the Eisenhower era, at least until he passed a mother with a shaved head and tribal tattoos on her scalp pushing twins in a double stroller.

Irena Posokovanovich's sister lived in a small, one-story frame house with a small covered porch that had jasmine vines growing up trellises on either side and springing off into the air like morning-after-sex hair. The rest of the tiny yard was meticulously groomed, from the holly hedge at the sidewalk to the red geraniums that lined the concrete path up to the house.

Charlie parked a block away and walked to the house. On the way he was nearly run over by two different joggers, one a young mother pushing a running stroller. They couldn't see him — he was on track. Now, how to go about getting in? And then what? If he was the Luminatus, then perhaps just his presence would take care of the problem.

He checked around back and saw that there was a car in the garage, but the shades were drawn on all the windows. Finally he decided on the frontal approach and rang the doorbell.

A few seconds later a short woman in her seventies wearing a pink chenille housecoat opened the door. "Yes," she said, looking a little suspicious as she eyed Charlie's walking cast. She quickly flipped the lock on the screen door. "Can I help you?"

It was the woman in the picture. "Yes, ma'am, I'm looking for Irena Posokovanovich."

"Well, she's not here," said Irena Posokovanovich. "You must have the wrong house." She started to close the door.

"Wasn't there a death notice in the paper a couple of weeks ago?" Charlie said. So far, his awesome presence as the Luminatus wasn't having much of an effect on her.

"Well, yes, I believe there was," said the woman, sensing an out. She opened the door a little more. "It was such a tragedy. We all loved Irena so much. She was the kindest, most generous, most loving, attractive — you know, for her age — well-read —"

"And evidently didn't know that it's considered common courtesy when you publish a death notice to actually die!" Charlie held out the enlarged driver's-license picture. He considered adding *aha!*, but thought that might be a little over-the-top.

Irena Posokovanovich slammed the door. "I don't know who you are, but you have the wrong house," she said through the door.

"You know who I am," Charlie said. Actually, she probably had no idea who he was. "And I know who you are, and you are supposed to have died three weeks ago."

"You're mistaken. Now go away before I call the police and tell them that there's a rapist at my door."

Charlie gagged a little, then pushed on. "I am not a rapist, Mrs. Poso . . . Posokev — I'm Death, Irena. That's who I am. And you are overdue. You need to die, this minute if possible. There's nothing to be afraid of. It's like going to sleep, only, well —"

"I'm not ready," Irena whined. "If I was ready I wouldn't have left my home. I'm not ready."

"I'm sorry, ma'am, but I have to insist."

"I'm sure you're mistaken. Perhaps another Mrs. Posokovanovich."

"No, here it is, right here in the calendar, with your address. It's you." Charlie held his date book turned to the page with her name on it up to the little window in the door.

"And you say that that is Death's calendar?"

"That's correct, ma'am. Notice the date. And this is your second notice."

"And you are Death?"

"That's right."

"Well, that's just silly."

"I am not silly, Mrs. Posokovanovich. I am Death."

"Aren't you supposed to have a sickle and a long black robe?"

453

"No, we don't do that anymore. Take my word for it, I am Death." He tried to sound really ominous.

"Death is always tall in the pictures." She was standing on tiptoe, he could tell the way she kept bouncing up by the little window to get a look at him. "You don't seem tall enough."

"There's no height requirement."

"Then could I see your business card?"

"Sure." Charlie took out a card and held it against the glass.

"This says 'Purveyor of Fine Vintage Clothing and Accessories.'"

"Right! Exactly!" He knew he should have had a second set of business cards printed up. "And where do you think I get those things? From the dead. You see?"

"Mr. Asher, I'm going to have to ask you to leave."

"No, ma'am, I'm going to have to insist that you pass away, this instant. You're overdue."

"Go away! You are a charlatan, and I think you need psychological help."

"Death! You're fucking with Death! Capital *D*, bitch!" Well, that was uncalled for. Charlie felt bad the second he said it. "Sorry," he mumbled to the door.

"I'm calling the police."

"You go ahead, Mrs. — uh — Irena. You know what they'll tell you, that you're dead! It was in the *Chronicle*. They hardly ever print stuff that's not true."

"Please go away. I practiced for a long time so I could live longer, it's not fair."

"What?"

"Go away."

"I heard that part, I mean the part about practicing."

"Never you mind. You just go take someone else."

Charlie actually had no idea what he would do if she let him in. Maybe he had to touch her for his Death abilities to kick in. He remembered seeing an old *Twilight Zone* as a kid, where Robert Redford was Death, and this old lady wouldn't let him in, so he pretended to be injured, and when she came to help him . . . *ALA-KAZAM!* She croaked, and he peacefully led her off to Hole in the Wall, where she helped him produce independent movies. Maybe that would work. He did have the cast and the cane going for him.

He looked up and down the street to make sure that no one could see him, then he lay down, half on the little porch, half on the concrete steps. He threw his cane against the door and made sure that it clattered loudly on the concrete, then he let out what he thought was a very convincing wail. "Ahhhhhhhhh, I've broken my leg."

He heard footsteps inside and saw gray hair at the little window, bouncing a little so she could see out.

"Oh, it hurts," Charlie wailed. "Help."

More steps, the shade in the window to the right of the door parted and he saw an eye. He grimaced in fake pain.

"Are you all right?" said Mrs. Posokova-novich.

"I need help. My leg was hurt before, but I slipped on your steps. I think I've broken something. There's blood, and a piece of bone sticking out." He kept his leg below the level where she could see it.

"Oh my," she said. "Give me a minute."

"Help. Please. The pain. So — much — pain." Charlie coughed the way cowboys do when they are dying in the dirt and things are getting all dark.

He heard the latch being thrown, and then the inner door opened. "You're really hurt bad," she said.

"Please," Charlie said, holding his hand out to her. "Help me."

She unlatched the screen. Charlie suppressed a grin. "Oh, thank you," he gasped.

She threw open the screen door and blasted him in the face with a stream of pepper spray. "I saw that *Twilight Zone*, you son of a bitch!" The doors slammed. The latch was thrown.

Charlie's face felt like it was on fire.

When he could finally see well enough to walk, as he limped back to his van, he heard a female voice say, "I'd have let you in, lover." Then a chorus of spooky-girlish laughter erupted from the storm sewer. He backed against the van, ready to draw the sword from the cane, but then he heard what sounded like a small dog barking in the sewer.

"Where did he come from?" said one of the harpies.

"He bit me! You little fucker!"

"Get him!"

"I hate dogs. When we take over, no dogs."

The barking faded away, followed by the voices of the sewer harpies. Charlie took a deep breath and tried to blink the pain out of his eyes. He needed to regroup, but then he was taking the old lady down, pepper spray or not.

It took him the better part of an hour to get into position, but once he was ready, he put down the cinder block, flipped open his cell phone, and dialed the number he'd gotten from information.

A woman answered. "Hello."

"Ma'am, this is the gas company," Charlie said in his best gas-company voice. "My grid is showing pressure loss at your address. We're sending a truck right out, but you need to get everyone out of the house, right now."

"Well, I'm the only one here right now, but I'm sorry, I don't smell gas."

"It may be building up under the house," Charlie said, feeling proud of himself for being quick on his feet. Is there anyone else in the house?"

"No, just me and my kitty, Samantha."

"Ma'am, please take the cat and go out by the street. Our truck will meet you there. Go right now, okay?"

"Well, all right."

"Thank you, ma'am." Charlie clicked off. He could feel movement inside of the house. He moved right to the edge of the porch roof and raised the concrete cinder block over his head. *It'll look like an accident,* he thought, *like a cinder block fell off the porch roof.* He was glad that no one could see him up here. He was sweating from the climb, his armpits stained, his

458

trousers wrinkled.

He heard the door open and got ready to throw the cinder block as soon as his target emerged from under the roof.

"Good afternoon, ma'am." A man's voice, out by the street.

Charlie looked down to see Inspector Rivera standing at the sidewalk, having just climbed out of an unmarked car. What the hell was he doing here?

"Are you the gas company?" said Mrs. Posokovanovich.

"No, ma'am, I'm from the San Francisco police." He flashed his badge.

"They told me there was a gas leak," she said.

"That's been taken care of, ma'am. Could you step back inside and I'll check with you in a minute, okay?"

"Well, okay, then."

Charlie heard the doors open and close again. His arms were trembling from holding the cinder block over his head. He tried to breathe quietly, thinking that the sound of his wheezing might attract Rivera's attention, make him visible.

"Mr. Asher, what are you doing up there?"

Charlie nearly lost his balance and went over. "You can see me?"

459

"Yes, sir, I certainly can. And I can also see that cinder block you're holding over your head."

"Oh, this old thing."

"What were you planning on doing with that?"

"Repairs?" Charlie tried. How could Rivera see him when he was in soul-vessel-retrieval mode?

"I'm sorry, but I don't believe you, Mr. Asher. You're going to have to drop the cinder block."

"I'd rather not. It was really hard getting it up here."

"Be that as it may, I'm going to have to insist that you drop it."

"I was planning on it, but then you showed up."

"Please. Indulge me. Look, you're sweating. Climb down and you can sit in my air-conditioned car with me. We'll chat — talk about Italian suits, the Giants — I don't know — why you were about to brain that sweet old lady with a cinder block. Air-conditioning, Mr. Asher — won't that be nice?"

Charlie brought the cinder block down and rested it on his thigh, feeling his trousers snagging beyond repair as he did so. "That's not much of an incentive. What am I, some primitive Amazon native? I've had air-conditioning before. I have air-conditioning in my own van."

"Yes, I'll admit it's not exactly a weekend in Paris, but the next choice was that I shoot you off the roof, and they put you in a body bag, which is going to be sweltering on a warm day like this."

"Oh, well, yes," Charlie said. "That does make air-conditioning sound a lot more inviting. Thanks. I'm going to toss my brick down first, if that's okay?"

"That would be great, Mr. Asher."

Disillusioned with *DesperateFilipinas*, Ray was browsing through the selection of lonely first-grade teachers with master's degrees in nuclear physics on *Ukrainian-GirlsLovingYou.com* when she came through the door. He heard the bell and caught her out of the corner of his eye, and forgetting that his neck vertebrae were fused, he sprained the left side of his face trying to turn to see her.

She saw him looking and smiled.

Ray smiled back, then, out of the corner of his eye, saw the monitor with the photo of the first-grade teacher holding her breasts, and sprained the right side of his face trying to turn in time to punch the power button before she passed the counter.

"Just browsing," said the love of his life. "How are you today?"

"Hi," Ray said. In his mental rehearsals, he started with "hi," and it just sort of burped out of him before he realized that it put him behind a beat. "I mean, fine. Sorry. I was working."

"I can see that." Again the smile.

She was so understanding, forgiving — and kind, you could just tell that by her eyes. He knew in his heart that he would even sit through a hat movie for this woman. He would watch *A Room with a View* AND *The English Patient*, back-to-back, just to share a pizza with her. And she would stop him from eating his service revolver halfway through the second movie, because that's just how she was: compassionate.

She made a show of browsing the store, but two minutes hadn't passed before she made for Charlie's special shelf. Even the sign said SPECIAL ITEMS — ONE PER CUSTOMER, but it didn't say if that was a per-day policy, or one per lifetime. Charlie hadn't really specified, now that Ray thought about it. Sure, Lily had yammered on about how important it was that they adhere to the policy, but that was Lily, she might have grown up some, but she was still disturbed.

After a short time she picked up an electric alarm clock and brought it over to the counter. This was it. This was it. Ray heard the back door open.

"Will this be everything?" he said.

"Yes," said the future Mrs. Ray Macy. "I've been looking for one like this."

"Yep, you can't beat a Sunbeam," Ray said. "That's two-sixteen with tax — aw, heck, call it two even."

"That's very nice of you," she said, digging into a small purse woven from colorful Guatemalan cotton thread.

"Hi, Ray," Lily said, suddenly standing there beside him like some evil phantom who appeared out of nowhere to leech every potentially joyous moment out of his life.

"Hi, Lily," he said.

Lily clicked some keys on the computer. Slowed down by his freshly sprained face, Ray wasn't able to turn before she'd hit the power button on the monitor.

"What's this?" asked Lily.

With his free hand, Ray thumped Lily in the thigh under the counter.

"Ouch! Freak!"

"I'm sure you'll enjoy waking up with that," Ray said, handing the alarm clock to the woman who would be his queen.

"Thank you so much," said the lovely brunette goddess of all things Ray.

"By the way," Ray said, pushing on, "you've been in a couple of times, I was wondering, you know, because I'm curious that way, uh, what's your name?"

"Audrey."

"Hi, Audrey. I'm Ray."

"Nice to meet you, Ray. Gotta go. Bye." She waved over her shoulder and headed out the door.

Ray and Lily watched her walk away.

"Nice butt," Lily said.

"She said my name," Ray said.

"She's a little bit — I don't know — *unimaginary* for you."

Ray turned to the nemesis Lily. "You have to watch the store. I have to go."

"Why?"

"I have to follow her, find out who she is." Ray began to gather his stuff — phone, keys, baseball cap.

"Yeah, that's healthy, Ray."

"Tell Charlie I — don't tell Charlie."

"Okay. So is it okay if I switch the computer from the UGLY Web site?"

"What are you talking about?"

Lily stepped back from the screen and pointed to the letters as she read, "Ukrainian Girls Loving You — U-G-L-Y, ugly." Lily smiled, a perky, self-satisfied smile, like that kid who won the spelling bee in third grade. Didn't you hate that kid?

Ray couldn't believe it. They weren't even being subtle about it anymore. "Can't talk," he said. "Gotta go." He ran out the door and headed up Mason Street after the lovely and compassionate Audrey.

Rivera had driven up to the Cliff House Restaurant overlooking Seal Rocks and forced Charlie to buy him a drink while they watched the surfers down on the beach. Rivera was not a morbid man, but he knew that if he came here enough times, eventually he'd see a surfer get hit by a white shark. In fact, he sorely hoped that it would happen, because otherwise, the world made no sense, there was no justice, and life was just a tangled ball of chaos. Thousands of seals in the water and on the rocks — the mainstay of the white shark diet — hundreds of surfers in the water, dressed like seals, well, it just needed to happen for all to be right with the world.

"I never believed you, Mr. Asher, when

you said that you were Death, but since I couldn't explain whatever that thing was in the alley with you, didn't want to explain, in fact, I let it slide."

"And I appreciate that," said Charlie, showing a little discomfort at drinking a glass of wine with handcuffs on. His face was candy-apple red from having been burned by the pepper spray. "Is this normal procedure for interrogations?"

"No," Rivera said. "Normally the City is supposed to pay, but I'll have the judge take the drinks off your sentence."

"Great. Thanks," Charlie said. "And you can call me Charlie."

"Okay, and you can call me Inspector Rivera. Now, braining the old lady with the cinder block — just exactly what were you thinking?"

"Do I need a lawyer?"

"Of course not, you're fine, this bar is full of witnesses." Rivera had once been a *by-the-book* kind of cop. That was before the demons, the giant owls, the bankruptcy, the polar bears, the vampires, the divorce, and the saber-clawed woman-thing that turned into a bird. Now, not so much.

"In that case, I was thinking that no one could see me," Charlie said.

"Because you were invisible?"

"Not really. Just sort of not noticeable."

"Well, I'll give you that, but I don't think that's any reason to crush a grandmother's skull."

"You have no proof of that," Charlie said.

"Of course I do," Rivera said, holding up his glass to signal to the waitress that he needed another Glenfiddich on the rocks. "I saw pictures of her grandchildren, she showed me when I went in the house."

"No, I mean you have no proof that I was going to crush her skull."

"I see," said Rivera, who did not see at all. "How did you know Mrs. Posokovano-vich?"

"I didn't. Her name just showed up in my date book, like I showed you."

"Yes, you did. Yes, you did. But that doesn't really give you a license to kill her, now does it?"

"That's the point, she was supposed to be dead three weeks ago. There was even a death notice in the paper. I was just trying to make sure it was accurate."

"So in lieu of having the *Chronicle* print a correction, you thought you'd bash in granny's brains."

"Well, it was that or have my daughter

say 'kitty' at her, and I refuse to exploit my child in that way."

"Well, I admire your taking the high ground on that one, Charlie," Rivera said, thinking, *Who do I have to shoot to get a drink around here?* "But let's just say that for one millisecond I believe you, and the old lady was supposed to die, but didn't, and that because of it you were shot with a crossbow and that thing I shot in the alley appeared — let's just say I believe all that, what am I supposed to do about it?"

"You need to be careful," Charlie said. "You may be turning into one of us."

"Pardon?"

"That's how it happened to me. When my wife passed away, in the hospital, I saw the guy that came to collect her soul vessel, and *wham,* I was a Death Merchant. You saw me today, when no one else could, and you saw the sewer harpy, that night in the alley. Most of the time, I'm the only one who can see them."

Rivera really, really wanted to turn this guy over to a psychiatrist at the hospital and never see him again, but the problem was, he had seen the woman-thing, that night and another time on his own street, and he had seen reports of weird stuff happening in the City over the last two weeks.

And not just normal San Francisco weird stuff, but really weird stuff, like a flock of ravens attacking a tourist in Coit Tower, and a guy who slammed his car through a storefront in Chinatown, saying that he had swerved to miss a dragon, and people all over the Mission saying that they'd seen an iguana dressed like a musketeer going through their garbage, tiny sword and all.

"I can prove it," Charlie said. "Just take me to the music store in the Castro."

Rivera looked at the sad, naked ice cubes in his glass and said, "Anyone ever tell you that it's hard to follow your train of thought, Charlie?"

"You need to talk to Minty Fresh."

"Of course, that clears things up. I'll have a word with Krispy Kreme while I'm there."

"He's also a Death Merchant. He can tell you that what I'm telling you is true and you can let me go."

"Get up." Rivera stood.

"I'm not finished with my wine."

"Leave the money for the drinks and get up, please." Rivera hooked his finger in Charlie's handcuffs and pulled him up. "We're going to the Castro."

"I don't think I can work my cane with these things on," Charlie said.

Rivera sighed and looked down on the surfers. He thought he saw something large moving in a wave behind one surfer, but as his heart leapt at the prospect, a sea lion poked his whiskered face out of the curl and Rivera's spirits sank again. He threw Charlie the handcuff keys.

"Meet me in the car, I have to take a leak."

"I could escape."

"You do that, Charlie — after you pay."

22

Reconsidering a Career in Secondhand Retail

Anton Dubois, the owner of Book 'em Danno in the Mission, had been a Death Merchant longer than anyone else in San Francisco. Of course he hadn't called himself a Death Merchant at first, but when that Minty Fresh fellow who opened the record store in the Castro coined the term, he could never think of himself as anything else. He was sixty-five years old and not in the best health, having never used his body for much more than to carry his head around, which is where he lived most of the time. He had, however, in his years of reading, acquired an encyclopedic knowledge of the science and mythology of death. So, on that Tuesday evening, just after sundown, when the windows of his store went black, as if all the light had been sucked suddenly out of the universe, and the three female figures moved toward him through the store, as he sat under his little reading light at the counter in the back, like a tiny yellow island in the vast pitch of space, he was the first man in fifteen hundred years to know exactly what — *who* — they were.

"Morrigan," Anton said, with no particular note of fear in his voice. He set his book down, but didn't bother to mark the page. He took off his glasses and cleaned them on his flannel shirt, then put them back on so as not to miss any detail. Just now they were only blue-black highlights moving among the deep shadows in the store, but he could see them. They stopped when he spoke. One of them hissed — not the hiss of a cat, a long, steady tone — more like the hiss of air escaping the rubber raft that is all that lies between you and a dark sea full of sharks, the hiss of your life leaking out at the seams.

"I thought something might be happening," Anton said, a little anxious now. "With all the signs, and the prophecy about the Luminatus, I knew something was happening, but I didn't think it would be you — in person — so to speak. This is very exciting."

"A devotee?" said Nemain.

"A fan," said Babd.

"A sacrifice," said Macha.

They moved around him, just outside his circle of light.

"I moved the soul vessels," Anton said. "I guessed that something had happened to the others."

"Aw, are you disappointed because you're not the first?" said Babd.

"It will be just like the first time, pumpkin," said Nemain. "For you, anyway." She giggled.

Anton reached under his counter and pushed a button. Steel shutters began to roll in the front of the store over the windows and door.

"You afraid we'll get away, turtle man," said Macha. "Don't you think he looks like a turtle?"

"Oh, I know the shutters won't keep you in, that's not what they're for. The books say that you're immortal, but I suspect that that's not exactly true. Too many tales of warriors injuring you and watching you heal yourself on the battlefield."

"We will be here ten thousand years after your death, which starts pretty soon, I might add," said Nemain. "The souls, turtle man. Where did you put them?" She extended her claws and reached out so they caught the light from Anton's reading lamp. Venom dripped from their tips and sizzled when it hit the floor.

"You'd be Nemain, then," Anton said. The Morrigan smiled, he could just see her teeth in the dark.

Anton felt a strange peace fall over him. For thirty years he had, in some way or another, been preparing for this moment. What was it that the Buddhists said? *Only by being prepared for your death can you ever truly live.* If collecting souls and seeing people pass for thirty years didn't prepare you, what would? Under the counter he carefully unscrewed a stainless-steel cap that concealed a red button.

"I installed those four speakers at the back of the store a few months ago. I'm sure you can see them, even if I can't," Anton said.

"The souls!" Macha barked. "Where?"

"Of course I didn't know it would be you. I thought it might be those little creatures I've seen wandering the neighborhood. But I think you'll enjoy the music, nonetheless."

The Morrigan looked at each other.

Macha growled. "Who says things like 'nonetheless'?"

"He's babbling," said Babd. "Let's torture him. Take his eyes, Nemain."

"Do you remember what a claymore looks like?" Anton asked.

"A great, two-handed broadsword," said Nemain. "Good for the taking of heads."

"I knew that, I knew that," said Babd. "She's just showing off."

"Well, in this time, a claymore means something else," Anton said. "You acquire the most interesting things working in the secondhand business for three decades." He closed his eyes and pushed the button. He hoped that his soul would end up in a book, preferably his first edition of *Cannery Row*, which was safely stored away.

The curved claymore antipersonnel mines that he had installed in speaker cabinets at the rear of the store exploded, sending twenty-eight hundred ball bearings hurtling toward the steel shutters at just under the speed of sound, shredding Anton and everything else in their path.

Ray followed the love of his life a block up Mason Street, where she hopped on a cable car and rode it the rest of the way up the hill into Chinatown. The problem was that while it was pretty easy to figure out where a cable car was going, they only came along about every ten minutes, so

Ray couldn't wait for the next one, jump on, and shout, "Follow that antiquated but quaint public conveyance, and step on it!" And there were no cabs in sight.

It turned out that jogging up a steep city hill on a hot summer day in street clothes was somewhat different from jogging on a treadmill in an air-conditioned gym behind a row of taut fuck puppets, and by the time he got to California Street, Ray was drenched in sweat, and not only hated the city of San Francisco and everyone in it, he was pretty much ready to call it quits with Audrey and go back to the relative desperation of Ukrainian Girls Loving Him from afar.

He caught a break at the Powell Street exchange, where the cable cars pick up in Chinatown, and was actually able to jump on the car behind Audrey's and continue the breathtaking, seven-mile-per-hour chase, ten more blocks to Market Street.

Audrey hopped off the cable car, walked directly out to the island on Market, and stepped onto one of the antique streetcars, which left before Ray even got to the island. She was like some kind of diabolical rail-transit supervixen, Ray thought. The way the trains just seemed to be there when she needed them, then gone when he got there. She was master of some sort of evil, streetcar mojo, no doubt about that. (In matters of the heart, the Beta Male imagination can turn quickly on a floundering suitor, and at that point, Ray's was beginning to consume what little confidence he had mustered.)

It was Market Street, however, the busiest street in the City, and Ray was able to quickly grab a cab and follow Audrey all the way into the Mission district, and even kept the cab for a few blocks when she was on foot again.

Ray stayed a block away, following Audrey to a big jade-green Queen Anne Victorian building off Seventeenth Street, which had a small plaque on the column by the porch that read THREE JEWELS BUDDHIST CENTER. Ray had his breath and his composure back, and was able to watch comfortably from behind a light post across the street as Audrey climbed the steps of the center. As she got to the top step, the leaded-glass door flew open and two old ladies came rushing out, frantic, it seemed, to tell Audrey something, but entirely out of control. The old ladies looked familiar. Ray stopped breathing and dug into the back pocket of his jeans. He came up with the photocopies he'd kept of the driver's-license photos of the women Charlie had asked him to find. It was them: Esther Johnson and Irena Posokovanovich, standing there with the future Mrs. Macy. Then, just as Ray was trying to get his head around the connection, the door of the Buddhist center opened again and out charged what looked like a river otter in a sequined minidress and go-go boots, bent on attacking Audrey's ankles with a pair of scissors.

Charlie and Inspector Rivera stood outside Fresh Music in the Castro, trying to peer in the windows past the cardboard cutouts and giant album covers. According to the hours posted on the door, the store should have been open, but the door was locked and it was dark inside. From what Charlie could see, the store was exactly as he had seen it years ago when he'd confronted Minty Fresh, except for one, distinct difference: the shelf full of glowing soul vessels was gone.

There was a frozen-yogurt shop next door and Rivera led Charlie in and talked to the owner, a guy who looked entirely too fit to run a sweetshop, who said, "He hasn't opened for five days. Didn't say a word to any of us. Is he okay?"

"I'm sure he's fine," Rivera said.

Three minutes later Rivera had obtained Minty Fresh's phone numbers and home address from the SFPD dispatcher, and after trying the numbers and getting voice mail, they went to Fresh's apartment in Twin Peaks to find newspapers piled up by the door.

Rivera turned to Charlie. "Do you know of anyone else who could vouch for what you've been telling me?"

"You mean other Death Merchants?" Charlie asked. "I don't know them, but I know of them. They probably won't talk to you."

"Used-book-store owner in the Haight and a junk dealer off lower Fourth Street, right?" Rivera said.

"No," Charlie said. "I don't know of anyone like that. Why did you ask?"

"Because both of them are missing," Rivera said. There was blood all over the walls of the junk dealer's office. There was a human ear on the floor of the bookstore in the Haight."

Charlie backed against the wall. "That wasn't in the paper."

"We don't release stuff like that. Both lived alone, no one saw anything, we don't know that a crime was even committed.

But now, with this Fresh guy missing —"

"You think that these other guys were Death Merchants?"

"I'm not saying I believe that, Charlie, it could just be a coincidence, but when Ray Macy called me today about you, that was actually the reason I came to find you. I was going to ask you if you knew them."

"Ray ratted me out?"

"Let it go. He may have saved your life."

Charlie thought about Sophie for the hundredth time that night, worried about not being there with her. "Can I call my daughter?"

"Sure," Rivera said. "But then —"

"Book 'em Danno in the Mission," Charlie said, pulling his cell phone out of his jacket pocket. "That can't be ten minutes away. I think the owner is one of us."

Sophie was fine, feeding Cheese Newts to the hellhounds with Mrs. Korjev. She asked Charlie if he needed any help and he teared up and had to get control of his voice before he answered.

Seven minutes later they were parked crossways in the middle of Valencia Street, watching fire trucks blasting water into the second story of the building that housed Book 'em Danno. They got out of the car and Rivera showed his badge to the police

480

officer who had been first on the scene.

"Fire crews can't get in," the cop said. "There's a heavy steel fire door in the back and those shutters must be quarter-inch steel or more."

The security shutters were bowed outward and had thousands of small bumps all over them.

"What happened?" Rivera asked.

"We don't know yet," said the cop. "Neighbors reported an explosion and that's all we know so far. No one lived upstairs. We've evacuated all the adjacent buildings."

"Thanks," Rivera said. He looked at Charlie, raised an eyebrow.

"The Fillmore," Charlie said. "A pawnshop at Fulton and Fillmore."

"Let's go," Rivera said, taking Charlie's arm to help speed-limp him to the car.

"So I'm not a suspect anymore?" Charlie asked.

"We'll see if you live," Rivera said, opening the car door.

Once in the car, Charlie called his sister. "Jane, I need you to go get Sophie and the puppies and take them to your place."

"Sure, Charlie, but we just had the carpets cleaned — Alvin and —"

"*Do not* separate Sophie and the hellhounds for one second, Jane, do you understand?"

"Jeez, Charlie. Sure."

"I mean it. She may be in danger and they'll protect her."

"What's going on? Do you want me to call the cops?"

"I'm with the cops, Jane. Please, go get Sophie right now."

"I'm leaving now. How am I going to get them all into my Subaru?"

"You'll figure it out. If you have to, tie Alvin and Mohammed to the bumper and drive slowly."

"That's horrible, Charlie."

"No, it's not. They'll be fine."

"No, I mean they tore my bumper off last time I did that. It cost six hundred bucks to fix."

"Go get her. I'll call you in an hour." Charlie disconnected.

"Well, claymores suck, I can tell you that," said Babd. "I used to like the big sword claymore, but now . . . now they have to make them all splody and full of — what do you call that stuff, Nemain?"

"Shrapnel."

"Shrapnel," said Babd. "I was just starting to feel like my old self —"

482

"Shut up!" barked Macha.

"But it hurts," said Babd.

They were flowing along a storm sewer pipe under Sixteenth Street in the Mission. They were barely two-dimensional again, and they looked like tattered black battle flags, threadbare shadows, oozing black goo as they moved up the pipe. One of Nemain's legs had been completely severed and she had it tucked under her arm while her sisters towed her through the pipe.

"Can you fly, Nemain?" asked Babd. "You're getting heavy."

"Not down here, and I'm not going back up there."

"We have to go back Above," said Macha. "If you want to heal before a millennium passes."

As the three death divas came to a wide junction of pipes under Market Street, they heard something splashing in the pipe ahead.

"What's that?" said Babd. They stopped.

Something pattered by in the pipe they were approaching.

"What was that? What was that?" asked Nemain, who couldn't see past her sisters.

"Looked like a squirrel in a ball gown,"

said Babd. "But I'm weak and could be de-lusional."

"And an idiot," said Macha. "It was a gift soul. Get it! We can heal Nemain's leg with it."

Macha and Babd dropped their uni-dexter sister and surged forward toward the junction, just as the Boston terrier stepped into their path.

The Morrigan backpedaling in the pipe sounded like cats tearing lace. "Whoa, whoa, whoa," chanted Macha, what was left of her claws raking the pipe to back up.

Bummer yapped out a sharp tattoo of threat, then bolted down the pipe after the Morrigan.

"New plan, new plan, new plan," said Babd.

"I hate dogs," said Macha.

They snagged their sister as they passed her.

"We, the goddesses of death, who will soon command the all under darkness, are fleeing a tiny dog," said Nemain.

"So what's your point, hoppie?" said Macha.

Over in the Fillmore, Carrie Lang had closed her pawnshop for the night and was waiting for some jewelry she'd taken in that day to finish in the ultrasonic cleaner so she could put it in the display case. She wanted to finish and get out of there, go home and have dinner, then maybe go out for a couple of hours. She was thirty-six and single, and felt an obligation to go out, just on the off chance that she might meet a nice guy, even though she'd rather stay home and watch crime shows on TV. She prided herself on not becoming cynical. A pawnbroker, like a bail bondsman, tends to see people at their worst, and every day she fought the idea that the last decent guy had become a drummer or a crackhead.

Lately she didn't want to go out because of the strange stuff she'd been seeing and hearing out on the street — creatures scurrying in the shadows, whispers coming from the storm drains; staying at home was looking better all the time. She'd even started bringing her five-year-old basset hound, Cheerful, to work with her. He really wasn't a lot of protection, unless an attacker happened to be less than knee-high, but he had a loud bark, and there was a good chance that he might actually bark at a bad guy, as long he wasn't carrying a dog biscuit. As it turned out, the creatures who were invading her shop that evening were less than knee-high.

Carrie had been a Death Merchant for nine years, and after adjusting to the initial shock about the whole phenomenon of transference of souls subsided (which only took about four years), she'd taken to it like it was just another part of the business, but she knew from *The Great Big Book of Death* that something was going on, and it had her spooked.

As she went to the front of the store to crank the security shutters down, she heard something move behind her in the dark, something low, back by the guitars. It brushed a low E-string as it passed and the note vibrated like a warning. Carrie stopped cranking the shutters and checked that she had her keys with her, in case she needed to run through the front door. She unsnapped the holster of her .38 revolver, then thought, *What the hell, I'm not a cop,* and drew the weapon, training it on the still-sounding guitar. A cop she had dated years ago had talked her into carrying the Smith & Wesson when she was working the store, and although she'd never had to draw it before, she knew that it had been a deterrent to thieves.

"Cheerful?" she called.

She was answered by some shuffling in the back room. Why had she turned most of the lights out? The switches were in the back room, and she was moving by the case lights, which cast almost no light at the floor, where the noises were coming from.

"I have a gun, and I know how to use it," she said, feeling stupid even as the words came out of her mouth.

This time she was answered by a muffled whimper. "Cheerful!"

She ducked under the lift gate in the counter and ran to the back room, fanning the area with her pistol the way she saw them do in cop shows. Another whimper. She could just make out Cheerful, lying in his normal spot by the back door, but there was something around his paws and muzzle. Duct tape.

She reached out to turn on the lights and something hit her in the back of the knees. She tried to twist around and something thumped her in the chest, setting her off balance. Sharp claws raked her wrists as she fell and she lost her grip on the revolver. She hit her head on the doorjamb, setting off what seemed like a strobe light in her head, then something hit her in the back of the neck, hard, and everything went black.

It was still dark when she came to. She

couldn't tell how long she'd been out, and she couldn't move to look at her watch. *Oh my God, they've broken my neck,* she thought. She saw objects moving past her, each glowing dull red, barely illuminating whatever was carrying them — tiny skeletal faces — fangs, and claws and dead, empty eye sockets. The soul vessels appeared to be floating across the floor, with a carrion puppet escort. Then she felt claws, the creatures, touching her, moving under her. She tried to scream, but her mouth had been taped shut.

She felt herself being lifted, then made out the shape of the back door of her shop opening as she was carried through it, only a foot or so off the floor. Then she was hoisted nearly upright, and she felt herself falling into a dark abyss.

They found the back door to the pawn-shop open and the basset hound taped up in the corner. Rivera checked the shop with his weapon drawn and a flashlight in one hand, then called Charlie in from the alley when he found no one there.

Charlie turned on the shop lights as he came in. "Uh-oh," he said.

"What?" Rivera said.

Charlie pointed to a display case with

the glass broken out. "This case is where she displayed her soul vessels. It was nearly full when I was in here — now, well . . ."

Rivera looked at the empty case. "Don't touch anything. Whatever happened here, I don't think it was the same perp who hit the other shopkeepers."

"Why?" Charlie looked back to the back room, to the bound basset hound.

"Because of him," Rivera said. "You don't tie up the dog if you're going to slaughter the people and leave blood and body parts everywhere. That's not the same kind of mentality."

"Maybe she was tying him up when they surprised her," Charlie said. "She kind of had the look of a lady cop."

"Yeah, and all cops are into dog bondage, is that what you're saying?" Rivera holstered his weapon, pulled a penknife from his pocket, and went to where the basset hound was squirming on the floor.

"No, I'm not. Sorry. She did have a gun, though."

"She must have been here," Rivera said. "Otherwise the alarms would have been set. What's that on that doorjamb?" He was sawing through the duct tape on the basset's paws, being careful not to cut him.

He nodded toward the doorway from the shop to the back room.

"Blood," Charlie said. "And a little hair."

Rivera nodded. "That blood on the floor there, too? Don't touch."

Charlie looked at a three-inch puddle to the left of the door. "Yep, I think so."

Rivera had the basset's paws free and was kneeling on him to hold him still while he took the tape off his muzzle. "Those tracks in it, don't smear them. What are they, partial shoe prints?"

"Look like bird-feet prints. Chickens maybe?"

"No." Rivera released the basset, who immediately tried to jump on the inspector's Italian dress slacks and lick his face in celebration. He held the basset hound by the collar and moved to where Charlie was examining the tracks.

"They do look like chicken tracks," he said.

"Yep," Charlie said. "And you have dog drool on your jacket."

"I need to call this in, Charlie."

"So dog drool is the determining factor in calling in backup?"

"Forget the dog drool. The dog drool is not relevant. I need to report this and I need to call my partner in. He'll be pissed that I've waited this long. I need to take you home."

"If you can't get the stain out of that thousand-dollar suit jacket, you'll think it's relevant."

"Focus, Charlie. As soon as I can get another unit here, I'm sending you home. You have my cell. Let me know if anything happens. Anything."

Rivera called the dispatcher on his cell phone and asked him to send a uniform unit and the crime-scene squad as soon as they were available. When he snapped the phone shut, Charlie said, "So I'm not under arrest anymore?"

"No. Stay in touch. And stay safe, okay? You might even want to spend a few nights outside of the City."

"I can't. I'm the Luminatus, I have responsibilities."

"But you don't know what they are —"

"Just because I don't know what they are doesn't mean I don't have them," Charlie said, perhaps a little too defensively.

"And you're sure you don't know how many of these Death Merchants are in the City, or where they might be?"

"Minty Fresh said there was at least a dozen, that's all I know. This woman and the guy in the Mission were the only ones I spotted on my walks."

They heard a car pull up in the alley and Rivera went to the back door and signaled to the officers, then turned to Charlie. "You go home and get some sleep, if you can, Charlie. I'll be in touch."

Charlie let the uniformed police officer lead him to the cruiser and help him into the back, then waved to Rivera and the basset hound as the patrol car backed out of the alley.

23

A Fucked-up Day

It was a fucked-up day in the City by the Bay. At first light, flocks of vultures perched on the superstructures of the Golden Gate and Bay Bridges, and glared down at commuters as if they had a lot of goddamn gall to still be alive and driving. Traffic copters that were diverted to photograph the ranks of carrion birds ended up covering a spiral cloud of bats that circled the Transamerica pyramid for ten minutes, then seemed to evaporate into a black mist that floated out over the Bay. Three swimmers who had been competing in the San Francisco Triathlon drowned in the Bay, and a helicopter camera photographed something under the water, a dark shape approaching one of the swimmers from below and dragging him under. Numerous replays of the tape revealed that rather than the sleek shape of a shark, the creature had a wide wingspan and a distinctly horned head, unlike any ray or skate that anyone had ever seen before. The ducks in Golden Gate Park suddenly took to the wing and left the area, the hundreds of sea lions that normally lounged in the sun down at Pier 39 were gone as well, and even the pigeons seemed to have disappeared from the City.

A grunt reporter who had been covering the overnight police blotter noticed the coincidence of seven reports of violence or missing persons at local-area secondhand stores, and by early evening the television stations were mentioning it, along with spectacular footage of the Book 'em Danno building burning in the Mission. And there were hundreds of singular events experienced by individuals: creatures moving in the shadows, voices and screams from the sewer grates, milk souring, cats scratching owners, dogs howling, and a thousand people woke up to find that they no longer cared for the taste of chocolate. It was a fucked-up day.

Charlie spent the rest of the night fretting and checking locks, then double-checking them, then looking on the Internet for clues about the Underworlders, just in case someone posted a brand-new ancient document since he'd last checked. He wrote a will, and several letters, which he walked outside and put in the mailbox out on the street rather than with the outgoing mail on the counter of the store. Then, around dawn, completely exhausted yet with his Beta Male imagination racing at a thousand miles an hour, he took two of the sleeping pills Jane had given him and slept through the fucked-up day, to be awakened in early evening by a call from his darling daughter.

"Hello."

"Aunt Cassie is an anti-Semite," said Sophie.

"Honey, it's six in the morning. Can we discuss Aunt Cassie's politics a little later?"

"It is not, it's six at night. It's bath time, and Aunt Cassie won't let me bring Alvin and Mohammed into the bathroom with me for my bath, because she's an anti-Semite."

Charlie looked at his watch. He was sort of glad that it was six in the evening and he was talking to his daughter. Whatever happened while he was sleeping at least hadn't affected that.

"Cassie is not an anti-Semite." It was Jane on the other line.

"Is too," said Sophie. "Be careful,

Daddy, Aunt Jane is an anti-Semite sympathizer."

"I am not," Jane said.

"Listen to how smart my daughter is," said Charlie. "I didn't know words like *anti-Semite* and *sympathizer* when I was her age, did you?"

"You can't trust the goyim, Daddy," said Sophie. She lowered her voice to a whisper. "They hate baths, the goyim."

"Daddy's a goyim, too, baby."

"Oh my God, they're everywhere, like pod people!" He heard his daughter drop the phone, scream, and then a door slammed.

"Sophie, you unlock this door this instant," Cassie said in the background.

Jane said, "Charlie, where does she get this stuff? Are you teaching her this?"

"It's Mrs. Korjev — she's descended from Cossacks and she has a little residual guilt for what her ancestors did to the Jews."

"Oh," Jane said, not interested now that she couldn't blame Charlie. "Well, you shouldn't let the dogs in the bathroom with her. They eat the soap and sometimes they get in the tub, and then —"

"Let them go with her, Jane," Charlie interrupted. "They may be the only thing that can protect her."

"Okay, but I'm only letting them eat the cheap soaps. No French-milled soaps."

"They're fine with domestic soap, Jane. Look, I drew up a holographic will last night. If something happens to me, I want you to raise Sophie. It's in there."

Jane didn't answer. He could hear her breathing on the other end.

"Jane?"

"Sure, sure. Of course. What the hell is going on with you guys? What's the big danger Sophie's in? Why are you being spooky like this? And why didn't you call earlier, you fucker?"

"I was up all night doing stuff. Then I took two of those sleeping pills you gave me. Suddenly twelve hours are gone."

"You took two? Never take two."

"Yeah, thanks," Charlie said. "Anyway, I'm sure I'll be okay, but if for some reason I'm not, you need to take Sophie and get out of the City for a while. I mean like up in the Sierras. I also sent you a letter explaining everything, as much as I know, anyway. Only open it if something happens, okay?"

"Nothing better happen, you fuck. I just lost Mom, and I — why the hell are you talking like this, Charlie? What kind of trouble are you in?"

"I can't tell you, Jane. You have to trust me that I didn't have any choice in the matter."

"How can I help?"

"By doing exactly what you're doing, taking care of Sophie, keeping her safe, and keeping the hellhounds with her at all times."

"Okay, but nothing better happen to you. Cassie and I are going to get married and I want you to give me away. And I want to borrow your tux, too. It's Armani, right?"

"No, Jane."

"You won't give me away?"

"No, no, it's not that, I'd pay her to take you, it's not that."

"Then you don't think that gay people should be allowed to get married, is that it? You're finally coming clean. I knew it, after all —"

"I just don't think that gay people should be allowed to get married wearing my tux."

"Oh," Jane said.

"You'll wear my Armani tux and I'll have to rent some piece of crap or buy something new and cheap, and then I'll go through eternity looking like a total dork in the wedding pictures. I know how you guys like to show wedding pictures — it's like a disease."

"By 'you guys,' you mean lesbians?" Jane said, sounding very much like a prosecuting attorney.

"Yes, I mean lesbians, dumbfuck," said Charlie, sounding very much like a hostile witness.

"Oh, okay," Jane said. "It is my wedding, I guess I can buy a tux."

"That would be nice," Charlie said.

"I'm sort of needing the pants cut a little looser in the seat these days anyway," Jane said.

"Thatta girl."

"So you'll be safe and give me away."

"I'll sure try. You think Cassandra will let me bring the little Jewish kid?"

Jane laughed. "Call me every hour," she said.

"I won't do that."

"Okay, when you can."

"Yeah," Charlie said. "Bye." He smiled to himself and rolled out of bed, wondering if this might be the last time he would ever do that. Smile.

Charlie showered, ate a peanut-butter-and-jelly sandwich, and put on a thousand-dollar suit for which he had paid forty bucks. He limped around the bedroom for a few minutes and decided that his leg felt pretty good and he could do without the foam walking cast, so he left it on the floor by the bed. He put on a pot of coffee and called Inspector Rivera.

"It was a fucked-up day," Rivera said. "Charlie, you need to take your daughter and get out of town."

"I can't do that. This is about me. You'll keep me informed, right?"

"Promise you won't try to do anything stupid or heroic?"

"Not in my DNA, Inspector. I'll call you if I see anything."

Charlie disconnected, having no idea what he was going to do, but feeling like he had to do something. He called Jane's house to say good night to Sophie.

"I just want you to know that I love you very much, honey."

"Me, too, Daddy. Why did you call?"

"What, you have a meeting or something?"

"We're having ice cream."

"That's nice. Look, Sophie, Daddy has to go do some things, so I want you to stay with Aunt Jane for a few days, okay?"

"Okay. Do you need some help? I'm free."

"No, honey, but thank you."

"Okay, Daddy. Alvin is looking at my ice cream. He looks hungry, like bear. I have to go."

"Love you, honey."

"Love you, Daddy."

"Apologize to Aunt Cassie for calling her an anti-Semite."

" 'Kay." *Click*.

She hung up on him. The apple of his eye, the light of his life, his pride and joy, hung up on him. He sighed, but felt better. Heartbreak is the natural habitat of the Beta Male.

Charlie took a few minutes in the kitchen to sharpen the edge of the sword-cane on the back of the electric can opener he and Rachel had received as a wedding present, then he headed out to check on the store.

As soon as he opened the door to the back staircase Charlie heard strange animal noises coming from the store. It sounded as if they were coming from the back room, and there were no lights on, although he could see plenty of light filtering in from the store. Was this it? Sort of solved the problem of what he was going to do.

He drew the sword from his cane and

crept down the stairs in a crouch, moving along the edge of each step to minimize squeakage. Halfway down he saw the source of the animal noises and he recoiled, leaping nearly halfway back up the staircase.

"For the love of God!"

"It needed to be done," Lily said. She was astraddle Ray Macy, her plaid pleated skirt (mercifully) draped out over him, covering the parts that would have caused Charlie to have to tear his eyes out, which he was thinking about doing anyway.

"It did," Ray agreed breathlessly.

Charlie peeked down into the back room — they were still at it, Lily riding Ray like he was a mechanical bull, one bare breast bouncing out of the lapel of her chef's coat.

"He was despondent," she said. "I found him giving himself hickies with the shop vac. It's for the greater good, Asher."

"Well, stop it," Charlie said.

"No, no, no, no, no," said Ray.

"It's a charity thing," Lily said.

"You know, Lily," Charlie said, covering his eyes, "you could exercise your charity in other ways, like Salvation Army Santa or something."

"I don't want to fuck those guys. Most of

them are raging alcoholics, and they stink. At least Ray is clean."

"I don't mean *do* one, I mean *be* one. Ring the bell with the little red kettle. Jeez."

"I *am* clean," said Ray.

"You shut up," Charlie said. "She's young enough to be your daughter."

"He was suicidal," Lily said. "I may be saving his life."

"She is," Ray said.

"Shut up, Ray," Charlie said. "This is pathetic, desperate pity sex, that's all it is."

"He knows that," Lily said.

"I don't mind," said Ray.

"I'm doing this for the cause, too," Lily said. "Ray was holding out on you."

"I was?" said Ray.

"How?" Charlie said.

"He found a woman who was buying all the soul vessels. She was with the clients you missed. Somewhere in the Mission. He wasn't going to tell you about her."

"I don't know what you're talking about," Ray said. Then added, "Faster, please."

"Tell him the address," Lily said.

"Lily," Charlie said, "this isn't really necessary."

"No," Ray said.

There was a loud smack. Charlie opened his eyes. They were still there, doing it, but Ray's right cheek was bright red and Lily was winding up to slap him again.

"Tell him!"

"It's on Guerrero Street, between Eighteenth and Nineteenth, I don't know the number, but it's a big green Victorian, you can't miss it. Three Jewels Buddhist Center."

SMACK!

"Ouch, I told him," Ray whined.

"That's for not getting the address, BITCH!" Lily said. Then to Charlie: "There you go, Asher. I want a prime position when you take over the Underworld!"

Charlie thought that one of the first things he was going to change when he took over was expanding *The Great Big Book of Death* to include how to handle situations like this. But instead he said, "You got it, Lily. You'll be in charge of dress code and torture."

"Sweet," Lily said. " 'Scuse me, Asher, I have to finish this." Then to Ray: "Hear that? No more flannel shirts for you, grommet!" SMACK!

The grunts coming from Ray increased in frequency and intensity.

"Sure," Charlie said. "I'll just go out the other door."

"See ya," Ray said.

"I'm never going to look either one of you in the eye again, okay?"

"Sounds good, Asher," Lily said. "Be careful."

Charlie crept back up the steps, went out the front door of his apartment and down the elevator to the street entrance, suppressing his gag reflex the whole way. On the street he flagged down a cab and rode into the Mission, trying to wipe the image of his shagging employees out of his mind.

The Morrigan had followed the *gift souls* that had escaped through the drains to a deserted street in the Mission. Now they waited, watching the green Victorian building from storm-drain grates at either end of the street. They were more cautious now, their rapacious nature having been dampened somewhat by having been severely blown up the night before.

They called them the *gift souls* because the little patchwork creatures brought the souls right to them in the sewers — the gifts showing up in the Morrigan's weakest moment. After the accursed Boston terrier had chased them through miles of pipelines, leaving them battered and exhausted on a high ledge at a pipe junction, along marched twenty or so of the darling little nightmares, all dressed up in finery and carrying just what they needed to heal their wounds and replenish their strength: human souls. And thus renewed, they were able to scare away that obnoxious little dog. The Morrigan were back — not to the strength they'd achieved before the explosion, maybe not even enough to fly, but certainly enough to venture Above once again, especially with so many souls at hand.

No one was out on the streets tonight except the junkies, the hookers, and the homeless. After the fucked-up day in the City, most everyone had decided that it was just a better idea to stay in, safer. To the Morrigan (for all they cared), they were safer in their homes the same way a tuna fish is safer in a can, but no one knew that yet. No one knew what they were hiding from except Charlie Asher, and he was getting out of a cab right in front of them as they watched.

"It's New Meat," said Macha.

"We should give him a new name," said Babd. "I mean, he's really not that new anymore."

"Hush," hushed Macha.

"Hey, lover," Babd called out of her drain. "Did you miss me?"

Charlie paid the cabbie and stood in the middle of the street looking at the big jade-green Queen Anne. There were lights on in the turret upstairs and in one window downstairs. He could just make out the sign that read THREE JEWELS BUDDHIST CENTER. He started to step toward the house and saw movement in the lattice under the porch — eyes shining. A cat maybe. His cell phone rang and he flipped it open.

"Charlie, it's Rivera. I have some good news; we found Carrie Long, the woman from the pawnshop, and she's still alive. She was tied up and thrown in a Dumpster a block from her store."

"That's great," Charlie said. But he wasn't feeling great. The things that had been moving under the porch were coming out. Moving up the stairs, standing on the porch, lining up and facing him. Twenty or thirty of them, a little more than a foot tall, dressed in ornate period costumes. Each had the skeletal face of a dead animal, cats, foxes, badgers — animals Charlie couldn't identify, but just the skulls — the eye sockets empty, black. Yet they stared.

"You won't believe what she said put her there, Charlie. Little creatures, little monsters, she said."

"About fourteen inches tall," Charlie said.

"Yeah, how'd you know?"

"Lots of teeth and claws, like animal parts stuck together, all dressed up like they were going to a grand costume ball?"

"What are you telling me, Charlie? What do you know?"

"Just guessing," Charlie said. He unclipped the latch on his sword-cane.

"Hey, lover," came a female voice from behind him. "Did you miss me?"

Charlie turned. She was crawling out of the drain almost directly behind him.

"The bad news," Rivera said, "is we found the junk dealer and the bookstore guy from Book 'em Danno — pieces of them."

"That *is* bad news," Charlie said. He started moving up the street, away from the sewer harpy and the porch full of Satan's sock puppets.

"New Meat," came a voice from up the street.

Charlie looked to see another sewer harpy coming out of the drain, her eyes

508

gleaming black in the streetlight. Behind him he heard the clacking of little animal teeth.

"Charlie, I still think you should leave town for a while, but if you don't, and don't tell anyone I told you this, you should get a gun, maybe a couple of guns."

"I think that would be a great idea," Charlie said. The two sewer harpies were moving very slowly toward him, awkwardly, as if their nerves were short-circuiting. The one closest to him, the one from the alley in North Beach, was licking her lips. She looked a little ragged compared to the night she'd seduced him. He moved up the street away from them.

"A shotgun, so you won't need to learn to shoot. I can't give you one, but —"

"Inspector, I'm going to have to get back to you."

"I'm serious, Charlie, whatever these things are, they are going after your kind."

"You have no idea how clear that is to me, Inspector."

"Is that the one who shot me?" said the closest harpy. "Tell him I'm going to suck his eyeballs out of the sockets and chew them in his ear."

"You get that, Inspector?" Charlie said.

"She's there?"

"They," Charlie said.

"This way, Meat," said the third sewer harpy, coming out of the drain at the far end of the block. She stood, extended her claws, and flicked a line of venom down the side of a parked car. The paint sizzled and ran where it hit.

"Where are you, Charlie? Where are you?"

"I'm in the Mission. Near the Mission."

The little creatures were coming down the steps now, down the walk toward the street.

"Look," said a harpy, "he brought presents."

"Charlie, where exactly are you?" said Rivera.

"Gotta go, Inspector." Charlie flipped the phone closed and dropped it in his coat pocket. Then he drew the sword from the cane and turned to the harpy from the alley. "For you," he said to her, whipping the sword in a flourish through the air.

"That's sweet," she said. "You always think about my needs."

The 1957 Cadillac Eldorado Brougham was the perfect show-off of death machines. It consisted of nearly three tons of steel stamped into a massively mawed, high-tailed beast, lined with enough chrome to build a Terminator and still have parts left over — most of it in long, sharp strips that peeled off on impact and became lethal scythes to flay away pedestrian flesh. Under the four headlights it sported two chrome bumper bullets that looked like unexploded torpedoes or triple-G-cup Madonna death boobs. It had a noncollapsible steering column that would impale the driver upon any serious impact, electric windows that could pinch off a kid's head, no seat belts, and a 325 horsepower V8 with such appallingly bad fuel efficiency that you could hear it trying to slurp liquefied dinosaurs out of the ground when it passed. It had a top speed of a hundred and ten miles an hour, mushy, bargelike suspension that could in no way stabilize the car at that speed, and undersized power brakes that wouldn't stop it either. The fins jutting from the back were so high and sharp that the car was a lethal threat to pedestrians even when parked, and the whole package sat on tall, whitewall tires that looked, and generally handled, like oversized powdered doughnuts. Detroit couldn't have achieved more deadly finned ostentatia if they'd covered a killer whale in rhinestones. It was a masterpiece.

And the reason you need to know all that, is that along with the battle-worn Morrigan and the well-dressed chimeras, a '57 Eldorado was rapidly approaching Charlie.

The bloodred lacquered Eldo slid around the corner, tires screaming like flaming peacocks, hubcaps spinning off toward the curb, engine roaring, spewing blue smoke out of the rear wheel wells like a flatulent dragon. The first of the Morrigan turned in time to take a bumper bullet in the thigh before she was dragged and folded under the car and spit out the back into a black heap. The headlights came on and the Caddy veered toward the Morrigan nearest Charlie.

The animal creatures scurried back up the sidewalk and Charlie ran up onto the hood of a parked Honda as the Eldo smacked the second Morrigan. She ragdoll-whipped over the hood as the car's brakes screamed, then flew twenty yards down the street. The Caddy peeled out and hit her again, this time rolling over her with a series of thumps and leaving her tossing down the tarmac, shedding pieces as she rolled. The Caddy blazed on toward the final Morrigan.

This one had a few seconds on her sisters and started running up the street, her shape changing, arms to wings, tail feathers trying to manifest, but she didn't seem able to make the transformation in time to fly. The Eldo plowed over her, then hit the brakes, reversed, and burned rubber on her back.

Charlie ran up on the roof of the Honda, ready to leap away from the street, but the Caddy stopped and the blacked-out electric window wound down.

"Get the fuck in the car," said Minty Fresh.

Minty Fresh hit the final Morrigan again as he speeded off down the block, took two screeching lefts, then pulled the car to the curb, jumped out, and ran around to the front.

"Oh, goddamn," said Minty Fresh (*damn* on the downbeat, with pain and sustain). "Goddamn, my hood and grille are all fucked up. Goddamn. I will tolerate the rising of darkness to cover the world, but you *do not* fuck with my ride."

He jumped back in the car, threw it into gear, and screeched around the next corner.

"Where are you going?"

"I'm going to run over the bitches again. You *do not* fuck with my ride."

"Well, what did you think would happen when you ran them over?"

"Not this. I never ran over anyone before. Don't act like that's a surprise."

Charlie looked at the gleaming interior of the car, the bloodred leather seats, the dash fitted with walnut burl and gold-plated knobs.

"This is a great car. My mailman would love this car."

"Your mailman?"

"He collects vintage pimp wear."

"So what are you trying to say?"

"Nothing."

They were already on Guerrero Street and Minty floored it as they approached the target block. The first Morrigan he had hit was just getting to her knees when he hit her again, knocking her over two parked cars and into the side of a vacant building. The second one turned to face them and bared her claws, which raked the hood as he rolled over her with a drumroll of thumps, then he ran over the third one's legs as she was crawling back into the storm sewer.

"Jeez," Charlie said, turning and looking

out the back window.

Minty Fresh seemed to turn his full attention to driving safely now. "What the hell are those things?"

"I call them sewer harpies. They're the things that call to us from the storm sewers. They're a lot stronger now than they used to be."

"They're scary is what they are," said Minty.

"I don't know," Charlie said. "Have you gotten a good look at them? I mean, they got the badonkadonk out back and some fine bajoopbadangs up front, know what I'm sayin', dog? Buss a rock wid a playa?" He offered his fist for Minty to buss him a rock, but alas, the mint one left him hangin'.

"Stop that," Fresh said.

"Sorry," Charlie said.

"*Talk Like a Playa in Ten Days or Less* — Stone Thug Edition?" Minty asked.

Charlie nodded. "We got the CD into the store a couple of months ago. I practice in the van. How am I doing?"

"Your Negro-osity is uncanny. I had to keep checking to make sure you're still white."

"Thanks," Charlie said, then, as if a light went on: "Hey, I've been looking for you

— where the hell have you been?"

"Hiding out. One of those things came after me on the BART a few nights ago when I was coming back from Oakland."

"How'd you get away?"

"Those little animal things, a bunch of them attacked her in the dark. I could hear her screaming at them, tearing them to ribbons, but they held her off until the train pulled into the station, which was full of people. She bolted back into the tunnel. There were pieces of the animal creatures everywhere in the train car."

Minty turned onto Van Ness and started heading toward Charlie's side of town.

"So they helped you? They're not part of the Underworlders trying to take over?"

"They don't appear to be. They saved my ass."

"So you know some of the Death Merchants have been killed?"

"I didn't know. It wasn't in the paper. I saw where Anton's shop burned up last night. He didn't make it out?"

"They found pieces of him," Charlie said.

"Charlie, I think I caused this." Minty Fresh turned and really looked at Charlie for the first time, his golden eyes looking forlorn. "I failed to collect my last two soul vessels, and all of this started."

"I thought it was me," Charlie said. "I missed two as well. But I don't think it's us. My two clients are alive, I think they're in that house where I was going when you saved me: the Three Jewels Buddhist Center. There's a woman there who's been buying up soul vessels, too."

"Cute brunette?" Minty asked.

"I don't know. Why?"

"She bought some from me, too. Tried to disguise herself, but it was her."

"Well, she's in that house back there. I've got to go back there."

"I don't want anything to do with those bitches with the claws," Minty said.

"True dat," Charlie said. "I had a thing with one of them."

"No."

"Yeah, she got all up in my grille and shit — had to cut da ho loose."

"Stop that."

"Sorry. Anyway, I've got to go back."

"You sure? I don't think they're dead. Doesn't look like they can be dead."

"You could run over them again. By the way, how did you know where to find me?"

"After I heard about Anton's place burning, I tried to call him and got a disconnected message, so I went to your store. I talked to that little Goth girl you have working for you. She told me where you went. Talked to her for about ten minutes. She knows about me — I mean us? The Death Merchants?"

"Yes, I told her a long time ago. Wasn't she, uh, busy when you got there? With a guy, I mean."

"No. She seeing anyone?"

"I thought you were gay?"

"I never said that."

"Yeah, but you didn't go out of your way to deny it either."

"Charlie, I run a music store in the Castro, I'd do more business as a gay Death Merchant than a straight shopkeeper."

"Good point. I never thought of that."

"Color me surprised. So, she seeing anyone?"

"She's half your age and I think she's a little twisted — sexually, I mean."

"So is she seeing anyone?"

"She's like a little sister to me, Fresh. Don't you have employees like that?"

"Have you never met anyone who works in a record store? There's no greater repository of unjustified arrogance in the world. I'd poison my employees if I thought I could find replacements."

"I don't think she's seeing anybody, but since the world is about to be taken over by the Forces of Darkness, you may not have time for dating."

"I don't know. She seems like she might have an in with the Forces of Darkness. I like her, she's funny in a sort of macabre way, and she likes Miles."

"Lily likes Miles Davis?"

"You don't know that about your little sister?"

Charlie threw his hands up. "Take her, use her, throw her away, I don't care, she's only part-time. You can date my daughter, too. She's going to be six and probably loves Coltrane for all I know."

"Calm down, you're overreacting."

"Just turn around and take me back to that Buddhist center. I've got to stop this thing. It's all on me, Fresh. I'm the Luminatus."

"You are not."

"I am," Charlie said.

"You're the Great Death — with a capital *D?* You? You know this to be true?"

"I do," Charlie said.

"I knew there was something different about you, but I thought that the Luminatus would be — I don't know — taller."

"Don't start with that, okay."

Minty swung the car off Van Ness into a hotel turnaround.

"Where are you going?" Charlie said.

"To run over some sewer harpies again."

"Back to the Buddhist center?"

"Uh-huh. You have any weapons besides that stupid sword?"

"My cop friend told me I should get a gun."

Minty Fresh reached into his moss-green jacket and came out with the biggest pistol Charlie had ever seen. He placed it on the seat. "Take it. Desert Eagle fifty-caliber. It'll stop a bear."

Charlie picked up the chrome-plated pistol. It weighed like five pounds and the barrel looked big enough to stick your thumb in.

"This thing is huge."

"I'm a big guy. Listen, it holds eight shots. There's a round in the chamber. You have to cock it and release the safety before you fire. There and there." He pointed to the safety and the hammer. "Hold on to it if you have to shoot. It will knock you on your ass if you're not ready."

"What about you?"

Minty patted the other side of his coat. "I have another one."

Charlie turned the gun in his hand and watched the streetlights playing off its chromed surface. (Beta Males, who inherently feel they are always at a competitive disadvantage, are suckers for showy equalizers.) "You have a lot going on under the surface, Mr. Fresh. You are not just the run-of-the-mill seven-foot-tall Death Merchant in a pastel-green suit."

"Thank you, Mr. Asher. Very kind of you to say."

"My pleasure."

Charlie's cell phone rang and he flipped it open.

Rivera said, "Asher, where the hell are you? I've been circling the Mission and there's nothing here but a lot of black feathers flying in the air."

"Yeah, it's okay. I'm okay, Inspector. I found Minty Fresh, the guy who owns the music store. I'm in the car with him."

"So you're safe?"

"Relatively."

"Good. Lay low and I'll call you, okay? I want to talk to your friend tomorrow."

"You got it, Inspector. Thanks for coming to help."

"Careful, Asher."

"Gotcha. I'm laying low. Bye."

Charlie snapped the phone shut and

turned to Minty Fresh. "You ready?"

"Absolutely," said the fresh one.

The street was deserted when they pulled up in front of the Three Jewels Buddhist Center.

"I'll go around to the back," Minty said.

"Well, cars suck, I can tell you that," said Babd, trying to keep herself together as the Morrigan limped back to the great ship. "Five thousand years, horses are fine, all of a sudden we have to have paved streets and cars. I don't see the attraction."

"I'm not even sure that we need to rise and let Darkness rule," said Nemain. "Apparently darkness isn't qualified yet. Speaking as an agent of Darkness, I think it needs more time." She had been crushed into a half-woman, half-raven form and was shedding feathers as they limped through the pipe.

"It's like that New Meat has someone watching over him," said Macha. "Next time Orcus can deal with him."

"Yeah, let's get Orcus to go after him," Babd said. "See what he thinks of cars."

24

Audrey and the Squirrel People

Charlie could hear things scurrying under the porch as he walked to the front door of the Buddhist center, but the weight of the enormous pistol he'd stuck down the back of his belt reassured him, even if it was pulling his pants down a little. The front door was nearly twelve feet tall, red, with reeded glass running the length, and there were arrays of colorful Tibetan prayer wheels, like spools, on either side of the door. Charlie knew what they were because he'd once had a thief try to sell him some hot ones stolen from a temple.

Charlie knew he should kick down the door, but then, it was a really big door, and although he had watched a lot of cop shows and movies where door kicking had been done, he was inexperienced himself. Another option was to pull his pistol and blast the lock off the door, but he didn't know any more about lock blasting than he did door kicking, so he decided to ring the doorbell.

The scurrying noises increased and he could hear heavier footsteps inside. The door swung open and the pretty brunette he knew as Elizabeth Sarkoff — Esther Johnson's fake niece — stood in the doorway.

"Why, Mr. Asher, what a pleasant surprise."

It won't be for long, sister, said his inner tough guy. "Mrs. Sarkoff, nice to see you. What are you doing here?"

"I'm the receptionist. Come in, come in."

Charlie stepped into the foyer, which opened up to a staircase and had sliding double doors on either side. He could see that straight back the foyer led to a dining room with a long table, and beyond that a kitchen. The house had been restored nicely, and didn't really have the appearance of a public building.

The inner tough guy said, *Don't try to run your game on me, floozy. I've never hit a dame before, but if I don't get some straight talk quick, I'm willing to give it a try, see.* Charlie said, "I had no idea you were a Buddhist. That's fascinating. How's your Aunt Esther, by the way?" *He had her now, didn't even have to slap her around.*

"Still dead. Thanks for asking, though. What can I do for you, Mr. Asher?"

The sliding door to the left of them opened an inch and someone, a young man's voice, said, "Master, we need you."

"I'll be right there," said the alleged Mrs. Sarkoff.

"Master?" Charlie raised an eyebrow.

"We hold receptionists in very high regard in the Buddhist tradition." She grinned, really big and goofy, like she didn't even believe it herself. Charlie was totally charmed by the laughter and open surrender in her eyes. Trust there, with no reason for it.

"Good God, you're a bad liar," he said.

"Guess you could see right through my moo-poo, huh?" Big grin.

"So, you are?" Charlie offered his hand to shake.

"I am the Venerable Amitabha Audrey Rinpoche." She bowed. "Or just Audrey, if you're in a hurry." She took two of Charlie's fingers and shook them.

"Charlie Asher," Charlie said. "So you're not really Mrs. Johnson's niece."

"And you're not really a used-clothing dealer?"

"Well, actually —"

That's all Charlie got out. There was a crashing sound from straight ahead, glass and splintering wood. Then he saw the table go over in the next room and Minty Fresh screamed "Freeze!" as he leapt over the fallen table and headed toward them, gun in hand, oblivious, evidently, to the fact that he was seven feet tall and that the doorway, built in 1908, was only six feet eight inches high.

"Stop," Charlie shouted, about a half second too late, as Minty Fresh drove four inches of forehead into some very nicely finished oak trim above the door with a thud that shook the whole house. His feet continued on, his body swinging after, and at one point he was parallel to the floor, about six feet off the ground, when gravity decided to manifest itself.

The chrome Desert Eagle clattered all the way through the foyer and hit the front door. Minty Fresh landed flat and quite unconscious on the floor between Charlie and Audrey.

"And this is my friend Minty Fresh," Charlie said. "He doesn't do this a lot."

"Boy, you don't see that every day," said Audrey, looking down at the sleeping giant.

"Yeah," Charlie said. "I don't know where he found raw silk in moss green."

"That's not linen?" Audrey asked.

"No, it's silk."

"Hmm, it's so wrinkled, I thought it must be linen, or a blend."

"Well, I think maybe all the activity —"

"Yeah, I guess so." Audrey nodded, then looked at Charlie. "So —"

"Mr. Asher." A woman's voice to his right. The doors on Charlie's right slid open, and an older woman stood there: Irena Posokovanovich. The last time he'd seen her he was sitting in the back of Rivera's cruiser, in handcuffs.

"Mrs. Posokov . . . Mrs. Posokovano—Irena! How are you?"

"You weren't so concerned about that yesterday."

"No, I was. I really was. Sorry about that." Charlie smiled, thinking it was his most charming smile. "I hope you don't have that pepper spray with you."

"I don't," Irena said.

Charlie looked at Audrey. "We had a little misunderstanding —"

"I have this," Irena said, producing a stun gun from behind her back, pressing it to Charlie's chest and sending a hundred and twenty-five thousand volts surging through his body. He could see animals, or animal-like creatures, dressed in period finery, approaching him as he convulsed in pain on the floor.

"Get them both tied up, guys," Audrey said. "I'll make tea."

"Tea?" Audrey said.

So, for the second time in his life, Charlie Asher found himself tied to a chair and being served a hot beverage. Audrey was bent over before him, holding a teacup, and regardless of the awkwardness or danger of the situation, Charlie found himself staring down the front of her shirt.

"What kind of tea?" Charlie asked, buying time, noticing the cluster of tiny silk roses that perched happily at the front clasp of her bra.

"I like my tea like I like my men," Audrey said with a grin. "Weak and green."

Now Charlie looked into her eyes, which were smiling. "Your right hand is free," she said. "But we had to take your gun and your sword-cane, because those things are frowned upon."

"You're the nicest captor I've ever had," Charlie said, taking the teacup from her.

"What are you trying to say?" said Minty Fresh.

Charlie looked to his right, where Minty Fresh was tied to a chair that made him look as if he'd been taken hostage at a child's tea party — his knees were up near his chin and one of his wrists was taped near the floor. Someone had put a large ice pack on his head, which looked vaguely like a tam-o'-shanter.

"Nothing," Charlie said. "You were a great captor, too, don't get me wrong."

"Tea, Mr. Fresh?" Audrey said.

"Do you have coffee?"

"Back in a second," Audrey said. She left the room.

They'd been moved to one of the rooms off the foyer, Charlie couldn't tell which. It must have been a parlor for entertaining during its day, but it had been converted into a combination office and reception room: metal desks, a computer, some filing cabinets, and an array of older oak office chairs for working and waiting.

"I think she likes me," Charlie said.

"She has you taped to a chair," Minty Fresh said, pulling at the tape around his ankles with his free hand. The ice pack fell off his head and hit the floor with a loud thump.

"I didn't notice how attractive she was when I met her before."

"Would you help me get free, please?" Minty said.

"Can't," Charlie said. "Tea." He held up his cup.

Clicking noises by the door. They looked up as four little bipeds in silk and satin scampered into the room. One, who had the face of an iguana, the hands of a raccoon, and was dressed like a musketeer, big-feathered hat and all, drew a sword and poked Minty Fresh in the hand he was using to pull at the duct tape.

"Ow, dammit. Thing!"

"I don't think he wants you to try to get loose," Charlie said.

The iguana guy saluted Charlie with a flourish of his sword and pointed to the end of his snout with his free hand, as if to say, *On the nose, buddy.*

"So," Audrey said, entering the room carrying a tray with Minty's coffee, "I see you've met the squirrel people."

"Squirrel people?" Charlie asked.

A little lady with a duck's face and reptilian hands wearing a purple satin evening gown curtsied to Charlie, who nodded back.

"That's what we call them," Audrey said. "Because the first few I made had squirrel faces and hands, but then I ran out of squirrel parts and they got more baroque."

"They're not creatures of the Underworld?" Charlie said. "You made them?"

"Sort of," Audrey said. "Cream and sugar, Mr. Fresh?"

"Please," Minty said. "You make these monsters?"

All four of the little creatures turned to him at once and leaned back, as if to say, *Hey, pal, who are you calling monsters.*

"They're not monsters, Mr. Fresh. The squirrel people are as human as you are."

"Yeah, except they have better fashion sense," Charlie said.

"I'm not always going to be taped to this chair, Asher," Minty said. "Woman, who or what the hell are you?"

"Be nice," Charlie said.

"I suppose I should explain," Audrey said.

"Ya think?" Minty said.

Audrey sat down on the floor, cross-legged, and the squirrel people gathered around her, to listen.

"Well, it's a little embarrassing, but I guess it started when I was a kid. I sort of had this affinity for dead things."

"Like you liked to touch dead things?" asked Minty Fresh. "Get naked with them?"

531

"Would you please let the lady talk," Charlie said.

"Bitch is a freak," Minty said.

Audrey smiled. "Why, yes; yes, I am, Mr. Fresh, and you are tied up in my dining room, at the mercy of any freaky thing that might occur to me." She tapped a silver demitasse spoon she'd used to stir her tea on her front tooth and rolled her eyes as if imagining something delicious.

"Please go on," said Minty Fresh with a shudder. "Sorry to interrupt."

"It wasn't a freaky thing," Audrey said, glancing at Minty, daring him to speak up. "It was just that I had an overdeveloped sense of empathy with the dying, mostly animals, but when my grandmother passed, I could feel it, from miles away. Anyway, it didn't overwhelm me or anything, but when I got to college, to see if I could get a handle on it, I decided to study Eastern philosophy — oh yeah, and fashion design."

"I think it's important to look good when you're doing the work of the dead," Charlie said.

"Well — uh — okay," Audrey said. "And I was a good seamstress. I really liked making costumes. Anyway, I met and fell in love with a guy."

"A dead guy?" Minty asked.

"Soon enough, Mr. Fresh. He was dead soon enough." Audrey looked down at the carpet.

"See, you insensitive fuck," Charlie said. "You hurt her feelings."

"Hello, tied to a chair here," Minty said. "Surrounded by little monsters, Asher. Not the insensitive one."

"Sorry," Charlie said.

"It's okay," Audrey said. "His name was William — Billy, and we were together for two years before he got sick. We'd only been engaged a month when he was diagnosed with an inoperable brain tumor. They gave him a couple of months to live. I dropped out of school and stayed with him every moment. One of the nurses from hospice knew about my Eastern studies course and recommended we talk with Dorje Rinpoche, a monk from the Tibetan Buddhist Center in Berkeley. He talked to us about *Bardo Thodrol*, what you know as the Tibetan *Book of the Dead*. He helped prepare Billy to transfer his consciousness into the next world — into his next life. It took our focus off of the darkness and made death a natural, hopeful thing. I was with Billy when he died, and I could feel his consciousness move on — really feel it

— Dorje Rinpoche said that I had some special talent. He thought I should study under a high lama."

"So you became a monk?" Charlie asked.

"I thought a lama was just a tall sheep," said Minty Fresh.

Audrey ignored him. "I was heartbroken and I needed direction, so I went to Tibet and was accepted at a monastery where I studied *Bardo Thodrol* for twelve years under Lama Karmapa Rinpoche, the seventeenth reincarnation of the bodhisattva who had founded our school of Buddhism a thousand years ago. He taught me the art of *p'howa* — the transference of the consciousness at the moment of death."

"So you could do what the monk had done for your fiancé?" Charlie asked.

"Yes. I performed *p'howa* for many of the mountain villagers. It was a sort of a specialty with me — along with making the robes for everyone in the monastery. Lama Karmapa told me that he felt I was a very old soul, the reincarnation of a superenlightened being from many generations before. I thought perhaps he was just trying to test me, to get me to succumb to ego, but when his own death was near and he called me to perform the *p'howa* for him, I realized that this was the test, and he was trusting the transference of his own soul to me."

"Just so we're clear," said Minty Fresh. "I would not trust you with my car keys."

The iguana musketeer poked Minty in the calf with his little sword and the big man yelped.

"See," Charlie said. "When you're rude it comes back on you — like karma."

Audrey smiled at Charlie, put her tea on the floor, and folded her legs into the lotus position, settling in. "When the Lama passed, I saw his consciousness leave his body. Then I felt my own consciousness leave my body, and I followed the Lama into the mountains, where he showed me a small cave, buried deep beneath the snow. And in that cave was a stone box, sealed with wax and sinew. He told me that I must find the box, and then he was gone, ascended, and I found myself back in my body."

"Were you superenlightened then?" Charlie asked.

"I don't even know what that is," Audrey said. "The Lama was wrong about that, but something had changed me while performing the *p'howa* for him. When I came out of the room with his body, I could see a red spot glowing in people, right at their heart chakra. It was the same thing I had followed into the mountains, the undying consciousness — I could see people's souls. But what was more disturbing to me, I could see that the glow was absent in some people, or I couldn't see it in them, or in myself. I didn't know why, but I did know that I had to find that stone box. By following the exact path into the mountains that the Lama had shown me, I did. Inside was a scroll that most Buddhists thought — still think — was a myth: the lost chapter of the Tibetan *Book of the Dead* . . . It outlined two long-lost arts, the *p'howa of forceful projection,* and one I hadn't even heard of, the *p'howa of undying.* The first allows you to force a soul from one being to another, and the second allows the practitioner to prolong the transition, the *bardo,* between life and death indefinitely."

"Does that mean you could make people live forever?" Charlie asked.

"Sort of — more like they just stop dying. I meditated on the amazing gift I'd been given for months, afraid to try to perform the rituals. But one day when I was attending the *bardo* of an old man who was dying of a painful stomach cancer, I could watch the suffering no longer, and I tried the *p'howa of forceful projection*. I guided his soul into the body of his newborn grandson, who I could see had no glow at his heart chakra. I could actually see the glow move across the room and the soul enter the baby. The man died in peace only seconds later.

"A few weeks later I was called to attend the *bardo* of a young boy who had taken ill and was showing all the signs of imminent death. I couldn't bear to let it happen, knowing that there might be something I might be able to do, so I performed the *p'howa of undying* on him, and he didn't die. In fact, he got better. I succumbed to the ego of it, then, and I started to perform the ritual on other villagers, instead of helping them on to their next life. I did five in as many months, but there was a problem. The parents of the little boy summoned me. He wasn't growing — not even his hair and nails. He was stuck at age nine. But by then the villagers were all coming to me with the dying, and word spread throughout the mountains to other villages. They lined up outside of our monastery, demanding I come see them. But I had refused to perform the ritual, realizing that I was not helping these people, but in fact freezing them in their spiritual progression, plus, you know, kind of freaking them out."

"Understandably," Charlie said.

"I couldn't explain to my fellow monks what was happening. So I ran away in the night. I presented myself to be of service to a Buddhist center in Berkeley, and I was accepted as a monk. It was during that time that I saw, for the first time, a human soul contained in an inanimate object, when I went into a music store in the Castro. It was your music store, Mr. Fresh."

"I knew that was you," said Minty. "I told Asher about you."

"He did," Charlie said. "He said you were very attractive."

"I did not," Minty said.

"He did. 'Nice eyes,' he said," Charlie said. "Go on."

"There was no mistaking it, though — the glow in the CD — it was exactly the same presence that I could sense in people who had a soul. Needless to say, I was freaked out."

"Needless to say," Charlie said. "I had a similar experience."

Audrey nodded. "I was going to discuss all of this with my master at the center, you know, come clean about what I had learned in Tibet — turn the scrolls over to someone who perhaps understood what was going on with the souls inside of objects, but after only a few months, word came from Tibet that I had left under suspicious circumstances. I don't know what details they gave, but I was asked to leave the center."

"So you formed a posse of spooky animal things and moved to the Mission," said Minty Fresh. "That's nice. You can let me loose from this chair now and I'll be on my way."

"Fresh, will you please let Audrey finish telling her story. I'm sure there's a perfectly innocent reason that she hangs out with a posse of spooky animal things."

Audrey pressed on. "I was able to get a job as costumer for a local theater group, and being around theater people, basically a bunch of born show-offs, can put you back into the swing of a life. I tried to forget about my practice in Tibet, and I focused on my work, trying to let my creativity drive me. I couldn't afford to make full-sized costumes, so I began to create smaller versions. I bought a collection of stuffed squirrels from a secondhand store in the Mission, and used those as my first models. Later I made my models out of other taxidermied animal parts — mixing and matching them, but I'd already started calling them my squirrel people. A lot of them have bird feet, chicken and duck, because I could purchase them in Chinatown, along with things like turtle heads and — well, you can buy a lot of dead-animal parts in Chinatown."

"Tell me about it," Charlie said. "I live a block from the shark parts store. Never actually tried to build a shark from spare parts, though. Bet that would be fun."

"Y'all are twisted," Minty said. "Both of you — you know that, right? Messin' with dead things and all."

Charlie and Audrey each raised an eyebrow at him. A creature in a blue kimono with the face of a dog skull gave Minty the critical eye socket and would have raised an eyebrow at him if she'd had one.

"All right, go on," Minty said, waving Audrey on with his free hand. "You made your point."

Audrey sighed. "So I started to hit all of the secondhand stores in the City, looking for everything from buttons to hands. And at at least eight stores, I found the soul objects — all grouped together at each store. I realized that I wasn't the only one who could see them glowing red. Someone was imprisoning these souls in the objects. That's how I came to know about you gentlemen, whatever you are. I had to get these souls out of your hands. So I bought them. I wanted them to move on to their next rebirth, but I didn't know how. I thought about using the *p'howa of forceful projection,* forcing a soul into someone who I could see was soulless, but that process takes time. What would I do, tie them up? And I didn't even know if it would work. After all, that method was used to force a soul from one person to another, not from an inanimate object."

Charlie said, "So you tried this forceful-projection thing with one of your squirrel people?"

"Yeah, and it worked. But what I didn't count on is that they became animated. She started walking around, doing things, intelligent things. Which is how they came to be these little guys you've seen today.

"More tea, Mr. Asher?" Audrey smiled and held the teapot out to Charlie.

"Those things have human souls?" Charlie asked. "That's heinous."

"Oh yeah, and it's better that you have the soul imprisoned in an old pair of sneakers in your shop. They're only in the squirrel people until I can figure how to put their souls into a person. I wanted them saved from you and your kind."

"We're not the bad guys. Tell her, Fresh, we're not the bad guys."

"We're not the bad guys," Minty said. "Can I get some more coffee?"

"We're Death Merchants," Charlie said, but it came out much less cheerful-sounding than he'd hoped. He was very desperate for Audrey not to think of him as a bad guy. Like most Beta Males, he didn't realize that being a good guy was not necessarily an attraction to women.

"That's what I'm saying," Audrey said, "I couldn't just let you guys sell the souls like so much secondhand junk."

"That's how they find their next rebirth," Minty said.

"What?" Audrey looked at Charlie for confirmation.

Charlie nodded. "He's right. We get the souls when someone dies, and then someone buys them and they get to their next life. I've seen it happen."

"No way," Audrey said, overpouring Minty's coffee.

"Yep," Charlie said. "We can see the red glow, but not in people's bodies like you. Only in the objects. When someone who needs a soul comes in contact with the object, the glow goes out. The soul moves into them."

"I thought you'd trapped the souls between lives. You're not holding these souls prisoner?"

"Nope."

"It wasn't us after all," Minty Fresh said to Charlie. "She was the one that brought all of this on."

"What on? What?" Audrey said.

"There are *Forces of Darkness* — we don't know what they are," Charlie said. "What we've seen are giant ravens, and these demonlike women, we call them sewer harpies because they've come out of the storm sewers. They gain strength when they get hold of a soul vessel — and they're getting really strong. The prophecy says they are going to rise in San Francisco and darkness will cover the world."

"And they are in the sewers?" Audrey said.

Both Death Merchants nodded.

"Oh no, that's how the squirrel people get around town without being seen. I've sent them to the different stores in the City to get the souls. I must have been sending them right to these creatures. And a lot of them haven't come home. I thought they just might be lost, or wandering around. They do that. They have the potential of full human consciousness, but something is lost with time out of the body. Sometimes they can get a little goofy."

"No kidding," said Charlie. "So is that why iguana boy over there is gnawing on the light cord?"

"Ignatius, get off there! If you electrocute yourself the only place I have to put your soul is that Cornish hen I got at the Safeway. It's still frozen and I don't have any pants that will fit it." She turned to Charlie with an embarrassed smile. "The things you never think you'll hear yourself say."

"Yeah, kids, what are you gonna do?" Charlie said, trying to sound easygoing. "You know, one of your squirrel people shot me with a crossbow."

Audrey looked distraught now. Charlie wanted to comfort her. Give her a hug. Kiss her on the top of the head and tell her that everything was all right. Maybe even get her to untie him.

"They did? Crossbow, oh, that would be Mr. Shelly. He was a spy or something in a former life — had a habit of going off on his own little missions. I sent him to keep an eye on you and report back so I could figure out what you were doing. No one was supposed to get hurt. He never came home. I'm really sorry."

"Report back?" Charlie said. "They can talk?"

"Well, they don't talk," Audrey said. "But some of them can read and write. Mr. Shelly could actually type. I've been working on that. I need to get them a voice box that works. I tried one out of a talking doll, but I just ended up with a ferret in a samurai outfit that cried and kept asking if it could go play in the sandbox, it was unnerving. It's a strange process, as long as there's organic parts, stuff that was once living, they knit together, they work. Muscles and tendons make their own connections. I've been using hams for the torsos, because it gives them a lot of muscle to work with, and they smell better until the process is finished. You know, smoky. But some things are a mystery. They don't grow voice boxes."

"They don't appear to grow eyes, either," Charlie said, gesturing with his teacup at a creature whose head was an eyeless cat skull. "How do they see?"

"Got me." Audrey shrugged. "It wasn't in the book."

"Man, I know that feeling," said Minty Fresh.

"So I've been experimenting with a voice box made out of catgut and cuttlebone. We'll see if the one who has it learns to talk."

"Why don't you put the souls back in human bodies?" asked Minty. "I mean, you can, right?"

"I suppose," Audrey said. "But to be honest, I didn't have any human corpses lying around the house. But there does have to be a piece of human being in them — I learned that from experimenting — a finger bone, blood, something. I got a great deal on a backbone in a junk store in the Haight and I've been using one vertebra for each of them."

"So you're like some monstrous reanimator," Charlie said. Then he quickly added, "And I mean that in the nicest way."

"Thanks, *Mr. Death Merchant.*" Audrey smiled back and went to the nearby desk for some scissors. "But it looks like I need to cut you loose and hear how you guys got into your line of work. Mr. Greenstreet, could you bring us some more tea and coffee?"

A creature with a beaver's skull for a head, wearing a fez and a red satin smoking jacket, bowed and scampered by

Charlie, headed toward the kitchen.

"Nice jacket," Charlie said.

The beaver guy gave him a thumbs-up as he passed. Lizard thumbs.

25

The Rhythm of Lost and Found

The Emperor was camped in some bushes near an open culvert that drained into Lobos Creek in the Presidio, the land point on the San Francisco side of the Golden Gate where forts had stood from the time of the Spanish, but had recently been turned into a park. The Emperor had wandered the city for days, calling into storm drains, following the sound of his lost soldier's barking. The faithful retriever Lazarus had led him here, one of the few drains in the city where the Boston terrier might be able to exit without being washed into the Bay. They camped under a camouflage poncho and waited. Mercifully, it hadn't rained since Bummer had chased the squirrel into the storm sewer, but dark clouds had been bubbling over the City for two days now, and whether or not they were bringing rain, they made the Emperor fear for his city.

"Ah, Lazarus," said the Emperor, scratching his charge behind the ears, "if we had even half the courage of our small comrade, we would go into that drain and find him. But what are we without him, our courage, our valor? Steady and righteous we may be, my friend, but without courage to risk ourselves for our brother, we are but politicians — blustering whores to rhetoric."

Lazarus growled low and hunkered back under the poncho. The sun had just set, but the Emperor could see movement back in the culvert. As he climbed to his feet, the six-foot pipe was filled with a creature that crawled out and virtually unfolded in the creekbed — a huge, bullheaded thing, with eyes that glowed green and wings that unfurled like leathery umbrellas.

As they watched the creature took three steps and leapt into the twilight sky, his wings beating like the sails of a death ship. The Emperor shuddered, and considered for a moment moving their camp into the City proper, perhaps passing the night on Market Street, with people and policemen streaming by, but then he heard the faintest barking coming from deep in the culvert.

* * *

Audrey was showing them around the Buddhist center, which, except for the office in the front, and a living room that had been turned into a meditation room, looked very much like any other sprawling Victorian home. Austere and Oriental in its decor, yes, and perhaps the smell of incense permeating it, but still, just a big old house.

"It's just a big old house, really," she said, leading them into the kitchen.

Minty Fresh was making Audrey feel a little uncomfortable. He kept picking at bits of duct-tape adhesive that had stuck to the sleeve of his green jacket, and giving Audrey a look like he was saying, *This better come out when it's dry-cleaned or it's your ass.* His size alone was intimidating, but now a series of large knots were rising on his forehead where he'd smacked the doorway, and he looked vaguely like a Klingon warrior, except for the pastel-green suit, of course. Maybe the agent for a Klingon warrior.

"So," he said, "if the squirrel people thought I was a bad guy, why did they save me from the sewer harpy in the train last week? They attacked her and gave me time to get away."

Audrey shrugged. "I don't know. They were supposed to just watch you and report back. They must have seen that what was after you was much worse than you. They are human, at heart, you know."

She paused in front of the pantry door and turned to them. She hadn't seen the debacle in the street, but Esther had been watching through the window and had told her what had happened — about the womanlike creatures that had been coming after Charlie. Evidently these strange men were allies of a sort, practicing what she had taken on as her holy work: helping souls to move to their next existence. But the method? Could she trust them?

"So, from what you guys are saying, there are thousands of humans walking around without souls?"

"Millions, probably," Charlie said.

"Maybe that explains the last election," she said, trying to buy time.

"You said you could see if people had one," said Minty Fresh.

He was right, but she'd seen the soulless and never thought about their sheer numbers, and what happened when the dead didn't match with the born. She shook her head. "So the transfer of souls depends on material acquisition? That's just so — I don't know — *sleazy.*"

"Audrey, believe me," Charlie said, "we're both as baffled by the mechanics of it as you are, and we're instruments of it."

She looked at Charlie, really looked at him. He was telling the truth. He had come here to do the right thing. She threw open the pantry door and the red light spilled out on them.

The pantry was nearly as big as a modern bedroom, and every shelf from floor to ceiling and most of the floor space was covered with glowing soul vessels.

"Jeez," Charlie said.

"I got as many as I could — or, the squirrel people did."

Minty Fresh ducked into the pantry and stood in front of a shelf full of CDs and records. He grabbed a handful and started shuffling through them, then turned to her, holding up a half-dozen CD cases fanned out. "These are from my store."

"Yes. We got all of them," Audrey said.

"You broke into my store."

"She kept them from the bad guys, Minty," Charlie said, stepping in the pantry. "She probably saved them, maybe saved us."

"No way, man, none of this would be happening if it wasn't for her."

"No, it was always going to happen. I saw it in the other *Great Big Book*, in Arizona."

"I was just trying to help them," Audrey said.

Charlie was staring at the CDs in Minty's hand. He seemed to have fallen into some sort of trance, and reached out and took the CDs as if he were moving through some thick liquid — then shuffled away all but one, which he just stared at, then flipped over to look at the back. He sat down hard in the pantry and Audrey caught his head to keep him from bumping it on the shelf behind him.

"Charlie," she said. "Are you okay?"

Minty Fresh squatted down next to Charlie and looked at the CD — reached for it, but Charlie pulled it away. Minty looked at Audrey. "It's his wife," he said.

Audrey could see the name Rachel Asher scratched into the back of the CD case and she felt her heart breaking for poor Charlie. She put her arms around him. "I'm so sorry, Charlie. I'm so sorry."

Tears splattered on the CD case and Charlie wouldn't look up.

Minty Fresh stood and cleared his throat, his face clear of any rage or accusation. He seemed almost ashamed. "Audrey,

I've been driving around the City for days, I could sure use a place to lie down if you have it."

She nodded, her face against Charlie's back. "Ask Esther, she'll show you."

Minty Fresh ducked out of the pantry.

Audrey held Charlie and rocked him for a long time, and even though he was lost in the world of that CD that held the love of his life, and she was outside, crouched in a pantry that glowed red with cosmic bric-a-brac, she cried with him.

After an hour passed, or maybe it was three, because that's the way time is in grief and love, Charlie turned to her and said, "Do I have a soul?"

"What?" she said.

"You said you could see people's souls glowing in them — do I have a soul?"

"Yes, Charlie. Yes, you have a soul."

He nodded, turning away from her again, but pushing back against her.

"You want it?" he said.

"Nah, I'm good," she said. But she wasn't.

She took the CD out of his hand, pried his hands off of it, really, and put it with the others. "Let's let Rachel rest and go in the other room."

"Okay," Charlie said. He let her help him up.

Upstairs, in a little room with cushions all over the floor and pictures of the Buddha reclining amid lotuses, they sat and talked by candlelight. They'd shared their histories, of how they had come to be where they were, what they were, and with that out of the way, they talked about their losses.

"I've seen it again and again," Charlie said. "More with men than with women, but definitely with both — a wife or husband dies, and it's like the survivor is roped to him like a mountain climber who's fallen into a crevasse. If the survivor can't let go — cut them loose, I guess — the dead will drag them right into the grave. I think that would have happened to me, if it wasn't for Sophie, and maybe even becoming a Death Merchant. There was something bigger than me going on, something bigger than my pain. That's the only reason I made it this far."

"Faith," Audrey said. "Whatever that is. It's funny, when Esther came to me, she was angry. Dying and angry — she said that she'd believed in Jesus all her life, now she was dying and He said she was going to live forever."

"So you told her, 'Sucks to be you, Esther.'"

Audrey threw a cushion at him. She liked the way that he could find the silliness in such dark territory. "No, I told her that He told her that she'd live forever, but He didn't say how. Her faith hadn't been betrayed at all, she just needed to open to a broader understanding."

"Which was total bullshit," Charlie said.

Another cushion bounced off his forehead. "No, it wasn't moo-poo. If anyone should understand the significance of the book not covering everything in detail, it should be you — us."

"You can't say 'bullshit,' can you?"

Audrey felt herself blush and was glad they were in the dim orange candlelight. "I'm talking faith, over here, you want to give me a break?"

"Sorry. I know — or, I think I know what you mean. I mean, I know that there's some sort of order to all this, but I don't know how someone can reconcile, say, a Catholic upbringing with a Tibetan *Book of the Dead*, with a *Great Big Book of Death*, secondhand dealers selling objects with human souls, and vicious raven women in the sewers. The more I know, the less I understand. I'm just doing."

"Well, the *Bardo Thodrol* talks about hundreds of monsters you will encounter as your consciousness makes its journey into death and rebirth, but you're instructed to ignore them, as they are illusions, your own fears trying to keep your consciousness from moving on. They can't really harm you."

"I think this may be something they left out of the book, Audrey, because I've seen them, I've fought with them, wrenched souls out of their grasp, watched them take bullets and get hit by cars and keep going — they are definitely not illusions and they definitely can hurt you. The *Great Big Book* isn't clear about the specifics, but it definitely talks about the Forces of Darkness trying to take over our world, and how the Luminatus will rise and do battle with them."

"Luminatus?" Audrey said. "Something to do with light?"

"The big Death," Charlie said. "Death with a capital *D*. Sort of the Kahuna, the Big Cheese, the Boss Death. Like Minty and the other Death Merchants would be Santa's helpers, the Luminatus would be Santa."

"Santa Claus is the big Death?!" Audrey said, wide-eyed.

"No, that's just an example —" Charlie saw she was trying not to laugh. "Hey, I've been bruised and electrocuted and tied up and traumatized tonight."

"So my seduction strategy is working?" Audrey grinned.

Charlie was flustered. "I didn't — I wasn't — was I staring at your breasts? Because if I was, it was totally by accident, because, you know — there they were, and —"

"Shh." She reached over and put her finger on his lips to shush him. "Charlie, I feel very close to you right now, and very connected to you right now, and I want to keep that connection going, but I'm exhausted, and I don't think I can talk anymore. I think I'd like you to come to bed with me."

"Really? Are you sure?"

"Am I sure? I haven't had sex in fourteen years — and if you'd asked me yesterday, I'd have told you that I'd rather face one of your raven monsters than go to bed with a man, but now I'm here, with you, and I'm as sure as I've ever been of anything." She smiled, then looked away. "I mean, if you are."

Charlie took her hand. "Yeah," he said. "But I was going to tell you something important."

"Can't it wait till morning?"

"Sure."

They spent the night in each other's arms, and whatever fears or insecurities they had been feeling turned out to be illusions. Loneliness evaporated off of them like the steam off dry ice, and by morning it was just a cloud on the ceiling of the room, then gone with the light.

During the night someone had picked up the dining-room table and cleaned up the mess Minty Fresh had made when he crashed through the kitchen door. He was sitting at the table when Charlie came down.

"They towed my car," said Minty Fresh. "There's coffee."

"Thanks." Charlie skipped across the dining room to the kitchen. He poured himself a cup of coffee and sat down with Minty. "How's your head?"

The big man touched the purple bruise on his forehead. "Better. How're you doing?"

"I accidentally shagged a monk last night."

"Sometimes, in times of crisis, that shit cannot be avoided. How are you doing besides that?"

"I feel wonderful."

"Yeah, imagine the rest of us all bummed about the end of the world, not being cheerful."

"Not the end of the world, just darkness over everything," Charlie cheerfully said. "It gets dark — turn on a light."

"Good for you, Charlie. Now 'scuse me, I got to go get my car out of impound before you start with the whole *'if life gives you lemons you make lemonade'* speech and I have to beat you senseless."

(It's true, there is little more obnoxious than a Beta Male in love. So conditioned is he to the idea that he will never find love, that when he does, he feels as if the entire world has fallen into step with his desires — and thus deluded, he may act accordingly. It's a time of great joy and danger for him.)

"Wait, we can share a cab. I have to go home and get my date book."

"Me, too. I left mine on the front seat of the car. You know those two clients I missed — they're here. Alive."

"Audrey told me," Charlie said. "There's six of them altogether. She did that *p'howa of undying* thing on them. Obviously that's what's been causing the cosmic shit storm, but what can we do? We can't kill them."

"No, I think it's what you said. The

battle is going to happen here in San Francisco and it's going to happen now. And since you're the Luminatus, I guess this whole thing is riding on your shoulders. So I'd say we're doomed."

"Maybe not. I mean, every time they've almost gotten me, something or someone has intervened to pull out a victory. I think destiny is on our side. I feel very optimistic about this."

"That's just because you just shagged the monk," said Minty.

"I'm not a monk," said Audrey, bounding into the room with a sheaf of papers in hand.

"Oh, shit," said the Death Merchants in unison.

"No, it's okay," Audrey said. "He did shag me, or, I think more appropriately — we shagged — but I'm not a monk anymore. Not because of the shagging, you know, it was a preshag decision." She threw her papers on the table and climbed into Charlie's lap. "Hey, good-looking, how's your morning going?" She gave him a backbreaking kiss and entwined him like a starfish trying to open an oyster until Minty Fresh cleared his throat and she turned to him. "And good morning to you, Mr. Fresh."

"Yes. Thank you." Minty leaned to the side so he could see Charlie. "Whether they were here for you, or for our clients who didn't die, they'll be back, you know that?"

"The Morrigan?" said Audrey.

"Huh," said the Death Merchants, again in chorus.

"You guys are so cute," Audrey gushed. "They're called the Morrigan. Raven women — personifications of death in the form of beautiful warrior women who can change into birds. There are three of them, all part of the same collective queen of the Underworld known as the Morrigan."

Charlie leaned back from her so he could look her in the eye. "How do you know that?"

"I just looked it up on the Internet." Audrey climbed out of Charlie's lap, picked up the papers on the table, and began to read. " 'The Morrigan consists of three distinct entities: Macha, who haunts the battlefield, and takes heads of warriors as tribute in battle — she is said to be able to heal a warrior from mortal wounds in the field, if his men have offered enough heads to her. The Celtic warriors called the severed heads Macha's acorns. She is considered the mother goddess of the three. Babd is rage, the passion of battle and killing — she was said to collect the seed of fallen warriors, and use its power to inspire a sexual frenzy for battle, a literal bloodlust. And Nemain, who is frenzy, was said to drive soldiers into battle with a howl so fierce that it could cause enemy soldiers to die of fright — her claws were venomous and the mere prick of one would kill a soldier, but she would fling the venom into the eyes of enemy soldiers to blind them.' "

"That's them," said Minty Fresh. "I saw venom come from the claws of the one on the BART."

"Yeah," Charlie said, "and I think I remember Babd — the bloodlust one. That's them. I have to talk to Lily. I sent her to Berkeley to find out about them, but she came back with nothing. She must have not even looked."

"Yeah, ask her if she's seeing anybody," Minty Fresh said. To Audrey: "Did it say how you kill them? What their weaknesses are?"

Audrey shook her head. "Just that warriors took dogs into battle to protect against the Morrigan."

"Dogs," Charlie echoed. "That explains why my daughter got the hellhounds to protect her. I'm telling you, Fresh, we're going to be okay. Destiny is on our side."

"Yeah, you said that. Call us a cab."

"I wonder why of all the different gods and demons in the Underworld, the Celtic ones are here."

"Maybe they're all here," Minty said. "I had a crazy Indian tell me once that I was the son of Anubis, the Egyptian jackal-headed god of the dead."

"That's great!" Charlie said. "A jackal — that's a type of dog. You have natural abilities to battle the Morrigan, see."

Minty looked at Audrey. "If you don't do something to disappoint him and mellow his ass out, I'm going to shoot him."

"Oh yeah," Charlie said. "Can I still borrow one of your big guns?"

Minty unfolded to his feet. "I'm going outside to call a cab and wait, Charlie. If you're coming, you better start saying good-bye now, because I'm leaving when it gets here."

"Swell," Charlie said, looking adoringly at Audrey. "I think we're safe in the daylight anyway."

"Monk shagger," Minty growled as he ducked under the doorway.

Auntie Cassie let Charlie into their small

home in the Marina district and Sophie called off the greeting hump of devil dogs almost as soon as it started.

"Daddy!"

Charlie swept Sophie up in his arms and squeezed her until she started to change color; then, when Jane came out of the kitchen, he grabbed her in his other arm and hugged her as well.

"Uh, let go," Jane said, pushing him away. "You smell like incense."

"Oh, Jane, I can't believe it, she's so wonderful."

"He got laid," Cassandra said.

"You got laid?" Jane said, kissing her brother on the cheek. "I'm so happy for you. Now let me go."

"Daddy got laid," Sophie said to the hellhounds, who seemed very happy at hearing the news.

"No, not laid," Charlie said, and there was a collective sigh of disappointment.

"Well, yes, laid," and there was a collective sigh of relief, "but that's not the thing. The thing is she's wonderful. She's gorgeous, and kind, and sweet, and —"

"Charlie," Jane interrupted, "you called us and told us that there was some great danger and we had to go get Sophie and protect her, and you were going on a date?"

"No, no, there was — is danger, at least in the dark, and I did need you to get Sophie, but I met someone."

"Daddy got laid!" Sophie cheered again.

"Honey, we don't say that, okay," Charlie said. "Auntie Jane and Auntie Cassie shouldn't say that either. It's not nice."

"Like 'kitty' and 'not in the butt'?"

"Exactly, honey."

"Okay, Daddy. So it wasn't nice?"

"Daddy has to go to our house and get his date book, pumpkin, we'll talk about this later. Give me a kiss." Sophie gave him a huge hug and a kiss and Charlie thought that he might cry. For so long she had been his only future, his only joy, and now he had this other joy, and he wanted to share it with her. "I'll come right back, okay?"

"Okay. Let me down."

Charlie let her slide to the floor and she ran off to another part of the house.

"So it wasn't nice?" Jane asked.

"I'm sorry, Jane. This is really crazy. I hate that I put you guys in the middle of it. I didn't mean to scare you."

Jane thumped him in the arm. "So it *was* nice?"

"It was really nice," Charlie said, breaking into a grin. "She's really nice. She's so nice I miss Mom."

"Lost me," Cassandra said.

"Because I'd like Mom to see that I'm doing okay. That I met someone who's good for me. Who's going to be good for Sophie."

"Whoa, don't jump the gun, there, tiger," Jane said. "You just met this woman, you need to slow down — and remember, this comes from someone whose typical second date is moving a woman in."

"Slut," Cassie murmured.

"I mean it, Jane. She's amazing."

Cassie looked at Jane. "You were right, he really did need to get laid."

"That's not it!"

Charlie's cell rang. "Excuse me, guys." He flipped it open.

"Asher, what the hell have you done?" It was Lily. She was crying. "What the hell have you let loose?"

"What, Lily? What?"

"It was just here. The front window of the shop is gone. Gone! It just came in, ripped through the shop, and took all of your soul thingies. Loaded them into a bag and flew away. Fuck, Asher. I mean FUCK! This thing was huge, and fucking hideous."

"Yeah, Lily, are you okay? Is Ray okay?"

"Yeah, I'm okay. Ray didn't come in. I ran into the back when it came through the window. It wasn't interested in anything but that shelf. Asher, it was as big as a bull and it fucking flew!"

She sounded like she was on the edge of hysteria. "Hold on, Lily. Stay there and I'll come to you. Go in the back room and don't open the door until you hear me, okay."

"Asher, what the fuck was that thing?"

"I don't know, Lily."

The bullheaded Death flew into the culvert and immediately fell to all fours to move through the pipe, dragging the bag of souls behind him. Not for much longer — he would not crawl much longer. The time had come, Orcus could feel it. He could feel them converging on the City — the City where he had staked his territory so many years ago — his city. Still, they would come, and they would try to take what was rightfully his. All of the old gods of death: Yama and Anubis and Mors, Thanatos and Charon and Mahakala, Azrael and Emma-O and Ahkoh, Balor, Erebos, and Nyx — dozens of them, gods born of the energy of Man's greatest fear, the fear of death — all of them coming to rise as the leader of darkness and the dead, as the Luminatus. But he had come here first, and with Morrigan, he would become the one. But first he had to marshal his forces, heal the Morrigan, and take down the wretched human soul stealers of the City.

The satchel of souls would go a long way toward healing his brides. He marched into the grotto where the great ship was moored and leapt into the air, the beat of his great leathery wings like a war drum, echoing off the grotto walls and sending bats to the wing, swirling around the ship's masts in great clouds.

The Morrigan, torn and broken, were waiting for him on the deck.

"What did I tell you?" Babd said. "It's really not that great Above, huh? I, for one, could do without cars altogether."

Jane drove while Charlie fired out phone calls on his cell, first to Rivera, then to Minty Fresh. Within a half an hour they were all standing in Charlie's store, or the wreckage that had been Charlie's store, and uniformed policemen had taped off the sidewalk until someone could get the glass swept up.

"The tourists have to love this," Nick

Cavuto said, gnawing an unlit cigar. "Right on the cable-car line. Perfect."

Rivera was sitting in the back room interviewing Lily while Charlie, Jane, and Cassandra tried to sort through the mess and put things back on their shelves. Minty Fresh stood by the front door, wearing shades, looking entirely too cool for the destruction that lay strewn around him. Sophie was content to sit in the corner and feed shoes to Alvin and Mohammed.

"So," Cavuto said to Charlie, "some kind of flying monster came through your window and you thought this would be a good place to bring your kid?"

Charlie turned to the big cop and leaned on the counter. "Tell me, Detective, in your professional opinion, what procedure should I use in dealing with robbery by a flying monster? What the fuck is the SFPD giant-fucking-flying-monster protocol, Detective?"

Cavuto stood staring at Charlie as if he'd had water thrown in his face, not really angry, just very surprised. Finally, he grinned around his cigar, and said, "Mr. Asher, I am going to go outside and smoke, call in to the dispatcher, and have her look that particular protocol up. You have stumped me. Would you tell my

570

partner where I've gone?"

"I'll do that," Charlie said. He went into the office with Lily and Rivera and said, "Rivera, can I get some police protection here at my apartment — officers with shotguns?"

Rivera nodded, patting Lily on the hand as he looked away. "I can give you two, Charlie, but not for longer than twenty-four hours. You sure you don't want to get out of town?"

"Upstairs we have the security bars and steel doors, we have the hellhounds and Minty Fresh's weapons, and besides, they've already been here. I have a feeling they got what they came for, but the cops would make me feel better."

Lily looked at Charlie. She was in total mascara meltdown and had smudged her lipstick halfway across her face. "I'm sorry, I thought I would handle it better than this. It was so scary. It wasn't mysterious and cool, it was horrible. The eyes and the teeth — I peed, Asher. I'm sorry."

"Don't be sorry, kid. You did fine. I'm glad you had the sense to get out of its way."

"Asher, if you're the Luminatus, that thing must be your competition."

"What? What is that?" Rivera said.

"It's her weird Gothy stuff, Inspector. Don't worry about it," Charlie said. He looked through to the door and saw Minty Fresh standing at the front of the shop, looking at him, shrugging, as if saying, *Well?* So Charlie asked: "Hey, Lily, are you seeing anyone?"

Lily wiped her nose on the sleeve of her chef's coat. "Look, Asher — I, uh — I'm going to have to withdraw that offer I made you. I mean, after Ray, I'm not sure I really ever want to do that again. Ever."

"I wasn't asking for me, Lily." Charlie nodded toward the towering Fresh.

"Oh," Lily said, following his gaze, now wiping her eyes with her sleeves. "Oh. Fuck. Cover for me, I've got to regroup." She dashed into the employee washroom and slammed the door.

Rivera looked at Charlie. "What the hell is going on here?"

Charlie was going to try to come up with some kind of answer when his cell phone rang and he held up his finger to pause time. "Charlie Asher," he said.

"Charlie, it's Audrey," came the whispered voice. "They're here, right now. The Morrigan are *here*."

26

Orpheus in the Storm Sewer

Charlie parked the van sideways in the street and ran up the steps of the Buddhist center calling her name. The huge front door was hanging askew by one hinge, the glass broken, and every drawer and cabinet had been opened and the contents scattered, every piece of furniture overturned or broken.

"Audrey!"

He heard a voice to the front of the house and ran back out on the porch.

"Audrey?"

"Down here," she called. "We're still under the porch."

Charlie ran down the steps and around to the side of the porch. He could see movement behind the lattice. He found a small gate and opened it. Inside, Audrey was crouched with a half-dozen other people and a whole crowd of the squirrel people. He scrambled into the crawl space and took her in his arms. Charlie had tried to keep her on the line during the drive over, but a few blocks away the battery in his phone had died, and he had tried, for those few terrifying moments, to imagine losing her — his future, his hope — after his hope had just been awakened again. He was so relieved he could barely breathe.

"Are they gone?" Audrey asked.

"Yes, I think so. I'm so glad you're all right."

Charlie led them out of the crawl space and back into the house, the squirrel people staying close to the walls and moving quickly so as not to be seen from the street.

Charlie felt a tap on his shoulder and turned to see Irena Posokovanovich smiling at him. He jumped up a couple of steps and screamed. "Don't shock me again, I'm a good guy."

"I know that, Mr. Asher. I was wondering if you'd like me to park your van for you before it gets towed away."

"Oh yes, that would be nice." He handed her the keys. "Thank you."

In the house, Audrey said, "She just wants to help."

"She's creepy," Charlie said, but then he

caught what he thought was a look of disapproval rising in Audrey's eyes and he quickly added, "In a completely sweet way, I mean."

They went directly to the kitchen and stood before the open pantry.

"They got them all," Audrey said. "That's why they didn't hurt us — they weren't interested in us."

Charlie was so angry he was having trouble thinking, but without an outlet, he just shook and tried to keep his voice under control. "They just did the same thing at my store. Something did."

"There must have been three hundred souls in here," Audrey said.

"They took Rachel's soul."

Audrey put her arm around his back, but he couldn't respond other than to walk out of the kitchen. "That's it, Audrey. I'm done."

"What do you mean, you're done, Charlie? You're scaring me."

"Ask your squirrel people where I can get into the storm sewer system. Can they tell you that?"

"Probably. But you can't do that."

He wheeled on her and she jumped back.

"I have to do that. Find out, Audrey.

Everyone into my van. I want you at my building, where you'll be safe."

They were all gathered in Charlie's living room: Sophie, Audrey, Jane, Cassandra, Lily, Minty Fresh, the undead clients from the Buddhist center, the hellhounds, and fifty or so of the squirrel people. Lily, Jane, and Cassandra were standing on the couch to get away from the squirrel people, who were milling on and around the breakfast bar.

"Nice outfits," Lily said. "But ewww."

"Thank you," Audrey said. Sophie was standing next to Audrey, looking her up and down as if trying to guess her weight.

"I'm a Jewess," Sophie said. "Are you a Jewess?"

"No, I'm a Buddhist," Audrey said.

"Is that like a shiksa?"

"Yes, I think it is," said Audrey. "It's a type of shiksa."

"Oh, I guess that's okay, then. My puppies are shiksas, too. That's what Mrs. Ling calls them."

"They're very impressive puppies, too," Audrey said.

"They want to eat your little guys, but I won't let them, okay?"

"Thank you. That would be nice."

"Unless you're mean to my daddy. Then they're toast."

"Of course," Audrey said. "Special circumstances."

"He likes you a lot."

"I'm glad. I like him a lot."

"I think you're probably okay."

"Well, right back at you," Audrey said. She smiled at the little brunette with the heartbreaking blue eyes and the attitude, and it was all she could do not to scoop her up and hug the bejeezus out of her.

Charlie jumped up on the couch next to Jane, Cassandra, and Lily, and then realized as he looked across the room at Minty Fresh that he still didn't stand taller than the Death Merchant, which was a little unnerving. (Minty seemed focused on Lily, which was also a little unnerving.)

"You guys, I'm going to go do something, and I might not come back. Jane, that letter I sent you has all the papers making you Sophie's legal guardian."

"I'm out of here," Lily said.

"No," Charlie said, catching her by the arm. "I want you here, too. I'm leaving you the business, but with the understanding that a percentage of the profits go to Jane to help with Sophie and will also go into a college fund for her. I know you have your career as a chef, but I trust you and you're good at the business."

Lily looked like she wanted to say something sarcastic, but shrugged and said, "Sure. I can run your business and cook, too. You do your Death Merchant thing and raise a daughter."

"Thanks. Jane, you'll get the building, of course, but when Sophie grows up, if she wants to stay in the City, you always have to have an apartment for her."

Jane jumped off the couch. "Charlie, this is crap, I'm not letting you do anything —"

"Please. Jane, I've got to go. This is all in writing, I just want you to hear what I wanted in person."

"Okay," she said. Charlie hugged his sister, Cassandra, and Lily, then went to the bedroom and gestured for Minty Fresh to follow him.

"Minty, I'm going into the Underworld after the Morrigan — after Rachel's soul, all the souls. It's time."

The big man nodded, gravely. "I'm right there with you."

"No, you're not. I need you to stay here and watch over Audrey and Sophie and the others. There are cops outside, but I think their disbelief might make them hesitate if the Morrigan come. You won't do that."

Minty shook his head. "What chance do you have down there alone? Let me come with you. We'll fight this thing together."

"I don't think so," Charlie said. "I'm blessed or something. The prophecy says, 'The Luminatus will rise and do battle with the Forces of Darkness in the City of Two Bridges.' It doesn't say, the Luminatus and his trusty sidekick, Minty Fresh."

"I am not a sidekick."

"That's what I'm saying," said Charlie, who wasn't saying that at all. "I'm saying that I have some sort of protection, but you probably don't. And if I don't come back, you'll need to carry on as a Death Merchant in the City — maybe get the scales tipped back for our side."

Minty Fresh nodded, lowering his gaze to the floor. "You'll take my Desert Eagles, then, for luck?" He looked up and was grinning.

"I'll take one of them," Charlie said.

Minty Fresh slipped out of his shoulder-holster rig and adjusted the straps until they fit Charlie, then helped him into the harness.

"There are two extra clips in here, under your right arm," Minty said. "I hope you don't have to fire it that many times down there or you will be one deaf mother-fucker."

"Thanks," Charlie said.

Minty helped him get his tweed jacket on over the shoulder holster.

"You know, you might be heavily armed, but you still look like an English professor — don't you have some clothes more appropriate for fighting?"

"James Bond always wears a tux," Charlie said.

"Yeah, I understand the line between reality and fiction seems a little blurred here lately —"

"I'm kidding," Charlie said. "There are some motocross leathers and pads in the shop that will fit me if I can find them."

"Good." Minty patted Charlie's shoulders, like he was trying to make them bigger. "You see that bitch with the poison claws, you light her up for me, okay?"

"I'll buss a cap in da hoe's ass," Charlie said.

"Don't do that."

"Sorry."

The hardest part came a few minutes later.

"Honey, Daddy has to go do something."

"Are you going to get Mommy?"

Charlie was crouched in front of his daughter, and he nearly rolled over backward at the question. She hadn't mentioned her mommy a dozen times in the last two years.

"Why would you say that, honey?"

"I don't know. I was thinking about her."

"Well, you know that she loved you very much."

"Yeah."

"And you know that no matter what, I love you very much."

"Yeah, you said that yesterday."

"And I meant it yesterday. But this time, I really do have to go. I have to fight some bad guys, and I might not win."

Sophie's lower lip pushed out like a big wet shelf.

Don't cry, don't cry, don't cry, don't cry, Charlie chanted in his head. *I can't handle it if you cry.*

"Don't cry, honey. Everything will be okay."

"Noooooooooooo," Sophie wailed. "I want to go with you. I want to go with you. Don't go, Daddy, I want to go with you."

Charlie held her and looked across the room to his sister, pleading. She came and took Sophie from his arms. "Noooooo. I want to go with you."

"You can't go with me, honey." And Charlie ducked out of the apartment before his heart broke again.

Audrey was waiting in the hall with fifty-three squirrel people. "I'm driving you to the entrance," she said. "Don't argue."

"No," Charlie said. "I'm not losing you after just finding you. You stay here."

"You creep! What gives you the right to be that way. I just found you, too."

"Yeah, but I'm not much of a find."

"You're an ass," she said, and she walked into his arms and kissed him. After a long time, Charlie looked around. The squirrel people were all looking up at them.

"What are they doing here?"

"They're going with you."

"No. It's too risky."

"Then it's too risky for you, too. You don't even know what could be down there — this thing that broke into your store wasn't one of the Morrigan."

"I'm not going to be afraid, Audrey. There might be a hundred different demons, but *The Book of the Dead* is right, they are only keeping us from our path. I think these things exist for the same reason I was chosen to do this, because of fear. I was afraid to live, so I became Death. Their power is our fear of death. I'm not afraid. And I'm not taking the squirrel people."

"They know the way. And besides, they're fourteen inches tall, what do they have to live for?"

"Hey," said a Beefeater guard whose head was the skull of a bobcat.

"Did he say something?" Charlie asked.

"One of my experimental voice boxes."

"It's a little squeaky."

"Hey!"

"Sorry, uh, Beef," Charlie said. The creatures seemed resolute. "Onward, then!"

Charlie ran down the hall so he wouldn't have to say good-bye again. Ten yards behind him marched a small army of nightmare creatures, put together from the parts of a hundred different animals. It just so happened that at the time they were reaching the staircase, Mrs. Ling came downstairs to see what all the commotion had been about, and the entire army stopped in the stairway and looked up at her.

Mrs. Ling was, and had always been, a Buddhist, and so she was a firm believer in the concept of karma, and that those lessons you did not learn would continually be presented to you until you learned them, or your soul could never evolve to the next level. That afternoon, as the Forces of Light were about to engage the Forces of Darkness for dominion over the world, Mrs. Ling, staring into the blank eyes of the squirrel people, had her own epiphany, and she never again ate meat, of any kind. Her first act of atonement was an offering to those she felt she had wronged.

"You want snack?" she said.

But the squirrel people marched on.

The Emperor saw the van pull up near the creek and a man in bright yellow motorcycle leathers climb out. The man reached back into the van and grabbed what looked like a shoulder holster with a sledgehammer in it, and slipped into the harness. If the context hadn't been so bizarre, the Emperor could have sworn it was his friend Charlie Asher, from the second-hand shop in North Beach, but Charlie? Here? With a gun? No.

Lazarus, who was not so dependent on his eyes for recognition, barked a greeting.

The man turned to them and waved. It *was* Charlie. He walked down to the creek-bank across from them.

"Your Majesty," Charlie said.

"You seem upset, Charlie. Is something wrong?"

"No, no, I'm okay, I just had to take directions from a mute beaver in a fez to get here, it's unsettling."

"Well, I can see how it would be," said the Emperor. "Nice ensemble, though, the leathers and the pistol. Not your usual sartorial splendor."

"Well, no. I'm on a bit of a mission. Going to go into that culvert, find my way into the Underworld, and do battle with the Forces of Darkness."

"Good for you. Good for you. Forces of Darkness seem to be on the rise in my city lately."

"You noticed, then?"

The Emperor hung his head. "Yes, I'm afraid we've lost one of our troops to the fiends."

"Bummer?"

"He went into a storm sewer days ago, and hasn't come out."

"I'm sorry, sir."

"Would you look for him, Charlie? Please. Bring him out."

"Your Majesty, I'm not sure that I'm coming back myself, but I promise, if I find him, I'll try to bring him out. Now if you'll excuse me, I'm going to open this van and I don't want you to be alarmed by what you see, but I want to get into the pipe while there's still some light from the grates. What you see coming out of the van — they're friends."

"Carry on," said the Emperor.

Charlie slid the door open and the squirrel people hopped, scampered, and scooted down the bank of the creek toward the culvert. Charlie reached into the van, took out his sword-cane and flashlight, and butt-bumped the door shut. Lazarus whimpered and looked at the Emperor as if someone who was able to talk should say something.

"Good luck, then, valiant Charlie," said the Emperor. "You go forth with all of us in your heart, and you in ours."

"You'll watch the van?"

"Until the Golden Gate crumbles to dust, my friend," said the Emperor.

And so Charlie Asher, in the service of life and light and all sentient beings, and in hope of rescuing the soul of the love of his life, led an army of fourteen-inch-tall bundles of animal bits, armed with everything from knitting needles to a spork, into the storm sewers of San Francisco.

★ ★ ★

They slogged on for hours — sometimes the pipes became narrow enough that Charlie had to crawl on his hands and knees, other times they opened into wide junctions like concrete rooms. He helped the squirrel people climb to higher pipes. He'd found a lightweight construction helmet fitted with an LED headlamp, which came in handy in narrow passages where he couldn't aim the flashlight. He was also bumping his head about ten times an hour, and although the helmet protected him from injury, he'd developed a throbbing headache. His leathers — not really leathers, but more heavy nylon with Lexan pads at the knees, shoulders, elbows, shins, and forearms — were protecting him from bumps and abrasions on the pipes, but they were soaked and rubbing him raw at the backs of his knees. At an open junction with a grate at the top he climbed the ladder and tried to get a look at the neighborhood to perhaps get a sense of where they were, but it had gotten dark out since they started and the grate was under a parked car.

What irony, that he would finally summon his courage and charge into the breach, only to end up lost and stuck in

587

the breach. A human misfire.

"Where the hell are we?" he said.

"No idea," said the bobcat guy, the one who could talk.

The little Beefeater was disturbing to watch when he spoke, since he really didn't have a face, only a skull, and he spoke without ever making the *P* sound. Also, instead of a halberd, which Charlie thought should have come with the costume for authenticity, the bobcat had armed himself with a spork.

"Can you ask the others if they know where we are?"

"Okay." He turned to the damp gallery of squirrel people. "Hey, anybody know where we are?"

They all shook their heads, looking from one to another, shrugging. Nope.

"No," said the bobcat.

"Well, I could have done that," Charlie said.

"Why don't you? It's your _arty," he said. Charlie realized he meant "party."

"Why no *P*s?" Charlie asked.

"No li_s."

"Right, lips. Sorry. What are you going to do with that spork?"

"Well, when we find some bad guys, I'm going to s_ork the fuck out of them."

"Excellent. You're my lieutenant."

"Because of the s_ork?"

"No, because you can talk. What's your name?"

"Bob."

"No really."

"Really. It's Bob."

"So I suppose your last name is Cat."

"Wilson."

"Just checking. Sorry."

" 'S okay."

"Do you remember who you were in your last life?"

"I remember a little. I think I was an accountant."

"So, no military experience?"

"You need some bodies counted, I'm your man, er, thing."

"Swell. Does anyone here remember if they used to be a soldier, or a ninja or anything? Extra credit for ninjas or a Viking or something. Weren't any of you like Attila the Hun or Captain Horatio Hornblower in a former life or something?"

A ferret in a sequined minidress and go-go boots came forward, paw raised.

"You were a naval commander?"

The ferret appeared to whisper into Bob's hat (since Bob no longer had ears).

"She says no, she misunderstood, she

589

thought you meant horn blower."

"She was a prostitute?"

"Cornet _layer," said Bob.

"Sorry," Charlie said. "It's the boots."

The ferret waved him off in a "no wor-ries" way, then leaned over and whispered to Bob again.

"What?" Charlie said.

"Nothing," Bob said.

"Not nothing. I didn't think they could talk."

"Well, not to you," said Bob.

"What did she say?"

"She said we're fucked."

"Well, that's not a very good attitude," Charlie said, but he was starting to believe the go-go ferret was right, and he leaned back into a semisitting position in the pipe to rest.

Bob climbed up to a smaller pipe and sat on the edge, his feet dangling over; water dripped from his little patent-leather shoes, but the floral pattern brass buckles still shone in the light of Charlie's headlamp.

"Nice shoes," Charlie said.

"Yeah, well, Audrey digs me," said Bob.

Before Charlie could answer, the dog had grabbed Bob from behind and was shaking him like a rag doll. His mighty spork clattered off the pipe and was lost in the water below.

27

Bitch's Brew

Lily had been looking all night for a way to approach Minty Fresh. She'd made eye contact with him a dozen times over the course of the evening, and smiled, but with the atmosphere of dread that fell over the room she was having trouble thinking of an opening line. Finally, when an Oprah movie of the week came on the television and everyone gathered around to watch the media diva beat Paul Winfield to death with a steam iron, Minty went to the break- fast bar and started flipping through his day planner, and Lily made her move.

"So, checking your appointments?" she said. "You must be feeling optimistic about how things will go."

He shook his head. "Not really."

Lily was smitten. He was beautiful *and* morose — like a great brown man-gift from the gods.

"How bad can it be?" Lily said, pulling the appointment book out of his hand and flipping through the pages. She stopped on today's date.

"Why is Asher's name in here?" she asked.

Minty hung his head. "He said you've known all about us for a while."

"Yeah, but —" She looked at the name again and the realization of what she was seeing was like a punch in the chest. "This is that book? This is your date book for *that?*"

Minty nodded slowly, not looking at her.

"When did this name show up?" Lily asked.

"It wasn't there an hour ago."

"Well, fucksocks," she said, sitting down on the bar stool next to the big man.

"Yeah," said Minty Fresh. He put his arm around her shoulders.

With Charlie pulling on the legs of the bobcat guy (who was doing some impressive screaming considering he had prototype vocal cords) and the squirrel people dog-piling onto the Boston terrier, they were eventually able to extricate their lieutenant from the jaws of the bug-eyed fury with only a few snags in his Beefeater's costume.

"Down, Bummer," Charlie said. "Just chill." He didn't know if *chill* was an official dog command, but it should be.

Bummer snorted and backed away from the surrounding crowd of squirrel people.

"Not one of us," said the bobcat guy, pointing at Bummer. "Not one of us."

"You shut up," Charlie said. He pulled a beef jerky from his pocket that he'd brought for emergency rations, tore off a hunk, and held it out to Bummer. "Come on, buddy. I told the Emperor I'd look out for you."

Bummer trotted over to Charlie and took the beef jerky from him, then turned to face down the squirrel people as he chewed. The squirrel people made clicking noises and brandished their weapons. "Not one of us. Not one of us," chanted Bob.

"Stop that," Charlie said. "You can't get a mob chant going, Bob, you're the only one with a voice box."

"Oh yeah." Bob let his chanting trail off. "Well, he's not one of us," he added in his defense.

"He is now," Charlie said. To Bummer he said, "Can you lead us to the Underworld?"

Bummer looked up at Charlie as if he knew exactly what was being asked of him, but if he was going to find the strength to carry on, he was going to need the other half of that beef jerky. Charlie gave it to him and Bummer immediately jumped up to a higher, four-foot pipe, stopped, barked, then took off down the pipe.

"Follow him," Charlie said.

After an hour following Bummer through the sewers, the pipes gave way to tunnels that got bigger as they moved along. Soon they were moving in caves, with high ceilings and stalactites in the ceiling that glowed in various colors, illuminating their way with a dull, shadowy light. Charlie had read enough about the geology of the area to know that these caves were not natural to the city. He guessed that they were somewhere under the financial district, which was mostly built on Gold Rush landfill, so there would be nothing as old-looking or as solid as these caves.

Bummer kept on, leading them down one fork or another without the slightest hesitation, until suddenly the cave opened up into a massive grotto. The chamber was so large that it simply swallowed up Charlie's flashlight and headlamp beams, but the ceiling, which was several hundred feet

high, was lined with the luminous stalactites that reflected red, green, and purple
in a mirror-smooth black lake. In the
middle of the lake, probably two hundred
yards away, stood a great black sailing ship
— tall-masted like a Spanish galleon —
red, pulsating light coming from the cabin
windows in the rear, a single lantern
lighting the deck. Charlie had heard that
whole ships had been buried in the debris
during the Gold Rush, but they wouldn't
have been left preserved like this. Things
had changed, these caves were all the result
of the Underworld rising — and he realized that this was just a hint of what was
going to happen to the City if the Underworlders took over.

Bummer barked and the sharp report
echoed around the grotto, sending a cloud
of bats into the air.

Charlie saw movement on the deck of
the ship, the blue-black outline of a
woman, and he knew that Bummer had led
them to the right place. Charlie handed his
flashlight to Bob and set his sword-cane on
the cave floor. He drew the Desert Eagle
from the shoulder holster, checked that
there was a round in the chamber, cocked
the hammer, then reset the safety and
reholstered the pistol.

"We're going to need a boat," Charlie said to Bob. "See if you guys can find something we can make a raft from." The bobcat guy started down the shore with Charlie's flashlight, scanning the rocks for useful flotsam. Bummer growled, tossed his head like he had ear mites or perhaps to indicate that he thought Charlie was insane, and ran out into the lake. Fifty yards away he was still only in water up to his shoulder.

Charlie looked at the black ship and realized that it was sitting way, way too high out of the water — that, in fact, it was sitting with its hull on the bottom in only about six inches of water.

"Uh, Bob," Charlie said. "Forget the boat. We're walking. Everyone quiet." He unsheathed his sword and sloshed onward. As they approached the ship they could make out details in its construction. The railings were fashioned from leg bones lashed together, the mooring cleats were human pelvises. The lantern on the deck was, in fact, a human skull. Charlie wasn't exactly sure how his powers as Luminatus were going to manifest themselves, but as they reached the hull of the ship he found himself very much wishing it would happen soon, and that levitation would be one of the powers.

"We're fucked," said Bob, looking up at the black hull curving above them.

"We're not fucked," Charlie said. "We just need someone to climb up there and throw us a rope."

There was some milling around amid the squirrel people, then a lone figure stepped out of the little crowd — this one appeared to be a nineteenth-century French dandy with the head of a monitor lizard. His outfit — the ruffles and the coat — actually reminded Charlie of pictures that Lily had shown him of Charles Baudelaire.

"You can do it?" Charlie asked the lizard guy.

He held out his hands and lifted one foot out of the water. Squirrel paws. Charlie lifted the lizard guy as high as he could up to the hull, and the little creature caught ahold in the black wood, then scurried up the side of the ship and over the gunwale.

Minutes passed, and Charlie found himself listening hard for some hint as to what was going on above. When the thick rope splashed down next to him, he leapt two feet in the air and barely contained blasting out a full-blown man-scream.

"Nice," said Bob.

"You first, then," Charlie said, testing

the rope to see if it would hold his weight. He waited until the bobcat guy was about three feet over his head before he tucked the sword-cane down inside the Lexan plate strapped over his back and started the climb himself. By the time he was three-quarters of the way up the rope, he felt as if his biceps were going to pop like water balloons and he entwined his motocross boot into the rope to rest. As if being granted a second wind by the gods, his biceps relaxed and when he resumed climbing he felt as if he might really be gaining his power as the Luminatus. When he reached the railing, he grabbed one of the bone mooring cleats and swung himself up until he sat straddling the rail.

He swung around and his headlamp caught the black shine in her eyes. She was holding the bobcat guy like an ear of corn, her claw driven through his skull, pinning his jaw shut. There was flesh and goo glowing dull red, running down her face and over her breasts as she tore another bite out of the Beefeater.

"Want some, lover?" she said. "Tastes like ham."

At the breakfast bar in Charlie's apartment, Lily said, "Shouldn't we tell them?"

"They don't all know about us. About this." Minty held the date book. "Just Audrey."

"Then shouldn't we tell her?"

Minty looked at Audrey, who was sitting on the couch entwined in a sleepy pile with Charlie's sister and one of the hellhounds, looking very content. "No, I don't think that would serve any purpose right now."

"He's a good guy," Lily said. She snatched a paper towel off the roll on the counter and dabbed her eyes before her mascara went raccoon on her again.

"I know," Minty said. "He's my friend." As he said it, he felt a tug on his pant leg. He looked down to where Sophie was staring up at him.

"Hey, do you have a car?" she asked.

"Yes, I do, Sophie."

"Can we go for a ride?"

Without any hesitation, Charlie whipped the sword-cane out of his back and snapped it down on the Morrigan's wrist. She lost her grip on the bobcat guy, who bolted, screaming, across the deck and over the opposite railing. The Morrigan grabbed the sword-cane and tried to wrench it from Charlie's grasp. He let her — pulled the sword free, then drove it into her solar plexus so hard that his fist connected with her ribs and the blade came out her back, sinking into the wooden hull of the lifeboat she was reclining against. For a split second his face was an inch from hers.

"Miss me?" she asked.

He rolled away just as she slashed at him. He got his forearm up just in time to deflect the blow away from his face, the thick Lexan plate on his forearm stopping the claws from taking off his hand. She lunged for him, but the sword kept her pinned to the boat. Charlie ran down the deck away from her as she screeched in anger.

He saw light coming from a door that must have led to the cabin at the aft of the ship — that same red glow — and he realized that it had to be coming from the soul vessels. Rachel's soul could still be in there. He was only a step from the hatch when the giant raven dropped in front of him and spread her wings out across the deck, as if trying to block the whole end of the ship. He backpedaled and drew the Desert Eagle from the shoulder holster. He tried to hold it steady as he clicked off the safety. The Raven snapped at him and he leapt back. The beak then pulled back, changed, bubbled into the face of a woman — but the wings and talons remained in bird form.

"New Meat," said Macha. "How brave of you to come here."

Charlie pulled the trigger. Flame shot a foot out of the barrel and he felt as if someone had hit him in the palm with a hammer. He thought he had aimed right between her eyes, but the bullet had ripped through her neck, taking half of the black flesh with it. Her head lolled to the side and the raven body flailed its wings at him.

Charlie fell backward onto the deck, but pulled the pistol up and fired again as the raven was coming down on him. This one caught her in the center of the chest and sent her flying backward, up onto the cabin roof.

The ringing in his ears felt like someone had driven tuning forks into his head and hit them with drumsticks — a long, painful, high-pitched wail. He barely heard the shriek from his left as another Morrigan dropped out of the rigging behind him. He rolled to the railing and brought the gun up just as she slashed at his face. The gun and his forearm pad absorbed most of the blow, but the Desert Eagle was knocked from his grasp and slid down the deck.

Charlie did a somersault to his feet and ran after the gun. Nemain flicked her claws at his back and he heard the sizzle as the poison strafed the Lexan pad down his spine and burned onto the deck on either side of him. He dove for the pistol and tried to roll and come up with it pointed at his attacker, but he misjudged and came up with the back of his knees against the bone railing. She leapt, claws first, and hit him in the chest just as he fired the Desert Eagle and he was driven backward over the railing.

He hit flat on the water. The air exploded from his body and he felt like he'd been hit by a bus. He couldn't breathe, but he could see, he could feel his limbs, and after a couple of seconds of gasping, he finally caught a breath.

"So, how's it going so far?" asked the bobcat guy, about two feet from Charlie's head.

"Good," Charlie said. "They're running scared."

There was a big chunk bitten out of the middle of Bob's torso, and his Beefeater uniform was in tatters, but otherwise he seemed in good spirits. He was holding the Desert Eagle cradled in his arms like a baby.

"You'll likely need this. That last shot connected, by the way. You took off about half of her skull."

"Good," Charlie said, still having a little trouble catching his breath. He felt a searing pain in his chest and thought he might have broken a rib. He sat up and looked at his chest plate. The Morrigan's claws had raked the front of it, but in one spot he could see where a claw had slipped under the plate and into his chest. He wasn't bleeding badly, but he was bleeding, and it hurt like hell. "Are they still coming?"

"Not the two you shot. We don't know where the one you stuck with your sword went."

"I don't know if I can make it up that rope again," Charlie said.

"That may not be a _roblem," Bob said. He was looking up to the ceiling of the grotto, where a whirlwind of squeaking bats was spiraling around the mast, but above them was beating the wings of another creature altogether.

Charlie took the pistol from Bob and climbed to his feet, nearly fell, then steadied himself and backed away from the hull of the ship. The squirrel people scattered around him. Bummer let loose with a fusillade of angry yapping.

The demon hit the water about thirty feet away. Charlie felt a scream rising in his throat but fought it down. The thing was nearly ten feet tall, with a wingspan of thirty feet. Its head was as big as a beer keg, and it appeared to have the shape and horns of a bull, except for the jaws, which were predatory, lined with teeth, like a cross between a shark and a lion. Its eyes were gleaming green.

"Soul stealer," it growled. It folded its wings into two high points behind its back, and stepped toward Charlie.

"Well, that would be you, wouldn't it?" Charlie said, a little breathless still. "I'm the Luminatus."

The demon stopped. Charlie took the hesitation to bring up the pistol and fire. The shot took the demon high in the shoulder and spun him to the side. He turned back and roared.

Charlie could smell the creature's breath, like rotting meat, wash over him. He backed up and fired again, his hand numb now from the recoil of the big pistol. The shot knocked the demon back a step. There was shrill cheering from above.

Charlie fired again and again. The slugs opened craters in the demon's chest. He wavered, then fell to his knees. Charlie aimed and pulled the trigger again. The gun clicked.

Charlie backed up a few more steps and tried to remember what Minty had shown him about reloading. He managed to hit a button that released the clip from the pistol, which plopped into the water. Then he unsnapped one of the pouches under his arm to retrieve an extra clip. It slipped out and fell into the lake as well. Bob and a couple of the squirrel people splashed forward and started diving beneath the water, looking for the clip.

The demon roared again, unfurled his wings, and, in one great flap, pulled himself to his feet.

Charlie unsnapped the second clip and, with his hands shaking, managed to fit it into the bottom of the Desert Eagle. The demon crouched, as if to leap. Charlie jacked a shell into the chamber and fired at the same time. The demon fell forward as the huge slug took a chunk out of his thigh.

"Well done, Meat!" came a female voice from above.

Charlie looked up quickly, but then back to the bullheaded demon, who was on his feet again. Then he braced his wrist and fired, and again, walking forward, pumping

605

bullets into the demon's chest with each step, feeling any second as if his wrist would just shatter into pieces from the recoil, until the hammer clicked on an empty chamber. He stopped, just five feet away from the demon when it fell over, facefirst into the water. Charlie dropped the Desert Eagle and fell to his knees. The grotto seemed to be tilting before him, his vision tunneling down.

The Morrigan landed on three sides of him. Each had a glowing soul vessel in her claw and was rubbing it on her wounds.

"That was excellent, lover," said the raven woman standing closest to the fallen demon. Charlie recognized her from the alley. The stab wound his sword had made in her stomach healed over as he watched. She kicked the bullheaded demon's body. "See, I told you that guns suck."

"That *was* well done, Meat," said the one to Charlie's right. Her neck was still knitting back together. She was the one he'd blasted up onto the cabin roof.

"You guys do bounce back with a certain Wile E. Coyote charm," Charlie said. He grinned, feeling drunk now, like he was watching all this from another place.

"He's so sweet," said the hand-job harpy.

"I could just eat him up."

"Sounds good to me," said the Morrigan to his left, whose head was still a little lop-sided.

Charlie saw the venom dripping from her claws, then looked to the wound below his chest plate.

"Yes, darling," said hand job, "I'm afraid Nemain did nick you. You really are quite the warrior to have lasted this long."

"I'm the Luminatus," Charlie said.

The Morrigan laughed, the one in front of Charlie did a little dance step. As she did, the bullheaded demon lifted his head from the water.

"I'm the Luminatus," said the demon, black goo and water running between his teeth as he spoke.

The Morrigan stopped dancing, grabbed one of the demon's horns, then pulled his head back. "You think?" she said. Then she plunged her claws into the demon's throat. He rolled and threw her off, sending her sailing twenty feet in the air to smash into the hull of the ship.

The Morrigan behind Charlie patted his head as she passed. "We'll be right with you, darling. I'm Macha, by the way, and we are the Luminatus — or we will be in a minute."

The Morrigan fell on the bullheaded demon, taking great chunks of flesh and bone off his body with each slash of their talons. Two took to the air and swept in, taking swipes at the demon, who flailed at them, sometimes connecting, but too weakened from the gunshots to fight effectively. In two minutes it was finished, and most of the flesh had been flayed from it. Macha held his head by the horns like she was holding the handlebars of a motorcycle, even as the demon's jaws continued to snap at the air.

"Your turn, soul stealer," Macha said.

"Yeah, your turn," said Nemain, baring her claws.

Macha held the demon head out in front of her, driving it at Charlie. He backed away as the teeth snapped inches from his face.

"Wait a minute," said Babd.

The other two stopped and turned to their sister, who stood over what was left of the demon's corpse. "We never got to finish."

She took one step before something hit her like a ball of darkness, knocking her out of sight. Charlie looked at the demon head coming at him, then there was a loud smack and Macha was yanked to the side as if she'd had a bungee cord attached to her ankle.

The screeching started again and Charlie could see the Morrigan being whipped around in the darkness, splashing, and chaos — he couldn't follow what was happening. His eyes wouldn't focus.

He looked to Nemain, who was now coming at him with her claws dripping venom. A small hand appeared at the edge of his vision and the Morrigan's head exploded into what looked like a thousand stars.

Charlie looked to where the hand had appeared before his eyes.

"Hi, Daddy," Sophie said.

"Hi, baby," Charlie said.

Now he could see what was happening — the hellhounds were tearing at the Morrigan. One of them broke, jumped into the air and unfurled her wings, then dove at Sophie, screeching.

Sophie raised her hand as if she was waving bye-bye and the Morrigan vaporized into a spray of black goo. The souls, thousands of them, that she had consumed over the millennia, floated into the air, red lights that circled the grotto, making the whole huge chamber appear to have been frozen in the middle of a fireworks display.

"You shouldn't be here, honey," Charlie said.

"Yes, I should," Sophie said. "I had to fix this, send them all back. I'm the Luminatus."

"You . . ."

"Yeah," she said matter-of-factly, in that Master of All Death and Darkness voice that is so irritating in a six-year-old.

The hellhounds were both on the remaining Morrigan now, tearing her in half as Charlie watched.

"No, honey," Charlie said.

Sophie raised her hand and Babd was vaporized like the others — the captured souls rose like embers from a bonfire.

"Let's go home, Daddy," Sophie said.

"No," Charlie said, barely able to hold up his head. "We have something we have to get." He lurched forward and one of the hellhounds was there to brace him. The whole army of squirrel people was coming around the bow of the ship, each carrying a glowing soul vessel he'd retrieved from the ship's cabin.

"Is this it?" Sophie said. She took a CD from Bob and handed it to Charlie.

He turned it in his hands and hugged it to his chest. "You know what this is, honey?"

"Yeah. Let's go home, Daddy."

Charlie fell over the back of Alvin. Sophie and the squirrel people steadied him until they were out of the Underworld.

Minty Fresh carried Charlie to the car.

A doctor had come and gone. When Charlie came to he was on his bed at home and Audrey was wiping his forehead with a damp cloth.

"Hi," he said.

"Hi," Audrey said.

"Did Sophie tell you?"

"Yeah."

"They grow up so fast," Charlie said.

"Yeah." Audrey smiled.

"I got this." He reached behind his chest plate and pulled out the Sarah McLachlan CD that pulsated with red light.

Audrey nodded and reached out for the disc. "Let's put that over here where you can keep an eye on it." As soon as her fingers touched the plastic case the light went out and Audrey shuddered. "Oh my," she said.

"Audrey." Charlie tried to sit up, but was forced back down by the pain. "Ouch. Audrey, what happened? Did they get it? Did they take her soul?"

She was looking at her chest, then looked up at Charlie, tears in her eyes. "No,

Charlie, it's me," she said.

"But you had touched that before, that night in the pantry. Why didn't it happen then?"

"I guess I wasn't ready then."

Charlie took her hand and squeezed it, then squeezed it much harder than he intended as a wave of pain washed through him. "Goddammit," he said. He was panting now, breathing like he might hyperventilate.

"I thought it was all dark, Audrey. All the spiritual stuff was spooky. You made me see."

"I'm glad," Audrey said.

"Makes me think I should have slept with a poet so I could have understood the way the world can be distilled into words."

"Yes. I think you have the soul of a poet, Charlie."

"I should have made love with a painter, too, so I could feel the wave of a brushstroke, so I could absorb her colors and textures and really see."

"Yes," Audrey said, brushing at his hair with her fingers. "You have such a wonderful imagination."

"I think," said Charlie, his voice going higher as he breathed harder, "I should have bedded a scientist so I would understand the mechanics of the world, felt them right down to my spine."

"Yes, so you could feel the world," Audrey said.

"With big tits," Charlie added, his back arching in pain.

"Of course, baby," Audrey said.

"I love you, Audrey."

"I know, Charlie. I love you, too."

Then Charlie Asher, Beta Male, husband to Rachel, brother to Jane, father to Sophie (the Luminatus, who held dominion over Death), beloved of Audrey, Death Merchant and purveyor of fine vintage clothing and accessories, took his last breath, and died.

Audrey looked up to see Sophie come into the room. "He's gone, Sophie."

Sophie put her hand on Charlie's forehead. "Bye, Daddy," she said.

EPILOGUE

THE GIRLS

Things settled in the City of Two Bridges, and all the dark gods that had been rising to erupt out over the world remembered their place and returned to their domains deep in the Underworld.

Jane and Cassie were married in a civil ceremony that was dissolved and sanctioned a half-dozen times over the years. Nevertheless, they were happy and there was always laughter in their home.

Sophie went home to live with her Aunties Jane and Cassandra. She would grow to be a tall and beautiful woman, and eventually take her place as the Luminatus, but until then, she went to school and played with her puppies and had a fairly wonderful time as she waited for her daddy to come get her.

THE SHOPKEEPERS

While Minty Fresh had believed in the adage that in every moment there is a crisis, his belief had been somewhat academic until he started seeing Lily Severo, when it became very practical indeed. Life jumped up several steps for him on the interesting scale, to the point where the Death Merchant part of his existence became the more prosaic of his pursuits. They became renowned around town, the giant in pastels always in company with the short, Gothic chef, but the City really stood up and took notice when they opened up the Jazz and Gourmet Pizza Place in North Beach in the building that had once housed Asher's Secondhand.

As for Ray Macy, Inspector Rivera set him up with a lady pawnbroker from the Fillmore named Carrie Lang, and they hit it off almost immediately, having in common a love of detective movies and handguns, as well as a deep mistrust for most of humanity. Ray fell deeply in love, and true to his Beta Male nature, was doggedly loyal to her, although he always secretly suspected her of being a serial killer.

RIVERA

Inspector Alphonse Rivera has spent most of his life trying to change his life. He'd worked in a half-dozen different police departments, in a dozen different capacities, and although he was very good at being a cop, he always seemed to be trying to get out. After the debacle with the Death Merchants and the strange, unexplainable things that had gone on around it, he was simply exhausted. There had been a brief time when he'd been able to leave police work and open a rare-book store, and he felt as if that might have been the only time he had ever truly been happy. Now, at age forty-nine, he was ready to try it again: take an early retirement and just read and live in a calm, unevent-filled world of books.

So he was somewhat pleased when, two weeks after the death of Charlie Asher, he went to his mailbox to find a substantial envelope that could only be a book. It was like an omen, he thought as he sat down at his kitchen table to open the package. It *was* a book — what looked like a very rare and bizarre children's book. He opened it and turned to the first chapter. *So Now You're Death: Here's What You'll Need.*

THE EMPEROR

The Emperor enjoyed a happy reunion with his troops and went on to rule benevolently over San Francisco to the end of his days. For leading Charlie into the Underworld, and for his boundless courage, the Luminatus gave Bummer the strength and durability of a hellhound. It would fall to the Emperor to explain how his now all-black companion — while he never weighed more than seven pounds soaking wet — could outrun a cheetah and chew the tires off a Toyota.

AUDREY

Audrey continued her work at the Buddhist center and did costuming for a local theater group, but she also took a volunteer job with hospice, where she helped people to the other side as she had done for so long in Tibet. The hospice position also, however, gave her access to bodies that had been recently vacated by their souls, and she used these opportunities to cycle the squirrel people back into the human flow of birth and rebirth. And for a while, there were remarkable instances of people recovering from terminal illness in the City, as she exercised the *p'howa of undying*.

She didn't give up her work with the squirrel people altogether, however, as it was a skill she had come to over a long time and a lot of work, and it could still be extraordinarily rewarding. At least that's how she was feeling as she looked over her latest masterpiece in the meditation room of the Three Jewels Buddhist Center.

He had the face of a crocodile — sixty-eight spiked teeth, and eyes that gleamed like black glass beads. His hands were the claws of a raptor, the wicked black nails encrusted with dried blood. His feet were webbed like those of a waterbird, with claws for digging prey from the mud. He wore a purple silk robe, trimmed in sable, and a matching hat with a wizard's star embroidered on it in gold thread.

"It's only temporary, until we find someone," Audrey said. "But take my word for it, you look great."

"No, I don't. I'm only fourteen inches tall."

"Yeah, but I gave you a ten-inch schlong."

He opened his robe and looked down. "Wow, would you look at that," Charlie said. "Nice."

Author's Note and Acknowledgments

As with any book, I owe a debt of gratitude to those who helped inspire the book, as well as those who actually helped in the research and production.

For inspiration, my deepest thanks to the family and friends of Patricia Moss, who shared their thoughts and feelings during the time of Pat's passing. Also thanks to the hospice workers in all capacities, who share their lives and hearts every day with the dying and their families.

The city of San Francisco is always an inspiration, and I'm grateful to her people for letting me stalk their neighborhoods and for being understanding about my teasing. While I've tried to "represent" the feeling of the neighborhoods in San Francisco, I'm quite aware that the actual locations in the book, like Charlie's shop and the Three Jewels Buddhist Center, are not at the addresses indicated. If you find it absolutely necessary to write me to inform me of my inaccuracies, I will be forced to point out that you won't find giant shampoo-slurping hellhounds in North Beach, either.

I did not go into the storm sewer to confirm the details of descriptions in scenes that take place there, mainly because IT'S THE SEWER! San Francisco is one of the few coastal cities that combine their sewer and storm-drain system — a fact that I completely ignored in my description of that underground world. If you're really that concerned about how it looks down in the sewers — well — eww. Just take my word for it, all that stuff could happen down there and don't ruin the story for yourself by being a stickler about the details. There's a squirrel in a ball gown, for Christ's sake, just let the sewer thing go.

As for other factual faux pas, I do not know if you can actually pinch a kid's head off in the electric window of a 1957 Cadillac Eldorado — I just thought it would be cool for this book if you could. Please don't experiment at home.

My sincere thanks go to Monique Motil, upon whose amazing art the squirrel people are based. I happened across her sculptures, which she calls Sartorial Creatures, at Paxton Gate, a gallery in the Mission district of San Francisco, and was so charmed by their macabre whimsy that I wrote to Monique and asked her if I could bring them alive in *A Dirty Job*. She graciously gave me permission. You can view Monique's art at http://www.monique motil.com/sartcre.html. You can read about her sideline career as a zombie lounge singer (I'm not kidding) and her passion to bring zombies the sensual gravitas that vampires enjoy at zombie pinups.com.

My thanks to Betsy Aubrey, for her line "I like my men like I like my tea, weak and green," which, once I heard it, I had to put in a book. (And thanks to Sue Nash, whose tea was, indeed, weak and green.)

For sending me an emergency package of books on Tibetan Buddhism and *p'howa* when I was under the gun and out of sources, thanks to Rod Meade Sperry at Wisdom Press.

For keeping me fed, my thanks to my agent, Nick Ellison, and Abby Koons and Jennifer Cayea at Nicholas Ellison Inc.

Thanks, too, to my brilliant editor, Jennifer Brehl, who continually makes me look smarter without making me feel stupid. Many thanks to Michael Morrison,

Lisa Gallagher, Mike Spradlin, Jack Womack, Leslie Cohen, Dee Dee DeBartolo, and Debbie Stier, who have all kept the faith and kept my books in front of you readers.

And, as usual, my thanks to Charlee Rodgers, for her tolerance and understanding during the writing of this book, as well as for her extraordinary courage and compassion in caring for both of our dying mothers — events that helped shape the very soul of this story.

The employees of Thorndike Press hope you have enjoyed this Large Print book. All our Thorndike and Wheeler Large Print titles are designed for easy reading, and all our books are made to last. Other Thorndike Press Large Print books are available at your library, through selected bookstores, or directly from us.

For information about titles, please call:

(800) 223-1244

or visit our Web site at:

www.gale.com/thorndike
www.gale.com/wheeler

To share your comments, please write:

Publisher
Thorndike Press
295 Kennedy Memorial Drive
Waterville, ME   04901